SIMONE LAZAROO was born in Singapore and lives in Fremantle, Western Australia. Her previous novels are *The World Waiting to be Made*, which won the 1995 Western Australian Premier's Award for fiction and the T.A.G. Hungerford Award; and *The Australian Fiancé*, which won the Western Australian Premier's Award for fiction and was shortlisted for the Kiriyama Pacific Rim Prize in 2000. *The Australian Fiancé* has been broadcast on radio and is being adapted for film. Her short stories have been anthologised in England and Australia. She teaches in the English and Creative Arts program at Murdoch University.

Also by Simone Lazaroo
and available in Picador

The Australian Fiancé

SIMONE LAZAROO

the travel writer

PICADOR

Pan Macmillan Australia

First published 2006 in Picador by Pan Macmillan Australia Pty Limited
1 Market Street, Sydney

National Library of Australia
Cataloguing-in-Publication Data:

Lazaroo, Simone, 1961–.
The travel writer.

ISBN-13: 978 0 330 42256 7.

ISBN-10: 0 330 42256 1.

1. Women journalists - Fiction. 2. Man-woman relationships
- Fiction. 3. Travel writers - Fiction. 4. Mothers and
daughters - Fiction. 5. Malacca (Malacca) - Fiction.
I. Title.

A823.3

Typeset in 12.5/13 pt Bembo by Midland Typesetters, Maryborough
Printed by McPherson's Printing Group, Maryborough

Papers used by Pan Macmillan Australia Pty Ltd are natural, recyclable products made from
wood grown in sustainable forests. The manufacturing processes conform to the environmental
regulations of the country of origin.

What gives light must endure burning.

Viktor Frankl

EMBARKATION
Fuzih – to flee, to escape

Just after Independence but before my mother was wise, a travel writer gave her the only dictionary and thesaurus she'd ever owned. My mother found herself in the thesaurus, *Eurasian*, wedged between *half-breed*, *mongrel* and *hybrid*.

–Aiya! It breaks my back, this English language, she had complained when she carried these books and her plaster saints in her bulging handbag towards the taxi taking us from Malacca to our London-bound plane in 1965. –No wonder he gave me all these words. They would've weighed him down when he travelled lah.

A faint burst of guitar and bells came to us on the southerly breeze.

–Listen to that, Isabelle. Someone in the Land of the Priest is playing fado. Our Portuguese ancestors' songs of fate.

–You could throw the books away, I'd suggested, sensing she wanted to leave every trace of the travel writer behind.

But her determination to make the most of the dictionary and thesaurus stayed with her, even years after we migrated to England. Recently, she'd underlined words that helped her describe those things in life that made no sense.

–What a *shemozzle*, she would say. A *rigmarole*, a *kerfuffle*.

–Bamboozling. Utterly bamboozling lah, she said that London morning in August 1985 in the oncologist's rooms, using the word she saved for life's most serious mysteries.

The oncologist's light box illuminated the blue scan of the pea-sized tumour tethered to my mother's optical nerve. I could just read the label on the film from where I stood. *Mrs Ghislaine de Sequeira. Right eye.* As he spoke, the oncologist's glasses reflected the scan, like windows mirroring a dark cloud in a bright sky.

–It's time to start thinking in terms of quality rather than quantity of life, Mrs de Sequeira.

The pores of my scalp contracted.

My mother nodded impassively.

–Be more exactly precise with your translation, doctor. You mean it's not long until I die lah.

The oncologist nodded and gathered his notes at his desk without looking at us. How cold and indifferent the world seems when life's extremity becomes apparent.

My mother and I walked out of his room and down the corridor of fluorescent lights and pale green linoleum.

–Time to start looking at quality rather than quantity of life! I could have told him that years ago. He is what you would call euphemistic, yes?

My mother had been a writer of obituaries and death notices back in Malacca. She had practised eloquence in the face of death for years, whereas I could do nothing but tremble in those minutes following the oncologist's prognosis. I hoped her eyesight was diminished enough not to notice.

–I would call him a wanker, I said finally.

She patted my hand. The lift's interior light flickered as we entered. I felt that momentary sense of false buoyancy as the lift began its descent and the numbered squares next to the closed doors lit up, seven, six, five, four. My mother and I were some place between cures and death, between a good strong cup of tea and nothing for it. For a few seconds I wished we could just stay there in that lift, going up and down, not having to arrive at anything, not having to face what lay ahead.

The lift doors sighed open.

—Do you know what Grandfather Wish used to say when he worked for the British colonial government as a medical assistant in Malacca? Sometimes death is the best result that can be hoped for, and death is not as hard as we think. So don't worry, anak.

Anak, the Malay word for child.

My mother's words take me back to Malacca: its drowning shore, its filigrees of smoke, mildew and rosewood; its enduring faiths and crumbling monuments to centuries of broken promises.

PART ONE

Tokah — to touch, to cost

THE TRUE BODY

✤ *The brightest star* ✤

Aloysius de Sequeira walked in his dark mourner's jacket along the dusty street that led out of the Land of the Priest kampong to the centre of Malacca town. This was years before he became a grandfather, but already he had the dignity usually associated with old age.

Standing on the edge of the kampong that afternoon in the January monsoonal breezes of 1958, he calculated it was just over seventeen years since he had first met Mathilde. His late wife, Mathilde had come from one of the poorest Christao fishing families in the Land of the Priest, but it was not her poverty that made her problematic to the eligible Catholic bachelors of Malacca. He remembered her proud sorrow over her divorce from the wealthy Chinese lawyer who'd found someone rich and Chinese to marry instead.

Mathilde Dolores Oliveira Chan had been one of the few divorced Christao women in living memory. When she met

Aloysius de Sequeira as he did his rounds one morning in the kampong, she was still mourning the loss of the fine menagerie of pets she'd had to leave behind in the mansion of her first husband, most of them gifts from his clients. But despite her grief, or perhaps because of it, she had the loudest, most unladylike laugh in the Land of the Priest.

'Aiya!' hissed Aloysius's cousin Hortense Oratio the Devout. 'That Mathilde only laugh so bold since her marriage broke into pieces. See how divorce itchifies a woman?'

But Aloysius was forty-five, old enough to appreciate the unusual. He was entranced by the warm brown of her skin and the unpredictable quivering of her lush eyebrows before she laughed or cried; and impressed by her fluency in both English and Christao, the sixteenth-century Portuguese-Malay dialect unique to their people, but spoken decreasingly by them. And, to Aloysius's ears, Mathilde's unladylike fighter's laugh sounded like a refusal to despair.

He courted her with the aid of his macaque monkey, Lucifer. Months previously, the English horticulturalist at Malacca's Botanical Gardens had been desperate for some samples of Holy Ghost orchids to send back to his superiors at the Kew Gardens. Finding no orchids within reach in the closest stand of jungle, Aloysius trained Lucifer to climb the trees and retrieve some samples. When Aloysius first brought Mathilde home to meet his parents, the macaque monkey brought Mathilde one of these orchids. Aloysius took it as an omen, a confirmation of the authority Mathilde already exerted over his heart, and he proposed to her the following day.

'Still too sad,' she replied. 'My ex-husband left all the birds to die in their cages.'

'What if I promise you a whole new menagerie?'

'Not just birds?'

'Anything you like.'

'Even a python and a racquet-tailed drongo?'

Aloysius nodded emphatically, one hand on his head, one over his heart. Lucifer sidled up to her and dropped a peanut on her lap. It clinched the deal.

※

Wish couldn't recall any thickening of Mathilde's long slender neck in the early months of their marriage, but he remembered pouring his urgent breath and coconut-flower toddy down her throat in the evenings when the constellations fizzed silver in the sky and his own white stars sparkled in Mathilde's dark bay, and he remembered that tide of their merging waters that rocked them, sometimes to sleep, sometimes towards the world beyond.

'Wish,' as she called him from the early days of their marriage, 'come stroke my aching neck, Wish.' The pain in her neck had seemed to Aloysius a fine excuse for lovemaking, but within a year Mathilde's long slender neck was discernibly changed in shape. Hortense Oratio the Devout snidely suggested it was becoming thickset and muscular from too much kissing.

'Dowager hump awreddy, but back to front,' she sniggered.

Aloysius was also a Malaccan Eurasian of Portuguese descent, but his family wasn't as poor as Mathilde's. He came from a long line of clerks who knew how to book-keep and hold their tongues in Christao, Malay and English for the British colonial government. His career as a medical assistant was both a departure from and an improvement on the lives of most of his relatives. It made some of his relatives respectful, but it made Hortense Oratio spiteful.

A few months after Mathilde became pregnant with Wish's brightest star, a coin-sized lump, shaped and marked like a baby turtle's shell, appeared on her neck. Doctor Arbuckle pronounced a goitre and prescribed iodine, but neither love nor medicine halted the slow advance of the turtle across Mathilde's neck. Hortense Oratio suggested the turtle was God's way of punishing Aloysius for taking a divorced woman for his wife. She was also sure Aloysius's falling for Mathilde had something to do with the influence of

Hollywood movies on Malacca. Malacca's church congregations dwindled whenever one of the new movies came to town.

'Aiya! Off again to take smut lessons from all those itchified actresses,' Hortense said when she arrived one Sunday in time to see Mathilde departing for the movies. She ran a critical eye over Mathilde's powdered face.

'But the censors always cut the naughty bits out,' protested Mathilde.

'Think you so clever. Still smutty, naughty bits or no. You think those actresses put all that make-up on for nothing? Like putting light bulbs on their skin! Glowing so promiscuously, ah-yah! Trap so many men like moths. Serve the women right they get moth-eaten. One man more than enough for a good woman. Some good women never get one.' Hortense Oratio referred to herself often in this way, but she had a point about the influence of the movies on the young Christao women of Malacca. It was true that in that year, 1941, the sales of English and American cosmetics in Malacca tripled and the centuries-old churches of Malacca rang out with the indignant cries of Eurasian babies being christened with the names of Hollywood film stars.

Mathilde and Aloysius's baby would be named after a minor French actress whose luscious mouth, imbued by the grainy black-and-white pearlescence of Paramount Pictures, had come to Mathilde's attention in the Cathay Picture Theatre. The Cathay had almost enough holes in its tin roof to be considered an open-air theatre. Inside, Mathilde sat sharing salted plums and starfruit juice with Mak Non, the middle-aged Malay confinement lady and servant Wish had found her. Mathilde's nine-months-pregnant belly protruded from her like a globe of the world, abbreviated yet significant. She was transfixed by the variety of ways in which the actress's mouth gave meaning to her silences, for Mathilde was a woman who had considered the meanings and uses of silence in the five years of her previous marriage to the precisely spoken Chinese lawyer. She counted and named the expressions on the actress's lips.

'Amused. He is amusing her. How you say in Malay?' she asked Mak Non.

'Menggeli hati. Tickle the heart.'

'Desire. She desires him.'

'Keinginan,' concurred Mak Non with a noisy slurp on her star-fruit juice.

'Shame. She is ashamed of herself.'

'Malu. Look at that man touching her! Ai-yee!'

This time Mathilde could only find the word for what was happening on the screen in Christao, the language of her parents, which she hadn't spoken during her marriage to her first husband.

'Tokah,' she whispered, pressing her fingers against the pricking of tears in her eyes.

'What tokah?'

'It means to touch, but it also means to cost. Christao word.' Until her first marriage, Mathilde had not believed her parents' dying language had any meaning that couldn't be more adequately expressed in English. She had spoken to no-one, not even Wish, about what the Chinese lawyer's touch had cost her.

The leading lady loomed larger on the screen, hands on hips, eyelashes thick with mascara, utterly silent but in full possession of herself.

'She wants revenge,' said Mathilde. 'How you say like that in Malay?'

'Membalas dendam. To take revenge. He wanted to go deep inside her so soon. Like he got no shame ah. Englishman of course.' There was a sudden flare of white on the screen and a jump in the soundtrack. A murmur went through the audience.

'Aiya! Government censor.'

'Kiss or murder lah?'

'How you say deep inside in Malay?' murmured Mathilde.

'Dalam. More than one meaning. Deep, inside, interior. You can use it for the private places in a house. Or in a woman ah.'

'Ah.' The unnamed baby turned suddenly in Mathilde, sending a needle-like jab along the length of her birth canal. She retrieved the salted-plum stone from her mouth. 'How deep? So deep that a baby doesn't touch it? So deep that a man can't go there? Sspphh!' She drew her breath in sharply through her teeth.

White-hot pain obliterated further speech as the brightest star of the love she'd shared with Wish surged suddenly in the darkness of her body.

᭧

Ghislaine Evangela de Sequeira. What a brilliant constellation of contradictory features Mak Non revealed when she wiped the vernix from her. Although the baby had her father's slightly perplexed expression, her cry rang with the same belligerence as Mathilde's laughter. But no-one could agree where her pale golden skin faintly tinged with green came from, and not everyone could get their tongue around her name. Ghislaine, pronounced with a 'J'. Although her name was never abbreviated, she would become used to being abbreviated by people in other ways after her mother's death. But she would always remember her mother called her Ghis-laine after the minor but brilliantly expressive actress who had imparted so many meanings to silence.

LONDON, SEPTEMBER 1985

Packing my mother's bag for the hospital. On her dressing table, one of her dark and one of her silver hairs wind through the teeth of a blue plastic Marks & Spencer comb, and the lenses of her reading glasses reflect the twilight sky and garden beyond her bedroom window.

The orchids and small palms she planted when we first came to England are almost overgrown by the more vigorous lavender and roses. When we first arrived at this house that my father the tea taster willed to us, there were only weeds and the skeleton of a small shrub in the garden. Our raking revealed a nameplate at the base of its trunk: *Camellia sinensis*, the plant from the tropics that tea is harvested from. We didn't know how long it had been dead. We supposed it wasn't suited to the climate.

My mother didn't pull out the skeleton of the camellia. She planted a tiny garden around it: two palms and two orchids facing south-east, towards Malacca.

−The seeds of palms sometimes float for months in the sea before they take root, she told me as she firmed the soil around these distant relatives of the plants from home.

She tended this new garden as if her life might depend on it. It was her escape from desolation: the unfriendliness of her neighbours; the London traffic and fumes; the love she'd lost in Malaysia. The palms struggled for life, barely making it through the first winter. She made them a bed of straw and woodchips, wrapped their trunks with blankets to keep them warm, and plastic to keep the frost out.

They bloomed and fruited spectacularly in spring. In the tiny greenhouse in the corner of the backyard, she potted the newly born orchid pseudo-bulbs and palm seedlings and left them on the cold stone steps of her neighbours. Although they wouldn't accept bargaining in their shops, or talk about love and losing it, her English neighbours would talk about a garden. Soon a gardenia, a Queen Elizabeth and White Rose of York grew in the same bed as the orchid and the palm. When it bloomed the next year, the white orchid was suffused with the palest of blushes.

–In the jungle near home some varieties of orchids are pollinated by male insects who mistake their colouring and shape for female insects' anatomy, my mother had told me as she watered the garden. Flowering is possible despite false love. Remember this.

※

By the time I return to the hospital the next day, the knots of pain on my mother's face have been smoothed over by something in the drip attached to her wrist.

On the television opposite her bed, the fleeting faces of the News of the World give way to a blonde weather-woman with a Princess Diana hairdo.

–An early cold snap, she smiles through her frosted lipstick as she points at the cold winds blowing in from the north on the weather map.

–Hope we're not in for a long winter. Shame we won't make it back to Malacca before I die. I could do with the warmth, my mother murmurs, pulling the sheets up higher. –And I'd like to have a true body made for me by the funeral-decoration makers there.

—A true body?

—A life-sized papier-mâché doll. A kind of effigy of the deceased the Chinese make for funerals. Some of the Chinese call them *zensheng*. They say a true body gives the spirit of the deceased somewhere to go after death. I would like a true body to return to when I die.

—But you're not Chinese, Mum.

—Christao Eurasians don't fuss like that lah. We've been borrowing from other cultures for centuries. We have blood from all over the world rushing through our veins. Anyway, I'd ask Father O'Reilly to sprinkle some holy water on the true body.

My mother has always kept an eye on life after death.

※

When I return home from the hospital that evening, the tall dark kitchen still smells faintly of coconut milk and cardamon, traces of the last meal my mother cooked. The night before, my mother had given me her New World-brand diary.

—My Malaccan life, she'd said.

Some of its pages have been torn out, revealing its yellowing spine and the threads of its binding. I wonder if she'd removed some secrets to leave me a respectable image of herself. Mother. She's fed me properly all my life and she wants to go on feeding me properly, even after she dies.

Near the beginning of the diary, I find tea-tasting notes and newspaper obituaries. Strewn throughout are oil-spattered recipes in my Grandmother Mathilde's ornate handwriting, and what seem to be cuttings from an article about travel safety:

Ascent — that interval immediately after departure in which we begin climbing to greater heights — is the time in which accidents are most likely to occur.

The more travellers <u>need</u> to see the signs of safe arrival, the more they are likely to be <u>deluded</u> that they have actually arrived.

And this, in my mother's handwriting, at the end of the book:

There are moments between us when it seems safest to keep my tongue in my tea.

It's apparent my mother's family found life in Malacca both delicious and dangerous. But why? What kind of book is this, exactly?

Then I remember my mother's desire for a true body. Does she think she'll be forgotten after she's gone? I write in blue ink, across the red globe of the world on the diary's cardboard cover: *The True Body*. Can I write a story in her image, another kind of true body for her to fly towards before she dies?

※

When I wake the next morning to my own voice saying *Philip Border will help*, it doesn't seem at all like the end of a dream. It seems as clear as the daylight illuminating my room, as true as my first encounter with Philip.

I'd been expecting someone lined and grey for a writing tutor, but there was a man who looked like a student, almost adolescent in his slenderness, his T-shirt emblazoned with a jet plane arcing over a map showing the great cities of the world. He was leaning back against the whiteboard, hands in the pockets of his jeans, watching his students leave at the end of their first class. He held his head to one side, as if considering something. A small gold earring glinted in his ear. His complexion came from somewhere sunnier.

He looked just foreign enough to be my familiar.

When I approached him, he smiled as if he recognised me.

–Sorry I missed the class, I said, still catching my breath after running from the tube station.

–Looks like life's a bit hectic for you at the moment. He touched my arm lightly with his hand. His touch, such easy forgiveness. His gaze trickling down my body like water.

Even then, he was something else besides my writing tutor.

A siren blares and gradually recedes in the direction of the hospital. Of course I'd been dreaming. No-one else would share this sense of urgency about writing my mother's life before she died, not even Philip.

As I slide out of bed, the siren's barely audible above the din of the daily traffic.

Underneath the fluorescent hospital light, my mother looks as cold as her plaster saints. I cross myself in the surreptitious de Sequeira way.

–Are you awake, Mum?

Her eyes flicker open, but her gaze is far away.

–Isabelle. I was just travelling.

–In your dreams?

–No. I wasn't asleep. Just visiting the old places and people in Malacca.

–Mum. Sssh.

It must be the drugs, I think to myself.

–Why? I've travelled back like that before lah.

Something invisible hovers over my skin.

–You and your old Malaccan superstitions.

–You and your Londoner's cynicism.

–Well. Just don't tell the doctors, Mum. They'll put you in a psychiatric ward.

She folds her hands and regards me patiently, neither smiling nor frowning.

–I was thinking, Mum. I could write your life.

–Good lord. Why would you do that? There's hardly anything there.

Against the white sheet, her hand trembles slightly as I reach for it.

–Because . . . how else will we hold you when you are gone?

Her thin fingers return the pressure of mine.

–Okay. But you have to understand. Mine isn't a story of heroism. Or grand romance. I've done nothing great. Just small things and big mistakes with lots of love lah. And my memory's not so good now. The drugs.

Sealed windows muffle a blackbird's song outside.

–Don't worry. I'll fill in any gaps in your story, I tell her.

She turns towards the window. The pale morning floods her eyes.

–I dreamed last night I had to retrieve a blind baby from the well in the courtyard of Grandfather Wish's house in Malacca. My amah, Ah Kwei, used to keep carp in that well. Anyway, the blind baby reminded me of a story from my childhood. When your Grand-mother Mathilde was alive, she used to get seaweed for the agar-agar in our birthday and Christmas jellies from near Pulau Besar, the island just off Malacca. She told me that in the old days, when being pregnant out of wedlock was highly shameful, unmarried women who were pregnant and abandoned by their lovers sometimes asked Christao fishermen to row them over to the island, on the pretext of gathering the special seaweed for jellies. If the fishermen refused to leave these women on the island to die, some of them jumped into the sea. Strangely, several of the women who tried unsuccessfully to drown or miscarry gave birth to babies whose eyelids wouldn't open properly. People said their blindness was a blessing in disguise, because those children would never see their fathers turn their backs on them in the street.

She closes her eyes.

–Do you think that's a true story? I ask.

–Well, your grandmother certainly seemed to believe it. If a

Christao fisherman ever carried one of these women in his boat, he'd sprinkle the bow and oars with holy water and blossoms blessed by a bomoh, to prevent the curse of a whole season of bad fishing. Those old Malay bomohs practised strong magic. They gave the unmarried mothers specially blessed limes and blossoms to bathe in, to wash the bad luck away. The Christao people even sang a fado about a woman who gives birth to a little girl who is blind.

My mother presses her fingers to her eyelids.

−This light is too bright, she says.

THE TRUE BODY

* *The cost of comfort* *

Even Hortense Oratio congratulated Mathilde for producing such a fair-skinned baby. After over a century of British government, Hortense wasn't the only Malaccan who saw good fortune in a pale complexion. But the value of pale skin had changed in Malacca many times since the sixteenth century, with successive Portuguese, Dutch and British colonisation, and was about to change again.

One morning when Ghislaine was just over a year old, her father went downstairs and tuned the wireless to the Malayan Broadcasting Corporation. The British newsreader reported *firm stands* and *strategic retreats* by troops against the Japanese in the northern peninsula. Aloysius filled his government-issue portmanteau with strips of clean old sheeting, suture thread and antiseptic. He had worked with British doctors full of cool reserve and implacable nerve in the Malacca Hospital for twenty years. He knew a British euphemism for impending disaster when he heard one.

✳

Two British soldiers and Aloysius's boss, Doctor Arbuckle, came knocking at the door of the de Sequeira house early the next morning.

'We're all getting out of here,' Doctor Arbuckle said. 'We don't stand a chance against the Japanese. But you do. Good luck, old chap.' Doctor Arbuckle's spectacles were smeared with blood and his shirtsleeves flapped open at the cuffs. His greying hair clung to his forehead with sweat, and the lines of his face had deepened with fatigue. He gave Aloysius his leather medical bag full of supplies and a key. 'Help yourself to the dispensary. You'll need it.'

'And take the stores in the hospital pantry before the Japs do,' said one of the soldiers.

'I'll never forget you, Doctor Arbuckle sir.'

The doctor shook his hand. 'Likewise, Aloysius. But now the Japanese are here. Pretend you never knew us.'

By the time Aloysius got to the hospital pantry, it had been ransacked by looters. But, on the backmost shelf, he found a box of unopened treacle tins from Australia and a small pile of Bing Crosby records. He carried them home to Mathilde.

'Aiya, Wish! How will all this syrupy stuff help us survive a war lah?' she cried, pushing the box under the stairs.

The next day, the decapitated heads of looters were displayed on lamp-posts throughout the town. The invaders had brought a new kind of justice to Malacca. Aloysius hid the records and the treacle under the stairs, but he slept with Doctor Arbuckle's bag next to the bed.

✳

Within days of the Japanese invasion of Malacca, some Japanese soldiers noticed dark-skinned Mathilde holding her pink baby as she alighted from a trishaw outside the de Sequeira bungalow in the Land of the Priest.

'Your baby very pale. Who is the father?'

'Aloysius de Sequeira, a medical dresser.'

'What nationality?'

'Eurasian. We come out all different shades in the wash.'

'Liar! How can the baby's skin be so pale if your husband is half-caste? Englishman's whore! You are hiding an Englishman somewhere in here. Search!' shouted the officer. Six bayonets sliced the air above the threshold of the house.

The soldiers of the Japanese Imperial Army tore down the ceilings and ripped the doors off cupboards with their bayonets in their search for the Englishman. Thick clouds of plaster drifted like mist over the well and the furniture. The baby screamed as the plaster dusted her eyes. Mathilde and Mak Non were unable to read the soldiers' faces clearly, even as they loomed closer and closer.

❋

Aloysius arrived home that evening to find Mathilde and Mak Non white with plaster from the torn ceilings.

'They rubbed it into our faces. They said it would make us paler for our English men.'

The fish in the well lay immobilised by a white sludge. A boat-shaped bloodstain grew larger across the back of Mathilde's sea-green skirt, as if the arrival of some unknown cargo drew closer by the second.

'Those bastards didn't . . .' Wish couldn't bring himself to say the word.

'No lah. The shock has opened her birth wound again, ah. Light some brand and incense in the burner,' Mak Non said, sponging Mathilde's thighs.

Mathilde shook her head. 'What if the soldiers come back lah?

Shouldn't we leave just in case?'

'The Japanese Imperial Army will need medical officers like me too much to imprison us. First things first.' Wish lit the incense burner and the stove and brewed five spoonfuls of Teacher-brand tea until the water was purple. He poured a whole can of Dutch Maid condensed milk and a tablespoon of Australian treacle into it.

'For the shock. Drink,' he told Mathilde. He took Ghislaine from her arms. Mak Non guided Mathilde to the burner.

'Stand astride. Like that. Ah. Dry the wound. You must always make time to heal. Especially deep inside. Dalam, ah.'

❋

Within days, Aloysius was working for the Japanese Imperial Army. All the English medical practitioners had fled with their families, causing such a shortage of doctors that Wish, who had only ever worked as a medical assistant, was called on to attend to the gynaecological needs of ten women after the invasion.

'These women also working for Japanese Imperial Army. For comfort and relaxation. All live in same house,' the Japanese soldier informed him cryptically as he drove Aloysius in the recommissioned government Austin. Wish did not know enough Japanese to translate the new sign on the door of the old hotel, but he knew where he was headed as he paused at the door, waiting for it to open. He'd heard soldiers around town refer to the comfort station and to the women inside variously as comfort women, whores, kuniangs, or prostitutes. In his bag he carried a small quantity of bandages, sanitary napkins and Epsom salts. He had no idea if these supplies would be sufficient. He could only guess at what ailments he might discover.

He was met at the door by another Japanese soldier with a face slim and stern as the butt of a rifle. In the hallway the mama-san hovered, the skin of her neck, jowls and wrists plumply quilted and dripping with gold chains. She reminded Wish of the statue of the pug dog in Wing's Melaka Professional Photographic studio.

Wish's first duty that morning was to write a death certificate for a Chinese woman who'd been shot through the vagina. The blood that ran from her birth canal across the grey concrete yard out the back was still shiny. It carried the colour from her skin towards the gutter.

'She had pox,' said the Japanese soldier. 'She didn't report it. She gave it to the sergeant and half his men.'

'You treat the women like animals for slaughter. No wonder they don't report it.'

The rifle butt between his shoulder blades winded Wish, but he did not stumble. He made a surreptitious sign of the cross by resting his closed fist against his chest, using just his bent thumb to trace the axis there. Generations of the de Sequeira family had kept their moments of prayer disguised like this. It was a useful sign to make when concealing fear or resolve from colonisers of various persuasions. It was a private way to reiterate one's determination.

The soldier and the mama-san watched him as he examined the women off duty in the back room. Nearly every woman's genitals were abraded to bleeding point. Three women had swabbed themselves with iodine in a bid to treat syphilis. Their gazes were recondite with terror.

'I suppose you're going to kill them all,' he said tersely to the mama-san.

She thrust a document into his hands. 'We treat women well. We keep them healthy. Each regulation number-one priority,' she insisted.

Wish did not allow his disdain for the document to show until he got to the end of the English translation of *Health Regulations for Malacca Station*:

1. *Each comfort woman room equipped with creosote soap solution and rubber hose for douching and condom washing.*
2. *Each comfort woman wash and disinfect necessary parts.*
3. *Forbid intercourse during menstruation 2 days only.*

4. *Baths five minutes long only to be taken once a day only.*
5. *Each comfort woman to clean bedding daily.*
6. *Proprietor and comfort woman bear cost of illness equally.*
7. *Condoms to be worn.*
8. *Kissing and love relationship forbidden.*
9. *No unreasonable demands to be made.*

He crushed the document in one hand.

'I do not have adequate supplies to treat these women. Take me to the hospital for more,' he commanded the driver.

※

Wish scrounged in the hospital dispensary for more condoms, a supply of antibiotics and Salvarsan cream, and an unused red New World-brand *Diary of Emergency Procedures* the thickness of a clay brick. He directed the driver to the Botanical Gardens, its rotundas already succumbing to jungle vines and weeds. He picked paw-paw from the trees to make poultices for easing the raw swelling between each woman's legs. But his most important remedy was his wife. Mathilde, with her resolve of steel forged by her first husband's abuse; Mathilde, with her eyes that saw everything but gave nothing away. As the soldier drove them through the streets of Malacca, Wish told Mathilde in Christao what he had seen in the brothel. He gave her the red New World *Diary of Emergency Procedures* to record the names and ordeals of the women and the dosages of the remedies he administered them.

'Don't say anything to the soldiers,' he warned her. 'I'll tell them you are my assistant nurse.'

On the verandah of the brothel, used condoms hung drying on a piece of string. The brothel was adjacent to the Japanese soldiers' canteen on one side and the prison on the other. As Aloysius and Mathilde visited each of the women in their lavatory-sized cubicles, they could hear the clanging of pots and pans, the scrape of ladles doling food onto plates, and the shouts and grunts of soldiers through the thin walls. It was difficult to distinguish which of the soldiers' appetites was being satisfied. Through this din, Aloysius and Mathilde heard the screaming of prisoners being tortured.

The women were Chinese, except for two Malays. Most of them came from further north, but Mathilde recognised four of them. She had seen them at the markets before the war, women buying food for their family, just like her. Wish spoke Malay and Cantonese well enough to ascertain the specifics of their suffering. His eyes smarted with anger and sorrow as he gave the women tubes of soothing antiseptic cream for the bleeding rawness of genitals and Terramycin for syphilis. He pronounced as many women too ill to work as he could invent feasible excuses for. When the soldier left the room for a few minutes, Mathilde listened to the women as she helped them apply the Salvarsan cream and poultices.

'You don't even get time to wash yourself between men at the busiest times of the day.'

'The high-ranking ones refuse to wear condoms. If you are lucky, they come to you before they eat, so they are quick and not belching the smell of their dinner and saki into your face while they have sex. If you are luckier still, you are ordered to cook in the kitchen and given a day off sex.'

Mathilde didn't get the time to record any of the women's stories, but she wrote their full names in the diary. As she dispensed sanitary napkins and cream to the next woman, she heard a high insistent gibbering from the rear of the building.

'Fatimah go latah,' the Malay woman they were treating said sorrowfully. 'Latah all the time now. She's forgotten who she is, aiyee.' She led Mathilde and Wish towards the noise.

The woman who'd forgotten who she was lay curled on a stained mattress in a small dark cubicle, like a creature protecting her wounds. She wore only a faded sarong. For a minute she looked at Mathilde with what seemed a lucid gaze. Then her eyes rolled mournfully, as a dog does when resigning itself to being punished.

'She's about four months pregnant,' Wish whispered to his wife.

'The soldiers go dalam,' the woman standing at the door whispered. 'Make Fatimah go latah.' She tapped her head and heart simultaneously.

'It is true. Rape can make you lose your mind. I know. My first husband nearly did it to me after I refused him when he started seeing his mistress lah.'

This was the first time Mathilde had mentioned this to Aloysius. He saw she'd kept more of her history hidden from him than he'd suspected, that he had married a woman who had almost forgotten who she was before her fighter's laugh had won out.

'Your name is Fatimah,' she murmured to the woman as she sponged her and stroked her brow, but Fatimah closed her eyes and moaned, as if remembering who she was caused her too much pain.

My name is Fatimah, Mathilde wrote in the notebook. *Remember me.*

On the drive home, Mathilde drew a woman's body inside a house on the next blank page. In the centre of the body she drew a small round space. She didn't have the Christao word for it.

Dalam, she wrote in Malay. *Deep inside.* She tried to write a prayer for the women, but only five words from her parents' language came to her. Next to them, she wrote their English translations.

Tokah — to touch, to cost
Perdidu — to be lost, naked
Fikah — to be, to become, to live
Largah — to release, to let go

Hardly a prayer.

She closed the *Diary of Emergency Procedures* abruptly. What prayer in what language could ever be adequate for those women?

❋

One evening about four months later, Wish arrived home with Doctor Arbuckle's supplies case in one hand and a bundle wrapped in white sheeting in the other. A thin mewing came from it. His shirt was soaked with sweat and spattered with blood. Mathilde held out her arms for the bundle. The baby had black hair and skin as pink as coconut ice. Its eyelids had the epicanthus fold of the Japanese.

'Fatimah's baby,' Aloysius said. Mathilde was suckling Ghislaine on one breast. She put Fatimah's baby immediately to the other.

'How is Fatimah?'

'I had to stitch her up. There wasn't any anaesthetic.' He sat at the kitchen table with his head in his hands. 'One of the Japanese sergeants claims this baby as his. He boasts all over town about how many babies he's sired to virgins during the war. Some of the Japanese soldiers believe that breaking in a virgin before battle gives them victory and invulnerability to death.' Mathilde could see the muscles working at his jaw and temple as he gritted his teeth. 'If we feed the baby, the sergeant will give me more rations. I'll be able to get better supplies for the women and the prisoners.'

✳

Fatimah died just after the war was declared over, and her baby was adopted by her childless sister and husband who lived a few villages away. Aloysius found work in the hospital for the local women who'd worked in the Japanese brothel during the war, for he knew of no man who would marry them.

The British returned, including Doctor Arbuckle, who'd grown greyer and plumper on English food. In the de Sequeira house, the racquet-tailed drongo and the Indian mynah birds sang in their wicker cages as the Malacca morning poured in through the windows, illuminating the newly repaired ceilings.

The days of peace became years. The British improved the supply of electricity throughout Malacca. In these times of light, neither

Aloysius nor Mathilde suspected that, by young womanhood, their daughter would be subject to a war more subtle but no less invasive than the Japanese one.

But her early adolescence was bright with hope. Mathilde and Ghislaine fed the motley menagerie, offered thanks to Mathilde's plaster saints, cooked miraculous food, and went to see the latest movie at the Cathay some Sunday mornings.

'What are they doing?' Ghislaine asked when the picture was obliterated by the censors' white flare just as Clark Gable's moustachioed lip approached Carole Lombard's impeccably lipsticked mouth.

'Kissing or lying down,' her mother murmured.

'Kissing or lying down? It sounds like they're dying.'

LONDON, SEPTEMBER 1985

My estranged husband, David, answers the door of his flat,
his cane-coloured hair awry. I notice the smudge of blue in
the skin under his eyes that suggests he hasn't slept well, a sign that
makes me feel wary, guilty and sorry for him all at once. Behind
him, a couple of self-help books and his hospital orderly's uniform
lie strewn across the sofa. He's swallowed such books whole since
our marriage started coming undone, leaving them open at the last
page he's read on the kitchen table, in the bathroom, on the bed.

−I can't see any help for this mess we're in, he'd said one day,
closing the books and packing them together. And so his answer
to the complications of our married life had been to leave it, with
apparently little rancour and a determination to apply the popular-
psychology truths that fitted so conveniently into his backpack.

This afternoon, as I wait on the threshold of his flat, David seems
almost transparent to me. Yet it hasn't always been so. I'd only
noticed those smudges of blue in his face when our marriage began
faltering. How long had they been there? How can it be that you
can share your life with another, but not read his face carefully until
it's too late?

—You're early, he mumbles to me as Clara clambers out of her pram.

—Did you forget? Mum's still in hospital. Tuesday. My writing class.

—You still doing that? Thought you'd finished weeks ago.

—I re-enrolled for a second semester. I told you last week.

—You could have reminded me.

—Sorry. Is it too much of a hassle for you to have Clara now?

Clara wraps her arms around his leg. He ruffles her hair and takes a deep breath.

—Well. What do you expect me to say?

We learned in the months before and after our break-up not to look at one another when feeling the particular pain or joy of being Clara's parents. As if we'd made an unspoken choice to experience this separately.

—You can look after her at Mum's place each time if you like. Would that be easier for you?

Clara and I had lived there since David and I separated.

—Yeah. It's all set up for her there. Her cot. Her toys.

I hand him the house keys.

—Thanks. Thanks very much, I say, trying in vain to make eye contact with him.

Outside, the fog has lifted to reveal patches of afternoon sun. Vendors of cut-price lingerie and food shout above the hum of traffic as I walk down Portobello Road past the Westway flyover.

—Don't get yer knickers in a knot, only fifty p to cover yer bot! chants a red-faced man with a cockney accent and a pair of lacy black underpants on his head.

—Hurry hurry hurry, come and get your curry! calls Aunty Kanti, the Malay woman my mother and I buy our spices from. She throws me a cellophane packet.

—Isabelle! Take these salted plums to your mother. Poor thing, all that English hospital food. Like porridge for every meal lah. Good afternoon, Mrs Lim. How's your restaurant?

She waves at me and turns to Mrs Lim.

A West Indian man balancing a bottle of Bacardi on his head lurches up to me near the EAT THE RICH posters leading to the tube station.

–Hoooo golden girl. Ever seen a black man blush? It's a white man's lie.

He takes a swig from his bottle before staggering towards the squat grey block of flats where the Asian and Caribbean migrants live.

This day feels hopeful to me, despite everything. The sun shines on the bitter and the sad; on the displaced people of the Empire; the mis-sized underclothes from China and fog-dampened spices from Asia, and I'm on my way to Philip Border again.

⁂

After class, Philip drives me in his silver car through the fast descent of evening. Headlights and streetlamps shine blue through a thin damp fog, but inside his car the warmth smells of leather and some other, almost imperceptible scent, like freshly mown lawns or sap. I look straight ahead as I sink into the heated seat, silenced by so much comfort.

We're caught in slow traffic somewhere between the fish-and-chip and X-rated shops just off the high street. In the glow from the dashboard lights, the skin on his wrists and his face is a warm gold, the colour of perfect toast. My stomach grumbles softly.

He pushes a button. A woman sings something in German on his car cassette player, her voice hoarse and knowing. We pass Hampstead Heath and streets of white porticoed houses. At the lights he turns and smiles at me, breaking the long proud line of his forehead, nose and chin, but his eyes are dark and ardent.

A few streets beyond Highgate Cemetery, we pull into the gravel driveway of his white Victorian house. A soft yellow light from inside illuminates the stained glass front door with its central lion flanked by a fleur-de-lis in each corner. For just a few seconds, I can't see into the cold darkness around the external basement stairs, and I feel as if part of me is falling away.

But then he smiles at me again as he opens the door, puts his hand on the small of my back to usher me in, and I'm warm again, warm all through.

His overfed Siamese cat mutters and rubs itself against our legs. Behind the gold Buddha, a large oval gilt-framed mirror hangs like a silvery bay on the wall, a dark grey blemish running along its bottom like a tidal mark or shoreline. Our reflected faces look mildly surprised at being framed next to one another.

−The mirror's Victorian. Come through. First time you've been here since last semester. A few changes since then. The renovations have really come along. An excellent investment of my inheritance, my accountant tells me.

The wooden floorboards give way abruptly to new, gleaming cold tiles. We tread carefully on the tiles in case they shift in their fresh grout.

There are stained glass windows in the new sitting room, repeating the front door's fleurs-de-lis motif. Carved wooden masks hang on high walls next to a Chinese silk painting showing three women walking beside a stream. As we look at the painting, he turns to me candidly.

−Your toes turn in like theirs. It makes you sway when you walk. I've never asked, but how Asian are you, anyway?

I can just see our reflections in the glass covering the painting. Next to his neat head, mine's shaped like half a loaf of bread. My forehead and cheekbones are too wide, my chin is too square. My eyes are grey. My hair looks like the only fine Asian thing about me.

It isn't the first time he's asked a question I'm not sure how to answer.

−These walls are very high, I say, sitting down, looking at my feet. They're pigeon-toed and slightly clenched, but too big to be Asian.

He ruffles my hair affectionately. For the first time, he gives me a smile that says *I know you*.

−Sorry. I didn't mean to put you on the spot, he murmurs.

So it appears he not only reads me, he feels for me. His silence, too, seems considered, like my mother's. My feet unclench. There's a long crescent-shaped scar I haven't noticed before on the edge of his right hand.

−How did you do that?

−Oh *that*. A childhood scar. My mother was always breaking things, and I was always picking up after her. To make a long story short.

−Really? Tell me the rest of it?

But he turns away and asks what I'd like to drink, and pours Bombay Sapphire without waiting for my reply. The ice cracks in the tall glasses. His scar turns pale purple with their cold.

−I briefed the architect to take the old house back to its original Victorian style and to give the additions a tropical feel that's still harmonious with the original house. Like the colonial buildings of the Far East.

−Well, you certainly know what you want.

−Took a while to get council approval. Come and look out the back. Be careful. There's only one light globe installed out there at the moment.

The glasses of gin and tonic clink and chime as he leads me to the new glass conservatory, cantilevered like a temple. There's a deep rectangular pit in the ground.

−That's a long dark fall, I say.

−That's the swimming pool. Concreted and tiled by next week. Heated after that. Just before winter sets in. I want tropical ambience. There'll be palms. Teak planter's chairs.

Standing looking back through the glass to his house, I'm reminded of the mansions of the expatriates in Malacca, high and ornate, gradually subsiding as the tropical termites and death-watch beetles gnawed behind the skirting boards. The loftiness of his new walls panic me as those old mansions did when I was a child. I think I can feel the foundations shifting and the gap widening between the old and the new.

−And you, of course, he grins.

And you. His words are so soft, I wonder if I've imagined them. I can't read his face clearly in the dimness. His glass doesn't make a sound as he puts it down.

−Me? Oh. You mean I'll add to the tropical ambience?

I don't intend this as a joke, but his loud laughter deepens the lines around his eyes and mouth. He places his hand on my head.

−I find you very amusing, you know. And you have lovely hair.

The pores of my scalp unknot as he lifts my plait and lets it drop against the nape of my neck. His smile shifts from his *I want you* smile to his *I know you* smile as he begins to speak softly, with authority, about my writing.

−It's very good. The relationships in it are emblematic, really. England doesn't understand the Far East, and vice versa, but the two are nonetheless complexly conjoined.

He brings his hands together, as if in prayer. Only part of his scar is visible.

−The more I read of your work, the more you interest me, Isabelle.

So he's interested in more of me than just my body. I feel that pang like unspeakable hunger at the glands near the base of my tongue again. I've been waiting for years for food like this.

−Don't look at me like that. Interpreting texts is my job, he says, laughing again, placing his hands over my eyes.

−Actually, I'm trying to write my mother's life before she dies. I don't know if I can do it.

−I can help you, Isabelle. I can help you in lots of ways. He removes his hands from my face, looks me in the eye.

My pulse quickens. *I can help you.* It seems such a confirmation of what I'd hoped for that morning. This time I'm certain I'm not dreaming. His hands are warm on mine. A car pausing on the side road shines its headlights through the autumn fog, illuminating us. I can see the lines of his smile deepening, and the jagged edge of the scar on his hand. Perhaps, over time, he will tell me more about what formed these marks on him. Perhaps this is even the beginning of love, this fascination with each other's histories and their inscription on our bodies, this pleasure in each other's happiness. We're still looking at each other when the headlights pass.

—We could really go places, he continues, with a sweep of his arm that seems to encompass his house and beyond.

My pulse is like applause, uncountable. Ever since migrating to London as a child, I've felt, somewhere deeper than my bones, that I belong nowhere. What I remember most about my father, the tea-taster, is his distance. But, with just a few sentences, this new Englishman, his success and family money surrounding him like a nation, shows me a way out of my statelessness.

Only when we return to his brightly lit interior do I notice his scar seems shiny and quite pink.

THE TRUE BODY

✤ *Light and darkness* *✤*

After putting Ghislaine to bed with a cium, the Christao embrace and sniff that helped them ascertain if she'd been eating hawker food on the sly, Wish and Mathilde spent their evenings cracking their knuckles in companionable silence as they sprawled bow-legged on their wooden planter's chairs listening to the radio, smoking their pipes, drinking the odd glass of toddy. Sometimes when the BBC news was over, they listened to Harry Belafonte or Bing Crosby on the gramophone; sometimes they made plans for their future. The days passed so fast they did not notice the slow advance of Mathilde's turtle-shaped goitre across her neck.

At odd times of the day, Mathilde noticed Ghislaine's gaze become glassy. Her daughter looked terrified. She would be unreachable during those moments, which sometimes stretched to over a minute, before she began shaking and crying long, inconsolable sobs too full of the knowledge of grief for such a child.

Looking into her eyes when this happened, Mathilde was sure Ghislaine was not in her body.

'She has gone to a foreign country,' she confided in Mak Non and Ah Kwei, Ghislaine's elderly Chinese nursemaid. 'What if she doesn't return one day? If anything ever happens to me, promise me you'll take care of her.'

❋

Sometimes after school at Our Lady Convent, Ghislaine went down to the old tree on the banks of the Malacca River with the children from Mak Non's kampong. Still dressed in her blue-and-white school uniform, she lined up with the Malay children in their sarongs and shorts and waited for her turn to swing out from the rope that someone had knotted around the lowest branch of the tree. None of these children knew that several years before the war, a young Chinese woman jilted by her wealthy expatriate lover had knotted the rope so thoroughly on the branch so that she could hang herself.

Beneath Ghislaine, the river was the colour of her veins, a milky golden green. She barely felt the rope burn her palms as she flew over the river until she felt herself entering the diamond-bright afternoon light.

❋

Mathilde's goitre grew gradually through the years of peace until it almost spanned the space between her jaw and shoulder clavicle. One morning as she ate chicken porridge with Ghislaine, Mathilde felt the goitre pressing against her windpipe. She swallowed hard. She put down her spoon. She smiled at her daughter.

'What do you see during your terrors, Ghislaine, anak?'

'Nothing. But just before them, I see a bright white flare, like the one on the picture-theatre screen that happens when a scene gets cut by the censors. And then there is a grey curtain and . . .

nothing. Darkness. When I come to again, I feel as if I don't know anything lah.'

Mathilde nodded and squeezed her daughter's hand. She saw that her daughter found death unspeakable, too.

※

On Ghislaine's fifteenth birthday, Mathilde took her into town to buy sweet kueh to eat with the family that evening. Ghislaine wore the new sky-blue dress Mathilde had given her that morning. She imitated her mother's loud fighter's laugh in between swallowing, without embarrassment, three pieces of kueh – one purple, one green-and-white-striped, one coffee-coloured. Her legs were long and knobbly-kneed as a giraffe's under the dress as it shifted like cirrus clouds across her body. Her hair spilt down her back like molasses; her future spread undifferentiated and shining as the Malaccan morning sea before her.

Mathilde wasn't sure if her daughter saw the pale man in the white Panama hat sitting in the coffee shop over the road, staring at her in her new dress. Mathilde thought she'd seen his photograph in the newspapers; an English journalist, perhaps. She hurried Ghislaine away from his gaze and into the fabric shop, on the pretext of choosing material for another dress. There amongst the bolts of cotton and silk, Mathilde watched in alarm as Ghislaine stiffened and sank into the longest faint she had seen her have. As on previous occasions, her eyes remained open but blank.

'It's adolescence,' Doctor Arbuckle pronounced when he made a house call later that day. He was stooped and his hair was the grey of windborne ash, but he was as dapper and gracious as he'd been before the war. 'Teenage girls are prone to low blood pressure. Give her a good sweet cup of tea next time, after she comes around. And don't worry,' he exhorted Mathilde kindly, patting her on the shoulder.

After that day, the frequency of Ghislaine's blank-eyed faints increased until they occurred almost daily. Besides a cup of tea and food, the only remedy Mathilde had for these blanknesses was to fill Ghislaine with stories about the lives of Malaccans who'd survived great hardship.

'A person without the story of her life is lost. This story binds you more closely to the world when love can't be found.' Mathilde did not imagine for a minute that her daughter was banking these stories as assiduously as money. They were already an unbroken silver thread running through the white flare and dark curtain that severed her own stories' beginnings from their conclusions.

LONDON, OCTOBER 1985

Precious Eyebrows. Gunpowder. Lapsang Souchong. Darjeeling. Broken Orange Pekoe. These are the teas David has brought over and lined up in their airtight tins on the kitchen windowsill. A torn packet of tea sits to one side. This one's mine. *PG Tips Teabags – Economy*, with the image of the woman in the sari fading out to nothing on the edge of the packet.

–One more cuppa for the road. I put Clara to bed half an hour ago, David says as I take my coat off after visiting the hospital. He heats the teapot with water and empties it before pouring boiling water from the kettle over three level teaspoons of the Darjeeling. He warms his cup while he puts the timer on for three minutes, and pours milk into his cup precisely up to the point where it widens.

He cleans his ears with a cotton bud until the timer goes off, and then pours the tea through the strainer until it's one centimetre below the lip of the cup. Making tea properly is something he learned from me. For a few seconds, the fresh cut-grass smell of the tea drifts on the steam between us.

He's made just one, for himself. *I am used to it now,* I tell myself. We've known each other for nearly nine years now.

I look for the flashing red light on the telephone answering machine, hoping Philip's left a message. Nothing. Just David, slurping his tea.

–Would you like something to eat before you go?

I open the fridge. A solitary boiled egg rolls off the shelf. I hear its shell crack as it hits the floor and rolls between us. We stand looking at it for a moment before I pick it up. He gulps the last of his tea.

–No thanks. I'll let myself out.

The cracked piece of shell lifts off as he shuts the door behind him, but the egg inside isn't even dented. I eat it and put on my pyjamas and yellow dressing gown because I can't afford to turn the heating on. In Malacca, that yellow was the colour worn by royalty; in London, it's the colour of a Marks & Spencer final markdown.

❋

My workmate Sunil wheels a barrow towards the wrought-iron-and-glass Palm House near the western end of Kew Gardens. Despite his gardener's uniform and boots, he always looks sleek as a seal with his short hair, dark, mournful eyes and freshly waxed moustache.

–New haircut, Sunil.

He pats it and twirls his moustache.

–Like it? The boss is in a savage mood this morning, Isabelle. We have to pick up the weekend rubbish. Can you clean up in here while I do the Oriental Gardens? The boss reckons the Chinese pagoda's only a few condoms short of a brothel.

The Victorian Palm House looks like an enormous ornate cage. Inside it smells faintly of treacle on toasted crumpets. I push the barrow around the towering central stand of palms with their leaves hanging like attenuated xylophone keys in the domed roof space. I start at the eastern wall, hoping to warm myself in the patches of sunlight there.

Two icecream wrappers and a condom on the ground; a piece of chewing gum stuck to the leaves of a Holy Ghost orchid.

I fantasise that one of these plants is descended from a sample retrieved by my grandfather's pet monkey. I love orchids for their strategies of adaptation and survival. Settling in the buttress roots or branches of some large tree, their aerial roots form lattice-like receptacles to catch plant debris to feed on. Shallowly rooted, so far from the ground, they often appear in danger of falling, but, by growing in such seemingly precarious positions, they avoid competition for light.

I wonder what Philip's doing as I pull off a dead leaf. Every time after I've seen him, I think of the things I should have said.

※

As I push Clara in her pram across the road from the monastery to the hospital, the black-frocked homeless woman sings in her foreign language next to the memorial. At the end of each line she strikes four notes on a triangle she carries in her pocket, *high low, high low.* They're so clear and pure I can hear them above the noise of the traffic.

For the first time, I recognise her song as one of yearning.

I take Clara into the hospital's childcare centre so I can be with my mother while the chemicals drip into her veins.

–I want gramma's sun-and-cloud dress, Clara wails, throwing herself on the cold yellow linoleum, gripping me by my legs and howling until her face is slimy with mucus and tears. The carer takes her from me.

–It's best just to go. Clean and fast, she says.

Clara's face presses against the glass window of the childcare centre as I head out towards the lifts. Her mouth blurs and elongates against the glass. The tracks of her fingers are red on my arms. I turn my face away so she can't see I am crying too.

There is a plaster crucifix above the door of the hospital chaplain's office. *Please. Help me. Please rescue us from too hard a death.*

The plaster Jesus looks mournfully towards the ceiling. Clara howls as insistently as an ambulance. The lift doors open to reveal a white-coated doctor standing by the controls. I press Level 3 and avert my face from his steady gaze as the lift ascends.

My mother's eyes are closed when I enter her room, but her face is tense. Every day might be the day she can't see who I am any more. A clear solution drips through plastic tubing into her wrist. I touch her hand to check whether she's awake or asleep. Her hand is cold.

Please. Not dead. Not yet. I squeeze her fingers.

She opens her eyes. I almost gasp in relief.

–I didn't mean to wake you. How are you?

–Not bad.

Someone's groaning on the other side of the blue curtain around the bed. A nurse checks my mother's drip and leaves.

The muscles in her face slowly relax as the painkiller takes effect.

–They treating you well here? There's a kind of heavy cloud of English Catholicism hanging over this place.

–That's not the cloud of Catholicism. That's the Holy Spirit.

It's an old joke of hers. She closes her eyes and opens them again to look directly at me as she speaks.

–So we are reduced to this. We are sugar and salt, we are nerves and cells. We say our lines. And we love each other. With all our limitations.

I open her old diary at a place that contains more torn-out pages than writing.

–Grandmother Mathilde's writing on that page, mine there. The torn pages are another story. The blank spaces are where unspeakable things happened.

–Can you talk about them now?

She shakes her head. She turns her face to the sunlight streaming through the window, leaving me again to imagine her past.

THE TRUE BODY

✦ *The sleeping dictionary* ✦

When Ghislaine was nearly sixteen years old, Mathilde finally began writing her story in what remained of the red New World *Diary of Emergency Procedures*. The war and the silverfish had claimed some of its pages. She smoothed over the names of the women in the comfort station she'd written all those years ago, turned the pages and began. But perhaps, as she began, she could feel how imminent her end was.

Perhaps her pen bumped over the holes the silverfish had eaten in the names.

The goitre had grown further. She could hardly swallow.

Give us all strength, her ornately seriffed script began. She paused. She could barely keep hold of the pen. She looked out of the bedroom window and tried to gather strength from the sky. She left a large gap on the page, writing where the pen fell. *I am going to fight*

The sentence was unfinished. Apart from the names of the women in the brothel and a few of her recipes, these were the only words written in her hand in the diary. They were the last weapons of a fighting woman, for hours after writing this, surrounded by frangipani flowers brought in by Ghislaine and cups of untouched tea made by Mak Non, Mathilde de Sequeira succumbed to the metastases from the turtle-shaped lump in her neck that Doctor Arbuckle had called a goitre. The doctor who wrote her death certificate rediagnosed it as a tumour, measured it with his callipers and drew the sheet up high over her chin to cover it.

Ghislaine refused the comforting arms of her father and other relations as she stood staring at her mother in her coffin on the dining table. The skin around Mathilde's closed eyes was dark as mildew with fatigue, and her lips were slightly open, as if she was thirsty, or preparing to receive a kiss. Aloysius placed her silver flask filled with toddy, her best clay pipe, and a Holy Ghost orchid next to her in the coffin. Last of all he placed a white cotton thread the exact length of Ghislaine next to the body. He was merely following an old Christao tradition to please the rest of the family. He did not really believe that the white thread would enable Mathilde to take Ghislaine's sufferings with her into the afterlife.

'Now my mother is dead,' said Ghislaine, 'can I go to sleep?'

But Ghislaine did not sleep for hours. She was old enough to know what she had lost. Her mother, devotee of the Silver Screen and Our Lady; cook and synthesiser of flavours from Europe and Asia; bestower of dresses, shoes and Clements Iron Tonic; speaker of hard-won wisdom, sixteenth-century Christao dialect and Malaccan-marketplace English. Her mother, of the soft embrace smelling of spices, of skin like rosewood and hair like a cloud, of laughter like a battle-cry and stories as tall as memorials to the past. Her mother, Mathilde Dolores Oliveira de Sequeira.

'Now she is gone,' Ghislaine asked the unanswering night just before sleep finally came, 'who will I find all this in?'

When she woke, Ghislaine saw the Englishman in the white Panama hat walking on the four-foot way across the road. He reminded her of some question she'd asked herself in the haze of sleep the night before, but couldn't recall. Neither could she recall her mother's loud fighter's laugh, as hard as she tried, although she thought she could sense its echo somewhere deep within herself.

And during the following days that fell towards the future like ill-dealt cards, Ghislaine's vision no longer filled with the white flare and dark curtain, for now she was living the long-suppressed terror of her mother's death.

※

Mathilde had been dead for several months on the afternoon that Aloysius de Sequeira extracted the maggots from Manuel Santiago's arm, but Aloysius still wore both his mourner's jacket and the name Wish, the nickname Mathilde had invented for him. He answered to it sorrowfully but gladly, like the patriot of a country that had cost him his youth.

The Christao people surmised that his grief over Mathilde's death drove Wish de Sequeira to behave in un-Christao ways. He took Ghislaine and the menagerie of pets and left the home he'd shared with Mathilde in the Land of the Priest. He took up residence behind the ruins of A Famosa, the old Portuguese fort, in one of the tall narrow shophouses built in the earliest days of the British colony. A promotion allowed him to buy the house unsubsidised. He employed Ghislaine's old, bespectacled Chinese nurse, Ah Kwei, to help Mak Non in the house. He gave up fishing and toddy drinking and he did not go to church, even at Easter and Christmas.

As the months and the worst of the grief passed, Aloysius took up horticulture and photography, weight-lifting and listening to music, as antidotes to Mathilde's absence. He had classical records and books mailed to him from the Theosophical Society and the Photographers' Guild in London, yet he disagreed with the belief held by his Malaccan contemporaries that England was the centre of the world. He founded the Malacca Conservation Society, whose brief was to propagate species of jungle plants threatened by land reclamation for the golf courses, rubber plantations and housing estates of the British expatriates of the Malayan civil service and the tin and rubber companies. It was a one-man society. He carried plants in his pockets from one medical assignment to another. He negotiated with the local schools to ensure they taught the Christao language that had been dying out ever since the first British governor had come to Malacca. In short, he became a semi-reclusive advocate for anything that might be threatened with extinction.

He began making regular visits to the medicine man Encik, who lived a hermitic life in the jungle beyond the rubber and palm plantations that skirted Malacca. This bomoh taught him how to see worlds beyond what most eyes saw. When he was visited one Saturday for afternoon tea by Hortense Oratio the Devout, who still lived in the Land of the Priest, she was insulted by the way he spent much of the afternoon listening to her speak with his eyes closed.

'And so I said to Father, I pay a stipend, I get a front pew lah.' Aloysius's closed eyelids formed a perfect unwavering seam as Hortense's mouth puckered with disapproval. 'Are you unwell, Aloysius?'

'To the contrary,' he smiled, his eyes still closed. 'I am just consulting my friends about your words.'

Hortense narrowed her eyes. This was surely proof that he was learning black arts from one of those primitive Malay bomohs living in the kampongs on the outskirts of town. She crossed herself, gathered her handbag and stood to take her leave.

'I wouldn't trust friends I can't see myself. When are you coming to church, Aloysius? Who will save you if you don't go to church?'

Hortense was always thorough and methodical at her evening ablutions, but she took the extra precaution of washing herself in holy water that evening.

Aloysius mastered cures for many ills including halitosis, vile thoughts and unfaithful spouses on his visits to the bomoh Encik. Soon he was in big demand for his cures. He built up a steady but covert stream of clients from amongst Malacca's Catholic and Anglican Eurasians – members from both congregations did not want others to know they found his black arts more effective than God in certain matters – but he didn't succeed in curing Ghislaine of living her mother's death as a continuous nightmare.

Wish de Sequeira never courted another woman after Mathilde died. She stayed in his blood despite her death, giving him itchy feet and restless nights. Every night, after a day spent dressing the wounds of fishermen and prisoners and helping Ghislaine with her homework, he shut the door to his high-ceilinged bedroom and practised the bomoh Encik's instructions for travelling out of his body.

To practise this travelling, Wish donned his loosest singlet and drawstring pyjama pants, opened the shutters to the stars and lay on his bed beneath the mosquito net, his arms angled at about sixty degrees to his body (how like an aeroplane, he thought to himself), the palms of his hands facing downwards. He flexed his elbows and knees and rolled his head from side to side in an attempt to release the burdens of the day. He closed his eyes and waited for his heart-beat to slow, for his blood and thoughts to begin swimming in memories of the sweet toddy and kisses trickling down Mathilde's long throat, and of muted nocturnal explosions like white shooting stars between their bodies. Sometimes inventories of bandages, surgical trusses and sterile maggots interrupted these reminiscences, or he found himself hypothesising theories of the relationship between the sweetness of life and despair, or formulae for fortifying Ghislaine against the enervating nightmare of life after her mother's death. Other urgencies would occur to him as he lay there – the necessity of making reparation to the expatriate neighbours after Ghislaine's pet python, King George, had swallowed their Persian kitten; the urgency of speaking to a local Chinese dying-house pro-prietor about the poor quality of the gruel he served to the almost dead; and of lobbying the governor for more taps per kampong.

Wish allowed all these thoughts to swim in his blood. In the beginning, as he lay in his dark room willing himself towards the tall dark rectangle of stars and sky framed by his bedroom window, he felt as if his soul was being stretched to breaking point by his anxiety over Ghislaine and his grief over Mathilde. It was almost more than he could bear. If he hadn't had Ghislaine to care for, he would have left to make a life in a new country. Australia, perhaps, or even America.

'How can you travel out of your body if your spirit is torn like this?' he asked Encik the bomoh.

'Loss makes you ask questions of life. Just don't expect answers. It'll only grieve you further,' replied the bomoh in his courtly old Malay dialect.

After that, Wish lay on his bed at nights watching his questions unfurl like an endless scroll, waiting patiently for their undulations to subside. Around midnight, his house became silent and deep as the well it was built around. But for six more months the questions kept coming at him, keeping him tied to his body, until one night, during the seventh month, he was so tired he forgot his questions.

Lying on his bed, he felt his muscles unknot and his bones sink into them so deeply that his spirit lifted and peeled off his body like mist. As he thinned out and drifted through the window, he felt the air move through him, temperate as silk. He was fascinated but unsurprised to find himself floating over the crumbling and mildewed walls and rooftops of Malacca's old colonial district. He made a note to fix the cracked terracotta roof tiles above his kitchen before drifting across the newer roofs of the expatriate bungalows towards Hortense Oratio's house in the Land of the Priest.

Hortense was in her bedroom, tossing and turning. Although her bed was in darkness, Wish could sense that she was awake, for her bitterness permeated the air as he floated into the square of light cast by the full moon through her window. She did not flinch or call out, confirming for him that when he travelled like this he was not visible to anyone else. He hung there in the pale blue light until her breathing became shallower and she began snoring. But, even in her sleep, she kept tossing and turning.

What a painfree way to visit troublesome relatives, he thought. *I don't need to speak, and I can see which of them have clear consciences. Poor Hortense, how you suffer in the gap between your piety and your lack of faith*, he murmured. He kissed her breath and floated through the wall into the night again.

Three houses away, he heard his sister Zeraphina's snores rumbling like distant thunder as she lay next to her husband, Theobald Albuquerque, in the light cast by the streetlamp outside their window. The forebodings of her dreams showed in the mobile lines on her forehead, but Wish apprehended that these had more to do with her anxiety over Theobald's impending loss of work than her conscience. Next to her, Theobald's face wavered beneath a cloud of alcohol fumes, but, for the first time, Wish could read the war that had continued inside Theobald ever since his internment by the Japanese sixteen years previously. Wish's vision was filled with a fleeting but startling image of Theobald burying his face in the dirt of the jungle as, nearby, his best friend's body exploded in a hail of Japanese bullets. In his bed, Theobald cried out and Wish understood he'd been shown a part of Theobald's recurring nightmare. As he exited their room, Wish resolved to offer his brother-in-law and sister the use of his recently acquired Cameron Highlands property to re-establish themselves in some business that took advantage of the expatriate tourist trade there. It was a little rundown, but it would give them a start.

But Ghislaine. What about motherless Ghislaine? Just as he thought he'd thinned out enough to be able to permeate and dissolve all problems and questions, he fell back to his bed with a shudder, dragged back from his floating body by his grief over his daughter and his dead wife. The problems of everyone he'd visited seemed either resolvable or bearable, except for Ghislaine's. *Ah Mathilde. If only you were here, Mathilde, Ghislaine would suffer less.* It was as if his daughter and his dead wife existed in some unreachable world, some unattainable site beyond his resolve.

❀

On her seventeenth birthday, Wish de Sequeira sat for hours telling Ghislaine stories about her mother.

He told her about their courtship and the menagerie, about Mathilde's courage during her first marriage and the war, about her despair over the comfort women and over the treacle. He told her about her determination to overcome Ghislaine's childhood terrors with stories and trips to the movies, about her pride over every step Ghislaine took into the world.

'These are all stories of love,' said Aloysius. 'I am telling them to you because you will hear other stories about your mother from people who loved her less. All stories have their truth, but the truest stories about a person are told by those who loved them most.' As the purple Malaccan dusk descended, he handed her a book spattered with oil and sticky with glutinous adhesions. 'She was a great cook. She taught herself how to cook as a way of consuming time after being divorced by that Chinese lawyer. She invented new recipes and menus during all those years of longing. When we married, she fed them to me. This is her recipe book.' Every story about Mathilde that he told Ghislaine was a memorial to his love for her.

In the nights that followed, Ghislaine lay awake under her mosquito net in her bedroom well past midnight. She thought her father was dropping the weights he lifted to keep himself fit when she heard him crash to the bed after his curtailed attempts to travel out of his body.

Some nights, she felt certain stirrings in her body that made her think about food. She fantasised about sinking her teeth into cakes that were firm yet soft. She took out Mathilde's recipes and read them under the sheets. The recipe for Putugal seemed an answer to her longing. Putugal was a glutinous tapioca and banana cake coloured with the small blue flower of the clitoria creeper that grew in the jungle on the outskirts of Malacca.

The next day, she showed the recipe to her father.

'It's called Putugal because the cake's blue and white, the colour of the Portuguese flag. Your mother baked it for the Tranquerah church's priests and congregation after mass. The priests ate it even though they wouldn't give her communion because she was divorced. *Imagine that, all the priests swallowing clitoria-coloured cake baked by a divorced woman,* she used to say.' Ghislaine sucked her plait in bewilderment. Aloysius saw he'd gone too far. He cleared his throat in embarrassment.

'Clitoria is, of course, the name the anatomically obsessed English expatriates give to what is really a species of pea flower the Malays called bunga telang,' he explained when he brought in a handful of the flower for her that Saturday morning. Ghislaine didn't need to try too hard to work out which part of the anatomy the English were obsessed with. A more instinctive creature than her father, she soaked and squeezed a handful of the blue clitoria flower until each petal was bruised and her fingers were stained with its juice, before soaking three cups of grated coconut in water to make one cup of thick milk. She was intrigued by the speed with which the liquid took on the sweetness and milkiness of the coconut. She put her finger in it several times and sucked it before grating a few pounds of tapioca, over which she poured the sweet white milk and one and a half cups of sugar. She mixed all this so vigorously she began dripping with perspiration. She cut the sticky mixture in half and coloured one half with the blue clitoria dye. She lined a cake tin with greased banana leaves before spreading a layer of banana over a layer of the uncoloured mixture. She laid the coloured mixture on top, patted it firmly down with her long tapered fingers until her mouth watered, and then steamed it on the stove for twenty minutes. When she had finished, her face was flushed and dripping with sweat. She cut it into diamonds and swallowed them while they were still warm. As she felt them slide past her tonsils, smoothly, sweetly, without resistance, she cried silently with longing for her mother, and for whatever love the future might hold.

In the back of her mother's recipe book she wrote:

Different kinds of Waiting.
Waiting for sadness to pass
Waiting for something to take the place of sadness
Waiting for what you want more than anything else in the world
Waiting for someone real to take the place of God

For Ghislaine had begun developing her own remedies for the grey curtain of bewilderment that severed the beginning from the end of so many of her days. All of them involved waiting: wait the grey curtain out; wait, drink Fauldings Effervescent Saline or Teacher-brand tea; wait, eat something cooked from her mother's recipe book or the hawkers' stalls; wait and trust that, somehow, she would rediscover her mother's fighter's laugh in herself; wait and trust that her beginning would be joined to her end, despite the link between them being lost forever.

By the time she was seventeen years and one week old, Ghislaine was a woman in possession of many facts relating to her mother and father's love for one another, but especially these: that longing and waiting can serve many purposes and take on many flavours; and that telling stories about the dead is the closest the living get to re-enacting their love for the dead.

※

A few weeks after her seventeenth birthday, Ghislaine walked back from town in the early evening with Olivia Skelchy, her wide-mouthed, worldly cousin who was the daughter of Mathilde's sister Lourdes Skelchy. A drunken Englishman wearing white rubber-planter's clothes was pissing in the gutter outside the Malacca Club. He buttoned up his fly casually and inquired festively: 'How's your nonok? How's your pukas?' before stepping into his own urine on his way back inside.

'That itchified white prick has been learning the Malay words for women's private parts from his sleeping dictionary,' Olivia Skelchy said.

'Sleeping dictionary? The English expats at the end of our street call our next-door neighbour Jamilah a sleeping dictionary.'

'Girl, why you so ignorant and pretend holy, ah-yah? The expats call your neighbour a sleeping dictionary because she sleeps with that English museum curator. Translation isn't the only thing he needs her for.'

'What do you mean lah?'

'Ah-yah! So hysterical! Like you got geragok shrimps for brains! Most English bachelors in this town have a sleeping dictionary, and some of the married men, too. They need them for talking business as well as for sex. How else do they come to know the Malay words to sweet-talk locals with? How else do they learn the Malay words for women's rude bits?' Olivia Skelchy spat in the direction of the retreating English planter. 'And how else does a poor east-coast kampong girl like your neighbour come suddenly to live in a good part of town so close to the expats?'

Her neighbour Jamilah never looked the same to Ghislaine after that evening. She appeared instead like a closed book, this woman with the dark interior life, full of hidden meaning, turnable, susceptible to mistranslation and tearing.

When Ghislaine heard other chapters of Jamilah's story days later, she was at the annual Malacca horse races sitting behind the members' stand with her father, who was on duty in case of accident or heat exhaustion amongst the mostly expatriate spectators. The pre-monsoonal northerly wind carried the aroma of tobacco smoke from the members' stand directly to her, making her long for a puff on a clay pipe. She dared not tell her father she'd taken up pipe smoking with Mak Non and Olivia Skelchy in the afternoons, before he returned home from work. The gossip of a group of expatriate planters' wives drifted with the tobacco smoke towards the de Sequeiras.

'Did you hear the museum curator's sleeping dictionary has run amok?'

'Amok!' How like squawking macaws the wives sounded as they opined beneath their hats of fine straw over tea and scones.

'Completely amok!' And their tobacco smelled so fine, no Rough Riders for them.

'I agree, amok! The Malays invented the word, after all.'

'What did she expect, that sleeping dictionary? That he would prefer her to a wife from his own people?'

'The next race has a few classy thoroughbreds in it.'

'My Malay houseboy says that sleeping dictionary kept a Hantu Pelesit. You could hear her talking to it at night before she had the baby.' The informant had a long nose and a narrow-brimmed cloche hat.

'A Hantu Pelesit?'

'A spirit some Malay women keep to make their man love them. Or so the fairytale goes,' the woman hooted down her nose.

'She needed *some* kind of magic. I don't know what the curator saw in her. So coarse. Too dark and dumpy.' The woman in the wide-brimmed hat might have been grading tea.

'That's where a Hantu Pelesit comes in handy. A Pelesit masks a woman with a false version of herself that makes her look attractive to her man. Or so my houseboy says.'

'I'd sooner use cosmetics.'

'Wouldn't mind putting my money on that thoroughbred owned by the Dunlop manager.'

'Do you believe in all that hantu talk?'

'Well,' said an elderly, quietly spoken woman whom Ghislaine recognised as Doctor Arbuckle's wife, 'there is a certain wisdom in the Malays' superstition.'

'These Malay women will resort to anything to get themselves an Englishman. Watch your husbands, ladies,' warned the long-nosed woman.

'They're off and racing.'

'My houseboy says she lost control of her Pelesit when the baby came. She had no time after the baby came to look after the Pelesit.

The fake beautiful version of herself shrank and disappeared into the jungle with the Pelesit. The museum curator was no longer bound to her,' the long-nosed woman concluded.

'Surely you don't believe all that primitive superstition?' one of the planters' wives asked.

When Doctor Arbuckle's wife spoke again, her voice was so soft that Ghislaine could only just hear it. 'I don't know that we can dismiss it as superstition. The Malays have been in this country a lot longer than us.'

'That doesn't stop them from being primitive. That sleeping dictionary simply let herself go, like all the native women do after they have babies. No wonder the Malay men take more than one wife.'

'So she isn't a sleeping dictionary any more.'

'She is a woman amok.'

'She can't even remember her own name. What was it, anyway?'

'What does it matter? She is the woman who went mad for love.'

'But don't you think that could happen to anyone?' demurred Doctor Arbuckle's wife.

All six women turned to watch the horses come down the straight. Ghislaine looked at her father to gauge his reaction. He rolled his eyes.

'Notice,' he whispered, 'Mrs Arbuckle is really first class, like her husband.' He paused. 'I remember when our neighbour changed from a mysterious sleeping dictionary to the woman who went mad for love, as some of these expat wives call her. That English curator robbed her of love not once, but twice.'

Wish de Sequeira told Ghislaine he had been at the harbour escorting a sick Malaccan sailor home when he saw a tugboat heading back from the open sea to the passenger dock. Nothing remarkable about this, except that someone stood on the tiny deck of the tugboat wailing so loudly he could hear it over the bustle and din of the harbour.

'Ai yeeeee! Aiyeeee!' He stood watching the colours of the

tugboat and the woman on board become brighter as the little boat swung around to face the morning light and the dock.

The woman was facing the horizon and screaming, her head back, her mouth dark with grief, her hands clawing the air at the end of her outstretched arms.

'Do you know this madwoman?' the tugboat pilot asked. 'She tried to stow away on the boat thinking her Englishman was on board, but wrong boat lah. He left yesterday morning with a child to catch the mailboat from Penang to England.'

Aloysius raised his hand to stop the man's gossip. 'This woman is my neighbour Jamilah.' The de Sequeiras had lived next door to the nocturnal comings and goings of Jamilah's expatriate lover for three years, and Wish had treated the illnesses of their illegitimate child, Yusef.

He knew her story well.

'Grief is deep. Deep and very private,' he admonished the pilot.

After her father recounted this tale to her at the expatriates' horse races, Ghislaine approached Jamilah, who was walking up and down the street looking into the distance, one hand shielding her eyes. As she drew closer, she noticed Jamilah murmuring.

'What love? Lies, all lies. Where Yusef? What love?' she repeated over and over, pausing sometimes to spit after the first question.

Ghislaine meant to console her, but she was shocked by the gaps in Jamilah's words and gaze. It was as if one could look straight through huge holes in her cover. It seemed to Ghislaine that grief had blown open this sleeping dictionary, and that everyone felt entitled to read her. There she was, falling open at the words her lover had marked in her as he undid her page by page, exposing her spine, leaving only this bad translation of her flapping in the wind.

LONDON, OCTOBER 1985

When I get home from Philip's house after the second class of the semester, I invite David to stay for dinner, but I burn the curry and forget to cook the rice until well after the curry is spoilt. I'm in the house I've shared with my mother for years, but I'm no longer at home in it.

–Oops. Sorry.

–Look, just put it on the table.

David's voice is higher than usual.

–Oooh. Black meat, says Clara.

I never feel I have to apologise to Clara, and suddenly I feel terrible about this. Clara, in the course of her short life, has learned to slide in and out of her parents' laps with their moods, and to tiptoe warily around their incompetencies, pointing out their most picturesque consequences.

–Look, for goodness sake, lend me a hand. Just this once, I hiss at David.

His fist comes at me suddenly, as if through the dark. I take it across my forearm; behind our colliding wrists I can see the grim snarl on his face. My arm is hot with the rush of blood.

–Oh.

Clara, so understated in her dismay and shock. It's not my forearm that hurts me as much as Clara's precocious restraint. Nearly two years old and she's learned how to repress her alarm at her parents' behaviour.

My voice comes from somewhere beyond this quaking.

–Go.

–I'm . . .

–Go.

David opens his mouth again, shrugs his shoulders and looks at the ground. All the colour has drained from his face. He turns, rushes down the hall and slams the front door.

Clara stands at the table twisting the hem of her sun-and-cloud-patterned dress, her face pale, her eyebrows raised and mouth turned down.

–Don't worry, Clara. Don't worry.

I cut her the most tender pieces of meat I can find on top of the burnt shell of the curry. She eats with her eyes lowered, pushing the meat jerkily into her mouth with her hands.

After splashing my face at the kitchen sink, I read her *Where the Wild Things Are*. In the aftermath of our savage family meal, the long-clawed and fanged monsters drawn there seem even more unconvincing.

When she's in bed, I retreat to the darkest corner of the kitchen. Through the window, this part of my mother's garden looks over-grown, as if the cultivars are returning to the jungle of their wilder ancestors. When I close my eyes, the face of my mother waiting patiently for her death comes to me, and my arm still throbs with the imprint of David's fist. But I don't weep, because the words Philip had spoken to me earlier that evening gleam at me through the darkness: *You look like you belong here.*

Promising enough words to begin a life together.

Philip Border: my escape from burnt leftovers and grief.

I open the kitchen door and walk through the night garden.

Inside my mother's small greenhouse, the seedling trays she'd placed there just before her most recent diagnosis are full of potting mix, waiting to nurture new life. She loves this little greenhouse because on a sunny day its humidity and the light shining through its greenery remind her of the jungle in the hills around Malacca. When I close the greenhouse door on the seedling trays, the hinges creak like someone weeping softly.

In the garden, I run my hands over the leaves of the palms my mother planted to symbolise renewal after long journeys and great tribulation, the orchids she'd planted to symbolise flowering despite false love and erratic sustenance.

It occurs fleetingly to me that my mother's garden is proof that paying attention to what one has bears more fruit than longing for what one has not.

THE TRUE BODY

✦ *The afternoon of the* ✦
Portuguese ambassador

After Mathilde died, whenever Ghislaine de Sequeira thought about her own destiny, she saw an overedited, flickering film of an actress in an imperfectly conceived minor role. All completeness and true meaning seemed to reside just beyond Ghislaine. Her father went to work, but he rarely brought the stories of others' lives or the news of the wider world back with him to illuminate the house in the evenings. After Mak Non and Ah Kwei had served the evening meal, he'd kiss his daughter on the forehead and retreat to his room immediately. The few relatives who visited dared not crack jokes or laugh in Aloysius's company; his stricken face canted towards the ground, his funeral jacket drooping from his diminishing frame. Six months after her mother's death, the rooms of the de Sequeira house were still shuttered and dark with her father's mourning, and the candles at the altar remained unlit.

Ghislaine began to fear that her destiny would be defined by this cloistered grief; the platitudes spoken by the nuns of Our Lady of

Sorrows Convent; and by the narrow, dusty streets she walked between school and home, with their crowded shophouses and kampongs, their history of incessant defeat and colonisation, and their sad but ineluctable aroma of incense and shit. It seemed to her she'd been left behind by the rest of the world as it went on turning towards the bright future.

All this changed on the day of the tea party for the Portuguese ambassador.

It was February. Outside, the heat evaporated fine droplets of rain before they hit the ground. Ghislaine had been withdrawn from choir practice with her cousin Olivia Skelchy and three other girls to prepare afternoon tea in the staffroom for the ambassador, who visited every five to ten years to keep alive the tenuous but four-centuries-old connection between his country and the Christao Eurasians of Malacca.

They could hear the first form's bored chant through the staffroom walls:

'Rubber is used for tennis shoes, bathing caps and bouncing balls.'

It was Ghislaine's job to slice the sugee cake she'd baked the day before, a whitish-yellow loaf dense with semolina and eggs. How gently she'd folded into the creamy dough the ground almonds and brandy, the rose essence, cinnamon and cloves. How diligently she'd creamed the semolina in the butter. How many times she'd stroked it with the curve of her spoon to make it rise.

She ran hot water from the kettle over the knife blade to help hasten its passage through the granular interior of the immense cake. She licked the knife when the nuns weren't looking. The gobbets of cake melted on her tongue as she smiled at the nuns with her lips closed. She finished cutting the cake. She was curious more than apprehensive. She had never met the Portuguese ambassador.

'First girl to see him tell me straight away. He is creamy-brown, like milky coffee,' said Sister Victorina. 'He comes in a dark blue suit with white shirt and a long black car with four staff carrying fans and papers and his wife.' She hurried off to make sure the new plastic flowers had been placed at the altar and the table of honour.

Ghislaine helped Olivia take from the oven the pang susis, the spiced meat buns.

'They look like your nonok,' whispered Olivia Skelchy. 'Plump and golden.'

'But not as hairy,' replied Ghislaine as the other girls set out coin-sized pineapple tarts amongst the cups and saucers.

'Stop wasting time on small talk, you two cousins,' shouted Sister Victorina. 'He'll be here any minute.' Ghislaine was putting the last warm pang susis on the platter when she saw through the window a pale man in a shirt and trousers. He wandered past the British and Straits Settlements flags hanging next to the newly laundered Portuguese flag and the freshly painted and flower-strewn grotto of Our Lady. He stuck out his chin and chest, as if he was determined to impress. He had his shirtsleeves rolled up and his straw Panama hat skewed like coincidence over one eye.

'The Portuguese ambassador has arrived, Sister Victorina!'

The man knocked on the door. Ghislaine opened it and curtsied low. The man looked slightly surprised, but pleased with himself. He thrust his chin and chest further forward. He'd taken off his hat. His gold-streaked hair was illuminated by the daylight more compellingly than the faded halo on the picture of Christ hanging on the wall. This was the first time Ghislaine had come close to eyes that were the blue of horizons and distance. They seemed closer to the sky than she had ever been. When he returned Ghislaine's smile, his teeth shone. She looked down quickly at his shoes. They were dusty brogues. She'd only seen shoes like this on the feet of Doctor Arbuckle. She thought, *How hot this man's feet must feel.* She wished her smile didn't take up so much space on her face. She wished her nose was shaped less like a chilli pepper, that her hair was neater, thicker, longer, smoother. She wished her abdomen didn't reveal her love of food, that her dark brown eyes were blue, that her olive complexion was as pale as Ginger Rogers' skin.

Sister Victorina hurried in, black moons of perspiration at the armpits of her grey habit. Ghislaine had never seen her sweating like this for the church. Sister Victorina exhaled loudly at the sight of the pale man.

'That's not the ambassador, you silly girl. Where's his black car? Where's his staff and wife? Where's his suit and white shirt? That's just another Englishman in a batik shirt and linen trousers. What is your business, young man?'

'I heard your after-school Portuguese language classes were available to members of the public,' the pale man said, slightly crest-fallen but speaking like the British governor, adamantly impressing his importance upon his audience. He took his eyes off Ghislaine for only a couple of seconds, but this was long enough for her to notice the way he held his head back slightly, as if he was both familiarising and distancing himself from everything he saw. A small gold filling glinted from his top left incisor. When he looked at her again, she saw how authoritative his gaze was. It was as if he knew her already.

'Why does an Englishman want to learn Portuguese?' asked Sister Victorina.

'I am a travel writer,' replied the man. 'Walter Humphries is my name. Actually, I want to learn Spanish for my next European journey, but someone said there has never been any Spanish in Malacca. Malacca only has the next best thing, right?'

'You'd better go before the Portuguese ambassador hears you,' said Sister Victorina. 'He is coming any minute now. No time for Portuguese classes today! Come back next Tuesday. Three-thirty.' She hurried out of the room, scowling.

The man smiled unabashedly now at Ghislaine de Sequeira. He was struck by the incandescence of her flushed cheeks against the strange green tinge in her golden skin. He wondered if she was unwell or excited.

'Are you feeling all right?' he murmured solicitously.

'Me?' she gulped, running her hand quickly across her face,

smoothing her hair, wishing for a mirror to show her what had prompted his question. 'I am fine. And you?'

He didn't waste his breath replying, but he knew how to use his eyes to smile and look at the same time, this man. He knew more about the world that turned beyond the dark shuttered mourning of her past months than she would ever know. Already she wanted some of this light.

'You'll be doing the language classes too, I trust?'

'Yes.' Up until then, she hadn't even contemplated them.

'Do you know any Portuguese?'

'Only some dialect.'

'You're Eurasian?' His smile didn't leave his face once. She nodded.

She decided, in the sudden, wilful way that some adolescent girls do, that his smile was kind and wise, that his nostrils were flared with desire, like that of an actor she'd seen in a Hollywood film once, and that his cinnamon-coloured freckles made his skin mouthwatering. His body struck her as being not unlike Doctor Arbuckle's Chesterfield sofa, compactly padded, comfortable and capacious; and his clothes as a little eclectic but international, those of a well-travelled man. She felt a sensation like motion sickness roll from her head to her belly. She nodded again. She felt she could go on saying yes to him forever.

Since childhood, Ghislaine had deduced that anything resembling true civilisation had come to Malacca through the English. At the opening of new roads and hospital wards, she'd watched the sweating pink-skinned officials in suits raise His Majesty's Straits Settlements flag, its white insignia shaped like an upside-down pair of men's underpants. She'd seen them unveil shiny new taps in kampongs with a flourish, or shake her father's hand as they promoted him to positions well below their own. It became apparent to her that these administrators of the colonial government determined the status of every Malaccan. Until she met Walter Humphries that afternoon, she was a Malacca girl who knew there were better places in life, but she could see no means of getting there. When the English travel writer exercised his voice and gold-filled smile on her, she grasped at his apparent interest in her with all the undiscriminating desperation of someone intent on leaving behind an inferior, grief-darkened past.

No-one else was looking. She lifted a pang susis from its plate and pressed it into the travel writer's hand. It fit perfectly. When he bit into the cleft running down its centre, it released a smell of hot dough and spicy meat.

Ghislaine did not meet the Portuguese ambassador that afternoon. His chauffeur had taken a long detour on the drive from Singapore to avoid some communist bandits rumoured to be waiting with their guns on the outskirts of Muar. It was nearly two years since Malaya's British governor had declared the Communist Emergency over, but communist bandits continued to resurface like rumours on the outskirts of towns.

She returned to the tall narrow shophouse on Jalan Koon Cheng that she shared with her father and their menagerie of pets. She ignored the crazed cries of Jamilah next door. She ignored the desperate greetings of the ravenous fat grey cat Winston Churchill; of Wimbledon the racquet-tailed drongo and Mata Hari the talking mynah in their wicker cages, and forgot to feed King George the python his weekly frozen mouse.

She sat and watched the traffic flicker only five feet beyond the shuttered front windows of the sitting room. She sucked salted plums until all the juices in her mouth ran. When it happened with the travel writer, it would be like this: sugar and salt dissolving in her saliva and blood, bearing away the grief of her past. She imagined the next Tuesday afternoon, the knowledge of the world the nuns never gave in Geography, and the perfect, light-filled escape from her father's dim, cloistered grieving for her mother.

✳

All through his first language class, the English travel writer stared at the way Ghislaine's lips formed around the Christao words for love, for heart, for very good. On the wall above his head, mildew grew on the glowing heart of the sun-faded Christ pulling aside his robes to reveal the affliction of his love.

'Coracao,' Ghislaine murmured, her voice getting fainter and fainter as his gaze grew more intense, 'subrosoo.'

At last he looked away from her. 'Is this the real Portuguese?' the Englishman asked Sister Victorina.

'This is more authentic than the Portuguese they speak today in Portugal. It is Christao, the dialect spoken by the Portuguese colonisers here in the sixteenth century.' Sister Victorina held her head high and imperiously as a queen as she turned with her chalk to the board.

The man tapped his lips with his Regal fountain pen and remained silent until the end of class. When Sister Victorina left the room, he turned to Ghislaine.

He wore a paler batik shirt than last time. 'I am a journalist specialising in travel writing. I will have travelled the whole world by the time I am fifty. Only a few years to go.' The travel writer's body bore marks of experience unlike any she had ever had. When he tugged at his left earlobe, Ghislaine noticed a tiny indentation in the skin, as if it had been pierced and had then grown over. His hair was bleached and his skin tanned and lined as if he'd spent hours out in the sun, but he didn't look nearly fifty years old. To Ghislaine, he looked like freedom from grief and duty.

'My name is Ghislaine de Sequeira. I haven't been anywhere much.'

'Well then,' he said magnanimously, 'I can teach you things, and take you places you've never dreamed of.'

✳

The following week, Walter Humphries waited until the end of the language class to give Ghislaine de Sequeira a scrapbook half full of cuttings of all the articles he had written since his arrival in Malacca six months previously. She did not thank him for it. She had to hide the scrapbook in her school satchel to conceal it from the eyes of her father.

Her convent was on the ocean side of the town. She passed the street of the laundries with its yards full of charcoal-burning coppers and steam on her way to the rickshaw parade, where some prostitutes already waited, leaning on rickshaws pulled by their wheezy cigarette-smoking permanent boys for the evening's trade. She walked through the makeshift stalls of Glutton's Corner and bought herself a portion of oyster omelette. The oysters squirted their briny juice over her tongue with every bite she took and slid like firm jelly past her tonsils. She didn't waste a drop, licking her lips and following it with a serve of roti chanai. She mopped the gravy with the flat pancake before rolling it to swallow in three mouthfuls.

'Hollow legs,' the Chinese and Malay cooks sniggered. 'Real Sirani girl will eat anything.'

Freshly moustached with piquantly spiced gravy, Ghislaine de Sequeira struck out past the laterite red statehouse and post office before circling the hill with its roofless old church that looked out west across the town to the sea. She picked her way over the ruins of A Famosa, scattered over its eastern base. The de Sequeiras' house was the last before the bend in a row of five shophouses, and the only one occupied by Eurasians in the area. She carefully hid her satchel in her wardrobe upstairs, helped Mak Non prepare and serve curry devil for dinner, and, citing tiredness, declined to sit with her father next to the radio as he cracked his knuckles and parodied the British newsreader's accent. She took a torch to bed and read the first article in Walter Humphries' scrapbook under the sheets before going to sleep.

A World of Choice in Singapore
by Walter Humphries

The dance floor of the Great World awaits every expatriate bachelor in Singapore every Friday and Saturday night in Chinatown. Drink, food, entertainment and especially women — from white through to black and all shades in between — are his for the choosing. Here, all colours mingle without the constraints of that other work-a-day world they have taken refuge from for a night.

At the entrance, you queue with other bachelors, mostly expatriate or Chinese planters, bankers and businessmen. You pay seventy cents and enter the Great World all awhirl with circling dancers and shadows from the ceiling fans. Above them, a gilded dragon and phoenix undulate through clouds towards the bar. At the bar, you can order whisky stengahs, Singapore slings or a wide range of international lagers. On the dance floor, white, black and brindle glide through the fumes of alcohol and cigarettes to the tune of some Oriental chanteuse howling songs from the silver screen, which are heard these days in nightclubs all over the Far East. Often the chanteuse is backed by a band of half-castes known here as Eurasians, who also strum Hawaiian rhythms on guitars at intervals.

This happy musical synthesis of West and East reinforces the sense that the World is yours for the taking as you eye the hostesses, also called taxi dancers, who sit on chairs on the circumference of the floor. A twenty-cent ticket entitles you to a dance with any one of these girls at a time. They are mostly Chinese or Eurasian, apart from one or two of the less rustic type of young woman of Malaya or Siam. The Chinese girls wear the tantalising yet demure long brocade gowns known here as cheongsams, frog-fastened at the neck, bust and waist. The Eurasian girls wear the same if they derive from Chinese stock; a sarong kebaya if from Malayan stock; or, most typically, Western evening dress, perhaps featuring the off-the-shoulder bodices and can-can petticoats currently in vogue here due to the latest spate of Hollywood films. These girls of modern Singapore wear their costumes in very untraditional ways: tight enough to reveal their curves. Though their chests are rarely generously endowed, their bodies sway elegantly because they are slender and taut, rather than prone to wobbling as girls of Anglo-Saxon stock are. These Asian maidens wear their hair bobbed or pulled back in a chignon, and just enough eyeliner and rouge to enhance their Oriental beauty. Even by this well-travelled Englishman's measure, they are a pleasure to behold.

I found myself vying with every other man for the same handful of willowy daughters of Cathay, but in the end I had to choose from two girls left behind, a Thai and a Eurasian. I eventually settled for the cheerful daughter of Siam, who was comparatively squat and dark complexioned, but also agreeably manoeuvrable on the dance floor.

An additional fee of around eighteen dollars entitles patrons to sit and converse with a girl. Many expatriate bachelors with limited contact with eligible expatriates of the fairer sex relish such opportunities, and I know of several who have met their regular partners, sometimes known as 'sleeping dictionaries', in this way. If it is conversation in good English you want, try the Eurasian girls, who are usually educated in the English language, as well as fluent in at least one other tongue. However, while many of the Eurasian girls have an indefinable attractiveness to them, they are a little less exotic than the Chinese, Siam or Malay girls, and many expatriate men I know find there are certain compensations for not having to converse with the girl you dance with. Lest you be in any doubt about what these compensations are, there are advertisements for 'potency medicines' behind the bar, and these medicines are available for purchase along with alcohol. One such poster exhorts: **Fortify Your Manhood With Tiger Brand Tablets**.

These posters remind you that if you have no luck in the Great World, just around the corner are the brothels where a girl of any race can be had for a small sum. For all her cleaning up by the British, Singapore still sits close to the bottom of the moral morass that is the East. Yes, it's the end of the working week in Singapore, and here the whole world is yours for the taking.

Ghislaine drew in her breath sharply. She surmised that Walter Humphries must be what her father called an experienced English bachelor. She believed the picture he painted of himself on the floors of the Great World dance hall, and did not know whether to be worried or relieved that she could not see herself there.

His article adjoined an advertisement for P&O Far East cruises, in which a pale woman on the deck of a ship nestled against a tall man's shoulder. Ghislaine thought the man looked like Walter Humphries. The couple smiled at the dark figure of a woman standing forlornly under a palm tree on the shore. Ghislaine imagined herself escaping with Walter Humphries on holiday, far away from the walls of her father's grief-shuttered house. She turned off the torch and breathed shallowly under the damp cotton sheet.

Would she be the sad woman left behind? Or the one to get away from it all?

❁

When Ghislaine went to town on Saturday morning with five dollars from her father and instructions from Mak Non to price a new rice saucepan, she'd already made up her mind. She'd had enough grief. She would not be the sad woman left behind. She dressed as if she might meet the travel writer at any moment: hair out, waistline nipped in over her full red can-can skirt. She hurried past the soothsayer at the Chinese temple who divined futures by suspending a cut piece of his clients' tongues in a jar of cloudy liquid; past the Malay bomoh who used boiled eggs and rice to predict what future awaited his clients in the Land of the Unseen; and paused, hand over her eyes, at the Cantonese face reader who could foretell one's luck in love. She hurried away when the face reader looked at her too intently, and turned the corner into the street of kitchenware and shoe repairs.

Embroidered tablecloths, charcoal burners, enamel buckets, clay pots, aluminium rice and steamboat saucepans balanced in unwieldy piles on the four-foot way. It was good luck for a young woman to be seen buying things for the kitchen. She looked around for Walter Humphries before bending over the saucepans and checking for dents in them.

But she was just pretending. She left the dull clank and squeak of household effects behind her and headed to the street of haberdashery and tailors with its shiny buttons and bolts of fabric, towards

King's with its flesh-coloured liquids, powders and foundation garments. She dabbed some foundation on the back of her hand. She told herself her skin was only a little bit darker than the colour the English manufacturers of cosmetics and foundation garments called flesh. She wanted to be as succulent as the film stars in *Silver Screen* magazine. She wanted the travel writer to want her. She fingered the petticoats and brassieres on their racks.

And then she saw the dress. It felt unctuous as fine-grade coconut oil, and was cut from silk along the lines of a Shanghai gown. *Colour: Flesh* it said on the label, but it was not the colour of her flesh. It was somewhere between the colour of bandages and the pale skin of movie stars she had seen at the Cathay Picture Theatre. She tried it on. Not too tight, not too loose.

She bought it with the five dollars her father had given her and the ten dollars' pocket money she had saved over months, asked the shop assistant to wrap it carefully, forgot the price of rice saucepans, and ran all the way back home with it hidden in her string shopping bag. But Jamilah was standing at the bend in the dogleg where their two houses joined. She gave her high-pitched wail and rushed towards Ghislaine, clawing at her string bag with her bony bird's claw of a hand. Ghislaine pulled her last three salted plums from the bottom of the bag and gave them to Jamilah, but her neighbour kept pointing at the bag. Ghislaine wondered if the woman knew she had a dress the colour of movie-star flesh in there.

She did not look her neighbour in the eye. She ran upstairs to hide the dress in the back of her old Dutch wardrobe.

Pausing at her bedroom window, Ghislaine saw the shadow of Jamilah against the lace curtain of the upstairs window in the adjoining shophouse. She wondered what it would be like to be that woman who went mad for love, standing there holding the lace curtain to her head, practising to be a bride; or bundling it in her arms, practising to be a mother again. Remembering what could have been hers if the museum curator hadn't decided she was uncollectable.

❋

Walter Humphries waited by the grotto for Ghislaine after the next language class. He'd noticed the narrowing of Sister Victorina's eyes whenever she saw him speaking to Ghislaine.

'Would you like afternoon tea with me? There's a coffee shop around the corner. I'll walk you home afterwards.'

'As long as you don't make me drink coffee or walk me home lah.' As they walked, Ghislaine de Sequeira didn't tell him she knew every coffee shop and hawker stall in Malacca. The travel writer guided her proprietorially to the Melaka Kedai Kopi, a dark narrow shop with creaky old bentwood chairs and small round marble tables. He pulled out a chair for her and stumbled over a table leg. He flushed and cleared his throat importantly, opening his mouth and closed it again.

Ghislaine was glad that her back was turned to the street. She hoped that no-one she knew would see her if she kept facing the wall behind the charcoal burner where the coronation photograph of Queen Elizabeth basted in the oil from the daily cooking of the coffee shop's specialty, nasi lemak. She ordered a teh tarik.

The old Malay proprietor poured Walter Humphries a thick black liquid of cardamon and coffee from a tall jug into a large glass and squirted a cloud of sweet condensed milk straight from the tube into it. As the travel writer sipped, he kept his eyes fixed on Ghislaine.

'So. Are your family originally from Malacca?'

Ghislaine nodded, and drank as gustily as if she were a child.

'I assume you are descended from the original In-Between people. The Mestiços, or topazese, as they were called a few centuries ago. What are you? Half caste? Quadroon? Octoroon?'

'One hundred per cent Eurasian mix,' she replied, utterly guileless, in a voice far bolder than she felt.

'How old are you, Ghislaine?'

'Seventeen.'

He smiled at the milk moustache on her finely chiselled top lip.

'What brought you to Malacca?' She felt slightly reckless, asking him a question like this. 'I mean, I didn't think that anyone . . . like you would be interested in Malacca.'

'You would be surprised. Far Eastern travel is a growing industry. And my father recommended the Far East as a place for a young man to begin a working life. Though I must say I prefer Paris myself.'

Ghislaine de Sequeira only blushed slightly when Walter Humphries pulled a handkerchief out of his shirt pocket, leaned over and wiped the moustache from her face. It was what her mother would've done. She ran her forefinger over her clean top lip and smiled.

The travel writer had seen many paintings of the Virgin in the chapels and museums of Europe.

'You have a madonna's smile,' he told her. But he didn't look more deeply; didn't wonder why, at her age, her smile held such pain.

'So, Ghislaine. Are *you* hoping to get away from here eventually?'

She took Walter Humphries' question as an invitation. 'Yes,' she answered. 'Oh yes.'

❋

When she went into town that weekend, Ghislaine stepped inside Pinky's Wedding Shop on the street of tailors and haberdashery. This was the first time she had ever stepped inside Pinky's. White dresses hung on dressmakers' dummies like inflated ghosts in the dim interior. She narrowed her choice down to two: it would be the dress with the peplum on the hip, or the one with the low back and neck. There would be a honeymoon in Paris.

Her nipples rose as the silk of the first dress rolled like water down her skin. She felt the flesh at her waist pucker as she fastened the dress. Too tight.

'Aiya,' she muttered to herself as she popped a fake pearl button, 'all that hawker food.' She would need larger fittings and firm foundation garments, but something told her she would not need a soothsayer.

Perhaps it was youth. Or perhaps it was her longing to escape grief that made her certain Walter Humphries was meant for her.

LONDON, OCTOBER 1985

 A tea trolley rattles past the doorway and wakes my mother just as I begin writing her a note.

–How are you?

–Sleeping a lot these days.

–You probably need it.

For just a few seconds, she doesn't conceal her despair.

–For what? Practising to die?

She sits up abruptly, as if ashamed, and tries to reassure me with a smile. But her smile looks strained. She holds the fold on the hospital sheet in place between her thumb and forefinger.

–Sorry. Grandfather Wish told me once that the terminally ill often feel ashamed of their condition. Well. What have you been up to?

–Oh, you know, the usual. Though my writing tutor, Philip Border, invited me to his house again the other evening.

–Oh? That must have been nice.

What can I tell her? Yes, I forgot who I was for a while? That it was like being in another world?

❋

Sometimes when the tutor takes me, no light is on except the little lamp next to the gold plated Buddha; sometimes the full glare of the ceiling lights makes my eyes ache as he enters me. Often as we lie in his new, dazzling white bedroom, I can hear the creaking of wood and hinges in the old, dark part of the house, as if it's straining to break away from the shell of the renovations that cocoon us. Sometimes the ornately carved Victorian mirror in the hallway or my reflection in the gleaming new windows show me my incongruity in his house. Often the artefacts of his travels seem to loom around us under their spotlights like museum exhibits, proof of the distinctiveness of his history, and the itinerary of his life fills our conversation after we make love. Sometimes I'm sure I can hear a scratching in the roof of his bedroom like a creature trying to escape some exitless space, but he tells me it's a figment of my imagination, or it's the branches of the oak tree against the eaves. Other times I think I can hear the wailing of a child, but the tutor assures me it's just my anxiety over Clara or my mother, and he strokes my face to calm me. Sometimes he talks to me about my writing or my body, sometimes about his own. If there is a moon, the shadow of the tree outside his bedroom window moves back and forth across his face. Often he turns his face to one side, as if to avoid being read by me. Sometimes he places his hands over my eyes. So that I never quite possess Philip Border's image as he enters me.

THE TRUE BODY
❦ *The journey towards silence* ❦

'Would you like to come out with me on Saturday night?'

Ghislaine feigned a casual shrug, but the sense of motion sickness she had felt since meeting Walter Humphries escalated. She took a desperate and noisy slurp of teh tarik to slow the spin of her blood, struggling to look perfectly composed as she sat across the table from him. She felt herself begin to splinter.

You don't even know Walter Humphries, she told herself, heeding her father. *Careful he doesn't slip a little white tablet into your milk.*

Perhaps her face went red, or pale; perhaps she looked too long at her tea. Walter Humphries knew how to read such signs of unease. He asked her about her family, school, he told her she was beautiful. All this and the attentiveness of his sky-blue eyes were almost overwhelming for her: she was only seventeen, just a Malacca girl, naïve enough to believe this man could help her escape the grief of her mother's death. He smiled at her, enjoying her youth, perhaps even realising he'd already begun needing her for the feelings of solicitation and tenderness she engendered in him. How long had it been since he felt this way? As if a woman had melted some time-hardened crust in him. When the travel writer wiped the milk moustache from her lip again, Ghislaine thought only fleetingly of her mother. Then she remembered the flesh-coloured silk dress under her bed and felt the blood jump under her skin again. He sat and watched these surges of blood in her face for almost two hours, talking her through them, listening with the patience middle-aged men cultivate for young women. He told her again there were places he could take her.

'Where?' she asked him.

'We shall see,' he said with a wink as he rose from the table. It sounded like a promise. She followed him out into the dimming light of the late afternoon.

Only minutes after they left the Kedai Kopi, there was a moment so dark that Ghislaine de Sequeira would not be able to see it clearly whenever she tried to recall it, a moment so unutterable she would not speak to anyone of it for her whole life. It occurred in the narrow alley between the Melaka Kedai Kopi and the Chinese medicine shop, where no sunlight fell and the damp mildewed walls pressed against her like fate.

'No,' she said, 'no,' but it had already happened. He'd spoken only a few words, but he'd done something irreversible with them, something that went against everything she'd been taught. Something so painful that it split her in two.

※

In the wrung-out heat of the early March days that followed, Ghislaine fell again and again into the darkness of her split self. In this darkness, every footstep, every voice sounded like the travel writer coming to assuage her dread and longing. On the eighth night, she resolved to make herself whole again. Her plan involved bringing the two men in her life together. She would do it with cake. She would use her mother's recipe for sugee cake, the queen of Christao cakes, the making of which involved as many taboos as ingredients. It would be a practice wedding cake. It would show the two most important men in her life how much she loved them.

Every afternoon after school that week, she crisscrossed the streets of Malacca buying ingredients for the cake: fifteen large eggs; the semolina, flour and ground almonds; the essences of rose, vanilla and almond; the stew spice, candied winter melon and cream. While her father was away on house calls on Friday night, she beat the white grains of semolina into the butter until her arms ached and the butter ran, and let them mingle overnight with one another for seven hours under her bed, next to the silk dress.

She waited until her father was out again the following day before she whipped the eggs and sugar into a lather and creamed the semolina and butter into it. She watched with satisfaction as the dry ingredients swelled with the creamy mixture. As she poured the mixture into the tin, bubbles surfaced from deep within the mixture and popped. She sighed as she licked the back of her spoon. The cake rose in the oven like a breast, but sank immediately she pulled it out.

She cut the cake in half to make the dent look less obvious, but each piece looked as if it were running downhill. All she could do was level them with thick icing. She chose yellow, the colour of royalty, for each man. She rehearsed her request to her father as she waited for him to return.

But Ghislaine never had the chance to give her father the cake and ask if she could go out with the travel writer. When he arrived home, Wish was thin-lipped with consternation, brandishing the travel writer's Taxi Dancing article, neatly cut and dated by Sister Victorina's hand.

Adamant as the mole on her lip, Sister Victorina had remembered Walter Humphries' name from the newspaper when he first introduced himself, noticed his exchanges with Ghislaine, and made it her job to read every article written by him in the newspaper.

'You told me Englishmen were good men,' Ghislaine murmured.

'You silly girl. I meant the first-class ones. You know what these second-class John Felt Hats do to Eurasian girls, don't you?' shouted Wish. 'Don't you? Don't you? They take them out for a drink and slip little white pills into their glasses of lemonade! They promise them a mansion in England, marry them and take them back to a tiny flat and a life as a dustman's wife! Or worse still,' his voice trembled, 'worse still, but even more common, they don't marry them. They get themselves a nice English mem from home, and keep the Eurasian girl on the side as their sleeping dictionary. If she's lucky. Do you know what happens to sleeping dictionaries? Just go down to the Land of the Priest and take a look at all the sleeping dictionaries there. They bear children out of wedlock. And lose the good name of their family forever.' Wish realised what was behind his words even as he spoke them. How strange to hear his anxiety over Ghislaine's lack of motherly guidance manifesting in this way. It occurred briefly to him that he had been listening to too many expatriate Englishmen boasting of their conquests of local women over whisky stengahs in the panelled wooden darkness of the Malacca Club, but he kept erupting dire warnings.

'Do you know what a sleeping dictionary is? A whore; an Englishman's whore.'

Ghislaine went to her bedroom upstairs and locked herself in with the sugee cake. She left it under her bed uneaten. She did not emerge for two days, except to pull in trays of food left at her door by her amah, Ah Kwei, or by Mak Non.

On the third day, she sat at the table but refused to speak to her father. After an hour, Wish de Sequeira compensated for his daughter's implacable speechlessness with another torrent of words. 'You will not return to Our Lady of Sorrows Convent again. The day after tomorrow, you will accompany Aunty Zeraphina and Uncle Theobald to my place in the highlands, where they will be setting up a tea shop. You will cool off your itchified behaviour up where the English are so first class they won't speak to a girl like you.'

Ah Kwei and Mak Non stood speechless at the entrance to the kitchen, gazing at Ghislaine from behind her father's shoulder with their ineffable spinsters' sadness and compassion.

Under her bedsheets that night, Ghislaine composed a brief note to Walter Humphries explaining what had happened, entreating him to write to her care of the Tanah Rata post office in the Cameron Highlands. She sealed it in a pale blue air-mail envelope, addressed it to Mr Walter Humphries, International Traveller, Scholar and Writer, and placed it with the best, carefully wrapped half of the sugee cake into Mak Non's hands the next morning.

'I do not know where he lives. Find out where and put these on his doorstep. Can?'

'Can.'

※

Wish was filled with remorse, but was determined to carry out his resolve to send his daughter far from the reach of Walter Humphries. The day before she was due to leave with her Aunt Zeraphina and Uncle Theobald Albuquerque, he gave Ghislaine two things.

'This was your mother's. I can't remember its name.' It was a stone carving of a heavy-breasted woman with feathered wings and tail like a bird's. It had sat on her mother's old dressing table for as long as Ghislaine could remember. In a halting speech of curiously strung emphases and pauses, her father said: 'It's a woman spirit, a poet and singer to the gods. Your mother's uncle, the sea captain, brought it to Malacca rolled up in a wad of tobacco when she became pregnant with you. A native somewhere in Indonesia gave it to him for luck. Your mother believed it helped her find her way between life and death when she gave birth to you, and helped her again in those months she knew she was dying.'

'How could you fly with tetek like that?' She pointed to the breasts.

'Your mother said that was the magic, finding the way to leave this life and body when its weight became too much.'

Her father handed her the old New World-brand book covered in red and marked *Diary of Emergency Procedures*. He'd torn out the comfort women's names and lists of symptoms, but overlooked the crumpled page of brothel regulations at the back of the book.

'Your mother was going to write her story in this, but she didn't get the chance. I thought you might . . . use this to record your own journey one day. Even when the outward journey is harsh, there is always the reward of one's own inward journey.'

Ghislaine did not look her father in the eye, let alone thank him, for she was sure now that he was mad.

※

Early the morning after Aloysius de Sequeira gave his daughter the stone spirit and the New World diary, Zeraphina and Theobald Albuquerque pulled up outside the house in their blue Mayflower. Ghislaine was waiting in the front room with one suitcase and three wicker cages containing her menagerie of pets. Theobald tied the baskets to the roof of the car. Wish placed the newly rediscovered tins of treacle from the war in the boot.

'It's in perfect condition,' he assured Zeraphina. 'So much sugar it will never go off. The expatriates in the highlands will love it.' Ghislaine sat flanked like a prisoner on the back seat by Ah Kwei and Mak Non. She did not turn to see the tears welling in her father's eyes. She did not hear him call, 'God bless, my dear daughter. God bless.'

It was a cool sunrise, the sky wan and bleached, the birds subdued in their song as the blue Mayflower left the gentle hills of Malacca for the dusty plain that stretched to Kuala Lumpur and beyond. Ghislaine did not speak to anyone else during the day-long journey, except to whisper to Mak Non as they approached Kuala Lumpur after passing litter-strewn jungle and plantations of rubber:

'I would rather show my arse to Theobald on the verge than squat inside one of those filthy bus-station lavatories.'

Her pets had even less self-restraint. Every now and then a rivulet of yellow urine or khaki and ash-coloured faeces trickled down the windscreen from one of the animals in the wicker cages.

'Ah yaaah!' cursed Theobald Albuquerque. 'Who allowed this spoiled child to bring her zoo? We'll be drowning in shit by Tanah Rata.'

As they drove, Ghislaine barely noticed the city looming ahead. She felt her throat constricting, as if it were trying to prevent someone driving a fine blade into it. Aunty Zeraphina had packed a five-layered tiffin carrier full of pakoras, curry puffs and kueh of assorted colours and glutinousness, but her niece had been struck by such lethargy and constriction around her throat that she could not be tempted.

By the time they reached the outskirts of Kuala Lumpur, Ghislaine was almost overwhelmed by the sense of motion sickness and loss of focus she had first experienced in the company of the travel writer. This unreadiness to say goodbye to what she knew echoed her feelings when she had watched her mother's coffin being lowered into the wet Malacca earth.

After the travellers had left the racket and screech of the capital behind them, the interminable order of rubber plantations planted by the British resumed: rows and rows of *Palaquium gutta*, rubber trees, their thick white sap silencing jungle and species that had never been catalogued. She thought of the tread of tennis shoes, the firm grip of bathing caps, the bounce of rubber balls, and dry-retched silently into her old school satchel.

The Mayflower passed army barracks and town bus stations where people ate food cooked over charcoal burners at makeshift stalls streaked in motor oil and clouded by fumes; and kampongs where buffalo and chickens took shelter from the sun beneath wooden stilted houses, while naked children sat in the storm drains with their fingers hooked like question marks in their mouths as they watched the traffic go by. Ghislaine saw all this with an increasing sense of distance, because her vision began to blur and she was overcome by a sweat that began as a heat and then settled in her as a chill. She became uncomfortably aware of her stomach, as if she could sense its precise outline within her. Mak Non noticed with alarm the pallor that had overcome her charge, but Ghislaine would not speak about this or anything else.

On the other side of Tapah, the grimy town at the foothills of the Cameron Highlands, the road began to climb steeply into clouds that hung like lumpy grey puddings from the unseen tops of serried peaks. It grew narrow and edged along the sides of hills that fell away on one side into valleys hundreds of feet deep. Every time they took a bend, their bodies swayed to one side so that Ghislaine was forced every now and then to suffer the indignity of rubbing shoulders with the others. Throughout the ordeal, Zeraphina Albuquerque gripped her rosary beads until her knuckles were white, murmuring the Hail Mary continuously as her husband sucked more and more frequently on his hip flask and swore hotly at every driver coming the other way. By this time, Ghislaine's symptoms had taken on a momentum of their own. A terrible queasiness had replaced the outline of her stomach, she felt her mouth awash with saliva, and the beads of sweat had turned into a thin sheet that wrapped around every square inch of her skin.

'Don't worry, anak. Travel sickness,' murmured Mak Non. 'You always did get it in high country.'

'Hoh! Travel sickness is caused by lack of moral fibre,' Theobald boomed from the front seat.

'Nonsense lah! Travel sickness thrives on an empty stomach.' Zeraphina's spurned offerings from the tiffin carrier sat on her lap. 'What she needs is soup made with horseradish, rice and fish. Or . . . remember our honeymoon lah? P&O recommended pickled onions and champagne to make a gas in the stomach to equalise the pressure.'

'Actually, it is to do with the upsetting of the organs of balance in the ear and the abdomen. The only certain remedy is to arrive,' murmured Mak Non.

But when they reached the hills glowing in the afternoon light with rows of tea-bushes that unfolded like sheets of green cotton wool spilling out of bales, Ghislaine knew her journey from Walter Humphries to silence had only just begun.

※

Theobald parked the car outside a double-storey weatherboard mansion bearing the brass nameplate Journey's End on its front door. This was Ghislaine's first look at her father's recently acquired retirement house. It was a sprawling weatherboard hexagonal house whose shape had been dictated by the hill on which it was perched. It had been named Journey's End by its previous owners, an English tea-plantation manager and his family, and it was still decorated with the furniture and ornaments of previous owners. Wish had bought it cheaply as the demands for Independence increased.

The house clung to the curve of a hill that overlooked a valley about halfway up the highlands, between the kampongs in the dust of the foothills and the clouds. Above the clouds were the rose gardens and the tennis courts, strawberry farms and mock-Tudor guesthouses where the English expatriates spent their holidays. Ghislaine strained her eyes looking for a gap in the clouds. There, in the very spine of Malaya, on the other side of the cloud, were so many ideas of England. Standing on the verandah of Journey's End, Ghislaine was struck by the distance between herself and these ideas. She sat and felt another wave of cold sweat wash over her. She smelled the white flowers stiff as wax and fragrant as coconut rice that grew in the bed against the verandah, but did not know their name.

Inside, she dropped a coin in the centre of the room next to the twisted ankle of the baby grand piano. The coin was one of the last she still had from Malacca. It rolled more quickly across the wide second-floor sitting room than it should have, gathering rather than diminishing in speed as the slope increased near the edge of the room. A lustrous white orchid straddled the wires of the grand piano near the window.

'A Holy Ghost orchid!' she exclaimed with surprise. She knew the flower from her mother's funeral. She thought she could smell the coffin oil: cool, woody, poignant. She struck a key. The note sounded dull and muffled.

Both these incidents showed Zeraphina and Theobald that Wish had bought a structurally unsound house to retire to, and that they would not be able to profit indefinitely from his generosity. They never spoke to one another about this. Each kept the image of the rolling coin and the strangled music to themselves as they unpacked and paced out the dimensions their teashop would take.

That first night at Journey's End, Ghislaine went to bed on a hard mattress and dreamed of empty envelopes. She woke the next morning even further adrift on the lassitude of the previous day, a lassitude that felt like travel sickness, only more intractable.

'What is her problem?' Zeraphina Albuquerque whispered to Mak Non.

'She's mourning both her mother and that John Felt Hat. She hasn't really left Malacca.'

※

A week later, Wish de Sequeira noticed an odour of rotting sweet-ness drifting from his daughter's bedroom. He supposed his grief over their separation was playing tricks with his olfactory nerves. He shut the door so he wouldn't have to look at the drawers full of little girl's dresses that no longer fit her, bought by Mathilde; or the drawings of brides dressed like queens on her walls. He did not see the furry grey mould feeding on the moist sugar of the sunken breast-shaped cake under her bed.

As for Walter Humphries, he had found the note from Ghislaine de Sequeira with the carefully wrapped cake on his doorstep when he came home from the office. He swallowed it in one sitting, dropping nearly as much on the floor as he had eaten. He interpreted the sugee cake's buttery, granular texture as failed sponge cake. Ghislaine's penned words blurred under the whisky he spilled from his glass. He was as ambivalent about her departure as he was about the passing of the cake down his throat. If Ghislaine had been there watching him eat, she would have seen he was a traveller accomplished at keeping the country he moved through at a distance.

❋

While their niece drifted on the stubborn residue of her travel sickness, Theobald and Zeraphina did what they could to sustain the illusion of their own soundness. They installed a flushing water closet and a tall earthenware Shanghai jar in the bathroom, an Arctic-brand refrigerator and Ah Kwei in the kitchen. Mak Non beat the spiders from their corners and laundered the heavy damask curtains. The Albuquerques had her plant a lawn of English blue couch under the trees. Theobald filled the crystal decanters the English had left at the built-in bar in the loungeroom, and took his place at it by midday every day, knees akimbo on the hinged leg rests of the teak planter's chair, whisky stengah perched on his white-singleted paunch. For Theobald had thrown away the old tin hip-flask full of brandy he'd used ever since the war to wash away his torrid memories and enduring nightmares of imprisonment by the Japanese, and he now sat at the bar as if he had finally reached his true station in life. There he gradually subsided until he fell off his stool or was dragged by Zeraphina to the bathroom to be sluiced with water and put into bed in his pyjamas, in plenty of time for Wish's invisible nocturnal visits.

Until her uncle was put to bed every night, Ghislaine lay awake listening to the breaking of glass in the bar and the voices of her aunt and uncle arguing, if her uncle was sober enough to reply.

Sometimes these noises merged with the sound of men shouting in the valley below the house. The voices both inside and outside ascended and descended into hope and terror, as if they were unsure whether they were being left to live or die.

When she mentioned what she'd heard to her aunt and uncle at breakfast one morning, they did not look at one another.

'The communist guerrillas,' her uncle said.

'*Communist Bandits Still Active*,' her aunt averred, pointing to the headline on the front page of the morning newspaper. It was the third time that month that the newspapers had reported communist bandits terrorising towns or destroying rubber trees on British-owned plantations. '*Again the communist bandits have failed in their bid to sabotage the post-war British governing of Malaya by disrupting the economy. The communist insurgents' senseless actions simply prolong the danger and inconvenience which has hampered both the reconstruction of Malaya since the end of the war and its moves towards Independence*,' Zeraphina concluded, before rolling the newspaper and funnelling spilled tea-leaves through it into a canister.

'Are we safe?' asked Ghislaine.

'They won't touch us here. This has been declared a White Area for years. Bandit free. And the Emergency is over, really. The bandits have retreated to Thailand since the end of the war. We're safe as houses.' As he spoke, Theobald's eyes slid across the room without focusing, and the rafters of Journey's End creaked in the wind.

LONDON, NOVEMBER 1985

In class, all eyes follow Philip Border. He cuts through late-afternoon stupor and hunger with his sharp talk and deft hands. Quotes and citations roll off his tongue; even his laughter sounds erudite, as if it's referenced. The earring glints against his warm gold skin. His repartee and the slogans on his T-shirts reveal he has been everywhere that counts. When he throws the class his quick epiphanies and jokes, he smiles at everyone.

But at the end of each session, when the last students have filed out, he gives me the smile that is for me alone.

※

Leaves in the wind; an early moon climbing the glass.

His phone rings, pauses and resumes.

−Expecting a call? I ask. On the wall above the telephone, numbers and names are scrawled on small yellow sticky-notepad squares.

−No.

Philip strokes my hair as the phone rings out. The distant

scratching noise like a branch against the eaves sounds so far off that I dismiss it.

–Tell me about your travels during the last break, I say.

He draws me onto the couch and speaks softly, his hand mapping my breast.

–In Paris, the districts fan out from the first arrondissement, which is centred on the Île de la Cité in the middle of the Seine, where Henri the Fourth kept his printing presses and a mistress whose name was lost to history. There's a hotel called Henri Quatre in that building now. The connection between sex and the dissemination of knowledge goes back a long way.

–I've never been there, I say, embarrassed by my limited knowledge and experience in these matters he speaks of with such easy authority.

–It doesn't cost much to get there, he replies.

I think of the unpaid gas and electricity bills sitting on top of the fridge. *Not much is all that I have.*

My words and my debts seem unspeakable.

–Is something wrong? he asks, his hands pausing like parentheses at my shoulders. But I shake my head and smile. Twenty–eight, and I still believe I might be rescued.

His fingers measure the gaps between my clothes and my skin. I'm suddenly aware of the holes along the seams of my old Marks & Spencer vest. I wish I'd listened to what my mother told me about thread count.

He undresses me slowly, almost courteously, his head inclined as if listening to distant music, his eyes on mine insistent and ardent as a child's.

All his sighs rising in me. A tide rushing underneath our skins, sweeping duty and death away.

The sea off Malacca, a flooded shore.

–What a good fuck, he says.

The meniscus of our mingled perspiration breaks as he rolls onto his side. In the dimness above the telephone, the names on the yellow paper squares are only just visible. Habiba. Pushpa. Lily.

He cups my chin and turns my face towards his.

−The pool's been tiled and filled with water. Come and look.

I pull on my shirt and stuff my shameful vest surreptitiously into my bag. His T-shirt glows a thick white as he leads me through to the conservatory.

Nets of departing daylight shift and glow softly in the pool's depths. He gestures across it.

−I think a tropical garden on that side.

−What a good idea. I could help you with that.

For a moment, he looks unnerved.

−Oh, I'll just get my gardener to do it.

Twisting his gold sleeper in his ear lobe, he stands immaculately sleek by the potted palm. *I have a place for you*, his smile seems to say. He has a fuller range of smiles than anyone I know.

−You look good next to the bamboo and teak, Isabelle.

Blood rushes through me like applause.

Spreading his arms like wings, he leads me back through the glass room.

−Just a bit more decorating left to do. I chose the furniture and the floor coverings myself. Tiles, sofas, the marble and stainless steel in the kitchen, everything.

−You never lose on investing in the kitchen, I say with false authority, thinking of the kitchen back home with one working burner on the stove, the floor running downhill, the cupboards that don't close properly.

−I'm redecorating in here, too.

He stands with his hand on the door handle of his study. There is a key in the lock. The room smells of leather and paper. Its walls are dark with books of literary criticism and photographs of bodies and destinations; its wooden desk is covered with notes in his emphatic, flowing handwriting. The new floor coverings and furniture are soft and perfectly proportioned, like his clothes. He has infinitely more threads per square inch than I.

His house, his body, his thoughts. Everything about Philip Border seems measured and collected.

❋

—Look at your mother's smile. She looks like a saint, doesn't she? A saint, the nurse nods adamantly.

The doctor shines his torch into my mother's eye.

—What's that look like? he asks her.

—Dim. Tell me, doctor. Is the human body dark inside?

—It's dark inside, no doubt about that.

He takes his gold-plated pen from the breast pocket of his jacket, turns to face me and draws a sphere.

—Let's say this big area is the vitreous body of the eye.

He sketches an ellipse at the front.

—Here's the lens. Here's the retina.

He draws a broken bracket at the back of the sphere.

—The retina is considered by many to be a specialised part of the brain, actually formed from it during gestation. It contains cells that deal with dim light and colourless vision, and others that deal with bright light and colour vision. Here at this break at the back of the retina is a small whitish area called the optic disc. It's also called the blind spot. All people have this blind spot. It's where the optic nerve begins.

He draws a small cloud over the beginning of the nerve.

—This is your mother's tumour. It's getting steadily bigger, gradually covering the blind spot and the retina, beginning to enter the nerve itself. Hence the steady diminishing of her vision.

—Can you see any of his diagram? I ask my mother after the doctor and nurse leave.

—Not very clearly.

—The tumour looks like a cloud, I explain.

—A cloud, slowly cutting the light from the nerve. Until you can't see. Until you're left with the darkness that's inside you.

THE TRUE BODY

+ *A connoisseur of women* +

After he had eaten the sugee cake, Walter Humphries' first reaction to the note Ghislaine sent to him before she left Malacca was one of alarm, followed by self-protection. He did not reply to her, changed his place of residence and told the newspaper office's receptionist not to give details of his new address to anyone requesting them. He ceased going to the Portuguese language classes. For weeks, twinges of remorse assailed him and the broad, expectant face and almond-shaped eyes of Ghislaine came to him as unpredictably as the weather, but he told himself he was acting in her best interests, too. *Beautiful but too young*, he murmured whenever her image arose.

In matters of Malaccan cuisine, the travel writer was prepared to try anything once, but, when it came to Malaccan women, he had just a few favourites. He overcame his desire for the immature buds and undisappointed expectancy of Ghislaine de Sequeira by renewing his attentions to those few women of Malacca whom he had already tried and whom he trusted well enough.

He supposed that these favourites represented nearly every race that lived in Malacca. He visited one of them whenever he felt need or boredom, which was usually once or twice a week and usually on a Friday or Saturday night; but he took care to visit these women in strict sequence, so that he felt that he was being faithful, in his own way, to each one of them. Now that he was only a few years away from fifty, he found making love more frequently than this interfered with his writing, and with his ability to transform his penis from comma to exclamation mark when occasion required.

So each of his four women waited sometimes for more than a month for a visit from him. Travel was his ready excuse, or dead-lines, and he found that these excuses and the fact he had been away from their bed for so long, lent a certain urgency to the ardour of each woman. These visits were the most mysterious, unreported journeys of Walter Humphries the travel writer, and were amongst the most indelibly impressed on his mind and body, apart from when he undertook them too drunk from too many whisky stengahs in the Malacca Club beforehand. To each of these women, he always managed to apply his expertise in the art of remaining unattached to every destination he moved through, without any of them suspecting this.

Pushpa Arasu, a short and fine-boned Tamil widow, supported her three adolescent sons by sewing blouses on her kitchen table for Marks & Spencer in England. The travel writer sometimes spent hours in the alley outside her blue weatherboard house in the Indian quarter, waiting until the light went off in her sons' bedroom. He held his offerings of grease-stained paper bags containing samosas and curry puffs away from his shirt.

'You have beautiful hair,' he would say if she needed more persuasion after eating. He was careful when he went to her bed not to make any noise that would wake her sons.

Pushpa Arasu greeted and farewelled him with a patient melan-choly, standing beneath the bunch of leaves that hung above her threshold to ward off the evil eye, her face slightly averted from him. He did not know the name or the purpose of the leaves. He assumed she was still grieving her dead husband. He did not for a moment suspect that Pushpa Arasu mourned his own recalcitrance but that she had too much grace to say so. He believed it suited both Pushpa Arasu and him that he left just after midnight, long before the sons awoke.

The following Friday or Saturday, Walter Humphries would visit the English nursing matron Lucille Towner-Jones in her bungalow at the foot of St John's Hill.

'You have lovely eyes,' he would say, always before and never after making love with her. He knew that, for all women, such compliments had different meanings before and after the act. His strategy was to use praise generously before lovemaking and very rarely afterwards.

Lucille was the most vain of all his women, except Lily Cheong. He supposed that at some point in her past, Lucille's vanity had superseded her desperation and explained her marriageless state. No one man could be good enough for Lucille Towner-Jones, and Walter Humphries knew he was no exception. He respected her despite her vanity, for he knew from inadvertently gossiping with them in the Malacca Club that she had two other expatriate lovers. He suspected she knew about his other women too, for she treated him with a contemptuous familiarity that bordered on disdain, often trimming her toenails and shaving her legs and armpits in his company.

The Malay seamstress Faridah, who would not reveal her surname to him, would only receive him during the day. She lived in the kampong of the sloping mangrove, beyond which the sea glittered diamond-like, overexposed in the midday light. She was the plump, round-cheeked first wife of a Malay who had another wife in another kampong. She directed him to enter her house through the side entrance facing the animal pen and the mangroves. He sometimes found himself waiting with assorted livestock – chickens, goats and a particularly shameless rat – in the overgrown gutter near her house, until her husband left for his second wife or the mosque. Her wooden kampong house was curtained with bright frills at every window, picturesque as a doll's house and open to the squawks of the livestock and chatter of the other kampong dwellers outside.

'It is necessary to chew the pillow here,' she warned him before they made love, 'and listen for the front door in case my husband comes from his second wife's house to visit me.' She sat above him with her long hair out, so that he felt as if he were lying in a tent.

It can wait was Faridah's favourite phrase. It was her unflappable response to his occasional impotency, and he was secretly grateful for this. She taught him how to say it in Malay: tidak apa. Faridah continued to see Walter Humphries because she felt sorry for him. She fed him nasi lemak in the bed draped with the same frilled nylon curtains that were at the windows, and soothed him as if he were a baby, both when he was unable to make love and after he had succeeded. He found that she lacked the technical finesse of Lily Cheong, the fourth woman he visited every month.

Lily Cheong was a Nonya, a Straits-born Chinese woman from one of the oldest families in Malacca. She was at pains to point out her aristocratic ancestry and the extent of her jade jewellery collection. She lived in a grand apartment at the back of her clan's kongsi, their temple. She made love with Walter Humphries on the embroidered red coverlet of an enormous rosewood marriage bed carved with peonies and bridges, under a ceiling decorated with the Cloud of Eternal Greenness. She made it clear to him that he would do only until a richer man proposed to her, and pointed out to him his deficiencies in gift buying, lovemaking and attentiveness.

Walter Humphries was a creature of such habit and high self-estimation that he'd had no compunction about visiting all these women in this way for years.

One night, about a fortnight after Ghislaine de Sequeira's departure for the highlands, Lily Cheong was even terser with him than usual. He had just presented her with a pair of green silk ribbons.

'What for you know me so long and you haven't learned to

make each gift finer than the before time.' She threw the ribbons on the marriage bed before filling the silver bowl of her opium pipe and turning away from him to face the window.

'I thought they'd look good against your dark hair. You have such beautiful hair.' He could see the corner of her mouth turn up. She looked pleased enough. Sometimes his words distracted women from his lack of true engagement with them. Lily Cheong looked at him for longer than usual. She saw the boy in his face, and not for the first time. She was nearly thirty years old. She would've liked to fall all the way into some kind of childlike, responsibility-free marriage in which they indulged one another in the exotic trappings of their respective cultures, but she knew this would cause too many consequences with her parents and her inheritance.

'Go. I have a headache.' She was already filling her opium pipe. 'Leave me to my consolation.'

Walter Humphries left the echoing walls of Lily Cheong's dark apartment physically replete but filled with a desolation that echoed that of his Orpington upbringing. This was neither coincidental nor an aberration, for what he sought in his visits to each of these women was an approximation to home, to something the same as, yet more than, the echoing shell of his childhood with his distant parents. Yet this time his abjection felt worse than usual.

He was filled with a nostalgia he couldn't account for when he saw some golden pang susis for sale on a hawker's barrow, but, as he walked home through the Malacca dusk that smelled of ash, he thought of Ghislaine de Sequeira: amenable and smelling like fresh bread. His forty-seven years felt heavy in his bones. When he turned his thoughts away from her, he knew he did so not due to any resolve on his part, but out of his inability to withstand the full weight of his sexual ache for her.

He was not sure which of his remaining Malaccan women he preferred. As he walked, he mused that the ingredient common to his feelings for all of them was diffidence, which he found a useful mask for furtiveness and guilt. But that night, as always, his conscience did not get in the way of sleep, for his conscience was almost always at least two women and several meals behind his libido.

※

Ghislaine found eight unopened jars of Horlicks, thirteen tins of Jacob's Crackers and five canisters of Twinings English Breakfast Tea in the pantry of Journey's End. All their labels bore the coat of arms of the British royal family. It was the crown she noticed most. All kings and queens, all mothers and fathers were so far away.

Upstairs, at the back of the house, Ghislaine discovered a study. It was dark and panelled, scattered with relics from the previous inhabitants: a large desk and chairs on squat legs carved with lion's feet, framed butterfly specimens on its walls. Mak Non rolled her eyes at the butterflies. 'Trust a John Felt Hat to kill butterflies and put them behind glass. Kill for beauty as well as food.'

On the narrow northern wall of the study, wooden bookshelves reached to the ceiling. They were full of old ledgers and copies of *The Tea and Rubber Mail* with their columns of figures and talk of rubber and broken orange pekoe prices, processing and marketing. On the highest shelf Ghislaine found a picture book with a paper cut-out map of England in its centre. These were the images of home that the expatriate English manager and his wife must have fed their children on. The cut-out showed her a country of green fields and grey cities, attenuated church spires and stocky men and women in hats. So civilised. She felt sure tea would be taken at regular intervals there. At London, a bridge opened itself in half and soldiers stood to attention in improbably tall black hats in front of a palace. This cut-out map of England was on thin paper, it tore as she unfolded it, but it re-ignited her longing for the rest of the world.

Next to this book was a thin cobalt-covered booklet. Its title had been eaten away by chains of bitemarks the size of pinheads. Crickets and silverfish, perhaps. Only a broken string of words remained: *sh Museum Provisional Oriental Antiquiti Catalogu*

A cloud of mildew rose from its pages as she picked it up and flicked through it. There were pages of items listed in black print under headings: Porcelain, Statuary, Metal Ware, Instruments, Jewellery. There were items from India, China, Java, Japan. She looked for Malaya. Nothing. At the back of the book, there was a brief note: *Limited holdings from Malaya and Singapore.* Adjacent to this, someone had written in blue fountain pen copperplate cursive that had been eaten by insects into more of the delicate lacework: *Suggest judicious supplementa*

Ghislaine turned the pages. She held her breath as she noticed how many of the items catalogued under Javanese statuary were described as winged women. *Naked from waist up, avian from waist down. Stand approx. one foot high.* Next to each item was an estimation of their monetary value. Which man would collect and catalogue the petrified spirits of stone women like this? Which man would put a price on them? And which nation had this '*sh Museum*' of women?

She read the first line of adjoining text.

We gathered together many fragments from ruined temples, palaces and houses that were neglected.

Who would write such coy explanations of possession?

She pushed the book to the back of the shelf.

On Saturdays and Wednesdays, when the Tanah Rata wet markets were open, Zeraphina allowed her niece a brief detour to Ashok's News of the World, the small post office and newsagency, to buy postage stamps. Every time Ghislaine walked into this shop, her pulse clamoured in her ears as she gave her name at the counter where the poste restante mail was held.

'Nothing again,' said Ashok, the Indian proprietor, mournfully when she gave him her name. 'Who you expecting, young lady? The king?'

'Have you checked?' she asked every time.

'There's nothing to check.'

She felt her blood slowing in her veins again as she walked to the pile of daily English-language newspapers and looked for Walter Humphries' weekly travel article in the weekend paper. He had written an article on the legendary Mount Ophir on the outskirts of Malacca, and several about Kuala Lumpur. She had been sure he must be drawing deliberately closer to her in the Cameron Highlands, until he confounded her by writing an article entitled 'Past or Future: the Straits Settlements of Singapore, Penang and Malacca'. She reread the article five times, looking for herself as a longing, a flavour, an absence noted, but it was full of his usual self-assured insider's knowledge of the English club bars in each city. There was a note at the end of the article: *Next Monday's article by Walter Humphries will be about the Eurasians of Malacca.*

Ghislaine approached Ashok with an unsteady voice.

'Please, can you keep for me next Monday's newspapers? I will pay when I come in next time.'

Ashok raised one elegant eyebrow. 'What you want them for?'

'Just the news.'

'It will be old news by Saturday.'

'I will pay you now if you like.' She left the newspaper she'd skimmed through on the shelf with the other copies, bought some stamps to satisfy her aunt, gave Ashok extra money, and returned to the wet markets in a blur of anticipation to help her aunt carry home the dripping vegetables and fish for the week's meals. From that moment, Ghislaine de Sequeira imagined the colour of her flesh, the shape of her body and the sound of her voice perfectly conveyed by the pen of Walter Humphries.

Back at Journey's End, she rushed to her room, closed the door and opened the newspaper at the article.

❋

Eurasians of Malacca
by Walter Humphries

The sixteenth-century Portuguese, the seventeenth-century Dutch and the nineteenth-century British have all colonised Malacca. Most Malaccan Eurasians trace their progenitors back to the Portuguese seamen of the sixteenth century, but some have Dutch or English ancestors. Those claiming English ancestry are known here as the Upper Ten, those of Portuguese descent are known as the Lower Sixes. Both nicknames are borrowed from a card game of cruel chance played here. The latter is sadly appropriate to describe the status of the Portuguese Eurasians or Christao, as they call themselves. The mixing bowl of East and West spawned these unfortunate mixed bloods, whom we expatriate Englishmen call stengahs, after the half whisky and water we partake of so fondly. The stengahs of Malacca live in simple wooden houses in the Land of the Priest and speak an ancient dialect of Portuguese called the Lingua de Christao, which, though grammatically incorrect, is understood by Portuguese travellers today. The passive fatalism of the Christao is reflected in this language, which is better suited to expressing suffering and sadness than success and joy.

The Christao people eat food that combines the spiciness of Malay cuisine with Portuguese. They are placed on a lower level socially and economically, on the grounds of their impure blood. At least half of them are fishermen, and some of them are employed as clerks by the government, due to their passable command of the English language. But even those few who are professionals well educated in England receive only a little more than half the wage of their English colleagues.

These Christao Eurasians are devout Catholics who enforce strict courtship rituals amongst their young, and discourage marrying with other races, unless with high-status English and Europeans. They range in hue from dark to light in both skin and eye colour, and their women, often indefinably beautiful, were sought after by soldiers of all races during the war. The British expatriate taking a Eurasian wife nowadays will probably keep his membership in the Malacca Club, that bastion of

Britishness, but he may still find himself ostracised by the expatriate community. Is it any wonder, under these circumstances, that so many expatriate men with Eurasian girlfriends prolong bachelorhood? It's a way of keeping a foot in both camps and keeping the needs of body and soul satisfied, unless of course the devout Catholicism of the Christao girlfriend prohibits such satisfactions, which is often the case. The devoutness of the Christao is a double-edged sword. It has sustained them through centuries of colonisation and hardship, along with their simplistic and almost desperate sense of humour. But it has kept them both servile to their colonisers and lacking in the courage needed to better their status in modern Malaya.

Ghislaine could not stop her hands shaking as she dropped the newspaper into the garbage tin outside Ashok's News of the World. Simmering with equal measures of rage and shame, she met her aunt outside the wet markets and carried the bags of vegetables and fish to Journey's End without speaking. Inside, she refused lunch and pulled shut as many doors behind her as she could. She sat at the window of her bedroom all afternoon and into the early evening, watching the changing light on the pitted stone of Mathilde's winged-woman carving, which she had positioned on her windowsill to look over the valley and hills.

She knew it was time for bed when the lamplight on the verandah was dulled by the droning squadrons of mosquitoes that rose from the jungle in the valley. Almost every evening she could hear her aunt and uncle as they sat on the verandah arguing in clouds of smoke from the mosquito coils. Beyond them, Winston Churchill the manx cat and the other cats of the neighbourhood slunk through the smoke and shadows, hunting rats and the flying brown tropical cockroaches longer than laundry pegs that flicked against the bamboo blinds of the verandah. But on that evening, mosquitoes did not arrive, and, all along the verandah, the teak-coloured cockroaches keeled over on their sides like fishing boats caught on low tide.

'The government anti-malarial teams sprayed dieldrin to kill the mosquitoes yesterday,' her uncle explained, unusually sober for that time of the evening.

For days the garden of Journey's End was strewn with the bodies of rats who'd eaten dieldrin-contaminated insects, but the most resilient rats didn't die. They could be seen running across the garden in the evening shadows, freighting the poison into the house.

A week later, Ghislaine found Winston dead on the backstep.

'Oh, the cats like the insect-spray taste too much,' said Mak Non, shaking her head sadly. 'That dieldrin full of bad hantu spirits. We must get Winnie a coffin.'

She placed Winston in an empty Blue Heaven Estate Premium Tea chest, with a white cushion for his head and a saucer of saltfish for his spirit, and helped Ah Kwei and Ghislaine bury him where the garden met the jungle. Ghislaine watched a plane recede in the blue sky until it disappeared, and wondered how many departures a single life could contain.

On the morning a small basket parachuted from the belly of a Royal Air Force plane into the backyard of Journey's End, Ghislaine de Sequeira was hoping for the best. It was nearly a month since they'd left Malacca. She walked across the dew-covered lawn towards the basket. What if it contained a gift from Walter Humphries, making use of his expatriate connections to deliver his rapture to her? Since reading the article, which had left her feeling vaguely insulted and misunderstood, she only allowed herself to entertain such hopes about him early in the morning, when she was still befuddled by recurrent dreams of travelling with him through strange cities. She pulled the cane catch on the basket to release a large marmalade-coloured tomcat and a tabby female. She saw the plane dropping more parachuted baskets through the air on the other side of town.

She did not name the cats after politicians, as her father would have. 'Fred Astaire,' she nodded to the thick marmalade; 'Ava Gardner,' she said to the tabby. They followed her into the house. There her aunt sat wanly over strong coffee and told her that her uncle had gone and wasn't coming back.

'Why has Uncle Theobald gone? Is it the poison or is the Emergency really here, still?'

'It's more than poison and the Emergency. It's war.' The cats yowled hungrily. 'The war never actually finished for us lah. Your uncle's been gone for years, really. Gone on his nightmares of the war. Gone on the whisky and low wages of His Majesty's Straits Settlements. Maybe the communist guerrillas are right.' Aunty Zeraphina was bitter and blue around her lips as if her mouth was frozen, and would say no more. Not that day or the next. Nothing about him, in all the days of residual Emergency and dieldrin that followed.

The cats grew fat as the mosquitoes and cockroaches multiplied into meals for the rats again. Every evening, Ghislaine looked along the road for signs of her uncle returning in the blue Mayflower, or Walter Humphries come to declare his love for her. She looked down towards Tanah Rata and the dusty plateau, and then up through the gaps in the clouds where the English took their holidays and planted their rose gardens.

'When is Uncle coming back?' she asked Mak Non and Ah Kwei. 'And when will Walter Humphries contact me?' Walter's promise to take her places endured as a memory, stronger than his slips of the pen.

Ah Kwei sucked her wrinkled lower lip and glanced at Mak Non.

'Anak, kekasih,' Mak Non murmured. Child, don't worry. 'Picture this, anak. These hills full of hantu spirit hiding from so many tea gardens and golf courses, waiting to take revenge on people for stealing their old jungle homes. Looking for soft bodies to make their new homes in. Damaged men and lost spirits behave the same way. Young women must make themselves strong against them.' She gave Ghislaine a silver cylindrical amulet containing a sharp nail and verses from the Koran. 'Say your prayers, wear this charm, live virtue. And drink Horlicks three times a day.'

✻

The garden of Journey's End backed onto a little valley of remnant jungle. The flagrant garden of yellow-blossomed angsana trees, purple bougainvillea and pink frangipani rained ruinously onto the lawns of English grass. Ghislaine, her aunt and Mak Non planted fruit and vegetables between the mansion's lawn and this jungle: strawberries, pak choy, pumpkin and carrots. In the heat of the day, a monitor lizard with scales that gleamed like emerald and topaz ate the ripe strawberries slowly and appreciatively. Mak Non had a secret name for this lizard. She left saucers of milk out for him, as if he was a pet.

'Drink it up, Walter Humphries,' she murmured when no-one was listening. 'Leave some strawberries for us.'

A few days after Theobald left, Ah Kwei made an announcement at the dinner table. She refused to eat any popiah, the vegetable-filled crepe rolls she'd just made. She offered her broken string of Malay and Cantonese, after the last popiah had been rolled and divided between the two de Sequeira women, with tears in her eyes and her head held high: 'Miss de Sequeira, you whom I have had the pleasure of serving since you were in nappies, your father and Mrs Zeraphina are too good to say what they can no longer afford, but I am old and will lighten your load by retiring.' Her round spectacles fogged over and she bowed her head.

The following Friday, Mak Non, Zeraphina and Ghislaine stood on the road pressing packages of siew mai and sui cao dumplings through the windows of the Malacca Express bus into Ah Kwei's hands as she sat with a Jacob's Cracker tin full of her life's savings on her knees.

After Ah Kwei left, it rained every day for a week just before evening, leaving an afterglow like a tincture of iodine in the air and trees.

'Hantu mambang. Evil spirits in the air. I will make special charms,' said Mak Non.

Ghislaine caught a fever that left her sheets soaked in perspiration. After three days, she began talking nonsense. Suspecting malaria, Aunty Zeraphina called in Doctor Lim. He took Ghislaine's pulse and temperature, pulled down her eyelids and listened to her heart.

'It is just a marsh fever or a monsoon virus,' he said. 'Give her cooling foods and plenty to drink.'

'Nonsense lah,' said Mak Non after Doctor Lim left. 'It is the same sickness she had in the car driving up here.'

At the height of her fever, Ghislaine saw hantu everywhere. They oozed out of the jungle disguised as mist, or as long grey streaks of dust adhering to greasy smears on the wall. She saw Hantu Kopek with her long pendulous breasts and the squat, fat Hantu Kengkeng swinging his testicles; Hantu Kookachi eating dung, and Hantu Bungkus, the ghost wrapped in a white shroud; but the most remarkable thing about all these spirits was that they all spoke to her earnestly through the face of the travel writer. Neither the remedies of Doctor Lim or Mak Non could help Ghislaine's fever. But, after a week, her fever abated, leaving her with dreams of being lost in a strange city of snow and cold blue light, where a bridge split in the middle and parted to allow enormous ships to pass as she tried to cross it to the travel writer's English afternoon tea party on the other side. She woke from this dream sweating, knowing that she had lost all points of reference, and that there was no-one in the strange city who would help her across the gap to the beautiful pale men and women living a real life.

LONDON, NOVEMBER 1985

In my mother's greenhouse, spiders are building webs between the seedling trays, and it's dark from the mildew and grime thickening on the glass roof and walls. David hangs Clara a swing from the branch of our neighbour's overhanging oak tree. I can't see her face through the murky glass as she soars for the first time on her new swing. The potting mix in the seedling trays is dry as dust. One of these days I will do something about all this, I say, closing the door on it again.

꽃

Another woman crooning in some foreign tongue on Philip's sound system.

—Is that French she's singing?

It's longing more than language that I recognise in her voice.

He nods, his lips pressed together in a bemused smile.

—My mother was French, you know. She was adopted by an English couple when she was a child, but she was southern French.

Olive complexion, dark hair. Not unlike your colouring. She would
have been beautiful, but she let herself go.

–Let herself go?

To me, it sounds like escape.

–She lived in her dressing gown, swallowed sedatives, waited for
my father to ring or come home, but his real emotional life was
with his mistresses in the city and the Far East. He collected artefacts for the museums. Before and after the war, the British were
amongst the most intrepid collectors.

I want to ask him why, but he looks over my shoulder and keeps
talking, fast.

–My mother only got pregnant with me to hold on to my father.
He kept seeing his mistresses regardless. He took me to visit two
of his women in London sometimes when I was a child. I always
wondered if my mother knew about them, but I was too frightened
to ask her.

Philip averts his eyes as he tells me about the day he came home
from school to find his mother sitting on the garden-shed floor
amongst his father's latest collection, five tea chests full of antique
stone goddesses, newly arrived from India. She was holding the bill-
hook used to poll the trees for winter. The bill-hook, her hair and
skin were grey with dust from the broken stone limbs and torsos
strewn on the ground around her, but he could see she was wearing
lipstick and her only evening gown, a rich green velvet, mottled like
lichen by the dust. Her eyes were open but quite still, as if she was
transfixed. When he spoke to her, she didn't respond. For a few
seconds he wondered if she was mimicking the statues.

He noticed an empty brown bottle on the workbench amongst
the chisels and hammers. Its label read *For the Relief of Nervous
Tension*. It took him a few more seconds to realise this had nothing
to do with hardware.

Philip's eyes are still averted as he tells me that his hand acciden-
tally pressed against the broken stone arm of a statue when he
leaned over to wipe the dust from his mother's face. Her skin was as

cold as the statue. Yes, the scar, the childhood scar. He didn't notice the blood flowing from the cut on his hand until at least a minute after he realised his mother was dead. It was easy to stop the blood from flowing. But the questions he'd never asked her remained.

He looks out the window as he says that eventually, he gave up trying to make sense of what had happened to his mother. She had always been beyond comprehension; what she knew no longer mattered to him.

Squeezing his hand gently, I'm careful not to touch the scar. As if it might still hurt.

Philip tells me then that he understands the pain of losing family, and of not belonging. When he says this, he looks directly at me. His eyes have another darkness behind their dark brown, yet for a moment it seems that nothing but our skins separate us. He turns my hand over, palm downwards, and places his next to it. They are nearly the same colour, the veins showing green through skins the colour of tea, one with just a little more milk in it, colder than the other.

THE TRUE BODY

✤ *The tea-tasters' terms* ✤

Ghislaine de Sequeira recovered from her fever, but now she woke to hear gunshots in the jungle drawing closer in the night. Aunty Zeraphina and Mak Non protected the household against these unnamed terrors in as many ways as they could.

'Don't bother your father with this. He's too busy earning a living in Malacca,' they told Ghislaine. Zeraphina retrieved an old Winchester rifle from the basement. Mak Non made each member of the household wear cylindrical invulnerability charms consisting of verses of the Koran and six special prayers for safety and well-being written in her tiny fastidious writing onto the finest paper, rolled up and sealed into bullet-sized silver cylinders with Tarzan's Grip glue. Aunty Zeraphina said novenas every night and had Mak Non fix Mathilde's five plaster statues of the saints and the Virgin Mary holding the Christ child onto some weighted tea chests on the back terrace overlooking the jungle, where it was rumoured some communist bandits had their hideout. The statues looked out across the valley with the same expressions of sorrowful imperturbability as Mathilde's stone carving, which sat just behind them at Ghislaine's window.

One night, there were gunshots and explosions from the valley. Too frightened to turn on any lights, Aunty Zeraphina insisted all three women sleep together in the library, the most hidden room in the house. Ghislaine agreed, but only if she could retrieve her menagerie of pets from their various nocturnal stations around the house to share the library with them.

'Aiya! Only if you lock them in their baskets, and even then, lah, even then we'll drown in animal shit by morning,' fumed Aunty Zeraphina.

Mak Non tempted King George to slide from the piano leg he was wrapped around by placing a frozen mouse in his wicker cage. Mata Hari the mynah and Wimbledon the racquet-tailed drongo were carried squawking in their cages from the conservatory. Only the cats, Fred Astaire and Ava Gardner, were allowed to remain uncaged. Ghislaine de Sequeira hung the two birds on the bookshelves behind her and set the python in his wicker cage on the other side of her makeshift bed.

She woke with a start in the dark calm to feel something silky and clammy wrapping itself around her armpit. Her first impulse was to scream, but she recognised the soft mooing breath as belonging to King George. How had he escaped? If she woke her aunt, she'd never let the animals sleep inside again. How could she untangle herself from King George's coils? The malty smelling shit of Wimbledon gave her an idea. She padded over to the bird's cage and placed the python's scales against it.

King George got the idea. He slid sinuously from her arm to the cage, tongue flicking. His head was too broad to fit between the bars, but he was so strong Ghislaine de Sequeira was afraid he would break the wicker to get to Mata Hari, who squawked as she pulled the snake from the cage. In the far corner of the room, behind the dark huddle of her aunt, she could see Fred Astaire's glowing, wide-awake eyes. By now her eyes had adjusted enough to see a grey tuft of fur suspended from the latch of King George's cage. Had Fred Astaire let the python out of his cage hoping to make a meal of him, or was it the other way around?

King George was not fully matured, but he had eaten the neighbour's kitten in Malacca. Fred Astaire, on the other hand, was corpulent and large-framed. She was afraid the cat would finish the python off, or vice versa. And now the snake was out, she didn't want to risk becoming entwined with him again.

There were still sporadic explosions coming from the valley behind the house. Ghislaine stayed awake, watching the python and the cat eye one another. Just before dawn, she grabbed her aunty's dressing-gown cord and tethered the python by his neck to the leg of the chair. She was surprised at the swiftness of Fred Astaire's approach from the opposite side of the room. Perhaps a tethered snake was as good as a dead one for him. She pushed the cat from the snake. Despite her fatigue, she stayed awake to ensure the survival of King George and Mata Hari, those living memorials of her childhood with her mother and father.

The three women of Journey's End rose the next morning to find the statues of the Virgin and the saints had been knocked from their upright stance. They leaned out almost horizontally on their warped metal stands from the tea chest, their arms outstretched in supplication. After so many nightmarish dawns, those unbroken saints leaning towards extremity were the image both of yielding and of transcendence for Aunty Zeraphina.

'It's a miracle,' she proclaimed.

'It's a disaster,' disagreed her niece.

'Either miracle or disaster happen,' said Mak Non diplomatically.

'It is a symbol of the effect of the war and the emergency on the innocent,' said Aunt Zeraphina, crossing herself, 'or perhaps it is a symbol of mercy. The saints are reaching out to catch the innocents as they fall.'

She sent Mak Non to fetch Father Texeiras from his slumber in his quarters in town.

'They are offering the Christ child as a sacrifice to stop the vice and sin of this country,' Father Texeiras pronounced, his bald head glistening with perspiration, the grey hairs in his nostrils quivering. 'The avarice and sloth and lust for power.' He ate all the green-and-white-striped jelly kueh that remained in Zeraphina's cake tin and emptied the crystal decanter of the last of the whisky left by Theobald, before plodding on his short legs trenchantly back down the hill towards his church.

'Priests tell us these stories because they need us to believe God cares for us,' murmured Ghislaine to Mak Non. 'But no-one in the world really cares what happens to us.'

'Aiya. Anak, so old woman already,' sighed Mak Non.

But Aunty Zeraphina was triumphant as she crossed herself. 'The leaning saints prove we are blessed. Father has confirmed it.'

Ghislaine de Sequeira snorted derisively at her aunt's response many times that day, but only in the privacy of her bedroom or the bathroom, as she smoked Mathilde's clay pipe and burned with shame at the blind piety her aunt had succumbed to since Uncle Theobald's departure. Yet, as she inhaled, she kept dreaming of rescue by the Englishman.

※

Nearly a month had passed since the women had arrived at Journey's End. Buoyed by the omen of the leaning saints, Zeraphina Albuquerque completed setting up the Miracle Tearooms in the old conservatory at the back of the house. She stood the leaning saints on the counter. Above the sink, she hung a badly executed painting she'd done, using the child's watercolour paints left behind by the previous inhabitants of the house. The painting showed the Virgin Mary sipping Cameron Highlands tea with a Malay bomoh dressed in a loincloth and the Queen of England cloaked in an ermine-trimmed map of the British Empire. The banner above them read:

Cameron Highlands Tea
for
Holiness Wisdom Wealth

The Virgin, the bomoh and the Queen were each haloed respectively by one of these words, ornately scripted in bright yellow paint that had run into their faces, imparting a satisfying incandescence that compensated for the obliteration of their eyebrows and the jaundiced weeping of their eyes. Zeraphina Albuquerque also stood a sign by the road:

Welcome to the Miracle Tearooms, Home of the Miracle of the Flying Saints.
Finest Quality Cameron Highlands Teas served English style.
Cakes, Biscuits and Cream Teas.

The tearooms were Zeraphina Albuquerque's defence against insignificance and obliteration. With her husband gone, the illusion of a front line to protect the household of women at Journey's End was gone, too. The women of Journey's End ran the tearooms by day and slept in shifts at night, keeping their eyes peeled for communist bandits, men in ragged clothes brandishing knives and guns. They did not suspect that the real danger for them might wear carefully tailored shirts and trousers and many hats, ranging from sola topees to felt Homburgs and quality straw Panamas.

In the evenings after they'd closed, Ghislaine added ingredients to the tea blend her aunt was trying to make from the local plantations' rejected pickings from the first flush of shoots and the new pickings from the second flush. She ground cinnamon quills and fat green cardamon pods in the stone tombok-tombok, because the cinnamon powder reminded her of the freckles on the travel writer's skin and the cardamon, so he'd told her, was what she smelled like. She stirred them through the tea leaves until her arm ached. The blend was her memorial to Walter Humphries. She inhaled the dry mixture deeply. It smelled both old and new, like another time and place. She scooped two teaspoons into a pot and poured boiling water over it. The late-afternoon sunlight slanting in through the tearoom windows illuminated the steam for a few moments as it spiralled into the air before evaporating. She took a sip. It caught in her throat and made her eyes weep. It was undrinkable. She spat it into the sink and washed the rest of it from the pot, but its otherworldly aroma still lingered when she began work the next morning.

❋

That weekend there was no article by Walter Humphries in the newspaper at Ashok's. In small print at the bottom of an earnestly written account of shopping in Singapore by a young Chinese cadet journalist was the note *Walter Humphries has taken extended leave to travel abroad.* There was a small photograph of him looking slightly more craven than she remembered him. His lips were closed, so that the gold filling above his left incisor wasn't visible, and there were dark circles under his eyes.

Ghislaine de Sequeira felt even colder and more desolate than she had on the evening of her arrival in the highlands. She forgot to buy postage stamps for her aunt, despite the expectant stare of Ashok Arasu. She returned to Journey's End without speaking to her aunt, went straight to the study, and climbed the bookshelves to retrieve the scrapbook of Walter Humphries' articles from its ungainly roost on the nest of *Tea and Rubber Mails*. She sat in the shaft of sunlit dust in the study reading his words, as if these could bring him closer to her. All that was left was to say goodbye to him, and she wouldn't even be able to do that.

❋

When Ghislaine de Sequeira stood between the pyramids of cumin and turmeric and the tubs of live turtle and eel at the Tanah Rata wet markets a few days later, she saw a man with skin the colour of pale rattan sampling goreng pisang at a stall. He was wearing a white jacket. She was so certain it was the travel writer made paler by illness that she could hardly bear to keep looking at him as she moved towards him with her pulse in her throat.

She dropped her newspaper-wrapped parcel of fenugreek into the tub of turtles. As she retrieved her parcel, the man moved closer to her, until he was at the stall directly opposite her. She felt a rolling motion from her head to her gut. She would not look at him. She would not let him see how desperate she was. From the corner of her eye she saw that he was looking at her. All those ungracious thoughts she'd harboured about him over the weeks since she'd left Malacca, and he'd taken leave to find her here, after all. She lifted her eyes to meet his.

Only then did she notice he was a taller man than the travel writer, that he wore a fine white cufflinked shirt and trousers rather than a batik open-necked shirt and shorts, and that he wore a felt hat instead of a straw one. But he held her gaze and nodded at her, as if they'd met before.

Two Malays hauling and pushing a buffalo entered the market, and Ghislaine moved back with the rest of the crowd. When she turned to look at the man in white again, he was gone. And then she remembered her father saying how common it was amongst the Christao people to see the ghost of someone beloved who had died recently.

Who had died, the travel writer or her? She caught a glimpse of herself in the window of the Chinese noodle house, a face floating in front of the preserved duck and saltfish that hung like dried skins behind the glass. She looked as if she had fallen to ground with no father, no mother, no past, no love or future.

※

It was the end of March, heavy with the humidity of a late-lingering monsoon. The road in front of the Miracle Tearooms was crawling with cars carrying expatriates seeking relief from the heat of the rubber plantations and towns: the administrators, planters and bankers of the Straits Settlements, men from Dunlop Rubber and Asia Petroleum and Boustead's driving their wives in Rovers, Austins and Morrises through the grey afternoon clouds that hung in the sky as warm and heavy as puddings.

Ghislaine de Sequeira saw all this through the mullioned windows of the tearooms. She covered the teapot with a woollen tea cosy shaped as an old grey cottage and embroidered with holly-hocks and roses. She could not get away from the sense that her aunt's tearooms were an inferior approximation of England. Even in this, the pouring of tea into fine porcelain from silver teapots, she was sure they were not being English enough.

Walter Humphries existed for her mostly as a sense of dulled expectation and motion sickness she felt some mornings when the night mists parted to reveal the expatriates' little England higher up the winding road. But she could almost imagine God living amongst the rose gardens, mock-Tudor guesthouses and tennis courts.

'The English,' panted Aunt Zeraphina, 'the English are coming. More milk and cream. More milk for the mems and the tuans. Ghislaine, clean the tannin stains off the tea cups with salt while I go to the shop lah.' Her pink dress had turned red under her arms with perspiration.

Aunt Zeraphina arrived back from the shop just as the first of the mems and tuans entered the tearooms. They were pungent with money, perfume and tobacco. She switched the ceiling fan on full. Soon their smell mixed with the scent of tea and the steam from the urn.

Ghislaine de Sequeira smiled at the mems and tuans from behind the curtain of steam and nervously carried them trays set meticulously with tea services, cutlery and scones cooked from a recipe

Aunt Zeraphina had learned years previously from the wife of the Malacca Botanical Gardens' horticulturalist.

A mem in a powder-blue dress and her husband in rubber-planter's whites wanted conversation as well as Devonshire tea.

'Were you born and bred here, dear?' the mem asked Ghislaine as she poured them two cups of the premium blend.

'We came here from Malacca about a month ago.'

'From Malacca, eh? Good place, Malacca. Full of Eurasians. Half-whisky half-water. Half-castes. That's why they call Malacca the place of slow runners and easy lays.'

'That's enough, William.' The wife narrowed her pale eyes. 'You are fair, even for a Eurasian. What percentage of you is European blood?'

'I've never had it measured,' said Ghislaine, looking at the cut on her finger with fresh curiosity.

'It's powerful stuff, Asian blood. Just one drop is enough to make you coloured,' said the planter. Ghislaine retreated behind the steam rising from the shiny Fortune urn. The talk at the tables turned to the price of rubber, tea and tin, and to the superiority of the clothes, roses, scones and cream back home.

At the end of that day, Aunty Zeraphina tapped her chest over her heart.

'They come to Malaya looking for wealth far away from their home because they are empty in here.'

But her niece was speechless with a sense of her own indefinability. It seemed that only England could give her a clear picture of what she really was. She imagined the pink passengers and customers of that day walking on the clouds and breathing the mist higher up the road. The thin air would be scented with the nectar of their roses. Their tables would be replete. They would want for nothing. She went to bed with a handful of rice lying at the bottom of her stomach, like confetti forgotten at the scene of a departed celebration. Sleeplessness. This longing. This distance between what she had and what she wanted. Every day it rose and filled her like a cloud that would not rain.

❋

Wish de Sequeira read in the newspaper that Walter Humphries had gone away. He guessed the news might reach his daughter in the highlands, and wondered about its effect on her. He wanted to take leave from his job to visit her, but it was impossible. For eight or nine nights he tried to travel to her outside his body, finally succeeding on that first night of the expatriates' annual vacation.

Wish was troubled to see that his daughter still lay awake, even though it was past midnight. Crickets called to one another from her bedroom ceiling like whistling kettles. He looked at her, the way she curled her body and head like a parenthesis, the way she looked out the window without really seeing; and he thought he knew what it meant. With his long experience of grief over Mathilde, he could have told his daughter that her longing was a variety of mourning. But he thought, even as he watched her tossing and turning on her bed, that he would not send her a letter to tell her what he knew. She would never credit him for having experienced more than she had in love.

❋

As she stood at the sink of the Miracle Tea Rooms the next day, Ghislaine found her longing had changed density. The small cut on her forefinger stung as she scrubbed the tannin from tea cups with salt and broke into the first lines of song she'd sung since leaving school. It was Mathilde's song, the only Christao one that Ghislaine could remember.

Anda com cinco sentido,
Causa di eu sa amor;
Si nunca toma cuidado,
Sentido; alma corpo bai perdido.

She could still remember Mathilde looking intently at her, translating the words:

Walk with your five senses alert,
Because of love
If one is not careful
Senses, body and soul will be lost forever.

Through the dusty windowpanes she could see the morning light raking across the green tea gardens and the encircling jungle-clad hills. Behind them more hills receded into the distance until they were blue. Just visible through the window, some Malay and Tamil labourers were finishing erecting the timber framework of the new guesthouse. The rumour she'd heard at the markets was that the English owners had gambled on Independence not being granted to the Malays, that they were aiming for years more of expatriate tourists from the hot dusty plains.

As she rubbed salt into the cups, Ghislaine moved closer to the window to try to gauge the size of the guesthouse. Three times the size of Journey's End, Mak Non had estimated. A locust hit a dusty pane of the tearoom's window hard, steamily. Its splayed legs and wings twitched for a minute before becoming perfectly still. She could see to the hills beyond through the framework of the guesthouse. It was too difficult to gauge its impact on the view.

Then the pale man in the felt hat entered the tearooms. Her heart leapt so that it seemed impossible it would ever return to its old beat. In that moment, it seemed her view of the future was clear.

Ghislaine was experiencing the same crisis of perception as she'd had in the markets. The man was the one she'd seen at the goreng pisang stall. He was the man who was not Walter Humphries. He was longer in the leg but narrower across his torso than the barrel-chested travel writer, so that he appeared more inward than expansive. His skin was paler, with a bluish tinge at the temples and eyelids. He did not wear his felt Homburg hat skewed like coincidence into the dimness; it sat perfectly straight on his head. But as Ghislaine de Sequeira watched him from behind the counter, she thought of smoky clubs, passenger terminals and foreign countries. Her longing for elsewhere had become as sharp as the edge of a new page.

He took a seat directly next to the window of the tearooms. When he lifted his hat, his hair was nothing like the travel writer's dishevelled halo. This new Englishman was balding slightly, and his dark silver-flecked hair was oiled and combed like Clark Gable's. He placed his grey felt hat on the table before him. As she approached him with the menu, his gaze flicked over the builders and the guesthouse, over the valley to the pillowy hills beyond. Another Englishman who had seen the world. But unlike the travel writer's sky-filled gaze, this new Englishman's eyes judged and catalogued. And in this new Englishman's eyes, she saw a kind of sadness, instead of Walter Humphries' appetite.

He sat with his hat placed like a barrier between them. Ghislaine was already predicting his reach, his voice, the breadth of his knowledge. She watched him carefully as he scanned the menu and the tasting notes written in Zeraphina Albuquerque's over-ornate serifs. She decided his eyes were the colour of lightly brewed Assam tips.

He smirked at the first entry.

Precious Eyebrows: finely shaped black tea leaves with quite light, bright liquor.

His eyes paused at In-Between Tea. This was the new one she and her aunt had blended from rejected pickings, and were trying to promote with the slogan *Double the taste for half the price.* In-Between was also another name the English called Eurasians.

'Would you be so kind as to read this to me? I can't make out the script.' His voice was deeper and rounder in its vowels than Walter Humphries' and more relaxed, as if he spoke from the back of his throat, rather than straining to protect himself. His mouth appeared to move without the aid of any other facial muscles. His wrists and ankles were elongated and languid beneath their cuffs.

She was struck by how his gestures differed from the travel writer's, whose stocky body had always seemed so animated by his determination to be noticed. This new paler Englishman leaned back in his chair and spoke with the graciousness of Doctor Arbuckle, as if he was far beyond any need to convince others of his worth. He wore a lined, cream-coloured jacket over a fine white cotton shirt with cufflinks. Perhaps it was just the cooler highlands climate. Or perhaps her first-class Englishman had finally arrived.

Ghislaine cleared her throat. 'An in-between tea that marries the greenness and astringency of young first-flush leaves with the more rounded maturity of the second-flush leaves that are picked in early summer. Blended from leaves from all the local plantations. Medium amber in colour. A hint of cardamon and . . .' she blinked to clear the memory of Walter Humphries' skin, 'cinnamon. Double the taste for half the price.' It was as if she was revealing herself. Her own skin was not dark or old enough to conceal the rising of heat in it. Everything about her had taken on new meaning. She was hearing herself, seeing herself as she imagined this new man might.

'In-Between Tea, hmm?' He smiled, only slightly condescendingly. She could not bring herself to read the last sentence out loud.

The champagne of teas, her desperate, teetotalling aunt had written on the menu. Ghislaine covered it with her hand. The Englishman stroked his top lip and placed his order. 'One of the Finest Tippy Golden Flowery Orange Pekoe from each plantation. And a clean cup, saucer and strainer for each of them, thank you.' He noted the astonishment on her face but did not explain himself.

At the privacy of the sink, she burned her hands on the kettle and dropped the lids of the canisters before putting an extra teaspoon of the leaves in each pot. *Hail Mary Mother of God, help me not to blush, spill tea or perspire under the armpits like Sister Victorina.* She included a complimentary pot of the In-Between Blend, taking care to remove the stalks, remembering Aunt Zeraphina's admonition:

With low-grade tea like this, what you leave out of the pot is as important as what you put in.

The tea strainers collided with the cups and saucers as she carried the tray over. The steam rose from the spouts of the three teapots between them. He looked at her as if he already knew her better than anyone else. It must be something Englishmen did, thought Ghislaine. He had a long, fastidious nose. She felt sure he wouldn't just settle for anything. She felt her pulse at her throat. She was already hoping that this Englishman, who seemed more English than Walter Humphries, would be truer than the travel writer.

'You are wondering why I have ordered three pots of tea, I'm sure.' She nodded politely. Nothing else had been further away from her mind. 'I am a tea broker, blender and taster. Rupert Balneaves is my name. I have shares in one of the plantations here. This is a good chance for me to do a little comparison of teas from all the local estates before the London auctions. You wouldn't happen to have a little spittoon handy, would you?'

The only spittoon Ghislaine had ever seen was a small brass one used by Mak Non for her chewed areca nut. She went through the back door of the tearooms into the house and found it on the upturned box that served as Mak Non's bedside table. It was dented and stained with the dull red juices. She hurried back into the tearooms with it and scrubbed it hard, watching the tea-taster in astonishment as he dug the leaves out of each pot of tea with a spoon and dumped them on a saucer.

The tea-taster wrinkled his nose with distaste. 'What in God's name is that?'

'A spittoon.'

'And I'm an Arab. Look, just a little bowl will do.'

She emptied sugar out of a bowl and hurried over with it. The tea-taster took a quick, noisy slurp of the Blue Valley Plantation premium, rolled it around in his mouth and spat it into the bowl.

Ghislaine swallowed hard. 'Sir, pardon me, but is that how the English do it back home?'

'My word. That's how the most discerning tea-tasters in the world taste tea.'

'Our tea is not usually . . . gargled like that.'

The corners of his mouth and the skin at the outer edge of his eyes twitched. 'It's not gargling. You slurp it up in a certain way so it hits your tastebuds.'

'I see.' In her short time working in the tearooms, she had grown accustomed to swallowing her disapproval. There was so much about first-class English behaviour that she had to learn. 'How did you find that one, then?'

'Fair body, brisk, though tending towards the brassy side.' He eyed her chest pensively as he spoke. What exactly was he judging here? She checked the top button of her blouse hadn't come undone. His gaze and his words seemed suddenly full of hidden meaning. She had a curious sense of wanting to both hide from and get closer to him. She supposed this was what the expatriate customers meant by *wishing for a bit of steam with someone.* She turned away and refilled the urn. 'Do you know what I mean by fair body, brisk, brassy?' he asked.

'Not exactly.'

'I'm using tea-tasters' terminology. A tea with body has a strong liquor, not a weak, thin one. Well-fermented teas are described as brisk, as opposed to flat teas. A brassy taste is a bitter one.'

His hat sat on the table with its two low peaks and central valley like a topological model. The In-Between Tea sat in the pot untasted, waiting to be recognised as so exotic he would take it home, let London taste it, sell it to the world. His nostrils dilated slightly. He wouldn't consume just anything. Ghislaine stood in the steam hoping for clarification and looked at him forthrightly, a sudden glint of genius in her eye. 'Could you write some of your . . . first-class terminology down?'

Rupert Balneaves shrugged. 'Why not? Nothing better than a young woman keen to learn. You haven't told me your name.'

'Ghislaine. Ghislaine de Sequeira.' She brought him a yellowed notepad and pen.

He wrote in a small, almost feminine hand:

Bright: refers to liquor not dull in colour.
Dull: an undesirable quality in colour.
Flat: a tea that has gone off with too much moisture.
Tainted: undesirable flavour caused by chemicals, damp etc.
Colory: special category teas with good bright liquor.
Plain: without desirable qualities.
Thin: an unflavoursome tea due to hard withering, under-rolling or too high a temperature during rolling.
Point: leaf with desirable briskness.

He looked at her chest again before writing his final line:

Tip: the end of the delicate young buds.

'What an interesting language,' she said.

He smiled at her guilelessness. 'And you, Ghislaine? A French name. What is your native tongue?'

'English.'

'How disappointing. Nothing more exotic than that?'

'My parents spoke some Christao, the dialect the Malaccan Eurasians speak. I know only a little of it. It's a dying language.'

'Do you speak Malay?'

'A little.'

'What is the Malay word for love?'

'Sayang.'

'And the Christao word?'

'Amor.'

'And what do you know of love?'

She blushed and looked out the window. What did she know about love? When her mother was alive, the Christao word for love had taken the place of eardrops. On her mother's tongue, *amor* sounded warm and tender.

Since arriving at Journey's End, Mak Non muttered *sayang*, the Malay word for love, as if she was warning Ghislaine away from it. She pronounced it 'sigh-ung', almost like sigh merging into hunger.

'Real sayang hard to find. Your mother had a Christao word for her bad first marriage,' Mak Non had told her the previous day when Ghislaine confided her grief over Walter Humphries again. 'Not sayang. Not amor. *Tokah*. To touch, to cost.'

To touch, to cost. Ghislaine felt this translation in her every nerve.

But she could not tell the tea-taster that she'd learned this about love. She could not tell him what Walter Humphries had cost her. She could not look Rupert Balneaves in the eye as he stood there, smoothing the brim of his hat expectantly.

'Nothing,' she said finally, the heat rising through her skin towards her eyes.

'Well,' the tea-taster murmured, putting on his hat, 'I'm charmed. But it's time for me to go. I hope I'll have the pleasure of your company again.' He left the money on the table and the peppery smell of his hair oil in the air. He left without tasting or telling her what grade he would give the special In-Between Tea blend.

PART TWO

Perdidu — to be lost, naked

LONDON, DECEMBER 1985

All the vendors along Portobello Road have shut up shop and gone home when I return from college. Philip had acknowledged me at the end of class with just a fleeting smile, as if he wasn't really behind it, before hurrying away.

Clearly something's not quite right, but I don't know what it is.

A woman scrounges amongst the refuse of the greengrocers' stalls; an old man spreads his threadbare blanket in front of a closed shop door as the dark and damp thicken.

−Back early tonight, I call out to David and Clara as I open the front door of the house.

David appears in the hallway with both his hands outstretched, a bunch of hothouse roses in one hand, something small and dented in the other.

−About that night when I hit you. I am sorry. Unforgivable. I have no good excuse.

He looks at his feet as he mumbles this, his eyes mournful and downcast. An apology out of the blue, so many days after the blow. It occurs to me how transparent he is compared to Philip Border, how unintimidated he makes me feel in comparison, despite his one recent display of physical violence. He hands the flowers to me awkwardly, as if he's presenting them both as an offering and a barrier between us.

So there is still a chance things might work out between us?

–Don't get me wrong, he says, as if he has read my thoughts. I just wanted to apologise. And . . . I thought I should return this to you.

He passes me the small dented thing. It's metal, cold to the touch. It is the tin queen my mother had given me when I was a child, the one relic from my childhood that had meant enough to me to give to David before we married.

When you are King, dilly dilly, I will be Queen.

Do the painted words on the tin have the nursery rhyme around the wrong way?

–I didn't know you'd taken it with you. Keep it. I want you to keep it, I say, my voice very small.

He holds it in his hand towards me until it's clear I won't take it. He puts it in his pocket and says goodbye without looking at me.

THE TRUE BODY

The new plan

As she set the tables in the tearoom the next morning, Ghislaine de Sequeira imagined a proper English tea with Rupert Balneaves. She would be served, not the server. There would be a well-laid table and ample time and space for the rituals of pouring, talking, sipping and looking at one another. There would be scones that parted as moistly as lips to take the whipped cream and jam from the full bowls. It would be held late in the afternoon, when the sun's disc had slipped behind a filter to suffuse their faces with gold and draw the shadows of their bodies into long monuments on the ground. This would take place in his mansion above the clouds. Perhaps, one day, it would even happen in the real England.

He wouldn't have noticed her blushing when he entered the tearooms that second time. It was dim inside so early in the morning. She hadn't even turned on the lights to welcome the early customers.

'Greetings,' he said, taking off his hat. 'How do you say that in Christao?'

'Nobas.'

'You never answered my final question yesterday.'

'I don't remember it,' she lied.

'I asked you what you know of love. Say-yang, isn't that how you say it?'

She turned her face to the window and squeezed her eyes shut. The memories of Walter Humphries were only just over a month old. Who was this Rupert Balneaves man anyway, extracting words from her as if she were a dictionary, stealing them for his own terrifying language?

'Nothing. And you didn't say it right.'

'It's difficult to have a conversation with you when you're facing the other way.'

She blinked her eyes clear of tears. She counted four mosquitoes on the other side of the window pane. Over the road, the earliest builder was facing the valley with his pants around his ankles, the fine arc of his urine a gold thread in the morning light.

'Dear girl,' the tea-taster murmured, 'dear girl.' He placed his hand on her chin and turned her face towards him. 'Have I offended you?' He smiled wanly, and it seemed to her his exhalation was humid with his own unspoken grief.

The bluish tinge under his eyes was more marked and a shadow ran along his lower jaw and chin, so that he appeared even more morose than he had the previous day. This made him look older. Perhaps he was older than Walter, even. The tea-taster cleared his throat. For a moment it seemed he might tell her something more about himself, but he lowered his gaze to the floor and squeezed the crown of his hat between his hands. He looked almost forlorn.

'Poor Mr Balneaves.'

'What do you mean *poor* Mr Balneaves?' He glanced sharply at her.

'Sorry. It's just . . . you look sad.'

'I am not happy. But that doesn't mean I am sad.'

Bewildered, she looked carefully at the downturned corners of his mouth.

'You grade feelings as well as tea?' she asked with a sudden flash of revelation.

He smiled but didn't reply.

'What makes you happy, Mr Balneaves?'

His smile grew more rueful.

'Life's taught me that happiness is not often possible, Ghislaine. But we could console one another, you and I. How do you say console in Malay?'

'Menghiburkan.'

'And in Christao?'

'I don't remember my parents ever using the Christao word for that. For all the time leading up to my mother's death and afterwards, we were, how you say? Not for consolation.'

'Inconsolable. Well.' He unfolded his hat. 'Let's have a cup of tea together one day, then. I brought this for you.' He retrieved a small metal canister from the pocket of his jacket. 'Best-quality Darjeeling. How would that be?'

'Oh, subezu!' she replied. 'That's Christao for more than enough.'

※

Ghislaine checked herself in the mirror. Did she have the appearance for taking a real English afternoon tea with Rupert Balneaves? The face? Well, there were things powder and shadow could do. Clothes? She needed one of those can-can petticoats mentioned in *Silver Screen* magazine and in Walter Humphries' article. Hair? She had the dark, straight hair and she cursed it. Well, there must be things a hairdresser could do.

Every time Zeraphina walked past her niece's room, she was in front of the mirror. She wondered what had gone wrong with Ghislaine, who came from a long line of women of exemplary frugality but spent her spare hours plotting the acquisition of can-can petticoats and permanent waves.

Mak Non thought she knew what was happening.

'Why fall for *this* Englishman, anak?'

'Because he is a *first-class* Englishman,' Ghislaine said, her eyes averted from Mak Non's in case she divined in them her unutterable desperation.

※

Ghislaine took the long, greasy bus down the narrow road that went through Tanah Rata and Ringlet to Tapah, the dusty foothills town. Her bus seat was thick with sweat and oil from fried snacks bought by previous passengers from the food stalls of numerous bus stations. Behind her, the lumpy, dark grey clouds shifted like a flock of sheep in the south-west trade wind.

She got off the bus at Lakshmi's Ladies' Fancy, the Indian tailor's on the main street. Through the window she could see the thin Chinese and Malay girls poring over magazines full of photos of buxom British brides. She opened the door a crack.

'Oh, like that, like that already: a bodice like that over a bust like that,' the Indian dressmaker exhorted a thin-chested Chinese girl.

Ghislaine stared at a blonde bride in a crinoline on the magazine cover closest to the door. The dress was jewelled and lustrous, but it was the tiara that caught her eye, the sovereignty of that particular bride that seemed so unattainable.

'What you want?' the Indian dressmaker asked, unrolling her tape measure as she approached her. Ghislaine pulled the latest issue of *Silver Screen* out of her bag and showed Bette Davis's can-can petticoat.

'Can do me one like that?'

'Ca-a-an.'

'How much?'

'Five dollars.'

'Too much lah.'

'First time I ever made one like this.'

'Four dollars.'

'Four dollars fifty. Good price lah.' The dressmaker pulled the measuring tape briskly around Ghislaine's waist. 'Ready for you tomorrow.'

'Okay lah. Best-quality tulle.'

'Can.'

Ghislaine closed the door behind her and walked along the four-foot way. She slid to a stop on a rain-sodden mound of dough, an offering to the Hungry Ghosts on the kerb outside Blossom's Asian Hair Transformation and Beauty Salon. She took a vinyl seat sticky with heat and thumbed through magazines full of Chinese girls curlier and fuller in the hair than she thought their genes would allow. She read in these magazines that a permanent wave could do wonders for thin straight Asian hair.

'Do I have the thin Asian hair?' she asked Blossom the Chinese hairdresser, who wore gold-streaked curls.

'Thin yes, but lighter colour. Chap cheng colour.' In the brightly lit mirror, Ghislaine noticed for the first time how softly it shone.

'This perm. Can do?'

'Ca-a-a-n.' Blossom fingered Ghislaine's long hair. 'Should curl up nice ah.'

'Make sure you do a good job.'

'I do brides and government wives all the time lah.' Blossom the hairdresser dug her fingernails into Ghislaine's scalp as she lathered up the shampoo, rinsed and wrung her hair dry like washing. She pulled skeins of hair around rollers and squeezed the perming solution into cold rivulets that smelled of cat's piss and ran down Ghislaine's scalp and behind her ears.

When the rollers were taken out the hair was dull and frizzy as steel wool.

'My-y-y,' said Blossom, 'my oh my. What a crowning glory I have done for you.'

'I'm not so sure,' said Ghislaine, her mouth puckering in dismay. 'Can you make it go back a bit the way it was?'

'This ni-i-ice,' said Blossom. 'Ve-ry Shirley Te-e-emple.'

Ghislaine pressed her hands against the curls and rose quickly. 'How much?'

'Ten dollars. Ten dollars not much to look like a Hollywood fillum star. I give you free eyebrow pluck too.'

But Ghislaine knew she did not look like a Hollywood film star. She looked like a Malacca girl's dream of Englishness gone wrong.

❋

'Aiya! What a breakfast you've made of your hair!' Aunt Zeraphina narrowed her eyes. 'And you've plucked your eyebrows. Such nice juicy Eurasian eyebrows shrivelled to a Chinese cracker! How much did that cost you lah?'

'Only two dollars,' lied her niece.

'Two dollars! Aiya! Don't forget the story of Hantu Langsuyar lah, girl! So interested in catching men that she sucked the blood from her own family to make herself attractive.'

❋

Ghislaine mixed some condensed milk and tea in a glass until the hot liquid was the colour of old silk. She poured it in a long arc through the air into another glass. She kept pouring from one glass to another, watching it fill with tiny bubbles, feeling it cool.

'What on earth are you doing?' The tea-taster had entered so stealthily she did not notice him until he spoke. He had one of his hands behind his back. She was struck by the ambiguity of his smile. It was as if he was being cautious, or holding part of his enthusiasm in reserve. It was, she decided, the half smile of a gentleman pre-occupied by important matters.

'Making teh tarik.'

'Oh *that*. That's no way to treat tea.'

'They've been treating tea like this for hundreds of years in Malaya.' She couldn't help but sound apologetic. 'Taste?'

An expression of unmitigated disdain crossed his face. 'No thank you. That's a milkshake, not a cup of tea. What does tarik mean, anyway?'

'Pull. Because of the way you pull the tea through the air into longer and longer arcs as you make it. It cools the tea and gives it bubbles.'

'I see.' He brought his hand from behind his back and held it out to her. In it he held a deep yellow rose. 'I thought yellow would look better than red against your skin.' She felt her heart knocking at her throat as she took the rose. She smiled but could not speak. She noticed that one of the petals was slightly burnt on the edge.

'What happened to your hair?'

She did not want to admit to her expensive mistake at the hair-dresser's. 'I slept on it while it was wet.'

'Looks kind of witchy.'

Ghislaine had never looked at the sink so studiously. She filled a Horlicks jar with some water and placed the rose in it.

'Don't worry. You still look beautiful.' He tapped his top lip with his forefinger, so that Ghislaine noticed the beads of sweat glistening there. He scanned her body as he did this, but did not meet her eyes. 'Totally captivating, as a matter of fact. Now, give me a good strong pot of that In-Between Tea.' He took a seat by the window, placed his grey felt hat on the table again and played with its topography, shifting the dent between its two small grey peaks with his thumb as she made the tea and brought it to the table.

'Any significance in the name? In-Between Tea?'

'Our special blend. My aunt named it after one of the British terms for Malaccan Eurasians. Also, the leaves are taken from the harvest between the first and –'

Rupert Balneaves cut across her explanation with a slurp. She rushed for an empty cup, but he swallowed all of the tea and exhaled loudly. 'This region will never produce the high-quality teas of Darjeeling. Your climate is too monotonous. It's those extremes in temperature that give the Darjeeling-tea flavours the edge. Bring me a pot of the premium tea, would you?'

The tea-taster watched her reach for the leaves with her spoon. 'You should warm the pot first, you know. That's the girl.'

The crockery clattered on the tray as she carried it over.

'Ah. The first cup moistens my lips and throat, the second cup breaks my loneliness . . . You are very unusual. Did you know that?'

Her feet felt hot. She was glad he didn't wait for an answer. He rose abruptly, locked the door of the tearooms from inside and turned the sign over to closed.

'My aunt will –'

He placed his forefinger on her lips and smiled. She could see his pulse in the vein near his temple. He swallowed hard. It seemed he was nervous, too. She felt suddenly less intimidated. She even felt sorry for him as his words tumbled out in a rush.

'The third cup searches my barren entrails but to find therein some five thousand volumes of odd ideographs. The fourth cup raises a slight perspiration, all the wrong of life passes away through my pores. At the fifth cup I am purified, the sixth cup calls me to the realm of the immortals. The seventh cup – ah, but I could take no more.' But, standing there with his hands cupping her shoulders, he looked as though he could consume the whole world.

'I only feel the breath of cool wind that rises. Where is heaven?' He was talking too fast for her to recover from her own deafening silence. 'By a Chinese poet in the time of Lo-yu.' She wondered if all Englishmen were as intent on displaying their knowledge as they courted, but by then his hands were on her hair, on her lips, unbuttoning her blouse as his words kept falling from his mouth: 'Let me waft away on this. I want you, I want you . . .'

She couldn't tell where the poetry ended and his own feelings began. And there was that blurring in her vision, the flickering shadow that she associated with the travel writer. As if she still had a choice to make.

'Please,' she pleaded, 'not yet,' but the tea-taster's tongue was at hers like a scythe, cutting down her protests as he pressed her back against the cool wooden floor. Her blood roared with hope shouting down fear, before the most silencing pain as he entered her.

This silence. It froze her. When he had finished, she felt it rise from her body and enter the air between them. Now it seemed there was no choice. She lay on her side searching the Englishman's face for her bearings while he stared at the blades of the ceiling fan cutting the light like a dying star. He turned his face to her and smoothed her hair.

'Are you all right, my dear?' The gentle half-smile was back on his lips. One hand on her hair, six words in her ear and his sad half-smile. These were all it took to show her with sudden clarity that everything she had longed for previously with Walter Humphries was nothing but a dream. A new and urgent plan had come to take its place.

She knew no-one she could tell about this plan. Not even Rupert Balneaves would know her desperation.

'Who is the man?' Zeraphina Albuquerque asked when she saw the stubble rash on her niece's chin. Ghislaine was as much surprised by the note of curiosity as by the lack of fury in her aunt's voice.

'He is a tea-taster. Rupert Balneaves.' She added with a whisper: 'English.'

Her aunt looked out the window of the tearooms and exhaled years of exhaustion and financial anxiety. She spoke with the resignation of someone for whom there was no longer any certainty.

'Sounds promising,' she said. 'Does he have money?'

Rupert Balneaves met Ghislaine de Sequeira in the tearooms every day, his words freighted with knowledge she could not measure.

'The Chinese place teas into five groups: red, green, yellow, red brick and green brick. Each group is subdivided into four grades . . .' He put his hands on her shoulders and moved them slowly over her clavicles towards her breasts '. . . rough, tender, old and new.'

He asked if she would marry him only two weeks after they'd met. She told herself that it didn't matter if it wasn't yet love she felt for him.

'Yes,' she said, but she didn't look him in the eye. Below them, the valley fell so steeply she couldn't see the bottom.

※

It was Maundy Thursday, and the road to Malacca was busy with people returning from afar to visit relatives and church for the Easter services. After she had walked Aunty Zeraphina from the Malacca bus station to Aunty Lourdes Skelchy's house, Ghislaine begged a ride with her cousin Olivia Skelchy in her fiancé Nazario Maximiano's shiny green Austin to the street of cakes, just around the corner from the street of tailors. She had been ordered by Aunty Zeraphina to buy a canister of cocoa and a dozen gelatinous kueh kos wee decorated with inky crosses for the Maundy Thursday ladies' tea party, so that Zeraphina and her friends could drink and eat purple, the colour of valour, as they sat gossiping victoriously and stoically in their mauve and lilac frocks.

In the padded red interior of the Austin, Ghislaine confided almost everything to Olivia. She told her she was not sure what love was, but she felt it was wrong to love two men. She told her that she did not love Rupert Balneaves as she loved Walter Humphries, but that Walter Humphries obviously did not love her as Rupert Balneaves did. She was about to tell her the deepest secret, when Olivia turned her wide smile and warm dark eyes from the road to face her.

'You're like a dog chasing its tail! What's love got to do with this lah! *Two* Englishmen!' Olivia slapped her thigh. 'You look as pure as the Madonna, but you are such an itchified whore lah!' They laughed as the Austin crossed the bridge over the Malacca River into town. They laughed as two young women who believe they know everything about one another do, until Ghislaine's chuckle subsided into a long, stuttering sob.

Olivia's eyes widened in sympathy. 'Aiya! Tell you what lah. There's a bomoh in the kampong near Bukit Bahru who specialises in the treatment of love. He sees people on Thursday after he gets back from the mosque. We take the kueh and cocoa back home first, then I'll take you to see him.'

They delivered the gelatinous kueh wrapped in old newspaper back to the Skelchy bungalow at the base of St John's Hill as the first guests were arriving. Soon the front room was full of redoubtable middle-aged Old Lady Convent ex-scholars, chewing and sipping on purple, their eyelids darkened by age as they commiserated with one another over the inconveniences of their bodies, the indiscretions of their husbands, the impieties of their children.

Ghislaine and Olivia left the house after helping pour the second round of cocoa. They did not tell any of the ex-scholars of Our Lady that they were going to the edge of town where the soothsayers and medicine men were, for they knew the ex-scholars of the Our Lady Convent would consider consulting soothsayers and bomohs on any day, let alone Maundy Thursday, the biggest impiety of all.

Olivia drove her cousin past the sprawling bungalows of the English expatriates and the Chinese businessmen and through the district of the soothsayers and fortune tellers. They drove past the temple where the Chinese deity sat with bottles full of cloudy solutions for his clients to drink, past the numerologist who dispensed lucky lottery numbers and the Indian astrologer who told lucky dates. Muslim, Catholic and Hindu soothsayers peered from the doors of their houses to assess the day and the likelihood of customers.

They turned right into the kampong of the bomoh Datok, parked the car in a patch of gravel and followed a muddy footpath that wound around the brown wooden houses perched on their stilts like long-legged birds. Only the voices of two women speaking inside one of the houses could be heard.

'Everyone else still at the mosque lah,' murmured Olivia. Along the sides of the path, thin brown hens clucked with consternation. Datok's house was the only house in the kampong painted lime green with pink and viridian glazed floral tiles on its steps.

The two cousins were the first of the day's clients to sit on the verandah that served as the bomoh's waiting room. His wife brought them cups of sweet black tea. She looked impassively at them from beneath her bright pink veil and spoke in fast Malay before going into the small room adjoining the verandah.

'He is late back from the mosque, but shouldn't be long now,' translated Olivia, who'd learned Malay from her neighbours in her childhood.

Ghislaine could see the wife lighting lumps of resin in the terracotta censer on a low table in the darkness of the room before she re-crossed the verandah and entered the rooms of the main house, shutting the door behind her. Soon a pall of grey smoke rose and drifted out of the room towards the verandah.

As they sat waiting, Olivia told her cousin what she knew of the bomoh.

'I'll have to translate for you. He speaks in an old poetic form of Malay. He is a customs officer most of the week, but he sets aside Thursday afternoon for his bomoh work. Any Muslims with problems come and see him when they're feeling at their purest, just after they've been to the mosque. Hope you're feeling holy lah!' She chortled before looking Ghislaine in the eye. 'Never, never tell Aunty Zeraphina or my mother I brought you here. They'd probably take us to Father Pereira to have us exorcised if they heard.'

'What does Datok do?'

'I came here with Faridah, that Muslim seamstress. Faridah

having man trouble, always having man trouble, lah. Datok cut some lime up on her stomach, bit it and sucked a big brown mass out of her, full of broken glass and God knows what else.'

Ghislaine felt her body growing tight and moist with fear as Olivia spoke.

'Did it hurt lah?'

'A little. Red mark on her stomach where he bit her lah. Then he gave some black liquid to drink. She vomited twenty minutes or so later. Everyone does. It's the spiritual impurities leaving your body lah.'

Ghislaine felt wet as a fish under her thin film of perspiration by the time a tall silver-haired man dressed in a white tunic, trousers and songket hat walked through the verandah and into the smoky room, beckoning them to follow. What if he divined her secret, the secret she could hardly admit to herself yet?

'What you want to ask him?'

Rupert Balneaves's ill-fitting engagement ring slipped around Ghislaine's finger, lubricated by the sweat of her prevarication and her fear of being found out. She was bursting with her question: Which man was for her, the travel writer or the tea-taster? But, after Olivia's reaction in the car, Ghislaine saw how such a question might reveal her as a woman so itchified she might crack the foundations of three of Malacca's most redoubtable institutions: the Holy Spirit Catholic Church, Our Lady of Sorrows Convent, and Aunt Zeraphina Albuquerque of the sorely tested but ineluctable faith and ambition.

'I don't know. I don't want to tell him about all this,' Ghislaine whispered.

'Just ask him a more general question then.' Olivia turned to Datok. 'She wants to know how things will go for her this year.'

Datok nodded, closed his eyes and bowed three times over the smoky censer, whispering as he did. He spoke peremptorily to Olivia, so that she had to translate fast to keep up with what he was saying.

'You do the same now. Lean over the censer as he did.' The smoke smelled of the dark saps and woods of the jungle. Ghislaine coughed and her eyes smarted as she bowed three times over it. The bomoh's wife entered and watched.

'Good. Now sit up on the floor. Legs straight out in front of you.'

Datok stood behind Ghislaine and placed his knee against her back and his hands on her shoulders. He took hold of her ears and tugged them suddenly, hard. When he spoke, it was in a voice that ascended and descended as if he was reciting a nursery rhyme.

'He says that a woman is very jealous of you. She's had someone do a charm to suck all the confidence out of you. Very strong charm. He says you do not sleep well at night because of this charm and some other secret you've hidden from everyone.'

'Who is jealous of me?'

Datok closed his eyes again before replying.

'He says that he will not tell you, in case it makes trouble between you and another person. He says to beware of a well-travelled man who seems to offer new horizons. He will take you through dark clouds to the Land of the Unseen. That,' Olivia hissed to her cousin, 'is where Malays believe people go after their death.'

Ghislaine felt her pulse jump. 'Ask him. Am I going to die soon?'

The bomoh closed his eyes when Olivia Skelchy put the question to him. His eyes remained closed as he spoke.

'You will die three deaths before your final death. You have died once already, you will die again soon. They are other kinds of death, years before your final death. Two men will leave you lost in places you don't want to go. Now, lie down and pull your blouse up just a little, just enough to show your stomach.'

Ghislaine shook as a cold sweat washed over her skin. She placed her hands over her stomach. She closed her eyes tightly, so that she felt rather than saw what came next. The bomoh lifted her hands away and rubbed an ointment briskly into a fist-sized area on her stomach. She felt the skin there grow warm and numb, as if Tiger

Balm ointment had been rubbed into it. He placed the lime on her stomach and cut through it so deftly she felt no blade.

'He wants to know, why are you so scared?'

Ghislaine could not say. Datok put his mouth against her stomach and sucked through his teeth once, twice. She was so alarmed she opened her eyes suddenly to see the bomoh's wife scooping a lump of congealed brownish paste from the surface of her stomach with a piece of newspaper. Ghislaine sat up to look as Datok broke up the lump with his knife. It fell apart to reveal pins, a piece of glass and a torn tie of cotton fabric.

'There is the string the maker of charms used to tie up your confidence with.'

The bomoh took a small phial from the table behind him as he continued speaking his old Malay.

'He says your suitor has a bad temper. You must take this oil and put a little bit of it on your brow before you talk to him, or anyone you want to impress. As you wipe the oil on your brow, you must say Minyak Makat Ramat Sayang. This means with this oil, this person will love me.' Datok handed her the tiny glass phial of oil tied at its neck with a piece of yellow cloth, and a small medicine bottle filled with black liquid in which irregularly sized particles floated.

'You must swallow this,' Olivia said. 'He says it is to get rid of any useless love, any love you have that isn't good for you. He says he doesn't know if medicine like this will work for siranis like us. Depends how much Malay we still have in our souls. Do you want, or no?'

'What you think lah?'

'Well, if this won't work, what will? The English doctors can't give us anything for the treatment of useless love. Take the black medicine. Try lah. In twenty minutes to half an hour's time, it will make you throw up. Then we can go home. He says praying to your Mary will help you, and that if I bring him a square of gold cloth and a square of white he will pray for you too.' Her voice dropped to a whisper. 'Leave five dollars in the plate on the way out.'

Datok's wife handed her a waxed bag as they walked through the door. 'For the vomit.' A paper bag to dispose of the useless love.

The waiting room was so full that people were sitting on the floor. Ghislaine and Olivia were the only women not wearing veils. The Muslim women in their bright tunics leaned out of their seats on the verandah, watching them avidly as they stood in the dirt amongst the chickens, waiting for the black emetic to work on Ghislaine. One by one the clients in the waiting room entered, exited, and vomited neatly at the back of the house into their little paper bags before leaving, but still Ghislaine's stomach would not oblige. She felt a sudden bright sweat break out all over her body, but nothing else followed. Perhaps she'd been so travel sick that morning on the bus that she had nothing left in her to throw up. There were only her feelings for the travel writer, deeper than her alimentary canal, that inconsolable panic like motion sickness she'd had since she first met him.

The sun dipped lower in the west. The waiting room was almost empty.

'No use lah. Shall we go?'

'You want? Don't you throw up in Nazario's new Austin lah!'

The interior of the car smelled of new vinyl baked by sun.

'That brown paste he sucked out of my stomach, Olivia. I don't think he did. I felt nothing come out of me. Looked like tamarind paste to me.'

'Aiya! No faith, girl, you have no faith! Not in Mary, not in bomohs. Who can help you lah?' Olivia slapped her on the leg and crashed through the gears as they drove along the road out of the kampong.

Ghislaine sat in the invisible vapours of the new red vinyl upholstery, her big question unasked, the disturbance in her vision like a flickering shadow behind her eyes again. She hoped this shadow of Walter would disappear when she married Rupert. She felt fraudulent, lacking in enough stomach and wisdom to discern the difference between useless and useful love. She desperately needed to believe that she had made the right decision, and that no-one would ever guess her secret.

⁂

Wish de Sequeira was waiting for his daughter in the front room of his house on Koon Cheng Road, windows and door open, when Olivia dropped her off after the visit to the bomoh. He saw her first, coming down the four-foot way on the other side of the road with her head held high in that way that reminded him so much of Mathilde when Hortense chided her for being a divorcee. Wounded pride, of course; it was wounded pride that made them hold their head in that way.

Oh Ghislaine, he thought to himself, how hard I have been on you.

He saw he would have to let her go her own way now.

He had been preparing himself to broach the subject of the travel writer's disappearance, but she pre-empted it with her own news.

'I am marrying,' she said defiantly, and was surprised at how sadly and knowingly her father nodded.

LONDON, DECEMBER 1985

–My gums are aching at the back, especially in the morning. Sunil and I are checking the tropical zone of the Princess of Wales conservatory, where some of the plants seem to be suffering from frost stress.

–How long's it been going on for?

–A few weeks at least. It feels like bruising.

–Go see Mr Gopalkrishnan the dentist, Isabelle.

–I don't know what it could be. There's no sign of any ulcers or decay. Only a few months ago he said my gums and teeth were in perfect condition.

I pull a weed out from under a fern.

–Maybe I could massage them at night while I'm waiting for Philip to ring.

–Oh dear. Like that is it? He's taken a mystery flight, yeah? Sunil pats me on the shoulder. –I worry about you. Still recovering from David leaving, aren't you?

I shrug. The ruins of my marriage, Clara crying for her father in the night, my mother dying. All these are freight too heavy to unload.

—What do you see in Philip Border, Isabelle?

The sudden apparition I have of Philip standing at the door to his house of words and light seems real and true.

—Escape, I guess. And home.

—Shit, mutters Sunil, snapping off a brown leaf. Another dead epiphyte. We need to get the thermostat checked.

❋

All over London, Asian is hip. Harvey Nichols's bandaid-pink display dummies wear heavy brocade cheongsams from China with carefully concealed price tags.

In her shop behind Mr Arasu's Indian restaurant a few blocks away from our house, Mrs Bakar always looks as if she means business. She wears metal-framed glasses, and her hair in the tight bun her mother would have worn back home. She has the no-nonsense manner of one who knows her customers best as a sequence of measurements. My mother and her Indian, Malay and Chinese friends who live in the flats near the Westway flyover go to Mrs Bakar for the clothes they wear to weddings, christenings and anniversaries. Lately, some of the Englishwomen, professionals from the recently gentrified streets around Portobello Road, have discovered her. Though Malay, Mrs Bakar has diversified. She does suits with shoulder pads; cocktail frocks and cheongsams as well as kebayas; but she refuses to do the plunging necklines so beloved by many of our more bosomy English neighbours. Does she disapprove, or is she simply intimidated, like me?

Previously, I have only ever visited Mrs Bakar when accompanying my mother for fittings. She barely conceals her surprise when I walk in alone and make my request.

—Can you sew me sarong kebaya, western style?

I lift a bolt of grey polished cloth from the neat pyramid of fabric behind her cutting table.

—Fitted skirt with a split at the hem. Kebaya fitted at the bust and waist. Like this but shorter hem, I say, drawing an airlines advertisement from my pocket.

–Oh, you mean like the new Singapore Girl uniform lah. Iv San Lorong design.

She pronounces its French designer's name like a suburban Malay address.

–And not batik.

–Why no batik?

–Too jungly village girl.

–This grey cotton. Good match for your eyes. Looks like silk but cheaper lah.

She runs her tape measure around my meagre chest as the smell of frying mustard seeds, ghee and garlic seeps under the back door of Mr Arasu's restaurant.

–Can you sew to make my tetek look bigger?

Mr Arasu clangs a saucepan lid like a gong on the other side of the door.

–Marks & Spencer has a new padded bra, she says without taking her eyes off the measuring tape. How's your mother?

All the rooms in my mother's house are cold. The phone rings. The sun is in Philip's voice, inviting me to that warmer place. It's been a week since he left so abruptly after class. Whatever might have been wrong between us seems suddenly inconsequential or imagined.

My new western-style kebaya fits like another skin when I visit. He scrutinises it unsmilingly for a moment, and I wonder if he's about to challenge its authenticity. But he just peels it off me. He runs his finger quickly up my spine to my neck. There's still all this language to learn.

–Say something French.

–I wouldn't mind more of that chicken tandoori, he replies.

Our smiles spread further than our faces. *Menggeli hati.* Tickling the heart in Malay. Warmed through, my muscles unclench, bones lighten. It seems I've almost found my true body.

–What are you doing next holidays? We could travel together. You could show me Malaysia. I could show you France, he says.

Beyond his bedroom window, the oak-tree branch cups the waxing moon and the clouds spread across the sky like a map of the world.

–That, I reply –would be a dream.

When I place my hand on his heart, it seems so close to the surface.

❋

The ache in my gums remains, but later that week I think I recognise other symptoms. I purchase a test kit from the pharmacy.

Give yourself certainty only fifteen days after a missed period, the blue words on the flowery mauve package read.

The little red plus sign takes only sixteen seconds to appear in the white plastic square under my droplet of urine. So much for my intra-uterine device. So much for certainty.

How far will Philip and I travel now?

❋

As I walk north along Portobello Road to the hospital, I'm carrying stolen flowers, red and pink cabbage roses from the nursery at work. My mother will surely guess. They are not the tight hothouse buds on the end of long stems the florists around the city sell. The roses I've stolen are monstrous and suburban by comparison, but their perfume is sweet.

It's early enough in the evening for the traffic to still be sluggish along Portobello Road. I look in the food shops for something that might help fatten up my mother. Pause outside the Lebanese cake shop, before remembering that pastries upset her stomach now. I buy a tub of strawberry gelati and a jar of saltfish pickle from the delicatessen a few doors down and ask the shopkeeper for two spoons.

I cross the square at the church opposite the hospital. At the foot of the hospital's stone stairs, the homeless woman in the black dress stands next to a portable tape recorder singing.

–*A-a-a-ve Mari-iiii-a . . .*

Her voice swells and falls through the air. One arm hangs straight at her side and she holds the other before her, as if she is keeping the noise of the city back. She doesn't drop one note, even in the din of revving motors and car horns.

Does my mother hold as firmly to the hymns and prayers of her Malaccan life as this disease engulfs her? If I could open her hospital window, she might hear the woman singing against the traffic with such courage, this song the de Sequeiras have sung for generations.

My heart skitters. I think I can feel the secret rolling in my belly. I pass the emergency wing, where someone has passed out on the floor, and the nurses calmly carry chartreuse-coloured kidney dishes and plastic tubes around patients. I take the lift and search for my mother's face through gaps in the blue curtains drawn around the beds.

My mother sits frowning slightly on her pillows in the flickering glow of the television mounted on the opposite wall. She turns and smiles when she hears my footsteps.

–You look like spring itself. What beautiful flowers.

I step around the plastic tube that hangs from her wrist to put the roses in the clumsy cut-glass vase on her bedside table.

–It's strange lah, becoming blind, knowing you will die soon. Every image you see becomes a rehearsal for loss.

I squeeze her hand.

–Roses. They smell like nectar. Izzy, your hands are sweaty. Are you nervous?

–No.

I can't bring myself to admit it.

Her eyes have grown larger with the loss of subcutaneous fat from her face. So this is what they mean by just skin and bone.

I sit down.

—Aunty Kanti sent more salted plums, and I bought these for you. Liven up that bland hospital food.

I put the saltfish pickle on the shelf next to the flowers, and hand her the gelati tub and a spoon.

—Share . . . with me? she suggests. She looks small and thin as a doll against the white pillow, but her hair is growing back dark and thick after the chemotherapy, as if she would come through all this younger than she was before.

I check the impulse to put my head on her chest and howl. *No, you can't die. Anyone but you.* A year before, I would have confided in her without hesitation about whatever was bothering me. Now, there are things I have to pretend. I have to pretend that I can bear her death. I have to pretend I know how to live my life.

I pull the lid off the gelati and begin spooning it into my mouth. On the television, David Attenborough's sonorous voice intones over images of orangutans courting.

—Anyway, good to see you, Izzy, my mother says.

How much of me can she see? A lump of gelati slides unmelted down my throat.

—What have you . . . been up to?

—Well. I exhale loudly and look out the window for the words to explain the tutor and our secret.

—So . . . what . . . is wrong with Isabelle today?

—Well. Ah. There is a man to consider, I guess.

And a terrible accident. The words are beyond me as I watch her face. There is no fat left under her skin to soften the sudden lines of concern in her face, and nothing between us but her dying vision to conceal my shame.

—Ah-yah. Here, eat, eat. More gelati. So. What . . . kind of man is involved with a woman like you?

The considered pauses in her voice do not condescend to me,

but I am grateful for more than this. I am grateful for the way in which she says *a woman like you*, giving my idiosyncrasies distinction, focusing so closely on me that I forget about her failing eyesight. This is what my mother has always done for people who need to confide in her: given them her undivided attention, until it becomes apparent to them that they are someone worth watching.

–He didn't propose it. He just . . . did it, I suppose you'd say.

–I . . . see. What kind of man is that?

–My writing tutor, actually. The one I mentioned before. Englishman. Forty-nine years old.

–Ah-yah! A teacher shouldn't do that to a student. Forty-nine? He's old enough to know better.

There is a tremor in her voice.

–He looks younger.

Who am I defending?

–And is proud of it, I bet.

–Now you come to mention it.

–Sounds like a warning to me. Too, too many precedents.

Her eyes are brimming with concern, as if she knows more about this than I.

I shouldn't confide in her at all. I decide not to tell her my newer secret.

–Precedents?

–The unwritten history of the British in Malaya. Middle-aged white man seeks young . . . half-caste woman to translate the exotic for him. Her voice drops to a whisper. –Sleeping dictionaries, the expatriates called us.

She unfolds and refolds the top hem of her hospital blanket.

–But you weren't one of *them*.

–If you ask me, no-one was. It all depended on who was talking about you. A sleeping dictionary was more an English rumour, gossip or fantasy than a true way to describe any woman. Walter called me a sleeping dictionary once or twice.

—Huh, Walter Humphries the third-rate travel writer. Why do you think you fell for a man like that in the first place?

—Maybe . . . maybe because I couldn't see him for what he was. Convent education and Malaccan society back then taught my generation that anything British was good. Being Eurasian, we weren't white enough for the British, nor Asian enough for the Malays or the Chinese. I was glad my skin was quite pale, and I was secretly ashamed of Grandfather Wish, can you imagine that? I was always trying to be someone else. And after Grandmother Mathilde's death, Grandfather Wish withdrew from life a fair bit. All that grief and shame lah. I couldn't see myself properly. How can we see our suitors properly if we can't see ourselves?

When she looks at me, it seems the sadness in her eyes might go on forever.

We? Typical mother, I think. *Always assuming my life will turn out like hers. Always assuming I suffer from the same weaknesses as she.*

My secret flutters in my belly again. There is no point in asking her advice about it. Philip Border is obviously a much more promising man than Walter Humphries. I won't tell her anything else about Philip and me. She won't understand, can't even be expected to.

—What makes you think my story will be the same as yours? I ask, regretting the harsh splinter in my voice as soon as I speak.

—Oh. I didn't mean that. I'm sorry. I hope it won't. One of the reasons I brought you to London was to try to give you a stronger sense of yourself. Show you that you belonged to the world your father had come from, too.

The gelati is almost finished, and my mother hasn't had a bit of it. Her eyes follow mine to the television. An old male orangutan creeps around the back of two younger males fighting one another for a female's favours. He mounts her successfully before running swiftly away.

—Sneaky rutters, some Malaccans called those old male orangutans who mate with the female while the other males are fighting it out. I can't remember the Malay term for it. Isabelle? I think that

I've overprotected you. I didn't want you to suffer the same kinds of misfortune I did with Walter and Rupert.

–So *that's* why you wouldn't let me go out alone with a man before David?

All those years, I'd thought my mother was adhering to some unspoken, antiquated courtship rules from the old country.

–Yes. But I think my protectiveness has made you more vulner-able. And your missing a father doesn't help, either.

–You think I'm still just a little girl in search of a father? Thanks, Mum.

She wrings her hands.

–No. I'm just warning you. Often when we think we've fallen in love, we're really seeking reconciliation with someone we've lost. Just as I fell for Walter Humphries when my mother died and Grandfather Wish withdrew.

–And how about Dad? Did you fall in love with Dad because you lost Walter?

–Well, yes and no. It's not always that simple. But you've got the idea. We're all blinded by loss to some extent. Be careful, Isabelle. Watch out for sneaky rutters.

She touches my hand.

–And, of course, you must look for the answers to your questions in yourself now. No-one else knows your story as well as you do.

My spoon scrapes on the bottom of the tub.

THE TRUE BODY

✤ The wrong flavour ✤

When Wish de Sequeira took delivery of the wedding photographs from Wing's Photographic Studio, his heart sank. Nearly every photograph reinforced his suspicion that his daughter had entered into an inexplicable new helplessness around the tea-taster, for in every one her hands were blurred, as if she did not know what to do with them. Nearly every photograph reminded Wish that his new son-in-law had not reciprocated Ghislaine's tentative touch on his arm, his hand, his shoulder. Every photograph except one, in which Rupert looked at her with an expression of . . . what was it? These Englishmen, their faces always so hard to read. Wish placed the photographs carefully into a leather-bound album, prayed over them and sent them to his daughter in the Cameron Highlands.

※

When he returned to the Cameron Highlands with Ghislaine after their fortnight's honeymoon in Penang, Rupert Balneaves was pleased to find Zeraphina had chosen to pack up her belongings and go to Singapore. The newly teetotalling Theobald had telegrammed her, beseeching her to join him in his shiny new Singapore flat. Rupert slapped the walls of Journey's End heartily, as if they were old friends. He walked from room to room, testing the floorboards, checking the flaky plaster of the walls with his thick fingers for rising damp. He paced the house in his shiny boots, each footfall a proclamation: I am the master. I am the master of the house.

He ignored the neat pairs of shoes lined up at the front door where people took them off to enter the house. He did not wear the house slippers Mak Non bought him specially from the market.

Mak Non followed him every day with the broom, sweeping up the dirt he brought in on his boots. Her bare feet made no sound.

❋

For weeks after the wedding, Ghislaine woke well before dawn, slick with sweat from her dreams of running through unfamiliar cities in search of Walter Humphries. The dream revisited her during the day with all the adamant, quiet persistence of a premonition. Every morning she got up, relieved her bladder and listened to the Lynx cistern purring as she smoked half a pipeful behind the locked door.

Just before dawn, the night mist was still at the windows but there was enough light in the bedroom to illuminate the paler surfaces in the room: the wall on either side of the Dutch armoire and mirror, Rupert's white shirt on the back of the door, and his sleeping face on the pillow. She could just make out his facial expressions, mobile as a child's, now disappointed, now hopeful. The crease at his brow puckered and he gave a low whimper. She was suddenly moved. She would make herself love him. She would prove her father's doubts and her own wrong. She would not go back to the dream of the travel writer. She put her hand on her husband's forehead as if she could smooth over the lines there. He opened his eyes and smiled at her.

'Good morning, my dusky-skinned one. Why is a beautiful young woman like you looking so anxious?'

'Am I?' How should she look? She rearranged her expression into a smile. 'I don't mean to be.'

'How do you mean to be, then?'

'I mean to . . . love you.'

He laughed. 'You make it sound a little bit like labour.' He brushed his hair back off his forehead. It was peppery smelling and heavy with the previous day's hair oil. 'Is it a labour? For a young woman like you to love an old chap like me?'

Ghislaine smiled uncertainly, both taken aback and disarmed. Despite his first-class way of speaking and dressing, her husband didn't seem as sure of himself as the travel writer, after all. In fact, he sounded almost grateful. Maybe he even loved her. Maybe things had worked out for the best.

'Forty-nine's not *that* old,' she said as reassuringly as she could.

'Why thank you,' he said, the corners of his mouth twitching. 'How do you say old in Malay?'

'Lusuh. Or tua.' She'd learned just enough Malay from Mak Non.

He pointed to himself. 'Lusuh.' Their faces were suddenly illumin-ated by the lemony light of the dawn breaking through a gap in the curtains.

'No-o-o,' she laughed. Walter Humphries had never played such self-effacing games.

'And how do you say beautiful?'

'Cantik.' She spoke seriously and clearly. The light in the room intensified as the sun cleared a cloud on the horizon. He ran his eyes along her body draped in the pale green cotton nightdress from the Chinese markets in Malacca.

'And breast?'

'Tetek.'

'Stomach?'

'Perut.'

'And what's the word for ugly?'

'Hodoh.' She hunched her shoulders and drew her knees up towards her belly, as if she might fold herself into something smaller.

He pointed at her. She held her breath.

'Cantik,' he said smoothly. She beamed. He ran his hand along her side. 'A little thick around the middle, perhaps, but an exotic prize nonetheless.' She drew the sheet hastily over herself.

'I like food.'

'That's okay. I've always liked women with a bit of flesh and appetite. But the chartreuse colour of that cheap nightdress really doesn't suit you.'

'It's just a nightdress. Clothes are just clothes.'

'You're wrong there. Clothes can say a lot about a person.'

She felt a new edge of panic rise in her.

'I'm going to the wet markets today with Mak Non to buy ingredients for popiah for your dinner tonight,' she said hastily. 'Have you ever eaten popiah?'

'I wouldn't know popiah from a pig's arse.'

'It–it's a kind of thin pancake rolled around shredded vegetables and meat.'

'I've never bothered to learn the names of lots of the food I've eaten in Malaya. I just eat it.'

'How do you order it then?'

'I just point to what I want. I always,' he smiled, 'get what I want. In food and in life.' But for a moment he looked past her to the window, and the L-shaped creases at the inner corners of his eyebrows deepened in consternation. *L for Love*, Ghislaine thought to herself. *L for Lies*.

She patted him on his arm. She might have been offering consolation. 'What about you? What are you doing today?'

The blue veins showed through the milky underside of his wrist as he stretched his arms above his head and yawned. A dense, sad smell like the damp earth of her mother's freshly dug grave rose from him, quite unlike the travel writer's odour of meaty panic. But the pale rise of her husband's chest reminded her of the uncooked breast of a freshly plucked chicken.

'I'm meeting some of the tea-pickers from one of the plantations today. How do you say tasty in Malay?'

'Rasa.'

'And bitter?'

'Pahit.'

'Do you know any Tamil? Most of the pickers are Tamil, from the Indian plantations.'

She shook her head. He spoke to the ceiling. 'There's so much to be done around here, too. Improvements to be made. I will get some workers in when the harvest is finished.'

※

At the breakfast table, Rupert drew a plan. He relocated the bar to one end of the living room, put a bathtub in the bathroom. He removed Mak Non's room to make way for a dining room, and turned the closet-sized old pantry at the rear of the kitchen into Mak Non's room. When he had finished, the intricate lines he'd drawn on the page looked like a cage.

'Selling all that land to the rear of the block will finance the rebuilding, of course.'

'But it's still in my father's name. And . . . not all that land is part of the block. Mak Non cleared some of the jungle to use it to grow vegetables in.' Ghislaine was alarmed by the thinness of the line he pressed his lips into after her explanation. He returned home that evening with it still in place.

'Keeping Mak Non is costing too much money,' he said. 'Anyway, you can do the cooking. I thought all Asian women could cook.'

Ghislaine had watched her aunt and Mak Non struggling with the mysteries of domesticity and triumphing, yet, since both her uncle and Walter Humphries had disappeared without saying goodbye, it seemed to her that women received nothing but abandonment and punishment for slaving over the stove.

'Dusting, cooking. I do not like doing these things lah. Dust and food repeat themselves.'

※

Ghislaine tried compensating for her reluctance to cook by cultivating more vegetables and sewing her own clothes. She managed only two dresses: one with a frilled collar, the other a blue dress for serving in the tearooms. Both were puckered with her impatience along their seams. But she made sure to spread treacle on her husband's toast every morning.

Most of the time, Ghislaine was gripped with an insatiable need for sleep. She would sink whenever she was able into the soft white bed with its mist of mosquito netting, often with tears of relief in her eyes. Her new husband often arrived home to find her in bed with the green tinge in her skin more marked than it had been when he left.

'You're thin on keeping house and getting even fatter around the middle. And those home-sewn dresses don't help.'

The little bird fluttered in her belly. She scrutinised his face carefully. There'd be no better time to tell him. 'I'm pregnant.'

'Already! I thought you'd be practising a few native precautions.' Despite the sola topee and the steel-capped boots he wore to supervise the tea-pickers, he looked like a little boy to her, disconsolate and baffled.

※

Rupert returned home every day to take off his fine white English shirt, his boots and sola topee after lunch, when the air grew warm. Since marrying his Eurasian wife, he was even more determined to prove to himself and the expatriate community of the highlands that he was not going native. He mail-ordered a dozen new shirts and trousers from Guthries Gentlemen's Outfitters in London. He turned his Noel Coward and Enrico Caruso records up so loud on His Master's Voice record player that the tea-pickers in the valley looked up in consternation.

'I am going to grade the harvest,' he said peremptorily. He bathed, dressed in fresh clothes and drove his Morris up the road beyond the clouds. Often he didn't return until Ghislaine was sleeping. He smelled of whisky and his talk was hot and angry.

※

One morning, Mak Non noticed the disappearance of Mathilde's stone carving of the bird woman, given to Ghislaine by Wish. She found it, finally, with the upright Madonna and the leaning Christ in a mound of rubble near the road. One breast had been dented, one eye had been chipped, one wing broken.

Ghislaine put the Christ, the Madonna and the kinnari on the altar in the tearooms. All day she felt the fluttering like wings in her belly. When her husband returned home late that afternoon, she suppressed the unladylike laugh that rose in her at the sight of the domed sola topee and steel-capped boots he wore to supervise the tea-pickers.

'Why did you throw the statues out?'

'They have no practical use. A woman that's a bird from the waist down? I'm getting rid of anything that doesn't serve a purpose.' His gaze was on his wife's belly.

'Stop looking at me like that lah.'

'Like what? I'll be honest. I'm a bit perturbed to find myself in this situation. Fatherhood approaching already. Not what I would have chosen.'

'It was the honeymoon that did it. We were careless.'

Mak Non heard all this from in the kitchen. She waited until she heard them both leave the dining room before clearing the table.

Ghislaine rushed past, sobbing. The tea-taster turned his Enrico Caruso to full volume. On the table were the plans for renovating the house.

❋

Ghislaine heard from the dark gossip of the local women at the wet markets that there was a Malay woman in Tanah Rata who had the right medicine for her problem. She took the bus to Tanah Rata the next day.

Siti Hajah lived in a wooden kampong house behind the shops of the main street. Her face was dark from the sun. Her gums were the purple of bruises.

'I only do if you give me the money first. Thirty dollars.' She stretched out her thin hand.

'Sit here.' She pulled up a peeling cane chair on the verandah and went inside.

Ghislaine watched three kampong children throw stones at a little mountain of empty Dutch Maid Powdered Milk and Ovaltine tins. Siti Hajah returned with an old brown glass medicine bottle full of a dull orange solution.

'Drink tonight.' She pointed between Ghislaine's legs. 'Bleed.'

Ghislaine hid the bottle in the study, on the shelf behind the English books and the yellowing copies of the *Tea and Rubber Mail*. Rupert came home smelling of whisky and perspiration just before midnight, in a gust of the first Sumatra wind of the season. Ghislaine heard him groan and the bedsprings creak as he rolled over. She shut the study door and retrieved the medicine. The liquid ran from the bottle down her long throat, sluggish and foul-smelling as swamp mud.

She sat in the chair and read the *Mother Goose Nursery Rhymes* and *Ten Important Facts about England*. Within half an hour, the pain in her lower abdomen was so intense that she lay down on the floor and drew her legs up to her chest. It was all she could do to moan as quietly as she could. The spasms clawed at her until her mind was empty of everything but broken lines of prayer.

'Holy Mary Mother of God . . .' She was unable to go beyond this. The Sumatra wind whooped through the treetops and blew the study window wide open with its cargo of moisture and hot air. It lifted the loose pages from the Bible and the *Tea and Rubber Mail* and scattered them over her like leaves.

Mak Non found Ghislaine half covered by the pages from Genesis and the tea-trading figures for 1954. The rug beneath her was dark with blood.

'Anak! What happen?'

'I got the medicine from Siti Hajah,' Ghislaine muttered through her clenched teeth. Mak Non brought towels and placed them between her legs, brought her hot sweet tea and sat next to her as she writhed and sweated and the blood seeped for hours into the dark. It eased, finally, when Ghislaine and the square of night sky through the window were the paleness of beaten tin, but the little bird still fluttered in her belly.

*

The woman with the pale orange hair kept bees that fed on the rose gardens of the expatriates. Her name was Divina Worth. Her own rose gardens grew in a stridently coloured half-acre around her white and green painted weatherboard house. Her Indian caretaker and cook lived in the garden shed with their family and made rose syrup and collected the honey from her hives for her to sell to the expatriates.

Before Ghislaine de Sequeira, Rupert Balneaves had slept with only one woman in his twelve years in Malaya. He'd visited Divina Worth in her bungalow next to the hives ever since he'd first started coming to the highlands just after the war.

'I don't give a damn for marriage,' she'd said then, 'and I don't give a sultan's sphincter for what people say.' This was a shame, for

Rupert had begun by then to think of himself as the marrying kind. Divina Worth wore her independent means the way she wore her Indian Army Bombay bloomers: as a coolly calculating affront to other English expatriate women. Rupert had known that he was just one of her several lovers. He'd suffered this for years partly because there were so few available Englishwomen in the highlands. But since he'd married a Eurasian, no other English person except Divina invited him home, and the Cameron Highlands Cricket Club had refused to renew his membership.

When Rupert visited Divina a few afternoons after his young wife had swallowed Siti Hajah's medicine, Divina handed the smoke bellows she used on her bees to her Tamil servant, who stood beside her bare-faced and solemn in her cerise sari. As Divina moved towards Rupert between the rows of little yellow wooden hives in her wide-veiled beekeeper's hat and long gloves, she looked like a matador in mourning. Her orange hair floated in the air like pale flames when she took her hat off with a wide sweep. He could see the fine nets of wrinkles in the skin around her eyes, the red blotches around her pink neck caused by the veil and the humidity.

Rupert embraced her and handed her a canister of tea he'd taken from the Miracle Tearooms.

'Precious Eyebrows tea for you.' He kissed her on her nose before fetching a white package from his shirt pocket.

'It's for your charm bracelet.' He'd been adding to it for years. Divina didn't thank him, but attached the tiny gold lips to her heirloom gold bracelet and slipped it back over her wrist without another glance at it.

'I have always appreciated you for your self-possession, and your mouth.' His smile was uneven but fulsome. 'Women who know their own mind and mouth are best in bed.' Despite his intimate way of addressing her, Rupert and Divina hadn't slept together since he'd announced his intention to marry Ghislaine. He knew she disdained sleeping with men who had sex with the natives. Nonetheless, he hoped to maintain the companionship he'd shared with her previously. He found himself slipping back into his pre-marital habit of trying to impress her, despite his wounded pride. But she breathed down her nose and he saw again that he could never charm her enough. She knew her own mind like she knew her own money.

'You have all the right sentiments and taste, but inadequate means to back them with,' she said bluntly. Rupert fingered his sweaty collar. It was not the first time she'd said this to him.

He had never seen Divina's other lovers, yet they had been the reason he had settled for Ghislaine. But from where he sat that afternoon, Divina looked like the reason he shouldn't have. She swaggered like a general, superbly aloof in her bloomers and heirloom gold chains. He wanted to protest the unfairness of it all. His years of wooing her felt like a massive failed military operation, full of nothing but errors of strategy.

She had her five best honeys and rose jellies set out in a row of little white sauce dishes next to the teapot on the front verandah. She held a silver teaspoon out to him.

'This one has a woody taste. Jungle nectar, most likely. Try some?' She stuck the teaspoon in his mouth as if he were a baby.

'I prefer it to the other,' he said. 'Not as sweet. I like a good strong flavour.' He took a long sip from the delicate cup she set before him. 'What is this tea setting? Not Royal Albert?'

'Limoges.'

'So delicate.' He traced the fine green pattern of leaves and white flowers with his blunt fingers.

Divina lit a cigarette in her silver holder and sat back in the rattan armchair. She blew a dense breath of smoke and looked at him calculatingly through it. 'My housegirl tells me some interesting things about your wife.'

'Oh? My wife could do with a bit of something interesting about her. She's put on too much weight with pregnancy.'

'Yati says that Mak Non has given your wife a special hantu to charm you.'

'Well, it hasn't worked yet.' He looked out the window as he spoke. 'You know I don't believe in all that hantu nonsense.'

'Anyone who doesn't believe in hantu hasn't lived here long enough. Yati!' she called.

The housegirl came into the room shuffling in her cloth house slippers.

'Tell the tuan what you know about his mem.'

Yati linked her forefingers and looked down at her feet as she spoke. 'I see your wife in Tanah Rata on market days. She not look when people speak to her. Her eyes bloodshot.' She drew her forefinger across her top lip. 'Kampong people talk. Say Mak Non give her Hantu Pelesit to fool you.'

'Which hantu is Pelesit?'

'Pelesit make women more attractive to men. That Mak Non powerful woman but evil. She left her first husband. Maybe she give your wife charms to trap you. Maybe she give her charms to get other man. Trust me. I know this country.' Yati looked hard at the strainer as she poured the tea. 'Not all I know, sir. Siti Hajah make women's medicine. She see your wife. Your wife no want your baby.'

Rupert laughed and turned to Divina. 'She's wrong there. Course she wants babies. Ghislaine's nothing if not a good Catholic girl from the backwaters of Malacca.'

The milk splashed over the edge of the jug as Yati pushed it towards him. 'Maybe not good. Chiap cheng women do this kine thing. They mixed up heart as well as blood.' She kept her eyes lowered as she left the room.

Rupert looked at Divina with a smirk like a streak of dirt on his face. 'Bit of native hocus-pocus. Anyway.' He patted her shoulder. 'Why should I worry? You're the sweetness in my life.' He sang this in a voice as syrupy as Enrico Caruso's, so that Divina's laughter poured thickly as the honey in the humid afternoon.

Divina Worth was the keeper not only of bees but also of the other half of Rupert Balneaves's smile. Divina Worth was the reason for the sadness in his eyes.

✳

When Divina told Rupert two days later that she'd met a man she wouldn't mind marrying after all, Rupert returned to Journey's End with his face mottled as if he'd been scalded.

'What's wrong?'

'Why can't you be like other women?' he shouted at his wife.

'Which other women?' He didn't answer her question. Ghislaine could hear nothing but his rage, long after her questions had thinned into air.

That was the week both halves of Rupert's smile disappeared. He looked even more like a lost little boy than when she'd told him she was pregnant. She put extra war-time treacle on his toast in the mornings. She played his favourite music loud. She helped Mak Non cook his favourite dishes every night.

It was only two months since Ghislaine had married Rupert.

All through that first week of the monsoon, so much Enrico Caruso and attempts at sweetness, but not even the ghost of his half-smile on the lips of her husband.

At the end of the week, Ghislaine went to the little church down the road overlooking the plantation in the valley, where she consoled herself by singing the hymns she'd learned in the Convent of Our Lady. The church was mostly empty on the afternoons of weekdays, and its walls usually contained her sadness and her voice like a cradle. But that grey afternoon her voice cracked against the bare surfaces of its walls after the last three lines of Mathilde's song:

Because of love
If one is not careful
Senses, body and soul will be . . .

The church could not contain her grief. The last two words reverberated unsung inside her.

. . . lost . . . forever.

※

As soon as Ghislaine asked her husband the question that evening, she knew she'd picked the wrong moment to ask for what she wanted more than anything.

He sat at the dining-room table with his back to her, reading a book titled *The Culture and Marketing of Tea*. She walked up behind him, put her arms around his shoulders and laid her cheek against the back of his head. He did not move.

'Do you love me?' she asked.

'I'm sick of this cheap Asian crockery,' he said, bringing his cup down hard on the table. 'And this sickly sweet treacle.' She waited, but he looked steadfastly at his book and did not speak. She saw the book was open at a page about withering. He kept studying it. She read it over his shoulder:

During the wither the permeability of the leaf increases. With a long wither of the freshly harvested leaf, the harmful effects on the briskness of the flavour can be reduced by a short fermentation, but the reverse does not hold, and the shortcomings of a rapid wither cannot be put right by extending the fermentation period.

She felt it all through her, unmarketable flavour gone to waste.

LONDON, DECEMBER 1985

How pliant and obliging my mother, Ghislaine de Sequeira, looks, how upright my father, Rupert Balneaves, appears in their one remaining wedding photograph. It is the only image I have of my father, besides my memory of his back. In the photograph, my mother inclines her head so far towards him that she looks in danger of losing her balance. My father's stance appears comparatively effortless, although he's looking sideways at her, maybe even a little proprietorially. A learned man, apparently, who might even have learned to love her for a while. All my life I've needed to believe that.

But in the photograph, he looks more than anything like a man who isn't really sure of what he's doing.

I put Clara in the pram and go walking and looking through the windows of other people's houses. I feel diminished and inadequate. My breasts have dropped since I weaned Clara. I can see the disbelief in David's face when he looks at my chest, his sleeves strewn with pale orange-blonde hair too long to be his. But my worst fear is this: what if my biggest lack is deep inside me? How brave my mother has been to keep loving the world. How unrewarded her struggle has been.

As I push Clara past the narrow-fronted houses on Chepstow Road, people nod at me as if I'm any mother following her daily routine, taking the baby out for a breath of fresh evening air, but I'm out to find the secret of how people love one another, of how one rises above past and present accidents.

The kitchen window of a house on the next corner is slightly open, letting out delicious smells of seasoned roasting meat and vegetables. It smells like a household that might know the trick of a whole heart, but I can only get a whiff of it. Clara leans out to sniff the air as I push the pram onwards in my search for stronger clues.

Through the window of a house a few doors up, I hear a man shouting:

–Have it your way then!

–Thanks, a woman replies.

I pause for a long time outside this one, wondering if this was an exchange loaded with bitterness or with the secret of loving. A door slams somewhere along the dim passage, but I am unsure whether or not it's just the way the wind is blowing.

❀

Christmas is only two days away, but the grey cloud whose edge I've felt encroaching since the pregnancy test has darkened with the image of Philip's back hurrying away from me after the last class. Again.

Clara's cries for attention seem muffled, as if they're coming to me through layers of cotton wool, and I can barely make myself get out of bed to attend to her. On Christmas Eve I call David and ask him to take her for a couple of days.

–There's something I should tell you, he says when he comes to pick Clara up. –I've met someone else. She'll be spending Christmas with me, too.

He brushes his fringe from his eyes with that careless gesture of his.

—That's okay, I say, my voice cracking only a little. I pull a long pale hair from his shirt and hand it to him. —I already guessed.

He grins sheepishly.

—I have some presents for Clara.

I hand him the gold plastic crown, the tea set and the rag doll. They're unwrapped, still rustling in the bags they came in.

—You all right? he asks. —You don't look so good.

I could tell him everything. I hand him more presents instead.

—There's one for you in there, too.

—I'm sorry, he says. —I haven't had time to get you one. I've been so busy with —

—Someone else. I smile at him to show I'm not bitter, and keep my arm outstretched as he gathers the bags in one hand. I turn and hug Clara.

—Bye bye, beautiful girl.

And David and I shake hands, quite formally, as if we barely know one another.

❋

I curl up and sleep through the remains of the day and the night, waking to the sounds of Christmas lunch being prepared in my neighbours' houses. I feel miles away from Christmas on Portobello Road, still on the edge of a dream of looking for home in some foreign country whose name I do not know.

As I have a cup of tea to help me make the transition from sleeping to waking, I notice the tin queen on the back corner of the kitchen counter. There's a small note in David's scratchy handwriting underneath the queen.

Thank you for this and _everything_.

Everything? Nothing. The queen has returned more dented than she was when David and I began loving one another. I push her to the back of the fridge behind the unpaid bills before walking through the melting grey snow to the hospital with my gifts of creams, lotions and a CD of hymns: my inadequate offerings for softening my mother's harsh, diminishing life.

–She's sleeping. She's been in a lot of pain again. We put a new morphine drip in, the nurse tells me, her green tinsel earrings winking.

My mother's smile as she sleeps is utterly fearless. I sit and watch her for almost an hour. Her hands move the way Clara's do when she sleeps, fingers moving as if to illustrate her thoughts.

The nurse re-enters to check her drip. I put the gifts down on the bedside table.

–Could you tell her . . . Isabelle came to say Happy Christmas?

–I'll give her the message. If she . . . when she wakes.

–What do you mean *if* she wakes?

But the nurse is already walking away down the cold corridor.

My mother is dying, and I'm not ready.

THE TRUE BODY

✤ Starved ✤

Standing in the doorway of the pantry that had become her room, Mak Non watched the tea-taster coming and going to and from the long afternoons he spent above the clouds.

'I am tasting tea. I am grading the leaves and pricing the crop. I am meeting with buyers.' All these excuses Ghislaine seemed to believe, but Mak Non knew better.

Mak Non knew that Ghislaine was almost mad with apprehension of something she could not see on the other side of the grey cloud. Mak Non knew the secrets laundresses come to know. Standing next to the stone tub she found long, shiny, apricot-coloured hairs on Rupert's shirts. She held the hair up to the light. It was the colour of sunset. It shimmered. She saw Ghislaine's ghost in it.

Mak Non murmured darkly to herself over the carbolic soap. 'Tasting flavours and grading crop all right, but I think not tea crop.'

Mak Non waited until the next morning to speak to Ghislaine.

'Anak. Excuse me. Excuse me for asking. I hear he shout at you late at night. His breath hot with whisky, no? He hit you?'

'Not physically, no.'

'More than one ways to hit a woman.'

'He tells me I look like a ghost. He tells me I disgust him with my big belly and homemade clothes.'

Mak Non looked at the dark circles under Ghislaine's eyes and could not bring herself to tell her about the orange hair on his shirts. 'Send him off. Get rid of him.'

'With this?' Ghislaine pointed to her belly and began a thin low howl broken by gasps for air.

'What do you know about my husband?'

Mak Non looked at her sorrowfully. 'Nothing worth telling until sure of it.'

❋

That morning when she brought Rupert his breakfast, Mak Non closed the dining room door behind her.

'A minute of your time, sir.' He noted Mak Non spoke not quite as a servant should. There was a ring of irony in the way she said *sir* that riled him. He looked up at her suspiciously.

'I won't run around the outside of this. Get straight to the point, you say yourself, sir. You won't thank me, I know. I know what you do above that cloud every afternoon. Doesn't matter what race, man look daft in face after pleasing self with other woman. Never mind, if that all. Difference between man and woman is woman put up with more. But that not all. You tell Ghislaine you don't love her. You tell her she look like a ghost. Nearly full bursting with your child and you tell her she look like a ghost. People with no club or money not really people for you. She your wife! Reckon it don't look so good against her, that colour of convent charity girl? You give her anything else to wear? Just more damnation and mean charity, like a church missionary. No wonder she ghost you.'

Rupert narrowed his eyes at her over his cup of tea. 'She's better off than ever she was. No more slaving in the tearooms. Where do you think the money for food and keeping you comes from?'

'Mr Balneaves, sir. She *soft* for you. Try some softness for her. For your good, for hers, for the baby in her belly.'

'How presumptuous of you. You have no idea what's going on.'

'I see the look on your face. See the long orange hair on your shirt,' Mak Non murmured.

'So much you do not see, Mak Non. You do not hear the rumours I've heard about Ghislaine. You do not see how Ghislaine has changed towards me since pregnancy. She's let herself go. Hair hanging down all over her face, lying in bed all day. Now get this straight.' He jabbed his finger in the air at her. 'I am only with Ghislaine at all because of the woman with the long orange hair.'

Rupert did not waste time after Mak Non left the room. He ate his spicy pork dumplings and his boiled egg, swallowed two cups of finest Assam-tips tea and went to Ashok's post office to send a telegram to an old school friend who worked as a journalist in Kuala Lumpur.

Then he caught a white taxi through the clouds to the woman with the pale orange hair.

※

Ghislaine wrote in the New World diary her father had given her: *Longing for what you had hoped for and thought you had, for a while. Sad love,* she wrote, *desperate love, non-existent love. Happy love?*

She retraced the question mark several times with her pen.

※

Rupert read the cutting from an old *Straits Times* his friend the journalist sent him a week after the confrontation with Mak Non. He read it in his office with the door locked:

Evidence was given by a witness in Malacca court last week that she had gone to the kampong of the Sloping Mangrove and visited the house of the woman bomoh Mak Non: 'Mak Non asked me about my affairs. I told her the reason I had come was to ask for a child. She told me how she was descended from the famous bomoh of Mount Ophir, on the outskirts of Malacca. She told me to pray at five prescribed times and to come again the following Thursday night to pick up a silver amulet, which she would fill with special prayers for me.'

Mak Non was found guilty in court of fraud and conduct in opposition to Christianity and the laws of the colonial government. She was fined $10 or a day's imprisonment, and cautioned that she could expect a much more severe penalty if she was found practising the black arts again.

The tea-taster folded the article carefully and put it in his wallet.

'As useful as money,' he murmured to himself.

※

Rupert read Mak Non the article with great relish. 'So. Do you think,' he spoke slowly, deliberately over-articulating each vowel, 'you'd better go back to where you came from?'

'This article nothing but bad excuse to sack me. You go long way on bad excuses, Mr Balneaves,' Mak Non replied.

The tea-taster stood at the window with his back to her. He was almost sure he could see the green gable of Divina Worth's house higher up the road. 'I'm glad you get my idea. If you speak to anyone else about my Englishwoman friend, I'll do more than sack you. I'll bring more charges against you in court. Now return to Malacca, and never come back.'

'So *sack* me.' She over-articulated the word as he had. '*Sack* me while your poor wife away visiting Ah Kwei in dying house.' She left the room murmuring 'Bless both their souls' so quietly that Rupert supposed she was insulting him in Malay.

✳

Shaken angrily from their cages and resting places by the new master of the house, one python, one racquet-tailed drongo, one mynah and three cats circled Journey's End for the last time, looking for the two servants who'd fed them ever since their owner was a small girl. As the afternoon drew into night, their circles elongated until they entered the thick shadows of the jungle in the valley where other hungrier animals lived.

LONDON, DECEMBER 1985

David is at the door, glowing and freshly scrubbed as a soap advertisement. It occurs to me he's much readier with his smile these days than he has been for years. Someone else is making him happy.

For a minute I plummet like a derailed train into the sense of failure I'd had when he first left me.

—What's the matter? He asks.

—I just . . . I'm sorry.

—For what?

—All the things that went wrong between us.

He flicks them away with his hand.

—It's just the way things were. Too much stress. We were both under too much stress. Clara being premature, your mother falling ill, me losing that job. A lot of couples just grow out of each other. That's life. You just have to embrace it and move on.

I wonder if he's had pop-psychology books or lovemaking for breakfast. I don't let my envy show on my face as I hand him the spoonful of Clara's baked beans.

As I catch the train to Philip's, I remember David's response to the onset of Clara's birth. We were queueing at the cash register with our trays of fast food in the cafeteria of Marks & Spencer when I felt a needle-like itch and trickle between my legs. I had a carton of milk in my hand and a plate of fish and salad on my tray. Still trying to eat for the baby. David was shaking salt onto his chips, unaware of the small pool of clear liquid forming on the white tiles between my swollen feet.

I'd read all the books and been to the pre-natal classes. It was a month too soon. I thought I knew all about bags of water breaking, but I had no idea it would feel like this.

—Have I lost bladder control? I whispered, frozen to the spot, gesturing towards the ground. David looked nonplussed at the puddle for only a few seconds before bending down, dipping his finger into it and smelling it.

—It's not urine. It smells salty, he whispered in my ear as he stood up.

I dropped my carton of milk on the floor as the first contraction began and the cash register rang.

—It's amniotic fluid. It smells like you do after we've made love, he said, smiling, crowning me with a kiss.

❋

Philip and I are in his bedroom above the tall giddy space again. My cup of tea is half empty.

—Look at you. You look like you belong here, he says.

For the third time. I'm counting.

Not *I love you*. Not yet. But his words and his hand on my cheek suggest he might. The scrabbling in the roof I'd heard the previous times I'd visited resumes intermittently, and the phone rings for the fourth time since I'd arrived, but these seem far away and of no consequence after he says this. He frames my face with his hands. I cannot see myself, but it is as if he has given me a photograph of myself at that instant; surely I have never been so close to being beautiful. Here we are, his lips soft against the lobe of my ear, his words ringing in the hollow between my cheek and ear. Here we are, that instant of resonance with one another captured and held. In that moment, my hopes seem entirely possible. But of course he doesn't know yet that I've come to tell him about the secret rolling like a die in my belly.

I tell him then, as his voice recedes in me. My news about our accident is apparently so terrible to him that he doesn't speak. Tiny beads of sweat break out along his forehead as he looks out the window at the snow falling sparsely from the dark sky. Our skins make a sound like the last page being torn from a book as he moves away from me.

−I don't know if I want another baby just yet, I say into the silence.

Is it relief I see on his face?

−Well then, if you *are* . . . do something about it.

I keep my tongue in my tea just then. And I don't look back to see where I've come from, for I can feel it just behind me, the long, empty fall back to nothing.

THE TRUE BODY

The dying house

What do you buy someone who is dying? Ghislaine paused outside the florist's stall, her pregnant belly rising under her dress like a red sail full of wind. Such weight, such lightness as she lingered amongst the strings of jasmine and frangipani on her way to visit Ah Kwei in the Chinese dying house. She steered herself past the workshops full of heavy wooden Chinese coffins buttressed at their base like tree roots, past the gaudy paper funeral decorations that bluffed and fluttered in the breeze.

The crickets ascended the notes of their noon song until the pre-monsoonal air was shrill with it. It was a sunny afternoon in Malacca, yet she felt a dull dragging ache from her abdomen down to her feet, as if her blood circulation had stalled. She was there, against the orders of the Malay midwife from the highlands, to visit Ah Kwei.

That morning as Ghislaine left the highlands, the midwife told her to put aside extra danger money for her. 'If you want me to

deliver after you take such risk lah! Visiting dying houses in the last
months of first pregnancy, ah-yah!'

So there was Ghislaine, enjoying disobeying orders one of the
few times since she'd married, not even thinking about where she
would find the extra danger money, following her belly and her
nose past the steam-filled laundry to the chartreuse-tiled kopi shop.
She finally bought two squares of bright green-and-white-striped
gelatinous cakes for Ah Kwei, but she swallowed one in two bites,
felt it fold and wobble like a jellyfish as it slid sweetly down her
throat. She carried the other in its waxed paper bag towards the
dying house.

On the corner was another Chinese funeral-decoration shop,
where the proprietor painted a stern red mouth on the face of a
papier-mâché true body.

'Going to a Cheena funeral, chiap cheng woman?' he called. She
didn't blink at the insult, but the baby turned inside her.

The man kept his eyes on the stern red mouth emerging from
his brush.

'Zensheng verree important for Cheena funerals. They give the
dead person's spirit somewhere to go.' He gestured towards the true
body. 'Best zensheng in Malacca.'

Ghislaine wondered if she could do with a true body for herself
as she caught sight of herself in the florist's window whilst turning
the corner into the street of dying houses. Her belly looked as if
it might burst any minute as the baby turned like a globe of
the world.

She felt detached from the heaviness of her limbs and belly, as if
she was floating, or out of her body. Such weight, such lightness as
she averted her eyes from the reflection of her belly and gathered
her red skirt into a curtain around it.

At the entrance of Happy Sleep, the proprietor was picking at his
teeth with a sharpened match. His gold fillings and the gold chains
resting on his impeccably white singlet glinted in the sun that fell
between the adjacent dying houses. Ghislaine remembered Ah

Kwei's life savings in the Jacob's Cracker tin, and wondered how much of this the man was already wearing in his teeth and on his chest. Behind him, empty coffins waited against the wall.

'Ah Kwei?'

'Down hall first turn left,' the proprietor muttered before resuming picking at his teeth.

Ghislaine walked past a low table bearing lanterns, stone name plaques and offerings of dumplings and oranges for the spirits of the recently dead, down the pale green painted corridor to Ah Kwei's room. She paused at the doorway to draw breath before entering the darkness of the long, narrow room lined on both sides with beds and the odour of urine and perspiration.

Near the entrance of the room, one old woman crouched on the side of her bed, her toes clenched around the mattress edge. She nodded almost imperceptibly to Ghislaine as she passed.

In every other bed was a body huddled under threadbare cloth, a wrinkled face shrunk by dehydration and age, grey hair thin as cobwebs. Most of the old women were still. Some of them rubbed old scars or dry skin, some slept, barely breathing. Others' eyes were feverish and huge with suffering. Someone in the room panted like some creature in terrible pain: *huuh huuh huuh*. As Ghislaine drew closer to the panting, she carefully searched each face for Ah Kwei's.

Huuh huuh huuh. Near the end of the row, the agonised breathing was loudest. The old woman's eyes were closed, but there were tears streaming from their corners and running into the grey wisps of hair at the sides of her face. When Ghislaine touched her on her hand, she opened her eyes. It was Ah Kwei, but her gaze showed no recognition and her tears did not stop.

'Ah Kwei, it's me, Ghislaine. You remember me.' Nothing. 'I have brought you kueh. The green coconut jelly one you like.' Not even a flicker of recognition in her tea-brown eyes. 'I have a baby in my belly.' The desperation of the motherless mother-to-be, bribing her nursemaid on her deathbed for blessings.

Ah Kwei closed her eyes. The tears kept leaking out between her eyelids.

All Ghislaine could do was put the kueh down on the floor, sit on the edge of the bed and gather her old amah in her bundle of rags against the bundle in her own belly. She couldn't feel or hear any sobbing, but the wet patch on her shoulder from Ah Kwei's tears spread from a bud into a continent whose borders kept expanding across her red bodice. As she held Ah Kwei, she watched the narrow windows cast small, gradually lengthening tunnels of sunlight on the walls.

The noise of the traffic was building gradually outside. It was almost evening when Ghislaine felt an emphatic kick in her belly that sent an acute, itching cramp into her vagina. She laid Ah Kwei back hastily on her bed and stood.

A warm gush of liquid flooded her thin cotton underpants and dripped into a small puddle around the wrapped kueh underneath her on the floor. She dipped her forefinger into the little pool and smelled salt, ants and almonds on it. She thought she would drown under the next wave of pain.

'Not yet. Too early; it's too early.' She felt as if she might implode into the pain, and yet she felt so far away from it. She did not have the words for this, could barely find the breath. Each contraction broke her breath in half, *hu-uh, hu-uh, hu-uh.* Behind her, Ah Kwei's breath sounded surer. Ghislaine's eyes were open wide, but her vision flickered as she gripped the wooden railing at the foot of the bed. In this thinning of air, in this dimming of sight, she felt herself enter the long, trembling opening of life, the long, trembling squeeze of death.

'Please,' she heard herself beg, but for Ah Kwei and herself there was only the fight to breathe, that sound like the wings of spirits flying towards their true bodies.

'Ah Kwei?' she whispered.

Huh huh huh.

A pain sharper and hotter than lightning and the baby slid from her, a flash of white and gold as the dying-house proprietor stepped into the room, picking his teeth, counting his money, a graceless angel ushering the doctor towards his daily rounds of the dying.

❋

Later, as she crouched before the doctor on the floor holding her baby, the sequestered mumbling and breathing of the dying came to Ghislaine again. She saw that Ah Kwei had turned to face the shadows on the wall, keeping her suffering to herself. The baby's face was fierce as a warrior's under the smearing of vernix. The skeins of the umbilical cord were blue and cream, almost alarmingly cool in colour against the pool of blood on the floor.

'Aiyee! What for you got make so much mess,' the proprietor admonished the new mother.

'Well, it's not a boy, but it's a beautiful baby. What nationality?' the Chinese doctor asked her.

'Eurasian.'

'Ah.' As if this explained everything: the ill-timed arrival, the enormousness of the baby, the thickness of the cord.

'Your husband?'

'English.'

The cord flexed like rubber under the doctor's scissors.

'Thick one,' he grunted.

'She came early,' said Ghislaine.

'Not too early,' said the doctor. 'Nice big baby. You need some rest now. We'll take you to the hospital. I am visiting from Singapore.' He gave her his card.

Dr S. Yip.
Kerbang Kerbau Hospital, Singapore

There was a translation for expatriates in smaller type: *The Pregnant Cow Maternity Hospital.*

'Your name?'

'Ghislaine Bal . . .' She swallowed the last syllable. 'My name is Ghislaine de Sequeira.'

While the doctor went downstairs to arrange a driver, Ghislaine watched Ah Kwei gasping for air as fine fissures formed in the drying vernix on her baby's skin.

'Live. Please live,' she murmured, her gaze on the pulses of the newborn and the dying.

LONDON, JANUARY 1986

I ring and leave a message on Philip's answering machine. With every passing day he does not reply.

The Kew lawns are white with frost, desolate as insomnia, their perimeters pegged by *Keep Off* signs.

*

—How astonishing. You've developed fine cracks in your teeth since I saw you only a few months ago. As if you've been in an accident. Had any falls lately?

Mr Gopalkrishnan's bald, domed head reflects the glare of his examination lamp as he bends over me.

—No. But my gums have been aching for a couple of months now. Especially when I first wake.

—Aha. Bruxism. Grinding your teeth in your sleep. Been under any stress recently? You're a single mother, yes?

—Yes.

I do not tell him that I've just realised the cracks in my smile show how intently I've been fleeing my mother's death, and how earnestly I've been pursuing Philip Border, even when I sleep.

–Hmm. We'll have to keep an eye on this. Might take some X-rays. Small cracks like these can widen and lead to decay.

※

–I always thought it was my fault that things didn't work between Dad and you.

–No. It wasn't your fault. When he found out Divina Worth was contemplating marriage after all, he figured he'd messed up his chances with her by marrying me. You might say that in his own way he was faithful, your poor father. Burning himself with a hidden torch for Divina all that time.

–How can you be so bloody forgiving, Mum?

–People have their reasons for doing what they do.

Snatches of the homeless woman's tender melody carry across the square during a lull in the traffic.

–Isabelle, could you bring me a few spare nightdresses from home? And my old Malaccan silk Shanghai gown.

She tilts her head towards the window.

–Listen, Isabelle. That sounds like the Christao song about the mother whose little girl is blind. The mother, who is dying, gives her eyes to her daughter.

The roar of traffic floods the homeless woman's voice again.

※

Sunil and I go for an early dinner at Mr and Mrs Arasu's restaurant that Friday evening after a discreet English doctor's given me two tablets to erase my secret. Friends of Sunil's mother, the Arasus give us combination platters of richly flavoured curries for the price of fish and chips. We sit down the back on the orange plastic chairs near the kitchen so Sunil can exchange gossip with Mr and Mrs

Arasu as they finish frying up curry puffs and pakoras for the evening rush.

–The second Seth girl's marrying a Punjabi boy. Not arranged, but werry nice chap. Accountant with an old London firm.

Beyond the bronze statues of Ganesha and Shiva in the kitchen, a small television broadcasts the cricket in India, and Mr Arasu clangs his tongs against the pan every time the Indian side scores a run.

The gravy on the lamb korma and the chicken vindaloo shimmers and spatters our Kew Gardens uniforms as Sunil and I slurp it down and mop it off the plate with paratha. Mr Arasu does the rest of the frying and shouts out the cricket scores while his sari-clad wife stands imperturbably over the large vats of curry, her face shiny from the steamy clouds of cardamon, turmeric and cumin.

Two men and two women enter when Sunil and I are midway through the meal. I recognise Philip's profile immediately. His head is raised and his nostrils flared, sniffing the air as he looks around. He appears not to have seen me. Are they university colleagues, those jacketed companions of his? He takes a look at the menu.

–That's him, that's Philip Border. The one wearing the leather jacket over T-shirt and jeans, I whisper to Sunil.

–Looks seriously hip. For a middle-aged academic, anyway. Aren't you going to say hello?

Philip leans solicitously towards his companions and murmurs. And then, just for a moment, his eyes skim over us, and he turns quickly and ushers his companions out the door.

※

Since erasing the tiny new life from my body, I feel even less at home in my mother's house.

Her bedroom smells of Joy perfume and Tiger Balm ointment when I enter. Opening her old Dutch armoire, I run my fingers over the faded love knots embroidered on her thin Malaccan cotton nightdresses. The silk of the Shanghai gown slips through my fingers like fine oil. It's taken on the subtle sepia tone that old Oriental silk does. I inhale deeply as I fold her clothes. They still smell of her skin, of roasted coffee and cardamon, but only very faintly. She is the only country I've known ever since I was born, but now even that scent I've breathed all my life is fading.

I don't know how to contain this loss. I flee from the vanishing smells and colours of my mother towards Philip's bright new world again.

※

Philip closes his front door quickly behind me. He looks as if he's aged years since I saw him last. There are creases under his eyes, as if he hasn't been sleeping well, and his shoulders are hunched.

–I saw you in Mr Arasu's last Friday, I say, unable to bring myself to ask if he'd seen me.

–Mr Arasu's?

–That Indian restaurant. You didn't stay.

–We checked a few out, as I remember.

He looks puzzled. Perhaps I'd been wrong in supposing he hadn't wanted to acknowledge me under the gaze of his peers.

–So did you get yourself fixed up, Isabelle? Or are you still . . . ?

Little beads of sweat have broken out across his forehead again.

–Two white tablets. I saw the doctor early enough, I say quickly, surprising myself with how clean I made it sound. Nothing like the bleeding caused by the pills.

–Good girl. It's no big deal these days.

As he strokes my hair, his smile looks like youth regained.

THE TRUE BODY

✦ *The architecture of the other* ✦

For years after Isabelle's birth, Ghislaine de Sequeira dreamed of Ah Kwei and Mak Non returning from the jungle with her pet cats, birds and python. The servants' and pets' movements were impeded by ornate but rusty cages that had punctured their skin when they'd tried to escape them.

'The Queen of England's cages,' Mak Non said balefully through her areca-nut red gums.

In these dreams, Ghislaine could never decide whether the cages had trapped the servants or protected them from the wild predators in the jungle. Their skins bled around the bars of the cage doors when she tried to prise them away. She woke, terrified that releasing them from the cages would kill them, certain that she was somehow more responsible for the servants' wounds than the Queen. She never recognised the dream as one about her fear of freedom and its costs.

✳

The man in the straw Panama hat was walking along the side of the road when he heard the woman singing in the church on the hill that overlooked the Blue Valley tea plantation. He had never heard that particular version of Ave Maria, brought to Malacca by Portuguese sailors in the sixteenth century and perpetuated by the Christao church congregations and Sister Victorina's resolute choral tuition of the erratic voices of Our Lady's students. He did not know it had been written by a twenty-two-year-old Portuguese composer shortly after he had been diagnosed with an unspecified but terminal wasting disease of the fifteenth century. He did not discern that its melody contained all the fervour and resignation of the true supplicant.

All he knew was that the woman sang it as if it had been written for her.

The man thought he had never heard a voice that combined such piquancy with such mysterious smokiness. He was seized by a desire to leave his mark on that voice. He peered through the half-open door but couldn't see anyone inside. The singing stopped and he heard the woman replying to the high expectant voice of a young child. He waited outside the church until he saw her go out through the side door, her head held high, the child on her hip, her dark hair unfurling in the breeze like a flag. He was shocked to be brought so unexpectedly to his most hidden reason for coming to the highlands. He followed her at a distance all the way to the tearooms, too scared to call her name.

Whenever Ghislaine tried to remember exactly how old she was that morning, she failed. It was after marriage, after giving birth, after years of dying had passed. Much later, she placed her age somewhere between the urgency usually associated with adolescence and the silent, resigned desperation that accompanies middle age. She was certain only that she had little in the way of knowledge. But if anyone had asked her how she felt that morning, she would have said she felt old. Rupert Balneaves had left for the tea plantations, passing judgment on the In-Between Tea she'd tried so hard to get right again that season.

It is thin. Too much hard withering. It is greenish and under-fermented. It's been corrupted by foreign material.

She no longer believed in Sister Victorina's God of stately cathedrals, or the gilded paintings of His son. For her, God was a reprieve from the chaos of the world, especially her marriage. This tiny, simplified church of frugal dimensions built in the sun by the hands of servants from local stone was more of a home to her than the house her husband was making grander.

After she returned from the little church that morning, her husband's words sat like sludge in her as she boiled the water and polished the teapots inside the dim tearooms. Across the road, the guesthouse stood, its completion stalled by the increasing likelihood of Britain granting Malaya Independence.

Ghislaine did not see the pale orange hair on the shoulder of her husband's shirts when he came home in the evenings, but every day she knew that in his eyes she'd been dead for a few years.

When she heard the knock on the door of the Miracle Tearooms, she was thinking about all the different kinds of dying. She was cold despite the warm cup of tea in her hands. She opened the door only as much as she needed to show her face. She saw that the man wore his Panama hat skewed like coincidence over one eye. There was a glint of gold on his left incisor. He had short arms. He had a camera slung over his shoulder.

She spilled tea down the front of her dress.

There he was, his hair on end when he lifted his hat, haloed by drizzle. There he was, smiling. Impossible.

Everything about her missed a beat: her heart, the view across the valley, the ground beneath her feet, her sense of who she was. She spilled more tea down the front of her dress. The voices of hope and fear roared in her head again. He took off his hat and tried to look around the door.

'The travel writer,' she said shyly, too shocked and proud to show she remembered his name, not opening the door any more widely. 'What are you doing here?'

'Work. I heard you singing in the church just a while ago. I didn't know you could sing. You have one of those voices that gets better and better with age.' His own voice was as she remembered, only wider, deeper, more far-reaching.

Walter Humphries saw with his hooded eyes that Ghislaine de Sequeira was already borne away by him. He was surprised by the upwelling of gratitude he felt for this, and for the fact that she hadn't learned to hate him during their years apart. He knew his body was beginning to erode in some places and thicken in others. It harboured tremors that surfaced inopportunely now in his hands and voice, and sentimental but troubling fondnesses for people he'd thought he'd long forgotten.

'And . . .' Now his jaw trembled as he stood before Ghislaine. He was suffering; he so needed to believe that he hadn't been as bad to women as his ex-lovers in Malacca claimed. 'I came to look for you, Ghislaine.' During his eight months of leave in England and Europe, his Malay lover had met his Indian lover in the small workshop where they sewed cut-price shirts and blouses for shipment to Marks & Spencer in London, and had discovered during lunch and tea breaks that they also shared the same cut-price lover. His English and Chinese women had taken up playing mahjong, drinking and smoking together. None of these women let him beyond their front doors any more. It was their clenched jaws he remembered most from these shunnings on cold thresholds, their smiles like bars that said: You shall not pass, Walter Humphries. Not now, not ever again.

Ghislaine knew none of this. All she wanted to know was what he'd just told her: he'd come to look for her. She found herself suddenly willing to believe there was a God after all, despite the tea soaking into the front of her dress. She put her hand out to him and he took it. She looked at the sparseness of the hairs on his olive-skinned forearm, his square nails with the pale crescents at their base.

'Where have you been?'

'Paris. London. Rome.'

She saw the tremor in his hands and the thickening around his waistline but she did not care, for her old dream of being rescued by him seemed almost to be coming true. He must have seen something of this delusion in her eyes, for his voice no longer shook when he spoke: 'Looking as lovely as the day I met you. The same beautiful hair.'

It was plain to her he expected to be asked in, but she did not want him to see the ruins of her marriage, or that she'd spilled tea down the front of her dress.

'Can you wait in the garden for a few moments?' She shut the door on her embarrassment firmly, before he had a chance to notice it, or to answer.

She took the door that led from the back of the tearoom to the house. She watched the travel writer from upstairs as she put on her blue dress with the frilly collar. He turned towards the valley. He had always liked taking in the view from somewhere high. He found a stone on the edge of the ragged lawn and threw it far into the air, watching it plummet towards the jungle canopy in the valley below. He raised his camera and looked at the valley through the viewfinder.

Ghislaine despised the frilled collar on her dress. She flexed her arms in the mirror, rehearsing flight, but it was sewn too tightly under the arms. She wondered if the moths had eaten the flesh-coloured Shanghai gown she'd left in her suitcase since leaving Malacca. She tugged at the collar as she headed to the tearooms.

The dark circles under her eyes and her pale green–gold skin against the blue dress were not lost on Walter Humphries as he stood in the doorway against the bright glare of the day.

'Bit of water under the bridge since last time I saw you.' He spoke as casually as if they were old neighbours, but he looked at her too long and hard. Behind him, Ghislaine could see the tea-pickers on the far hill moving between the rows of plants, their arms extended as they plucked at the tips and bent as they dropped them into the baskets slung over their shoulders to hang like early pregnancies at their bellies. Stretch and fold, stretch and fold, flexing their wings for flight.

'So, what is a beautiful woman like you doing here? Aren't you going to ask me in?'

'No.'

'Well then.' He only looked disconcerted for a few seconds. 'Can I take you away from all this for a while? Would you like to come into town with me for tiffin?'

Isabelle would be sleeping for at least another hour.

'Yes,' said Ghislaine. 'Oh yes.'

She felt light-headed as they walked away from Journey's End. By the time they got to the main street of Brinchang, she felt the giddiness like motion sickness she remembered after she'd first met him. The travel writer watched the way her gait made her narrow hips sway as she walked in front of him across the red tiled floor of the Indian kopi shop. He thought of the narrow arches and columns of Moorish buildings, and of dark wooden kampong houses rising high above flooding rivers on their stilts.

Inside the kopi shop, Ghislaine took a seat next to the ceramic tandoori oven, her back to the street. They ordered samosas, goat curry and saffron rice; a strong black coffee for him and teh tarik for her.

Her wrists were so fine as she raised her glass to her lips that Walter imagined them snapping in his hands.

'So. I am back.' He still had his self-congratulatory but amiable grin. 'And I must say you look slimmer than you did last time I saw you.' She saw for the first time how much whiter than his natural incisors his four false front teeth were. She did not tell him that marriage had diminished her in more ways than one.

'Tell me about your travels,' she said.

'Oh, you know. Everything from opera to haute couture.' He looked with bemusement at her dress. She pulled at her crooked collar and checked for traces of milk on her top lip.

'So why did you return to Malaya?' What was she hoping for?

'The paper offered me a promotion. I am in the highlands to write about the new guesthouse and the upgrading of the golf course.'

'What's the camera for?'

'My new Rolleiflex. To take photos to go with the article. To show how the natives live around here.' He kept his eye on the door as he shovelled his food into his mouth. 'And you? You are a married woman.' The last thing in her life she wanted to talk about. 'What do you do all day?'

She could have told him that every day she did everything she could to avoid despair over her marriage to the tea-taster. She could have told him that Isabelle had a smile that melted her heart and twisted it like wire with guilt, all at once. She could have told him about her husband and her customers, about hunger and feeding and cleaning up waste.

'I do my best to limit disasters,' she said instead. Walter laughed indulgently. 'And I am refining my own blend of tea.'

'Oh? Do you have a name for it?'

'It's called Double Jewel In-Between Tea.'

'In-Between's the English nickname for Eurasians.'

'Yes. And also because it's made from the tips of tea picked in between the first and second flushes.'

'I like it. Sounds like a contraceptive. Or the menopause.'

She felt the blood go to her face. She would not explain how she'd tried to memorialise him by including cinnamon in the tea. 'A flush is the appearance of the first new shoots. In-Between Tea's flavour lies between the astringency of the young first flush in April and the rounder flavour of the second flush.'

'You must give me a taste one day.' He raised an eyebrow. Ghislaine didn't know what a double entendre was, but she knew she didn't want to look Walter in the eye at that moment. 'I'm sorry.' He reached over and put his hand on her wrist. 'Have I offended you?'

'No. This blend doesn't have the flavour I am trying for yet.

I want something with a scented liquor, smoky notes, enduring body and good keeping qualities.' She was furious with herself for blushing.

'Well. Sounds a bit like the perfect lover,' he said as delicately as he could. 'Almost impossible, wouldn't you agree?' They looked at one another and laughed more openly, more equally than they ever had in Malacca. He was surprised at how knowing her laughter sounded. It seemed everything about her had deepened, her laughter and voice, the green tinge in her skin, her way of looking at him. He had to admit all this made him feel a little nervous.

'How *do* you find marriage?'

'It's . . . been nothing to write home about.'

'Ah,' he said. 'I see.' She thought, *He doesn't see, not really*, but his undivided gaze was like the sun shining on her after so many mornings of waking to find Rupert still so cold towards her.

※

It was only just dawn when she woke the next day. At first she didn't recognise the accelerated rhythm of her own heart. How can it be, she wondered, that when you've finally learned again how to put one foot in front of the other, you find that the steep mountain you've been climbing for years is just a thin shell? You see him again, your foot goes through and you fall, back to that foreign land again, where everything seems unprecedented and unpredictable.

The travel writer would not suffer like this, she supposed. He was accustomed to journeying through strange places, and he knew how to profit from them.

Rupert snored beside her, his mouth open in an expression somewhere between woe and disgruntlement, his fatigue showing under his eyes as faint bruises. His eyelids flickered as if he was dreaming of snow falling. She had been moved by this when they first married. She rose from the bed and crossed the floor before the heavily carved full-length mirror. The floorboard in front of the mirror always creaked. Her husband groaned and rolled over in bed, but did not wake.

In the bathroom, Ghislaine poured cold water from the Shanghai jar over herself. She took a long time in the bathroom that morning. It was the only room in the house besides the study that she could lock. She sat on the wooden stool in the coolness, smoking her mother's clay pipe, looking out of the high window at the pearlescent morning sky as she waited for the sound of her husband having his breakfast.

Only then did she dress herself and wake Isabelle for her customary breakfast of teh tarik and rice congee. Rupert wanted to take Isabelle that morning to visit a friend who lived higher up in the hills. She plaited Isabelle's hair and dressed her, and took her to the car where Rupert sat in his white clothes revving his black Austin impatiently.

As she stood near the front door, she could hear two crickets trilling out of time with one another somewhere up under the eaves.

❋

When Walter Humphries came to the door of Journey's End later that morning, Ghislaine took him by the outside path to the tearooms.

'So how's your personal life today?' he asked, closing the tearoom door behind them.

She shrugged abjectly.

'I find nothing is as difficult as bringing love to my life.'

He was both slightly frightened and greatly encouraged by this. He moved closer. Her skin still smelled of cardamon, but it merged with the metallic bite of tannin.

'That's a surprise,' he murmured nervously. 'I find that intriguing, that someone as young as you should know so much about love and its elusiveness.'

She stepped back to look at him. She waited for strong words from his heart. She waited for the coin that would make her sing.

But he looked at his watch intently, as if he was counting time, before smiling his most amiable smile at her and leaving as abruptly as he'd arrived.

※

During the next two days, Ghislaine brushed her hair copiously and used perfumed palm oil soap and a loofah on her body until her skin smarted. Every time she looked in the mirror, she tried to see how the travel writer saw her. She combed through the sparse words of his previous visit again and again. She was ready when he came to the door of the tearooms.

'Do you remember what you said about finding me intriguing?'

'Did I? What a thing to say.'

'You said you found me intriguing because I seemed to know so much about love and its elusiveness.'

She brought out every line she had remembered from their previous conversation and held them up like badges of honour for his scrutiny. It took her five minutes to realise he had forgotten most things he said to her only a few days previously. She felt her heart plummet. How would he ever come to love her without any memory of where they had been together?

She followed his gaze through the window. Across the valley, a steep jungle-clad hill bore a long wide gash on its near slope.

'There are landslides here. What you think is the immovable side of a mountain gives way, suddenly, without warning,' she said. A split in the travel writer had been revealed to her. She saw his ears were mostly attuned to something far beyond any words she spoke. 'You forget things I tell you from one minute to the next,' she continued matter-of-factly. Walter wondered fleetingly but with alarm whether he had inherited his father's Alzheimer's disease. He imagined his memory being eaten into lace, as the silverfish had eaten away his travel articles.

His hands had been surreptitiously on their way towards her breasts, but now they paused in mid-air, as if he were a dog that had learned the trick of begging. He felt his testicles shrink inside the cotton pouch of his Great Wall-brand underpants. His hands trembled again. He could not admit to himself that whereas he had always thought himself too young for finitude in his relationships with women, it now appeared certain he was getting too old. He took a step away from her, until his back was nearly up against the wall.

'You seem a little tense these days,' he muttered, taking a sidelong glance at the door. 'Well. I'd best be off and do my day's work.' He tapped his watch.

᛭

After he left Ghislaine that morning, Walter Humphries followed the road until it branched into three smaller roads. He took the one that wound between the hills, passing through pockets of jungle from which the dew and juices of the previous night were rising on the heat of the day, smelling sharp as limes in places, or thickly sweet like honey in others. He tried not to think of Ghislaine as he walked. He had his destination always in his sight as he followed the road around. The first time he had walked it, his arrival at the golf course on the hill seemed continually imminent because of this. He had been surprised when he looked at his watch to see an hour had already passed, and to find he was only halfway there. But this was his third visit to the highlands since he'd begun working in Malaya, and he was no longer fascinated by the illusion of imminent arrival at his destination, or by the way the highlands' circuitous roads swallowed time.

For Walter Humphries, this diminishing of fascination was now as true for the multitude of destinations he visited as it was with the women he had known in various countries. He was stricken as he walked that morning by sudden and intense ennui and awareness of his shortcomings with women. He couldn't go on like this any more. In those moments when he was halfway along the road between the golf course and the Miracle Tearooms, all the opportunities that he had missed for leading a settled life with someone became apparent to him, forcibly and without precedence. He was living in the wrong skin. A melancholy like ice settled in his bowels.

He returned in the thick yellow humidity of the afternoon to his room at the Olde English Inn. He concluded, more with the nerves of his itching skin than with his mind, that there was nothing for him to do about all this but to enter the green-tinged skin of Ghislaine de Sequeira with its unprecedented odour of tannin and cardamon.

*

Rupert Balneaves had grudgingly taken Isabelle for a drive by the time Ghislaine went downstairs to the tearooms the next morning. She washed the cups and saucers left from the few customers of the previous day. She set the tables with their lace cloths and single rose buds in cut-glass vases. She felt stricken by a sense that she had a choice to make, with no clear idea of the consequences.

This day is God's love, she told herself, looking out the window at the sun shining on places that she'd never been further up the road. 'In my heart is God's wisdom and it will guide me,' she murmured at the slow dull ache in her chest.

> *Anda com cinco sentido,*
> *Causa di eu sa amor . . .*

Ghislaine had only sung the first two lines of Mathilde's song when the bell on the back of the door jangled suddenly.

It was him, of course. The singularity of his gaze made her face burn again.

The travel writer found it remarkable that a woman with such an olive complexion could have such pink cheeks, but, after many years of having such observations misconstrued by women as a sign of undying love on his part, he kept them to himself unless he was drunk or desperate. This caution made him look cagey as he stood at the doorway to the tearooms. She interpreted it as shyness.

'Come in.' They smiled foolishly at one another.

'You sing remarkably well, for an untrained voice,' he said, standing immaculately sleek by the guava tree, so fair and considered, so finely discriminating. Ghislaine felt a rush through her body like a wave breaking. She opened the door wider.

'What language were you singing in?'

'Christao. My grandparents' language.'

'Sing it again?' He put the palm of one hand on her long thin throat and drew her hand to the same place. 'So you can feel the vibrations.' But his hand at her throat frightened her song away.

'What kind of song is it?' he asked solicitously, withdrawing his hand.

A song of longing and caution, she would have explained if she weren't so afraid to expose herself further.

'I don't know. I just sing it.'

'Sounds like a song I heard on the streets in Lisbon during my last European trip.' He looked nervously over his shoulder. 'Is there anywhere . . . around here we can go for some privacy?'

She shrugged. It was almost impossible for her to be mindful of the traps set by her desperation and grief over her desolate marriage.

'I have a room at the Olde English Inn,' he said. 'Shall we go?'

She only took seconds to close and lock the door behind her.

They didn't speak to one another as they walked. They passed Ashok's News of the World on the road out. Ghislaine averted her face from Ashok and the early-morning kopi-shop proprietor leaning on his broom. The front page of *The Straits Times* showed a photograph of an Englishman carrying a Malay woman in his arms away from a blaze lit by communist bandits. He carried her with the same expression on his face as the Christ statue's at Journey's End.

Walter Humphries' room was around the back of the mock-Tudor inn. He opened the door on to a room furnished with chintz armchairs and a brass bed, closed it and locked it again as soon as she was inside. The morning light edged underneath the lace curtains and fell on the plump bed. Ghislaine thought how much Aunty Zeraphina would love this room so full of lace antimacassars and doilies. The travel writer took off his hat and hung it on the hook on the back of the door. Ghislaine stood by the window. He pulled the curtains across and drew closer to her.

'Look at you,' he said. 'Why are you blushing?'

'My husband grades tea with his eyes closed. Tea and women.'

'Well, how foolish, to diminish one's pleasure like that. Colour is too important to my appreciation of flavour.'

'What's your favourite tea?'

Walter smiled condescendingly. 'All have their merits.'

Was he perhaps a more discerning connoisseur than the tea-taster?

'No,' she said as he leaned towards her, but his lips silenced her. All she could hear were the sounds of this new Emergency in her head, the air full of the range of human voice: of weeping, triumph, hope and fear.

'Please. I don't even know if you love me.'

He laughed, and ruffled her hair. 'You disappoint me, Ghislaine. Love? Who can say they know what love is? Seriously . . .'

'Talk to me,' she said. 'Please.'

'That's what women always say.' A mistake, he thought to himself. Women don't like to think they are one of many. But Ghislaine was more concerned about failing the unspoken tests he was setting her. He put one hand on her face.

'Don't be sad,' he said. 'Here's an idea. I'm going for another trip to England soon. You could come with me.'

She took this as a promise. He used this as much as he used his hands to skim her body like the pages of a book. He flooded her with words as he undressed them both. Another Englishman displaying his hard facts, she thought, but the travel writer's body revealed a soft secret.

'Help me, Ghislaine.' He didn't meet her eyes as he spoke, took her hand and drew it downwards.

She understood, for the first time, that the travel writer wasn't at home in his skin. She pulled a sheet over her to cover the silvery stretchmarks on her breasts. She withdrew her hand and put her ear to his chest.

'Tell me about your life,' she said.

Walter Humphries told her. He told her about his angry mother, who collected small porcelain dolls and dressed them better than she dressed him.

'She only had me in a desperate attempt to keep my father from *travelling so often*, as she put it.'

'What did she mean by travelling?'

'A good question. I only worked it out when I . . .' He was naked, yet he looked at her as if he was wondering how much of himself to reveal. 'When I was twelve or thirteen years old, I went through my father's pockets looking for money and sweets and found perfumed letters and telegrams from various towns. He sold fencing materials all around the south of England, but travelling really meant visiting his mistresses.' Walter pulled the sheet over his hips.

'Was he handsome?'

'Of course.' There wasn't a hint of irony in his voice. 'And charming.'

'And your mother?'

'She was sort of exotic looking. But she went to seed early.'

'Went to seed?' It sounded as full of ripeness and possibilities as a garden to Ghislaine.

'She ate fish and chips and cakes from the bakery all day. She was fat. She let sort of a . . . *moustache* grow. She read romance novels all the time. I think food and fiction were necessary to sustain her delusion that my father wasn't doing what she suspected he was doing.'

The rectangle of sunlight edging under the curtain shortened and receded from the bed as Walter Humphries continued telling the story of his life. He told her that mealtimes and bedtimes had been fatherless occasions of melancholy, of scraps of food fried in despair and lard, so that his alimentary canal moaned with unfulfilment and his tender skin erupted with separation anxiety and eczema. He told her how he had no-one to play with except snails in the dreary winters of Orpington; that Orpington was famous for nothing, except a speckled breed of chicken that took its name from the town; that his parents never painted their red-brick, two-up two-down house, as both believed they were going somewhere better, sooner or later. He told Ghislaine that he'd drawn pictures of passenger ships and foreign countries on the walls and dreamed of travel when he wasn't collecting snails, and that as he walked along the fence lines of the grey stone rowhouses plucking snails from the tiny square gardens, he'd heard a neighbour remark that the boy Walter Humphries had a smile that might have been the devil's, might have been an angel's.

'What did you do with the snails?'

'Dropped them into my mother's glass jug. Then I held the jug still in a dish of hot water to coax them out of their shells.' He continued with a kind of relish: 'I lifted the jug so I could watch their undersides gripping and blowing bubbles on the glass. The trails of mucus,' he winked at her as he spoke, 'fascinated me. I used to rub the mucus up and down their bodies quickly before they withdrew into their shells. Sometimes I pinned their eye-stalks and tails to a piece of cardboard so I could watch the mucus coming out in bubbles. Then I'd fill the jug with water and watch them writhe until they drowned.'

'Didn't anyone try and stop you?'

'My mother was too wrapped up in herself to care. There was a sweet shop on the corner near our house. I used to eat more sweets than meals. She used to tell me my toothaches were growing pains.'

'What happened to your teeth?'

'My mother didn't make a dental appointment for me until I was fifteen. The dentist extracted my teeth rather than filling them.'

He tapped his incisors. 'I have a Royal Doulton smile.'

His face had become shiny with enthusiasm. But he looked uneasy when Ghislaine asked: 'So who do you think has travelled best lah? Someone who has seen the whole world through the same tired eyes, or someone who has learned to look at the same place through different eyes?'

He wondered if she was referring obliquely to his women in Malacca.

'What do you mean? You mean you think you know more than me? You've gone no further than these tropical backwaters and you think you know more than me?' He glanced at her, rubbed his chin irritably and looked away again through the crack in the curtains.

But Ghislaine knew nothing of these women. *He was like the horizon*, she thought to herself. *Just when you think you are getting close, it becomes more distant.*

'And what gave you your wonderful mind lah?' she asked. He had many ideas about this. She kept listening to him as one who has been waiting all her life for love does, and, when he had finished, her eyes were full of him. He saw this instantly and moved onto her again.

'Please. Not yet.' But he put his hand on her mouth.

This day is God's love, she told herself, but the day did not protect her. *In my heart is God's wisdom and it guides me*, but she could only hear the travel writer's breathing.

❋

In his chintz-upholstered room in the highlands that night, the travel writer dreamed he had come home. There was such a familiarity about the house in which he found himself in this dream, yet it was nothing like the houses he had lived in in England or the Far East. It was a house built of thin branches to the scale of the Malaccan shophouses, but even the floor was made of thin branches. Through the gaps between the branches, he could see wild animals waiting hungrily underneath for something to fall through the floor.

A young woman with greenish-gold skin lived in the house. She was crouched unclothed, covering her face with her hands when he entered. The branches broke under his feet as he walked towards the woman, so that he could not go back. As he walked towards her, a baby bearing the face of a carved wooden idol emerged from her birth canal.

The fine, breakable branches of the floor, the cantilevering of the entrance leading to other unseen rooms. As he dreamt, the travel writer knew this was the architecture of Ghislaine de Sequeira's body. *Home or trap?* he shouted, waking himself before the birth was complete. He decided immediately that it was time to move on.

❋

Every day, Ghislaine stood behind the steam of the Fortune tea urn in the tearooms, waiting to be found again by the travel writer, his secret discovery. She dressed as if he might enter at any moment: in the flesh-coloured Shanghai gown she had kept in her suitcase ever since leaving Malacca, or in her old can-can petticoats under her blue dress. She wore her hair long and loose. As if he might come round the corner at last, carrying that bunch of long-stemmed flowers he hadn't given her yet; after so many years, walking towards her with that heart-fluttering solemnity he never showed her; finally, approaching her with his gaze upon her as only a man who knows his own mind can.

But, by the end of the week, the only trace she'd seen of him was in the newspapers in Ashok's News of the World. She bought one and read it on the cold tiles of the bathroom floor behind the locked door as she smoked Mathilde's old clay pipe.

The Cameron Highlands
by Walter Humphries

Ever since the formation of the Straits Settlements, English expatriates have journeyed to the Cameron Highlands to rejuvenate themselves when business allows a break of a few days. From the dusty foothills town of Tapah, the road circuitously ascends the hills for about fifty miles to Brinchang, the highest town. As the road clings precariously to the side of hills above jungle and vertiginous ravines, one feels a coolness in the air more akin to the beginning of an English spring than the sweltering tropics. This is a blessing for expatriates dreaming of England, for it allows them to sit before cheery fires and to sleep under quilts again. Quite unparalleled anywhere else in Malaya, this climate restores in one a sense of energy and virility. After a few hours, one feels ready to take on the world again.

Between Tanah Rata and Brinchang, the holiday houses, tennis courts and golf courses of English expatriates can be seen, and behind them, densely packed on the plummeting valleys and soaring hills, is the Malayan jungle. This is the virgin Malaya that has cost the British such an enormous expenditure of skill to tame over the past century. In the highlands, this skill has produced tea plantations rather than the rubber plantations and mines of the lowlands.

Along the road from Brinchang, which is more than 6000 feet high, I came upon terraced market gardens. Here, vegetables are produced in chequered plots that are agreeable in their resemblance to the East Sussex countryside, apart from the steepness of the terraces and the aberration of their Indian and Chinese cultivators in their coolies' hats.

In the next valley, I came upon an orang asli kampong. The orang asli are the truly aboriginal Malays, rather stunted in stature and Negroid in facial feature, followers of an animistic rather than Muslim faith. When I paused to photograph a bare-breasted orang asli woman carrying her baby in a sling, she demanded cash, apparently unashamed that she had been so corrupted.

Arriving back at Tanah Rata, I was relieved to retire to my hotel,

furnished tastefully in old-English style by its expatriate proprietor.
There, one can take tea and scones, drink a few glasses of Tiger beer over
the magazines and Somerset Maugham novels provided, and generally
enjoy the comfort of having a home away from home.

Below the article was the photograph of the orang asli woman in
front of her kampong. The woman was bent like a sapling in the
wind. She had pulled the sarong sling up to cover her baby's face
and her breasts, and her eyes were averted from the camera, as if she
was cowering from it. This did not look to Ghislaine like a photograph of how the natives lived. It looked like a photograph of how
a woman might die, frozen in time by the metal and glass eye of
men like the travel writer.

Ghislaine folded the newspaper in half and knocked the ash from
the pipe onto it. She supposed the article proved the travel writer
had returned to his office in Malacca. She tiptoed into the bedroom
to look at Rupert sleeping. The lines on his face looked even more
adamant than they did when he was awake. She knew she could no
longer put her arms around this man.

She heard Isabelle's footsteps on the landing. Ghislaine pulled on
her work clothes and took her down to the tearooms to breakfast
on the kueh of the previous day.

Isabelle pointed to the crowns on the canisters of the English tea.
'I like a crown like that.'

Ghislaine took some metal strapping from around the tea chests
under the counter. She bent it into a circle, fastened the gold lids of
empty canisters onto it with paperclips and placed it slowly, cere-
moniously, tenderly, on Isabelle's head as she sat before her plate of
coloured kueh, because she felt her daughter's desire to know sovereignty as deeply as if it were in her own bones.

LONDON, JANUARY 1986

I take Clara with me to the hospital, not sure if my mother will have the energy or the vision to see her. Clara carries her pink handbag containing her plastic fairy wand and my old tin king and queen like a talisman in front of her as we walk down the pea-green linoleum of the corridor.

My mother hears her footsteps.

–Hello, Clara!

Clara approaches her wordlessly, handing her the king, and buries her face in her lap. My mother runs her fingers quickly over the king.

–Ooh, you've brought the tin dolls.

–Doctor can listen to they hearts? Clara asks, her voice ringing out like a bell through the ward.

–Shall we ask him to if he comes? I've got a treat for you, Clara. My mother opens her bedside drawer and pulls out a plastic container full of melting moments. Clara takes them with a stealthy smile, sits on the vinyl chair, and begins working her way steadily through them.

My mother turns to me.

–There's something I want to tell you about Walter Humphries.

But it might be best to wait until you're on your own.

—Yeah, I wanted to ask you a few things about him and Dad, Mum.

Her hands tremble as she smooths the sheet between her fingers.

The doctor enters. Clara's smile is dark with the crumbs of melting moments as she holds the tin king up to the doctor's stethoscope.

❊

Sunil has a tray of fern seedlings in each hand when I enter Zone 6, the tropical section of the Princess of Wales Conservatory, to put my plan to him at the end of my shift.

—Some of these seedlings look quite phallic, yeah? Shall we take them and set them amongst the English roses? The only chance a queen like me gets to dabble in a bit of miscegenation. Heard from your tutor?

—Saw him yesterday. Finally.

—So he keeps you waiting, mmm? The English invented the controlled-crying approach to getting children to behave at bedtime, you know. Children and lovers. Ask me.

—Oh dear. How *is* it going with Daniel?

—All over, red rover. A flash in the bedpan.

—Oh, Sunil. You okay?

—Well, you know. Don't really want to talk about it. But hope springs eternal.

—Yeah, I know. Be gentle on yourself, Sunil.

—*You're* telling *me* to go gentle on myself?

—Well. I've been thinking, Sunil. It's Philip's birthday soon. He wants a tropical garden in his new conservatory.

—As an Englishman anxious about his sexual performance does.

One of the automatic mist sprinklers sprays suddenly into our faces.

—So you want to plant him this tropical garden for his birthday. Is he worth it?

—Yes. But I have no money.

—So I will turn a blind eye to the seedlings and cuttings you smuggle out of here. Stylish raincoat you're wearing. Nice big pockets. Open up now. Quick. While the mist sprinklers are hiding us.

He drops four bird's-nest ferns and three tilandera swiftly into the interior pockets.

—Zip up now. Wouldn't want them to get cold.

—Who owned the plants that these seedlings come from, anyway, Sunil? I'll bet the Royal Kew curator didn't pay the Malayans any money when he collected the original specimens.

—You have a point. But you make a better criminal than a lawyer.

We stuff more seedlings into my backpack and zip it up quickly as footsteps approach.

—Now. Don't give them all away to Philip. Smuggled tropical plants are part of your heritage, after all.

—So I'll keep some for propagation.

—Exactly. For your brilliant future.

I take the plants home and put some of them on the kitchen windowsill that afternoon. It's the sunniest, warmest place I can think of. I dig up and pot some palm seedlings from my mother's enclosed garden.

When I'm finished, the garden looks as bleak as the house, full of darkness and absence. I plant some of the seedlings from Kew in it, but the gaps are still apparent.

I'm suddenly stricken.

What if my plan doesn't work?

THE TRUE BODY

The censor's white flare

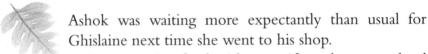Ashok was waiting more expectantly than usual for Ghislaine next time she went to his shop.

'I was serving food with my wife at the tea gardens' fancy dress ball. Your husband was there, dressed as a surgeon chappy. His partner was an Englishwoman dressed as a queen. Looked like a real crown on her head but werry werry shamefully unroyal low neckline. He poured her champagne all night.'

Ghislaine stammered her thanks, though she didn't feel grateful. She would not buy any more news of the world. On the plantation in the valley, the second flush was being picked before its most tender shoots turned bitter and unsaleable from being kept waiting more than a day too long. *Ashok is just an old gossip,* she told herself, but, as she walked above the valley, she knew all that remained for her to do with her marriage was to leave it.

She slept on the study floor and dreamed for a week of rescue by the travel writer, and of Mak Non and Ah Kwei trapped in the

Queen of England's cages. On the eighth morning, she packed up her most precious belongings in a cardboard suitcase. The eyeless kinnari with her broken wing and dented breast, the flesh-coloured Shanghai gown, Mathilde's clay pipe, the travel writer's articles stuffed into the New World *Diary of Emergency Procedures* next to Mathilde's recipes, the desiccated remains of Isabelle's umbilical stump in a Horlicks jar wrapped in the unfinished marriage bedspread Aunt Zeraphina made; all these were stored in the suitcase behind the study bookshelves.

Ghislaine woke early the next morning, dressed Isabelle and stoppered her bell-bright chat with a banana in the kitchen. She tiptoed in to take a last look at Rupert as he slept with his mouth open on the air. He looked hungry. She remembered Aunt Zeraphina tapping her heart in the tearooms. What had she said about the expatriates that afternoon? *They look for their fortune so far from their homes because they are empty in here.*

She almost put her fingertips on his temple one last time to feel his pulse, but she could no longer delude herself that she could touch his sadness. She pulled the doors closed behind her as quietly as she could and walked through the mist to the bus station with Isabelle to take the long, greasy bus back home to Malacca.

As the bus picked up speed on the straighter, flatter roads at the base of the highlands, she turned to try to catch a glimpse of everything she was leaving, but all was swathed in grey cloud.

※

Ghislaine de Sequeira arrived at her father's house late in the afternoon, but it was locked. She left her bags in the little lean-to out the back. Isabelle cried and clung to her so that she had to carry her as she walked around the base of the hill to Mak Non's kampong, beyond the Muslim cemetery with its knee-high grave-markers shaped like abbreviated spires.

Mak Non squinted through the glare, not recognising her at first.

Her smile broke across the wrinkles of her face in slow ripples. 'Ghislaine! Come.' She drew her into the yellow light of her house. 'Aiya! What happen to you? So thin lah! You were so plumpy before. Like Isabelle here. Ooh, Isabelle cantik.' She hoisted the child on to her own hip and hurried over to the stove to spoon out coconut rice and chilli-coloured chicken. 'Nasi lemak. Eat first, talk later.'

Mak Non fed Isabelle coconut rice and banana and put her to bed, while Ghislaine ate as she had not done since she had been a schoolgirl: smearing sauce on her face, sucking on the bones. Mak Non stayed silent until Ghislaine had finished eating. She made a cup of tea, sweetening it with condensed milk into a drink the tea-taster would not have acknowledged as tea.

'Have this while I bathe.'

When she drank that cup of tea, Ghislaine knew she was home. She could hear Mak Non sloshing water from the earthenware Shanghai jar with a metal dipper in the bath-house underneath the floorboards. She watched the cicak lizards scampering across the ceiling, their flesh-coloured feet shaped like stars, their chirping guttural and insistent.

Mak Non re-entered the room in a fresh sarong and baju, her hair dripping from her bath. She placed a small neat package wrapped in newspaper on the table.

'Now, what that John Felt Hat husband do to you? John Felt Hats say Malays run amok, but I say John Felt Hats run amok different ways.'

'What do you mean?'

'They more sneaky about it. None of this rushing around shouting to the whole kampong. Too worried what other John Felt Hats think about them for that. They run amok behind closed doors.'

'What do you know about Rupert?' Ghislaine hid her chin with her hand when she saw Mak Non looking at the fine scabs left there by the travel writer's stubble rash. 'You can tell me this time. I am not going back to him.'

Mak Non closed her eyes and saw all the secrets on the tea-taster's clothes, the orange hair and the lipstick and the honey soaking in the laundry trough at Journey's End.

'Excuse me, anak,' she murmured, opening her eyes, 'excuse me. Bad charms cast on you. Not talking Malay or Siam bomoh charms, I think. I think we talking Englishwoman's charms.' Mak Non closed her eyes again. 'Your husband. His woman above the clouds. His type. Fair hair, big money, big ideas about self. I smell the money and count the hairs. Smell the English club belonging.' She paused. 'Different John Felt Hats in Malaya. Some of them good men like Doctor Arbuckle. Some of them mix up with Malay, Chinese, Eurasian women. Open the women up and take what they can from them. Taste a happiness never tasted before, but only short time. Malacca Club and civil service, golf club and Anglican church, Dunlop Rubber and tennis club all shut out Englishman going native. Englishman in Malaya with no club to belong! Picture that, anak! They look for Englishwoman. Like your husband. Give them entry ticket back to club.'

Ghislaine felt her scalp and face tense and grow hot. Her eyes flooded with tears. It was as if a serious disease that she had registered the symptoms of only in her dreams had finally been confirmed. It was as if she had to leave the tea-taster all over again.

Mak Non saw the grey cloud spread across Ghislaine's face.

'I not saying he sleep with anyone else after he marry you. But he love the Englishwoman true.' Ghislaine slumped in her chair. Mak Non stood quickly and tugged her ears twice, hard.

'Don't be afeared, anak. Your spirit leave you long time search for true man. You cry like a baby being born, that's all right. Just your spirit coming back.' She pulled open the newspaper wrapping. Inside was a green lime chopped into quarters, and the petals of red roses, creamy frangipani and jasmine.

'Bathe. Put these in water and pour over your head. Scoop pieces up. Sunset tomorrow throw into river mouth. Tide carry old life away. Now relax. I look after Isabelle.'

❋

When Ghislaine came back from her bath, she felt as if her years in the highlands were a foreign country.

'Now you're true back I tell you this. You come right time, anak,' Mak Non said softly. 'I telegramming you tomorrow. Your father ill in hospital this morning.'

'What's wrong?'

'Stroke. But visiting hours finish now. You visit him tomorrow. Leave Isabelle here.'

'Can?'

'Can.'

'Will he . . . die?'

'I visit him this morning. Talking sense and seeing straight as usual. Strong as an ox your father.'

Ghislaine feigned casualness. 'Would you mind if I go and visit Walter Humphries now?'

'Go. Be careful.'

❋

Although the sea breeze was in and twilight falling, the Malaccan air was still warm and full of the aroma of incense and cooking. Ghislaine felt only a subdued elation when she smelled it, for her father's hospitalisation showed her that the life she thought she was returning to had changed. She knocked on the door of 35 St John's Hill, one of the wide, squat, stuccoed bungalows built by the British during the tin boom between the wars. When Walter Humphries answered the door, he struck her as being of similar architecture: squat, with a slightly lumpy skin. He stood at the door with a stengah in his hand and a packet of Jacob's Crackers digesting in his stomach beneath his sarong.

'Well hello,' he said, rubbing at a raw patch of skin on his neck. He noticed Ghislaine's bemused glance at the sarong. *Stomach of a*

Buddha, she thought to herself, recalling the plump rosewood statue in the town's Buddhist temple.

'I go native when I'm at home,' Walter Humphries said defensively, tugging the sarong more tightly around his thick waist. 'It's so much more comfortable. Come in, come in!' He made a sweeping gesture with his hand, as if he was offering this plush interior to her, as if he was offering himself.

Ghislaine, who had herself lived too long in a house echoing with lack, detected the anxiety of the homeless in Walter Humphries. As she paused on the threshold of his dark hallway, she was struck suddenly by the sense of familiarity that his aloneness engendered in her.

'I do love you,' she told him.

He looked startled, but saw his opportunity.

'*Love*, well. Love? What is that?' He kicked the front door shut. He embraced her and placed his hand on her breast.

'No, wait. Don't you want to hear the news first?' She removed his hand from her breast. She had been composing a headline for his ears alone, ever since he left the highlands. 'I've left my husband forever. I have come to travel with you.'

His complexion paled. 'Where?' It was as if the travel writer was a different man all over again.

'England. Don't you remember you said . . .'

He placed his hand back on her breast and spoke quickly. 'No harm if you do, I guess.' Why not? After all, which other woman in Malacca would have him now? And who else would have her, for that matter? A sleeping dictionary and a single mother to boot. Walter Humphries pressed his lips together. Had he settled for the lowest of the low? Well, yes and no. There was something else about her he'd never seen in his other four Malaccan women, besides the strangeness of her skin and her body, still fine and supple despite motherhood. Unlike his more worldly-wise lovers, this one seemed so obliging.

'I could be gone for a while, though. I want to travel through southern Europe again. Do some articles while I'm at it.'

Ghislaine felt the exaltation of arrival already.

'Come here,' he enjoined her, pulling her to his bed. 'Help me.'

Again? The flapping blinds against the streetlight cut the descent of his body and face towards her into a fast succession of light and dark.

She rubbed his stomach with the palm of one hand and crossed her chest with the thumb of the other, in the surreptitious de Sequeira way. Perhaps the light was dim enough so he wouldn't see her stretchmarks. But when they were undressed he pressed his lips together and looked out through the gap under the blinds.

'It's no good,' the travel writer said as he dropped onto the bed and rolled over, his arm bent under his head, staring at the ceiling.

'Bodies can be such a problem, can't they?' She meant to encourage him with this. She meant to share something with him. She lay down next to him and looked him directly in the eye, but he looked past her.

'I don't have any problem with mine,' he muttered tightly. She hastily pulled the sheet over herself.

He patted his stomach and turned his mind to thinking about the world. He remembered favourite moments in his travels: the turquoise Gulf of Naples with Vesuvius off to one side of the fumey city as he ate a sugary Saint Agatha's breast cake on the ferry back from Sicily; Notre Dame cathedral beyond the silvery Seine on a summer evening as he licked cream from an eclair; the little gated medieval towns in south-west France with their restaurants serving four courses of duck. All these moments were framed by the windows of hotels, boats, aeroplanes, trains or cars; negotiated and enjoyed through the exchange of foreign currency; experienced as the abbreviated kinds of judgments he made in his travel articles. When he was younger, this approach had sufficed for women, too. He had pretended he was interested in the places he wrote about, the women he slept with, but all he'd felt was a habitual but indifferent compulsion to cover as many sites as quickly and effortlessly as possible. Travel writing was a matter of making the world's underlying sameness look varied to his readers. A random and inconsequential string of destinies; how like women travel had seemed! Neither moved him very often; whatever lay between each reception terminal and departure lounge impressed him a little less each time. But women were not as willing or easy to read these days, and Lily Cheong, Pushpa Arasu, Lucille Towner-Jones and Faridah had revealed something about him he so disliked that he could neither name it nor look at it, except for his uneasy feeling that for his entire adult life he'd maintained the lack of engagement with places and people that he'd observed in travellers habituated to travelling first class.

Confronted by the travel writer's averted face and speechlessness as the streetlight through the blinds cast stripes on their skin, Ghislaine de Sequeira turned to thinking about the world, too. The world came to her as intimations of otherness, in the din of the day and in the breathing of the Malaccan night; in her dreams of her dead mother and the speechless raptures of Isabelle; through the predictions of bomohs and the singing of centuries-old hymns. Her world was full of such revelations.

'The Warner Bros film of Somerset Maugham's *The Letter* is on at the Cathay. It's based on the true story of a Eurasian adulteress by the name of Leslie Crosbie a few years ago. You should go and see it. You'll see yourself in it.' Walter Humphries said this with a knowing pursing of his lips, as if he meant more than he was saying. 'How *are* things with your husband, anyway?'

'Over. They were over a long time ago, before I knew it. Finished even while he courted me, now I look back on it.' Walter didn't look at her. Didn't he believe her? Surely he didn't think she was just having – what did the expatriate women call it? – *an extra-marital affair* with him. She was so embarrassed by this question that she couldn't ask it. She rose, covered her breasts with her clothes and went to the earthenware Shanghai jar in the corner of the bathroom. She dipped the old saucepan into it and poured the cold water over her shame. There were no towels. She dressed and re-entered the bedroom.

'When are you going to England?' she asked. She felt the fan-stirred air on her damp back.

'I'm leaving in a fortnight. Do you have a passport?'

'No.'

'Of course not. A Malacca girl all the way.' She wasn't sure if his smile tilted towards condescension or affection.

Naïve is the obvious word to describe her, he thought to himself. She actually seemed to trust that he would do the right thing by her. Unlike those other women.

'I'll help you organise a passport tomorrow.'

'What about Isabelle?'

'Isabelle?' His brow creased. 'Oh yes, the child. Do you think . . .' An expression of vagueness washed over his eyes. He'd rather not think too hard about the child. Underneath Ghislaine's loose dress, a drop of water ran from between her shoulder blades to her waist and paused there.

'I won't bring her. No. Of course not.' That would have been too much to hope for. A chill followed the water droplet down her spine to its base, but she was careful to smile as she left through the front door and entered the night.

❋

On her way to the hospital the next morning, Ghislaine bought a bunch of small red roses from an Indian flower vendor yawning at his stall overhung with garlands of frangipani, roses and jasmine for the devotees of the nearby Hindu temple. Against the base of the statue of Sir Stamford Raffles in the sandy garden of the hospital, a beggar crouched with her hand outstretched. Ghislaine gave her the change from the flowers and entered the chartreuse-painted dinginess of the wards.

She paused in the corridor. One of the roses dropped a petal.

'Aloysius de Sequeira?'

The short Chinese nurse stopped to answer her. 'You are Mr de Sequeira's daughter? Your father's mind is wandering a bit today.'

She nodded, and scratched the sign of the cross against her chest with her thumb apprehensively. The nurse led her past an old Malay man whose family sat mournfully next to his bed eating nasi lemak from the unstacked trays of a tin tiffin carrier. There was something festive about the way the food was arrayed across the foot of the bed, but the old man seemed unconscious and laboured in his breathing.

Wish de Sequeira sat up in his bed, his back against the square of morning at the window, his face dark against the white cloud of his hair, like a photographic negative of someone younger. Above him a ceiling fan stirred the soupy air, cutting the light on his face like a dying star.

'Oh, an angel. You must be an angel.' He smiled at her as she entered his room.

She bent to kiss him on his broad, lined forehead. He smelled of Tiger Balm ointment. He fixed her with a gaze clear as glass as she put the roses in a blue-and-white porcelain vase on his bedside table.

'You have come to say goodbye.' His voice was higher and thinner than usual, and it wavered.

'What makes you think that?'

'I still get around. The night flying, you know. When I have enough strength.'

She wondered if he'd seen the travel writer and her the previous night.

'You should be resting, not night flying. How are you, father?'

'Oh well, I put up with them . . .' he gestured towards the nurses' station, '. . . and they put up with me.'

He closed his eyes. 'How's the tea tasting?'

'Tainted.' She paused and looked at him. His closed eyelids looked almost transparent. Should she tell him?

'We're finished, Rupert and I.'

He opened his eyes just long enough for her to see that he was both grieved and unsurprised.

'I need love, Father.'

His eyes were closed again, but his brow furrowed in concern. 'Your mother and I loved one another because we could let ourselves

be vulnerable to each other.' He opened his eyes and turned to his
daughter again. 'I hope for the same for you.'

'I've been seeing Walter Humphries, the travel writer, again.'

'I know. What some people call love is a dangerous business.
More like a bad accident.'

'I'm going overseas with him for a while.'

'I will pray for you,' he said, knowing she would need much
more than this.

※

Ghislaine woke the following morning while Mak Non and
Isabelle still slept. She had been awake most of the previous night
as she lay in Mak Non's house puzzling over Walter Humphries'
words. 'It's no good,' he'd said after unbuttoning her blouse, pressing
his lips together as if he'd caught the aftertaste of something
unpleasant. She could remember his face clearly as he stood there,
trouserless and disdainful, looking suddenly away from her towards
the window.

She walked under the wan early-morning sky to the Land of the
Priest to confide all this to her cousin Olivia Skelchy Maximiano.
Rats scampered in the gutters amongst noodles, fish bones and
eggshells from the previous night's food hawkers. The last fishermen
of the morning pulled their painted wooden boats onto the sand as
she knocked on Olivia's door.

'Hello, you gorgeous old whore.' Olivia's optimism and talent for
bawdiness were unabated, despite her marriage to Nazario Maximiano, now a plodding and myopic clerk, and their three children.

'Give me a look at your poor old tetek then,' said Olivia, rubbing
the sleep from her eyes after Ghislaine had spilled her secrets over a
cup of Pupil-brand coffee. She unhooked Ghislaine's Great Wall-
brand brassiere.

'Aiya, Isabelle and Rupert have sucked all the fat out of them,
and they were never that big, anyway.' She peered more closely at

Ghislaine's breasts. 'Good de Sequeira skin though. Look at that, only a few stretchmarks, and the ones you do have are sort of silvery,' she marvelled enviously. 'Eat more kueh and go see the de Mello sisters at their shop on Bunga Raya Road. They'll sew you a bra to make your old tetek bounce again.'

'But what about when I have to take the bra off in front of him?'

'Nothing that sheets and darkness can't cover up. Keep the curtains drawn and the lights off. Either that, or hold on to your money and say goodbye to him. I mean, do you really want to spend yourself on such a half-hearted man lah?'

*

It was still early in the morning when Ghislaine arrived at the de Mello sisters' Melaka Personal Support Garment and Body Binding Shop, between the cobblers' and the drapers' shops on Bunga Raya Road. Mercedes and Maude de Mello were two elderly Christao women who had built their business upon their firm grasps, meticulous French seams and a reputation for keeping the personal details of their women customers confidential. Their clientele included everyone from the devout old girls of the Convent of Our Lady, to the prostitutes who lived in the alleys just beyond the streets where the lawyers and civil servants had their offices. The blue lettering on the sign outside the de Mellos' shop read:

> *Specialists in Partial Concealment and Fine Filigrees. We give the personal touch to the full support, enhancement and welfare of the female torso.*

Only old girls of Our Lady could make corsetry sound so wholesome. Despite her discussion with Olivia, Ghislaine was not exactly sure what she wanted from them, or what she could expect. The older, shorter sister, Maude, was sitting in her rattan armchair facing the morning sun, her face tattooed by the shadows of the laces and wires that hung from the shop front.

'Brassiere or binding?'

'Brassiere.'

'What kind?'

'What choice do I have?'

'Padded, unpadded, wired, unwired, with frills, without.'

'I just need something to give me more than I've got.'

Maude de Mello recognised the catch in her voice. 'Same old story,' she said. 'Go out the back with Mercedes lah.'

Mercedes led Ghislaine behind the curtain of rice sacks. The seamstress slipped her hand deftly between the underside of Ghislaine's breast and her ribs.

'Breastfeeding and starvation,' she said through the gap in her teeth to Maude as she hobbled up with a notebook. 'Half a fistful, B cup, wall-eyed and pointy, skin still quite elastic.' Her measuring tape cracked like a whip as she pulled it from the back of her neck and ran it around Ghislaine's chest.

'Thirty-two-and-three-quarters, all mostly rib cage.'

Ghislaine covered herself swiftly with her blouse as Mercedes de Mello pushed three different brassiere prototypes across the counter. They were unadorned, just wire and hooks. Another kind of cage.

'Which you want? This one squeezes. This one separates. This one uplifts.'

'Uplift.'

Maude de Mello spread an array of laces out on the table.

'Which lace you want lah? Sea-shell pink, powder blue, white?'

'Red,' said Ghislaine with certainty. 'The one with the little embroidered hearts.'

'Pelacur,' sniggered Mercedes, rehanging her measuring tape around her neck. 'Prostitute.'

'Cannot. Red is the prostitute's colour. In high demand right now, what with Lent coming up lah,' said Maude.

Ghislaine did not enquire about the mysterious connection between Lent and the prostitutes of Malacca.

'I'll pay you anything you like.'

'Aiya! Three dollars lah!'

'Red is the colour of a true heart,' she said, putting her money on the table.

※

After visiting the de Mello sisters, Ghislaine went to the Cathay Picture Theatre to watch the Warner Bros film adaptation of *The Letter*. She had ten dollars in her pocket and the rash on her chin from the travel writer's stubble smarted.

No dogs, durian, areca or patai nut allowed inside, the sign proclaimed in black lettering in English, Malay, Cantonese and Tamil.

She bought herself an orangeade from the lugubrious Malay man behind the counter and took it into the rustling twilight of the theatre. She sat on a canvas chair behind the more expensive padded seats preferred by the expatriates. The audience unwrapped ingeniously parcelled food. She had brought her own wrapped durian sweets, their flavour and odour contained by cellophane and sugar.

The heads of the tall expatriates in front of her obscured her view. Behind her, the Malay, Tamil and Chinese labourers and servants chattered to one another on their hard wooden benches. Her drink fizzed behind her nose as she sucked it through the blue-and-white-striped paper straw. Outside the dark coolness of the cinema, the Malacca morning was strident with heat and the song of crickets, the sky a bright, searing blue gash; but inside the Cathay Picture Theatre, after the lights were out, Ghislaine imagined she could be anywhere in the world. She relished hiding in the dark like this, savouring the privacy of her pleasure in the broad, blatant screen. She huddled low in her creaking seat, waiting for the Warner Bros logo to cast its cold blue light from the screen. Who would be the Eurasian adulteress Leslie Crosbie? Some unknown Eurasian actress?

On the screen, liquid rubber bled whitely, rhythmically from the trunk of a tree into a cup. The opening credits rolled over dark-skinned men and women playing rustic wooden instruments, or gambling, or sleeping in hammocks against a background of jungle and palms.

Bette Davis. Bette Davis would play the adulteress. Perhaps news of the adulteress's race hadn't reached Hollywood. Perhaps the rest of the world didn't know what a Eurasian was. Or perhaps Walter Humphries had been wrong.

The audience on the hard wooden benches behind her sniggered. She sank lower in her seat, slurped the rest of her orangeade through the straw, and tried watching the film as Walter might see it. But she cringed at the ominous bass trill of strings punctuated by one sonorous strike from a Chinese gong, at the picturesqueness of the plantation workers' camp and the Wild West cut of Bette Davis's clothes.

There was a crackle and jump like a dying motor in the soundtrack as a white flare cut the film to obliterate Bette Davis as she reached for a gun. A fizz like Fauldings saline solution followed as the flare receded and the film jumped jerkily to a long shot of a man lying on the ground. Ghislaine knew that brief white flare and jump in the soundtrack meant that the censors had cut some scene of passion or crime. The servants in the audience behind her laughed as the dark-skinned extras on the screen looked soulfully at the moon, as if it might tell them something.

'Coolies like us ah! What for they got camp like paradise?' a woman behind her exclaimed.

Bette Davis stood on the verandah, looking to Ghislaine like a kewpie doll dressed for a day out in town as she stared at the corpse of her lover. She went inside and poured a dark half-whisky half-water. Bette Davis drank more stengahs in the scenes that followed and her clothes changed to haute couture draped dresses, but all the way through she was smooth, her expressions spreading like butter over the adulteress's chasms of anxiety and terror.

You'll see yourself in it. What did Walter Humphries mean? Ghislaine felt herself evaporating into a caricature as the intrigue music with its eastern gongs played again. She sucked noisily on durian sweets and cursed the waste of her money on the ticket. And then, quite suddenly, Ghislaine heard words she could have sworn were her own being spoken from behind Bette Davis's pale mask.

'Every time I met him, I hated myself, and yet I lived for the moment I'd see him again. It was horrible. There was never an hour when I was at peace, when I wasn't reproaching myself. I was like a sick person with some loathsome disease.'

It seemed the actress had given a perfect account of the guilt Ghislaine had felt about being unfaithful to her own husband.

As Ghislaine sat in the dark listening to the audience around her sneering at the adulteress's plight, she saw how impossible it would be to explain what had happened between herself and the travel writer.

'Then I heard about his, his native woman.'

There was an expectant hush from the audience.

'I saw her walking in the street with those hideous bangles, that chalky painted face, those eyes like cobra's eyes.'

The native woman on the screen wore a sarong kebaya but she was not Malay, and she was not Chinese. There was a wave of vexed laughter from the Malay and Chinese audience at this version of native.

'What for a kampong woman got white face and charcoal on her eyes?' Ghislaine heard someone behind her sneer. 'Like she got to give everyone fright?'

'Ah. What for a kampong woman got silk-brocade kebaya? Like she wear it to feed chickens?'

Ghislaine had questions, too, but they did not leave her tongue. Which woman did the travel writer think she would see herself in? The speechless, brocade-clad native woman of indeterminate race who was the mother of the Englishman's child, or the almost-English, adulterous planter's wife played by Bette Davis?

'I hated him because he made me despise myself,' Bette Davis was telling the handsome, suited actor who played the English lawyer. Ghislaine put her hands on her cheeks and was grateful for the dark. She rose to leave, but the film reeled and crackled forward, not stopping where her courage did.

On the screen, the native woman hid with a knife in the garden in the dark of night in her silk clothes, immaculately soignée as the adulteress walked unwittingly towards her. The final scene was obliterated by another white censor's flare. Ghislaine left the picture theatre quickly as the credits rolled. As she walked out towards the strident heat of the Malacca day, she wondered if either woman won in the uncensored version.

※

Ghislaine let herself into her father's house with the key Mak Non had given her. The interior was cool and as meticulously ordered as before. She opened the shutters. Only then did she see her father had changed Ah Kwei's old bedroom behind the kitchen into a store-room for his photographs. She walked in and turned on the light. In a neat pile on the table were hundreds of photographs of faces. She flicked through the pile trying to make sense of it. They were all faces of people sleeping. Presumably, he'd taken them during his rounds as a medical assistant. There were wealthy Nonyas and Babars sleeping on silk pillows, coolies on woven mats, Malays and Indians on sheets strewn with the petals of flowers. She recognised a few of them: there was Grandfather Ezekiel, the Armenian Jewish jeweller; Bosco da Silva from the Eurasian settlement at the Land of the Priest; Mrs Lim, the Cantonese tailoress. The photographs of these familiars and of the strangers all had in common a sense of contained untouchability. Ghislaine wondered if there was anything as beautiful as the faces of people sleeping, the haunting sovereignty of the lone traveller on them.

But there was something else strange about these photographs, besides the fact they were all of sleeping people. They were all very formally composed. Few of the subjects were smiling; the hands of many of them were crossed over their chests. She almost overlooked the long white thread next to many of the Eurasians. Of course. These were people who had died, some of them during her absence in the highlands.

Why had her father taken all these photographs of people shortly after their deaths? She took the camera from the corner of the room. It was shaped like a box. Its leather case smelled of him, of malty sweat and antiseptic.

Mak Non was smoking her clay pipe on her verandah when Ghislaine returned to the kampong with the camera and the photographs.

'Mak Non, would you mind looking after Isabelle while I'm overseas with Walter?'

Mak Non's eyes were wry, as if she'd seen most of the tricks people played. She nodded and blew a fine plume of smoke towards the banana trees.

'Thank you so much. Mak Non, why do you think my father took all these photographs?'

'They his patients. He give their families memory of them.'

That afternoon, Ghislaine took some photographs of Isabelle. By the time she had finished, she thought she knew what other reasons her father had for photographing the people.

'He was both rehearsing his own departure and saying goodbye,' she told Mak Non. 'Could you take a photograph of me with Isabelle? For her to keep? For her to remember me by?'

'What for?' Mak Non asked gently. 'You dying?'

LONDON, FEBRUARY 1986

I arrange to meet Philip at the Palm House one grey Saturday afternoon. He's already standing at the top of one of the winding staircases inside when I arrive. I call out to him, but he doesn't hear. I walk further into the humid interior and tread as quietly as I can up the stairs. Halfway up I stop, almost afraid. Standing there in his black clothes with his hands spread out on the balustrade, the late-afternoon light streaming through the sixty-foot-high glass-and-iron dome above, he looks almost apocalyptic, like the priest of an enormous cathedral. Outside, the afternoon is darkening but there are fissures of gold between the leaden clouds to the west. I keep climbing towards him until my boot kicks the wrought-iron railing and he turns and sees me.

–Hello. So is this what jungle looks like in Malaysia? His face is flushed from the humidity.

–Well, they don't showcase species in glasshouses there.

–The wrought iron in this glasshouse is all iron deck-beam scantlings from when the first iron steamships were built, you know.

–Oh. I didn't know that.

He looks pleased.

—So which orchids do you like the best? he asks.

—The Holy Ghost orchid.

—A good Catholic orchid, hmm?

—It used to grow in the jungle near Malacca and in the highlands. They flower in quite dark conditions.

—Maybe I'll grow some in my conservatory.

I don't say: *They need too much care for someone as busy as you.*

—Come down here and I'll show you some of the smaller palms. Less showy, but more adaptable.

The iron stairs ring as we descend.

—*Diplothemium*, he says, craning his neck to look at a metal name plaque.

—The undersides are silver like the clouds in Malacca are some evenings. I have some potted at home. I'll bring them over. How about these?

—Too scrawny for me. *Cypripedium pubescens*, he mutters with a half smile, touching one of the few orchids that hasn't been removed by the head gardener.

—Such a delicate but optimistic flower, I say.

—They don't have many orchids in here.

—They don't allow different species to mingle so much here. It's a hangover from Victorian times, I guess. But I've been smuggling a few in from the tropical zone of the conservatory to mix them the way they do in the jungle. There are lots of orchids in the jungle outside Malacca. They're not rooted in the soil, but they're not parasitic, either. Their seeds are windblown, sometimes over big distances. They survive on bits and pieces that fall from plants higher above them, and so they sometimes suffer from shortages of nutrients.

He yawns. I surmise he's not used to being taught.

—Feel like cream tea in the Maids of Honour tearooms? I ask.

—Watching my cholesterol.

—Ah.

I've forgotten again how middle-aged he is. Not a grey hair

anywhere, though. Looking at the back of his hair as we depart, I wonder if he dyes it.

※

On the way home from the gardens, I notice a small restaurant advertising its food as *A Fusion of Far Eastern and Western Cuisine.* A new vision of the future comes to me as the smell of garam masala mingles with the rush-hour fumes. If Philip wants a tropical garden, other Londoners might, too. A small garden-design business might supplement my part-time income and pay all those bills.

After I put Clara to bed, it takes me less than an hour to design the leaflet for my new enterprise. I draw a Buddha nestled underneath a rose bower, but erase the face because it looks too like Philip's. Underneath it, I write:

> *My fusion gardens will bring the Far East close to you*
> *&*
> *add joy, spice and warmth to your life.*

And to Clara's and mine. I cross my fingers as the library photocopier churns out the leaflets the next day.

The slogan looks both desperate and cynical as I post it through the mail slots of all the houses that are within walking distance. Who am I kidding? The English love their English gardens.

–Bet there'll be no customers. Any English gardener will tell you that a jungle is not a garden, I say to Sunil at work on Monday.

He ruffles my hair.

–Of course it's not, silly. No garden is natural. They're all artificial recombinations of natural elements. But well-to-do English have been growing palms in their parlours for generations. They'll love your idea. You wait and see.

※

Eight people ring in response to the leaflets by the end of the week. As these first clients live nearby, where yards and conservatories are small, I avoid planting them the lawns so typical of English gardens and reserves. I design gardens like jewel boxes, grouping orchids and begonias in glazed terracotta pots as my relatives had done in their tiny backyards in Malacca when I was a child; or placing them in beds under bowers of climbing rose or frangipani. I plant swathes of tiger-striped croton, red ginger, white anthurium and cerise-edged cordyline ti around statues of miniature pagodas and Eastern deities souvenired by my customers during their package tours to Asia. I bring an easily controllable version of the Far East near to them.

THE TRUE BODY

Hantu Langsuyar in the Dorchester Hotel

It was done. Walter Humphries had bought Ghislaine de Sequeira a low-grade emerald ring and a plain alloy band from the younger Ezekiel on the street of jewellers and money-changers in Malacca. The emerald ring was too small for her and the plain band was too large, but they held one another in place. She journeyed with the travel writer to England with a layer of skin scraped off her knuckle.

Ghislaine hoped England would be a practice honeymoon. But England was the grey of nightmares. She shivered with cold inside her thin clothes and her new red brassiere decorated with love hearts. She didn't feel seasick until three hours after getting off the ship, but supposed it was the traffic fumes rising in the damp light. She could not bear to think that this was the return of the travel sickness Mak Non said would be remedied only by arriving at true love.

She was finally travelling with Walter Humphries, so hadn't she arrived?

The Dorchester Hotel was the colour of rust, rearing above the street and Hyde Park as steeply and imposingly as a cliff. They entered through a wood-and-glass door, panelled and hinged like a bank's. The porter was a smaller monument, standing straight in his top hat and tails. Behind him the stairs, carpeted in red, swept downwards like a cloak. They followed him up to their room draped in gold velvet.

'This hotel looks very expensive,' murmured Ghislaine.

'I inherited some money from an uncle recently,' said Walter airily. He took only two minutes to change his shirt.

'I am going down for a look around while you unpack,' he said, moving towards the door as he spoke, his averted face and squat, determined torso leaving no room for questions.

Ghislaine walked to the window. She would have liked to explore the city too, but the streets swirling with lanes of brightly lit traffic increased her sense of seasickness. She could feel the cold creeping in through a gap between the windows. She turned and sat at the Regency writing desk with its twisted ankles and its fountain pen and postcards of the Dorchester Hotel's imposing exterior, but she felt too over-awed to write.

※

On the second night, she began writing a postcard home.

Dear Isabelle, Father and Mak Non,

I cannot believe this refrigerator full of bad food is England. The days are colder and darker than it ever was inside the Arctic Defender at Journey's End. As for snow, I have seen none, but the food is white with cold fat and not very tasty. I wish I had a jar of belachan with me.

London is full of monuments and huge buildings, to remind everyone that a lot of important things have happened here. Walter has brought his camera to take photographs of home for the expatriate readers. He will take me to the museum soon to see what his father collected from the Far East.

She could not find the words to conclude with. She did not write that Walter Humphries, too, wanted her to know he was important. He wore waistcoats to match his suits, and spoke to the hotel's waiters in exclamation marks. He combed his sunbleached hair back off his forehead with pomade brought up by room service. He told her to grow her nails long so he could feel them on his back, to wear her hair out so he could hold it in his fist. He stood unselfconsciously naked under the chandelier in their room and made his demands.

Ghislaine told herself she was happy with him, that he had been kind enough to her in their poorly lit ship's cabin, especially first thing in the morning and last thing at night. But in the Dorchester Hotel the light was too bright on her imperfections. She could not bring herself to write to her father and Mak Non that with Walter Humphries she did not find herself in the great city she had dreamed of, the city of love. She kept hoping that this destination was somewhere ahead of them.

On that second night in the Dorchester Hotel, Ghislaine hurried to the four-poster bed well before Walter returned from the bar downstairs. She pulled the blank white sheet over her and hoped to dream of the sun glinting on the sea in Malacca: happiness, infinite and simple, without equivalent. But she did not dream of Malacca, because she had left more than Malacca behind.

The traffic hummed along Knightsbridge Road and the mattress sighed as she sank into it and drifted deeper into sleep. Ghislaine dreamed she was sitting on the roof of the Dorchester Hotel sucking blood from Isabelle's already dead body, hiding her own deformed breasts and her weeping from the travel writer so he would not abandon her.

When she woke, she knew who she was. She was Hantu Langsuyar, the ghost of the woman who'd died after killing and eating her child; Hantu Langsuyar who had been a mother before she became obsessed with making herself desirable to men. Walter Humphries slept beside her snoring alcohol fumes. There she was, inhaling his vapours, trying to be his idea of a woman.

※

After a rubbery breakfast of eggs and bacon, Walter hailed a cab and introduced Ghislaine to the sites of London as if they were esteemed relations of his, as if he was intent on showing her what a proud nation she might marry into.

'Take a photograph of me here,' she said when they got to Tower Bridge, 'so I can prove I was really here.' But he didn't. Because for him she wasn't. He walked on ahead of her. His back would be the sight she remembered most from this journey.

Not quite halfway across Tower Bridge, she became almost paralysed with fear. He didn't notice she had stopped walking until he was beyond the halfway mark. His brow was bent in annoyance as he turned back towards her.

'What's wrong?'

'What if the bridge opens before I get to the other side?'

'Don't be silly. It doesn't do it without warning. No-one's even allowed on the bridge when a ship's about to come through.' But she refused to go any further. Nothing seemed as certain to her that morning as the possibility of human error.

They walked silently through the drizzle to the British Museum. Outside its gates, an old man in a flat cap roasted chestnuts on a brazier. He watched Ghislaine with the speechless implacability of an old sea turtle as she paused next to him to look at the colonnaded entrance and portico from street level. She felt giddy with vertigo as she gazed up at the Ionic pillars. It looked both monumental and funereal, like an imitation of an ancient Greek temple she had seen once in a film in the Cathay Picture Theatre. In the centre of its gable was a bas-relief of men wearing Grecian drapes, holding aloft staffs, swords, spears. The further away from the peak the figures were, the more they were forced, by the angle of the gable, to recline. All the reclining roles were for women.

Walter Humphries bustled up the stairs past other visitors. He steered Ghislaine through the high-vaulted reception hall, past knots of people in a lofty room shiny with antique silver and gold inside glass showcases.

'Such wealth,' she murmured.

His smile was plump with satisfaction. 'It's a spiritual experience, looking at all this treasure.' He gestured to more lustrous rooms beyond, but Ghislaine sat down suddenly on the closest bench seat she could find. 'Something wrong?'

'Everything here seems to be stolen,' she whispered.

'The British paid for everything here. One way or another.' He glared at her. 'Haven't you been in a museum before?'

She would not answer. She was not being the grateful guest she should be. She allowed herself to be led into the rooms beyond.

The room marked Oriental Antiquities was empty of other visitors.

'The curators obviously had an eye for beauty,' Walter said, gesturing broadly at a showcase full of women's bodies in stone, porcelain, wood and brass. Side by side were princesses painted onto priceless pieces of porcelain from various Chinese dynasties, brass and stone goddesses from India, winged representations of spirits from Indonesia.

'They liked collecting breasts and wings,' she said.

'That's a very superficial observation.' He smiled. 'You are very funny, you know. Quite naïve.' She looked at the tip of his shoe. She'd never seen it so highly polished in Malacca.

'Where is their Malayan section?' she asked.

'There isn't one. The Malays just didn't have much to offer.'

Walter put his hand on the small of her back and steered her towards the Indian display, so that Ghislaine almost overlooked the stone carving of the bird with the breasts and face of a woman, displayed between tall pieces of brassware from Ceylon and Indonesia.

Exhibit 270. The kinnari, poet and singer to the gods, is part woman, part avian. It is found throughout Indonesia. Bequest of Reverend Flint from estate of Lady Raffles.

'Kinnari,' she breathed. 'It is like the statue that used to be my mother's.'

'A much better version.'

She bent closer to the glass. Did Walter say this just because the breasts were bigger? She felt the air grow cold with the beating of stone wings.

＊

Ghislaine did not own a coat to protect her from the London autumn. She wore three layers of Great Wall-brand underclothes from Malacca under her blouse and homemade dress, and two cardigans that used to be her mother's. She had brought with her the only two pairs of thin socks she owned, and she wore them both at once under her shabby vinyl pumps from Fong Li Wah's stall behind Bunga Raya Road. Walter looked down at her feet as their black taxi crawled past shops, hotels and churches of dark, rain-slicked brick.

'You could do with some decent footwear.' She felt her feet tense and curl. 'Those are all very well for Malacca. This is the country for quality clothes and shoes. You should go and buy some while I'm writing tomorrow.' He ran his hand over his coat sleeve. It was clear he was a man who knew how to dress for all weathers.

Ghislaine did not tell him she had neither the money nor the knowledge to buy clothes of the same quality as his. She'd travelled to be with him, not to shop. As she'd packed in Malacca, she'd been certain love would be more than sufficient cover for them both, that the climate wouldn't get any colder than the years with Rupert had been.

The cab stopped at the Dorchester Hotel, which was lit up like a ship against the descent of evening. She took Walter's hand as they walked up the steps, but he let it fall from her grasp, as he often did when they were walking in public.

In their suite, she washed her socks and underclothes in the bathroom and hung them over the radiator so they would be ready for the next day, dressed in her Flying Goose-brand nightdress embroidered with love knots, and sat against the pillows under the smooth, cold percale sheet. Walter sprawled in the armchair facing the window and smoked. She could see a small bald patch at the back of his head. When he turned and walked over to her, he was smiling, and his voice was smooth and low. He took her hand.

'So. What will you do with the land at the back of your father's Malaccan house when he dies, do you think? That land is big enough for four shophouses. You could make a small fortune.' He stroked her hair. 'You'll need help with these things. Your father's on his last legs, isn't he?'

His question was like a soft blow to the back of her head, frightening because it seemed to come from nowhere.

'Oh, but the doctors expect him to recover completely.' Walter looked bewildered. He dropped her hand and frowned until the two vertical lines between his eyebrows deepened into exclamation marks.

'Is there anything wrong?'

'Need some fresh air.' He got up, walked to the door and closed it behind him.

She sat in the middle of the bed in the enormous room, feeling cold and seasick, as if she were alone in a small boat in the middle of an unnavigable sea. She turned off the light and lay on the Dorchester Hotel's fine sheets weeping for Hantu Langsuyar, who had followed a man a whole life and death away from her true family, only to fail in her attempts at being his idea of a woman; Hantu Langsuyar who had become a ghost forever, unable to return to the woman she had been.

❄

The travel writer crashed into the antique writing desk of their Dorchester Hotel room in the dark, sending her unfinished postcards to the floor, trampling them underfoot as he made his way to the bed.

'Bloody hell! Nearly broke my crown jewels,' he muttered. He began humming a tune she couldn't recognise, then stopped as suddenly as he'd begun. She could hear his suspenders snapping off their buttons in the dark. The bed sank as he sat on it.

'Are you awake, Ghislaine?' She was surprised by the solicitation in his voice. Maybe things weren't as bad as they seemed. Perhaps she was letting her homesickness get the better of her. 'Listen to this. Someone downstairs just told me I look about thirty-five years old.' He paused. 'So what have you been doing?'

'Thinking about us. Do you love me?' she asked. She knew immediately that this lacked strategy.

'I don't think that's a fair question,' he replied. He put his hand on her cheek. It smelled of shortbread biscuits and whisky.

Would he have answered her question properly if there hadn't been that knock at the door? He dived, half dressed, under the covers. There was another knock at the door. She rose and wrapped a robe over her nightdress, turned the light on and opened the door.

'Ghislaine Humphries?' For a moment she forgot this was who she was supposed to be.

'That's me.' Her voice was small and reluctant, as if she were cowering in the sights of a gun. The bellboy handed her the pale yellow telegram and bowed.

Father dead stop Mak Non stop

There in the Dorchester Hotel, so many seas away from home, Ghislaine de Sequeira had forgotten who she'd ever been.

Philip flicks his television to news footage of an English rescuer helping a brown-skinned woman and her child from a devastated village. The volume is turned down to a low murmur. I sit on the edge of the chair buttoning my shirtsleeves as these images flicker like ghosts across his walls.

–Where's this? I ask.

He shrugs.

–Somewhere in Asia. I have work to do now, Isabelle. A conference paper to write.

–I'll be off then. Clara will be waiting to be fed, anyway.

–Yes. I thought it must be nearly time for you to go back to your family.

I pretend I'm getting ready to go, but I take longer than necessary to smooth the creases of my clothes.

–I was hoping to talk, actually.

–What about?

–Us.

–What about us in particular?

–Where do you think we're headed, Philip?

He pats my hand, but the muscles tense around his eyes.

—Isn't it a little early for that kind of thing? Look, Isabelle. I like you very much. But we hardly know each other.

How sensible he sounds. As I rise, the muscles around his eyes relax and he puts his arm around my shoulder reassuringly, like the rescuer on the News of the World.

He hands me my coat and backpack, opens the door on to an evening sky of clouds hanging like fine nets, and turns and looks at me gravely, as he had when I first entered his house all those months ago.

—Isabelle. Don't get me wrong. I do care for you. But it's best to let these things unfold in the fullness of time.

His expression softens: his wait-and-see smile.

The fullness of time. I put my hand out to him, but he's already stepping back into the warmth of his house, leaving me looking at my fingers outstretched and empty in the cold air.

※

Sometimes my garden-design customers ask me to do things that conflict with my sense of design. One elderly woman's father had been an administrator in the days of the Raj. Her cabinets are full of fine china and her skin powdered the paleness of porcelain. She insists on a squat statue of a skinny turbanned man taking a parasoled Victorian couple for a ride on an elephant in her waterlily pond.

That will look like something from a Spode tea set, not one of my fusion gardens, I want to protest, until I notice the tears welling in her eyes.

—I was only a child, but I remember our native servants so well. Their tongues were so sing-song and their food so spicy. And they were so affectionate.

As she speaks, her gold-framed spectacles magnify the facial powder suspended in her tears as they roll down the side of her nose.

—I understand, I say quickly, to cover the fact that I don't, not completely. Does her statue assuage her longing for the days when it seemed the Empire would prevail forever? Or do we have more in common with one another? Might we both be seeking respite in our gardens from more than one kind of English reserve?

※

Although it's only February, new green shoots are appearing on the branches of trees and shrubs, and some bulbs have begun budding. My mother spends most of her days sitting in a chair or in bed, turned towards the window without being able to see the signs of this early spring.

Inside, the freshness of the morning is lost in the hospital smells of stew and antiseptic. She turns her face to the door as soon as she hears my footsteps.

–You haven't brought Clara.

–Sorry. She's at a birthday party.

–It's okay lah. We can talk.

–You said there was something you wanted to tell me about Walter Humphries.

–Yes. I decided it was for the best to keep it to myself, after all. It's for me to think about, not you. Sorry, Isabelle.

She smooths the sheet between her fingers. I've finally realised she only does that when she's anxious.

–Fair enough. But what happened the night you heard about Grandfather Wish's death?

–Walter Humphries asked me to marry him that same night.

–Really? You never told me that!

–Years later I saw that it was only because he knew that Grandfather Wish's death meant I would inherit property and money. The travel writer had come to the East to make his fortune, had failed to find it for twenty years, and suddenly there it was.

–Oh no! Surely that's too cynical.

–Well. It's the way it was.

She turns her palms upwards in resignation and looks at me

almost beseechingly, as if pleading with me to believe this is the entire story.

—So what did you tell Walter that night?

—I refused his proposal, of course.

—Why?

She smooths the air with her hands as if she's trying to cover something with them.

—He put too many impossible conditions on it.

—What conditions?

—Can't remember now lah.

She looks away. What is she keeping from me?

—But your refusal in the Dorchester Hotel wasn't the end of it, was it? That wasn't the end of your romance with Walter Humphries, surely? He kept visiting us all those years afterwards in Malacca.

—It wasn't the end of him in my life, no. But I made it clear to him he was not the love of my life.

—But that's the end of the romance! Why end the romance in that way?

If there had been no other love for my mother, I want to believe there had at least been Walter Humphries.

—Because it became clear that night that I'd mistaken my dream of him for the man he really was.

—What do you mean?

—Aiya. Bamboozling, yes? But I think most women mistake the dream for the man at least once in their lives. I did it twice.

—Why do you think that was?

—I suppose because . . . I was desperate lah. With both Rupert and Walter. And the nightmares you don't learn from repeat themselves lah.

—Why were you so desperate?

She reaches over and places her hand on mine. I can see her arteries and bones as she squeezes my hand until the fate line deepens on my palm.

—Some things are better left unexplained, anak. But always remember this. Your father, Rupert, was not so much a bad man as a bewildered one. He had his reasons for behaving the way he did in the Cameron Highlands.

So I'd resented my father wrongly all these years? So I'd drawn him too harshly in the story of her life?

—What reasons, Mum?

—Enough lah. Grief is private.

I'm seized by a sudden wild hope, and can't restrain myself, beyond lowering my voice further.

—Was there someone else who loved you better than Rupert or Walter?

She crosses herself. That's a clue, surely. She's trying to protect us both from something she's hidden all these years.

—There was someone else I loved better than both of them, she says, her eyes filling with so many tears that there is no room for any more questions.

PART THREE

Fikah — to be, to become, to live

LONDON, FEBRUARY 1986

Philip lies next to me and looks into the middle distance, rubbing the wall behind the bed with the backs of his fingers. I trace the lines in his skin that fan out from his eyes as I listen to the almost imperceptible scratching above the ceiling.

—It's better to do it in this order. Sex first, eat later, he says, glancing at me, patting me peremptorily on the head. It's as if he's intent on showing me I've participated in something generic rather than personal. The brothel regulations at the back of my mother's diary come to me: *Kissing and love relationship forbidden. No unreasonable demands to be made.*

The noise in the ceiling grows louder, but he doesn't seem to hear it.

—About your writing. I've been thinking. She's too passive, this Eurasian woman.

He looks so sure of himself, my tutor. His learning and his money are there in his face, his body, his voice. Perhaps they're unbridgeable, the oceans between the de Sequeira's cramped shophouse built on a colonial budget, and the tutor's house of light-filled words and future built from family money.

–It's lack of opportunity, not passivity. I could describe her life further, but it might mean nothing to you, I murmur.

The scratching in the ceiling stops suddenly, but seconds later there's a high howl, beseeching, almost human.

–See. I told you a while ago some creature's up there, Philip. But now it's really suffering.

–Sounds like an animal of some kind, all right. Better grab the builder's ladder.

He sighs and wraps his sarong around his waist, and pulls the ladder in from the balcony.

I pull my clothes back on and follow him up the ladder. When he lifts the manhole cover in the ceiling, an overpowering stench of ammonia, faeces and mud descends, as if a marsh and all its creatures are dying in some terrible drought up there.

–Whatever it is, it's been trapped in here for a while. The builders must have closed it in when they finished the ceiling.

He pulls himself up through the manhole and crouches on a nearby rafter. I stand on the highest rung of the ladder, so that I'm leaning into the dark roof cavity. He turns on the torch. Its beam bounces around the rafters, isolating a chunk of foil-backed insulation here, a rafter there. Suddenly it picks out two small dim lights against the far edge of the roof. They come towards us stealthily, until midway across the roof space, they accelerate and glint an almost fluorescent green.

–Eyes. Some kind of animal, he says again, shifting on his rafters.

–A rat?

He shines the torch directly on it.

–Too big. A cat. A big one, a bloody big feral cat.

As it draws closer, it becomes clear there's something wrong with its mouth, something dark and crooked about it. A new smell comes towards us, one of fresh blood. In the torch-light, I see something hanging from its jaws. For a moment, I think the cat's bringing us a mouse. Philip shines the torch full in its face. It's a kitten hanging upside down from the cat's mouth, its eyes closed in its small round head. As the cat draws level with us, she bares her teeth and claws, hissing and snarling. In that moment, the kitten drops through the manhole onto the floor. It does not move when it lands.

–Shit! All over the Bokhara, Philip exclaims.

The cat's spine shows through its grey-striped fur as she hisses on her rafter. When I reach the floor, I notice there's only half a kitten there, and that one tiny entrail hangs like a purple string from its severed waist. The pink of its skin is still showing through its wet black fur. It was probably only born a few minutes previously. The cat hisses once more before she clears the ladder with a leap down to the floor and the stairs. Philip follows her, grabbing an umbrella from the hallstand as he goes. She leaps across the low table towards the study, toppling the gold-plated Buddha onto the floor in her wake. We pursue her into the study as she skitters across the desktop, sending a white wake of papers flying into the air. Hissing, she backs into the far corner, dislodging books of theory from the shelves. She arches her back and bares her teeth again as Philip draws closer to her. I see another kitten working its way slowly between her rear legs, hanging like a cocoon from the thin sticks of its mother's body. Philip lifts the umbrella over his head.

–Don't! She's still giving birth!

But he's already bringing down the full force of the metal umbrella spike hard into the cat's neck. She scratches him and lets out one long howl, bringing down more papers and books from the shelves as she throws herself against them in a desperate attempt to find escape. Philip drives the point home again, this time into her side. There's a soft rasping sound like a melon being cut and he lifts the umbrella just before she falls to the floor. Again he takes aim and the body lies motionless.

–I had to. These feral cats carry disease. The council's trying to eradicate a colony of them living in the cemetery. This one's probably a refugee from there.

Three thin bloody tracks run down Philip's forearm. He stands over the cat.

–Look at that. Crawling with fleas.

I bend closer, but not to look at the fleas. A hot smell of musk, metal and raw meat rises from the half-born kitten. I can feel the warmth coming from it. I can see the kitten's head tightly curled inwards, as if trying to close out the world. I wait to see if its mother's contractions will continue to push it out, but nothing happens. I don't know whether to help it finish being born, motherless, or to let it die still half inside its mother. The latter would be a kinder death, but I can hardly bear to keep looking, to watch for the moment it stops moving altogether. Then I notice it's quite still already, with no breathing visible in its tiny chest.

There's a loud choking sound from the toilet adjacent to the study. Philip's vomiting. A tap runs and an electric toothbrush whirrs as I take some tissues out of my pocket and place one over the severed kitten before mopping up the thin dribble of blood running from it onto the floor. I've almost finished when Philip stands at the door again, flapping his hands helplessly.

–Get me something to wrap them in, I say.

He comes back with a garbage bag. His lips are pale in his flushed face.

I hold the second kitten against its mother's cervix before sliding the bag underneath and over them. Together they weigh less than the book about bodies that had fallen during the struggle. I can feel their warmth through the green plastic of the garbage bag. I add the severed kitten and tie the opening of the bag into a knot.

–Where do you want them? You could grow a tree over them, maybe.

–How sentimental. Here.

He takes the bag gingerly by the knot, holding it at arm's length away from him.

I go to the bathroom to wash my hands. Through the window, I see him drop the bag into the bin.

–I had to kill them, he says again when he returns. Did you notice she was eating that first kitten?

–Like Hantu Langsuyar, the Malayan woman spirit who ate her baby when no man would love her.

–Oh that. In your story.

–She was hungry. For more than food.

–Look, Isabelle, I like cats. But these feral ones could infect Syrakit. She's a pedigree Siamese, for God's sake. Cost me two hundred pounds.

He wipes his forehead. Upstairs, he turns the spa taps on full and pours in some lotion from a bottle labelled in French. *LES ELIXIRS Bain Moussant Aux Extraits d'Algues.* Bubbles rise to the top of the tub as the mirrors cloud and the white bathroom with its shiny hard surfaces fills with steam.

–Care to join me?

I sit in the spa opposite him. We're both close and far enough away not to be able to avoid looking at one another.

I sink as low as I can under his expensive bubbles, to cover my breasts. But under his gaze I feel as if I'm on some hard butcher's slab.

We're silent for perhaps two minutes, not talking about the cat and motherhood, not talking about Hantu Langsuyar, love or unmet hunger. I wonder if Clara's playing in the sandpit, pouring yellow sand from the old aluminium teapot into her little white tin cups, the remains of lunch congealing into crusts at the corners of her mouth. Maybe David's sitting reading the paper on the back step with the door open in case I ring to say when I'll be home.

I listen to the sound of traffic going places, and I look at the glint in the tutor's eye.

–I don't think I can do this any more.

–I beg your pardon?

–Be your once-in-a-while woman.

He rubs me on the shoulder. For a few seconds it seems he might try going further, but he gives me just a final pat on my arm, as if he's pressing me back into myself.

–Once-in-a-while woman? I thought we were friends, Isabelle. Isn't that what we've always been?

His scar is pink and puckered, but his voice is as smooth as his spa.

–I was hoping for more, I say, but my voice sounds squeaky and desperate, as if it's been squeezed out of a plastic toy.

Sitting in the water on his white porcelain slab, I feel as heavy as the stone winged woman, and I can't work out what to do with my hands.

❋

–I'll ring you soon, he says with his *I promise* smile.

After he's hugged me and closed his front door, I walk around the side, reach into his dark green bin and retrieve the garbage bag with the dead cat and her babies in it. I take a shovel from his shed and begin digging a hole in the gap between his rose bushes. There's a tapping at the kitchen window.

–What are you doing? Gardening?

His face in the downlights looks pale as the moon against the dark rectangle of doorway behind him.

I lift the garbage bag up so he can see the outline of the unpedigreed cat's body through the plastic, and lower her gently back down onto the earth.

–I'm burying her. Giving her a proper farewell. She'll fertilise your roses.

❋

I wake the next morning wondering again how long my mother has left to live. I'll wait until visiting hours and see if she wants to talk about who she'd loved more than Walter Humphries and my father.

In the kitchen, Clara sits under the table drawing with a pencil, humming atonally. There's something about Clara I've never told anyone. I can barely admit it to myself: sometimes, since meeting

Philip Border, I'd found myself wishing I didn't have Clara.

I'm almost overcome with remorse for this as she looks up at me with her gummy smile. I dress her in the sun-and-cloud dress my mother bought her, tie a blue ribbon in her fine nut-brown hair, and sit with her in the sandpit pouring pretend cups of tea with sand from the teapot.

—We are two leddies. Having afternoon tea, she announces.

I pat some damp sand between my hands.

—Would you like a scone, Miss Clara?

She smiles so widely I can see the tips of her new teeth, white against her gums. She fills the teapot with more sand.

—How long til gramma home?

We watch as the sand pours through the spout.

—I don't know. I don't know if grandma will be coming home, Clara.

We wait together for the last grains of sand to fall.

❋

My mother is rubbing her eyes when I enter her room. She smiles as I greet her, but she focuses somewhere over my left shoulder. The tea lady rattles her trolley along the passageway and pokes her hair-netted head in through the doorway.

—One white and one black, please.

The tea lady pours a dull brown liquid from the aluminium teapot into the thick white cups and rattles her trolley away.

—What can you see, Mum?

She takes a sip of tea and rubs her eyes again.

—I can only see light and dark now. My days are light and dark and pain relief lah.

She says this as if it was a quip or an aphorism, but the sound of the nurse flicking the syringe or the drip full of morphine has almost become a substitute for hope. Otherwise, her headaches are so severe and frequent they make her vomit.

–You know, the doctor's wrong. There's more than darkness inside when you're blind. There's something else I can see, too.

–Oh?

–All our people. Grandma Mathilde and Grandfather Wish, Aunty Zeraphina and Mak Non. Ah Kwei, sometimes.

–But they're all dead.

Something like fear creeps up the back of my neck and settles in the roots of my hair as I try to explain her visions, to myself more than to her.

–The drugs are obviously making you hallucinate. Is it . . . frightening?

When I touch her hand, my hands are much sweatier than hers.

–No. It's real and approximately comforting.

I force myself to keep talking.

–Do you feel lonely?

–Not since I've been seeing those old faces lah.

The hair rises on the back of my neck. I glance quickly around the room.

–How do they . . . look?

–Sort of patient. As if they're waiting.

I swallow hard. I can't bring myself to ask what she thought they were waiting for.

–I had a letter from Olivia Skelchy in Singapore. The nurse read it to me. Olivia's just witnessed the exhumation of Aunty Lourdes's and Aunty Zeraphina's graves to make way for a new highway. It's more than twenty years since Aunty Zeraphina was buried there. She was all bones, but her dress and spectacles and her plaster Mary were still in the coffin in perfect condition. Aunty Zeraphina was wearing her spectacles when I saw her today, too.

–Oh.

–Olivia witnessed Theobald's exhumation, as well. His hip flask was still with him, she chuckles softly.

–What are they going to do with . . . Aunty Zeraphina and Uncle Theobald now?

—Cremation. There's a new multi-storey building with a drawer for each person's ashes there, Olivia said. That's the world now. Filing cabinets for the living and the dead. Isabelle, throw me to the wind in the hills near Malacca when I'm gone. So no-one can file me.

I feel my words roll unspoken from the base of my tongue to the pit of my stomach. She pats me on the hand.

—You sound tired. And I should get some rest myself. Would you mind fetching me the spare blanket from the closet?

I spread the blanket over her and pull it up over her thin arms.

—Before I go, Mum, I need to know. Who did you love better than Walter Humphries? You can tell me. I'm your daughter.

—I would have thought it obvious.

She ran her fingers lightly down the side of my face.

—You of course, Isabelle.

—Ohhh.

I don't know how to take this. I bend to kiss her lined forehead. I squeeze her hand until my grip gives out. I try to memorise every detail of her face as I look at her. I give her a smile, and then remember she won't be able to see that. I let the first few tears go, because she won't be able to see them, either.

—See you soon.

It's something we've said to each other all our lives, but I'm no longer sure of it. I rise to leave her with her visions and blindness, because she doesn't seem as frightened by them as I am.

—Mum? Thank you for . . .

I can't find the last words.

THE TRUE BODY

✤ *Death notices* ✤

While Isabelle explored her nostrils with her Flying Swallow-brand coloured pencils in Malacca's Holy Child Infants' School, Ghislaine de Sequeira looked for a job. Since Walter Humphries had returned from overseas, they had settled into an uneasy friendship in which they did not talk about their significance to one another, but Ghislaine woke from dreams about him with her fists still clenched from running after his departing boat, and Walter felt desolate with loneliness if ever he couldn't see her bedroom light on during his furtive insomniac strolls in the dark. He had no-one else who would listen to his boasts over his youthful appearance and good health. And Ghislaine put up with Walter because, as she told herself, he helped her with the finer details of applying for jobs in enterprises run by the British. But her real reason was more hidden than that, more desperate. A reason she could scarcely admit to herself.

After weeks of searching, Ghislaine found the job she was

looking for. The travel writer informed her that the local newspaper needed someone part-time to write obituaries and death notices. She suspected she had learned enough about writing and loss from Walter to demonstrate to the editor her capabilities.

Although Rupert Balneaves had been fit when she left him six months previously, and Walter Humphries visited her in robust health at least once a week to theorise and boast about himself over a cup of teh tarik, theirs were the first obituaries she practised on.

It gave Ghislaine some satisfaction to imagine them both dead and at the mercy of her pen and her charity. She was perturbed to find that, on paper at least, both men seemed almost indistinguishable from one another in certain aspects of their character, and that each of their lives seemed strangely insubstantial. Because of this, she combined their two names and obituaries into one:

Vale Rupert Humphries, connoisseur of teas and the flavours of women, esteemed writer and upholder of the Malacca Club bar, world traveller and accomplished bachelor about town, who died yesterday of a heart attack in an unknown woman's bed.

She swatted at an errant moth, absentmindedly streaking her cheeks with its wing powder like rouge as she wrote:

Always a man to take pride in his appearance and social standing, Rupert Humphries is also thought to have kept in business Malacca's abortionists and bomohs specialising in the treatment of women's madness, although he was careful not to take credit, or to pay, for either of these.

She crossed out this sentence before writing:

His door was always open to women of all races. He will be remembered for his way with words, both on the page and in the bedroom; for the wisdom and companionship he promised but never quite delivered; for his connoisseurship and his anthropological eye for anatomical detail; and for the example he gave us all of how to travel putting one's own comfort foremost. He lived by the maxim: 'It is much more realistic to love oneself than expect to be loved by another.' The women of this town who got to know him best found that this was exactly correct.

She deleted the most bitter phrases before submitting it to the editor. Her idiosyncratic obituary won her the job. Within a fortnight, she was writing about the real dead.

Ghislaine de Sequeira practised her considered silence when listening to the newly bereaved. She found that the principle she had learned during her years of making tea and cakes from poor-quality pickings for the Miracle Tearooms could be applied to writing obituaries and death notices: sometimes what was left out was as important as what was put in.

The relations of the recently deceased knocked on her shop-house door dressed in black or white, according to their race. Sometimes they carried photographs of the deceased to include in the newspaper's death notices, as was the custom in Malacca amongst Malay, Chinese and Eurasian families. Sometimes all they had was a photograph taken after death, and they would request Ghislaine's assistance in making the eyes of the deceased look as if they were still alive. Those who had photos of their dead when they were alive would sometimes ask her to add colour to the cheeks, or sparkle to the eyes. Ghislaine took the first few of these photos down to Wing's Photography Studio with some retouching paints and brushes she found in her father's darkroom. Her father had been one of old Mr Wing's best customers, and Mr Wing recognised her immediately from his memory of her wedding photographs. He showed her how to put pink into cheeks, gold and green into jade jewellery, and eyes onto lids that had closed forever.

'Hard ah,' he said. 'Have to guess how wide open their eyes were in life.'

Wish's darkroom and Ghislaine's careful observation of Mr Wing's photograph-retouching techniques allowed her to provide the extra services of creating photographic portraits of the dead. It wasn't uncommon for the family of the bereaved to discover after the death of the loved one that no photograph had ever been taken of him or her, so sometimes Ghislaine took her cosmetic case and her father's old camera down to the dying houses or dining-room tables where the deceased were laid out.

Usually though, Ghislaine sat the bereaved in her shuttered sitting room before taking notes for an obituary or death notice. The sun glared and the traffic rattled and honked only a few feet away from the front door, but there was a calm coolness to the room as she poured them Cameron Highlands tea in cups she'd meticulously scoured with salt.

'Tell me about your dear one,' she said to clients.

One afternoon, a woman came to her who looked as if she was from one of the wealthy Straits-born Chinese families. This Nonya wore a lustrous blue silk-brocade jacket that looked brand new, but stamped on her sharply featured face was an expression of long-suffering endurance that belied her first words about her husband. She held up a black-and-white photograph of a heavily eyelidded Chinese man with hair styled like Harry Belafonte's, and a grin like the travel writer's.

'He was a good man,' the woman said.

Ghislaine had already discovered that this was a common enough opening description of the deceased from the bereaved. It was usually accompanied by a flurry of handkerchiefs and tears, but this Nonya customer had eyes like ice. Why had this aloof woman chosen her instead of one of the Chinese scribes who lived near the temples of Jalan Hang Jebat? Ghislaine de Sequeira looked at her with intricate attentiveness as her story about her husband gathered steam like a cloud, waiting for it to become so heavy with lies that it rained and revealed a truer picture of the man. The Nonya had a small scar shaped like a bent wing in between the two wavy creases on her forehead, and two hairpins topped with small filigree phoenixes in her bun.

'He was a devoted father and husband.'

Devoted father and husband, Ghislaine wrote.

'When he was home.'

'When he was home?' Ghislaine knew it was time to put down her pen.

'Well, he wasn't home a lot of the time. He played around,' the woman murmured, 'he drank a bit, and gambled too much on mahjong, but he was still a good husband, no?'

'Some of the time, no doubt,' said Ghislaine. 'Would you like me to retouch the photograph before it's printed?'

'Just a little retouch around the chin and eyes, perhaps. He was a handsome man.'

'And what about you? How did you keep your sanity when he wasn't home?'

Usually, the good women of Malacca with philandering husbands shrugged, not looking her in the eye. But this woman looked at her as if she was giving her a warning before gazing into the distance, like someone who believed she had been to places no-one else had. She began and ended her story: 'There was an Englishman who visited me . . .'

LONDON, MARCH 1986

Sunil and I are in one of the Kew greenhouses repotting some newly shooting orchid pseudobulbs. We can see the sky darkening through the glass roof.

–So you're off to see your tutor this weekend?

–It's his birthday on Monday. I baked the cake this morning. A sugee cake. They keep well. I'm paying him a surprise visit.

–So what will you write on the cake? Happy Birthday Big Boy? Sunil slides some repotted pseudobulbs into my backpack as he speaks.

–Seriously, how are things now between you?

–He said we've just been friends all along. I don't get it. What about the sex?

–Oh no. He's showing his age, Isabelle. Twenty-something years old in the 1960s, forever twenty-something years old. For men like him, what's a bit of sex between friends?

–What if he's just damning my sexual performance with faint praise?

Sunil looks at me sternly.

—One thing I've learned, Isabelle. Never feel responsible for a lover's half-heartedness.

He zips up my backpack.

—Well, you've baked the cake. Might as well give it to him, I suppose. But don't do any more plant smuggling for him. Only for your paying customers, okay? Now get on your way before the rain. Good luck.

❃

Sugee cakes do not rise as high as most English cakes do, but the one I've baked for Philip has also developed a crack in the middle by the time I arrive home to ice it. I don't make the usual white marzipan icing used for sugee cakes, which are often wedding cakes back in Malacca and Singapore. I melt dark chocolate and cream it with butter and icing sugar. I apply the chocolate icing to the crack as if it's mortar, before smoothing the remainder over the cake, but the flaw's still obvious. I'd been too embarrassed to tell Sunil the cake was heart-shaped. Now it's a heart with a poorly concealed crack in the middle.

But thinking about all the eggs I'd broken, all the semolina I'd sifted, all the butter I'd creamed, it seems it's time to tell Philip about my feelings for him, no matter how imperfectly I express them. This will be a reckoning cake as well as a birthday cake. I stick twenty gold candles into it, because fifty might frighten him.

I put the potted orchids with the cake in Clara's old plastic baby bath for ease of carrying, and take a cab to his house. It's late afternoon on a spring day, but a freezing wind blows a thick blanket of cloud from the north as the cab drives past Hampstead Heath. In the distance, couples wrap themselves in picnic blankets against the approach of the evening chill and the first intermittent drops of rain. Others pedal home on bicycles past the Ladies' Pond with its clumps of reeds and duck feathers. A fine drizzle starts as the cab turns from Highgate Cemetery into Philip's street with its dark brick or white rendered houses and glossy front doors, its potted camellias and the gables of tasteful renovations peeking from behind the original frontages like discreet price tags.

Balancing the baby bath on my hip, I knock lightly on Philip's door. No answer. I tiptoe around the back until I come to the conservatory wall where he's planted the palms I've given him. They seem to have grown since my last visit. Their dark leaves fringe the aqua-blue rectangle of the pool and the carved Balinese day bed on the opposite side. The door opens without a squeak under my hand and I tiptoe into the conservatory with the baby bath full of my gifts to him under my arm.

Suddenly, I hear his voice.

—You look like you belong here.

Again. Pulse quickening, I put the baby bath down on the edge of the pool and look through the doorway leading to the rest of the house. He's nowhere to be seen.

—Where are you? I call softly. There's no answer.

Then a throaty, lilting voice drifts through the open window. A woman's voice, a voice of Asia.

—Show me your hand. Not like that, she laughs.

—The scar, from putting out my rubbish.

For the first time since I was a child in the Cathay Picture Theatre in Malacca, I feel the surge of the white-hot censor's flare that obliterates scenes of passion or violence.

I've been left out of the picture.

The woman's laughter floats down. Who is she? Her murmurs are too subdued to hear clearly.

—You have beautiful hair, he says, and then nothing but silence.

As I tiptoe closer to the open window, my foot knocks the baby bath full of orchids and birthday cake. It slides into the pool as gracefully as a ship, before sinking under a halo of bubbles. As the water clears, the heart with its golden candles looks like some ruined pillared city, shrouded by a jungle of orchids and a chocolatey cloud of dust.

I back out of the conservatory and crouch next to its door for a minute or two. Only faint murmurs come to me from above. But I no longer want to know more.

Now, let me see, I say, turning from the small cloud I've breathed on his window.

✳

Portobello Road at six in the evening, the air blue with fumes drifting down from the Westway flyover. An unexpected almond tree erupts from the grey pavement, its flowers glowing like dying embers in the evening light.

My heart is not breaking. How long can I go on pushing my baby along the road, against the traffic? Clara hums tunelessly in her pram as we pass the button and bead shops, the homeless people bedding themselves down for the night, the small family restaurants run by Indians, Malays and Chinese.

So the tutor is a collector of women, too. Why hadn't I noticed before? My mother's words all those months ago come to me. *Bamboozled. Utterly bamboozled.* I look up alleyways and into closed-up shops without really seeing, the white-hot flare surging again under my skin. Leaning against the darkened window of Aunty Kanti's shop, looking beyond the spice hills and anise stars for reasons for Philip's collecting habit. Another kind of scar, covering the wounds left by his parents?

This is more certain: somehow, I will let myself go. Somehow, I will find a truer body.

✳

Which loss really matters? The night is drawing in, but I wheel Clara, now sleeping in the pram, urgently towards the hospital. Towards my mother, the one that really matters.

But this is the evening that my mother's face begins to turn a dull, almost iodine yellow. Outside her window, the moon is blue with the vapour of remnant winter. There's a wheelchair near the foot of her bed. Two pale doctors with thin lips probe her with their sibilant questions and metal instruments, and draw me aside in the corridor to tell me the obvious with the full weight of their authority.

—She doesn't have long to go now. The cancer's all through her. She can't walk. Her body can't regulate its own temperature any more.

—Is that why her skin's gone yellow?

—Very common at this stage. Liver's closing down.

Her eyes are shut when I re-enter her room, but she opens them when I place my hand gently on her wrist.

It is too late to ask her certain questions now.

—Would you like me to bring you anything special? I ask her instead.

—There's no point buying me anything. Can't take it with me when I go.

That bleak smile, as if there are no longer enough cells in her skin to stretch across.

—Clara's here. Sleeping in the pram.

—Oh. I can't see her face any more, of course. Let me touch her?

I wheel the pram closer and guide my mother's hand to Clara's cheek. She closes her eyes and nods slightly, as if she's found a clearer image of Clara behind them.

—Bless her. Let her keep sleeping, she murmurs.

—The moon is lovely tonight, I say, sounding hollow.

—Oh? I would like to look at the moon with my five per cent vision. I haven't seen the moon for such a long time.

—Hang on a minute, then.

I wheel Clara, still sleeping, to the nurses' station across the corridor. A nurse is filing her nails there.

—Would you mind keeping an eye on my daughter for ten minutes? She'll probably stay asleep. I'm just going to . . . take my mother for a walk in the wheelchair.

–All right. Just a little walk, though. No longer than ten minutes.

–Thank you so much.

My mother is waiting with her hands clasped patiently in her lap. Or she might be praying.

–Let's go then.

I wrap my yellow mother's shoulders in her white chenille dressing gown.

–What fun. You'll have to help me to the wheelchair.

She holds her arms out to me like a child. She feels only a bit heavier than Clara as I try to lift her from the edge of the bed to the wheelchair, yet I can't quite make the distance with her, as if I lack the will for doing all these final things. She staggers the last few feet to it.

–Sorry.

We both say this at the same time. I wheel her out to the lift.

–The new nurse asked me if it was just my Asian complexion, or if I wanted some make-up to cover the yellow in my face. Have I turned urine yellow?

–No. Yellow's the colour of royalty in Malacca, remember?

We get out at the floor marked Rooftop Garden.

–An English moon always looks so different from a Malacca moon. It looks like ice here, more unreachable somehow. In Malacca, the moon is warm.

–Can you see it now?

–It's just a vague glow.

I look around for the garden, something familiar to tell her about. But there is no plant in this rooftop garden, except a dead geranium in a concrete pot. Who'd left this flower from a warmer climate to die in the English snow?

–Isabelle? I really would like my ashes to be scattered in the hills near Malacca. If it's not too much trouble.

So it's come to this. It is too late to ask her more about her life.

–Sure, I nod, forgetting she probably can't see me doing that, feeling as if I'm no longer behind anything I say.

−Could you make sure I just have a simple Catholic funeral service here? Neighbours and friends. Father O'Reilly could do the honours.

My mouth feels suddenly dry. I can find no voice in my throat except a broken croak.

−Of course.

I search the sky for a star. Why is it so difficult to put into words what matters most?

−Mum? I just want to say . . . how much you will always mean to me. Even after . . . probably even more after you've −

−I know, she says, looking at me so directly with her night-filled eyes that I have to remind myself all over again that she's almost blind.

My heart is not breaking, I think over and over to myself as I look at my mother's wasted face in the cold moonlight. *My heart is not breaking*, as if this might help me believe it.

❋

When I finally sleep in the early hours of the morning, I dream I am a tongueless bell. Rain runs down my neck and shoulders. Inside I am dark and hollow, trembling with undeclared mourning, my toll uncountable.

My face looks wan and lost in the bathroom mirror when I wake. I creak like an old woman, barely able to climb into the tub. Every part of me feels bent to breaking point; every part of me aches.

I've been in two accidents at once. I force myself to wash the body that has not been strong enough to carry my mother or beautiful enough to hold Philip Border for long, my inadequate breasts and arms, my stomach, all the tender flesh. I cry for all the care I will not be able to give my mother in the future, and all the care I will give Clara and myself. Then I pull out the plug and watch the previous day's waste run down the drain.

THE TRUE BODY

✦ *The man who was faithful to his house* ✦

The travel writer journeyed overseas more frequently, to
Paris and New York and Rome and all the other places
that were becoming fashionable in the 1960s as air travel
became more available, but he continued to visit Ghislaine de
Sequeira whenever he was in Malacca. He often found himself
having to queue when he visited her, for Ghislaine had become
more than a tactful yet evocative obituary writer and photograph
retoucher. In the long hours she spent retouching portraits of the
dead and listening to the bereaved, Ghislaine had become a great
exponent of empathy. She could read the extremity of others in the
lines that ran across their foreheads and down the sides of their
mouths, in their eyes and in the broken stories they told her about
their dead, and she knew how to communicate this to them
without speaking. People came to her for the great relief of being
understood.

Of course, it was not only her years of portrait retouching and death-notice writing that had taught her to acknowledge the urgency of every person's story. To every person she photographed, to every relation of the deceased she consoled, she brought the empathy she had learned from her parents, Mathilde and Wish de Sequeira, from the amah Ah Kwei and the soothsayer Mak Non, and from years of loving the wrong men.

※

The tea-taster Rupert Balneaves did not say goodbye to Ghislaine and Isabelle when he left Malaysia in the mid-1960s, on the slow tide of expatriates still receding from the nation's Independence. One monsoon morning in early 1969, Ghislaine was surprised to receive a letter from solicitors executing his will. She crossed herself and shook for an hour after reading the first half of the letter.

'My God, your father died already a few weeks ago. Sudden heart failure. Poor Rupert, his heart often failed him, if you ask me. But he cared for us after all, Isabelle. He's left us a small house in London with its study packed to the rafters with canisters of tea. This is how he shows he cares, poor fellow lah. Years late and with a semi-detached house full of semi-perishables. Aiya! Utterly bamboozling, the two Englishmen I've known. Semi-semi, half-hearted, maybe-maybe not. It must be the cold climate they come from. It makes their spirits and hearts slower than their minds.' Tears welling in her eyes, she did not divulge that she suspected she suffered from the inverse problem. She blew her nose sternly on a tea towel and cleared her throat. 'What are we going to do with a semi-detached house full of semi-perishables in London?' She read the rest of the letter. 'Good lord. He's left us some money too. And there I was thinking the English had cost us too much.'

Isabelle knew when her mother was talking to herself. 'Now my father is dead,' she said, looking at the drizzle receding like a curtain across the tin-coloured sky, 'can I go out and play?'

The sky looked as if it would go on forever.

✳

For weeks Ghislaine wondered what to do about the house in London, tantalising yet so far away from her present life, like one of her adolescent dreams of England. Perhaps it was time to live those dreams. She arranged passports and bought two Phoenix-brand cardboard suitcases from the markets.

But one morning, a few months after she received the letter from Rupert Balneaves's lawyers, she woke certain it was time for her to show her hand in love again instead. Without love, she thought to herself, what are fortune and ill fortune, what are two houses on opposite sides of the world?

She looked out her bedroom window at the new day shining on the centuries-old terracotta roofs of Malacca. Perhaps too many losses had made her cling to the familiar, but she was sure she wanted the travel writer more than London.

Seven years had passed since she had refused his proposal in the Dorchester Hotel. Seven years, the time it took for the princes and princesses in Malay legends to complete their journey to each other; seven years, the time it took for every cell of the body to be renewed. Seven years they'd had since the Dorchester Hotel to let go of the old hurts and get to know one another better. Surely she could claim to know and be known by Walter Humphries by now? Their friendship had deepened. They'd seen each other's failings and didn't care. Surely this counted as a truer kind of love than she'd felt for him before?

She soaked herself in lime and rosewater. She sloughed every square inch of her skin with one of the sea sponges she'd found during her solitary walks along the Malacca foreshore. She washed her hair and spread it over her shoulders in the sun to dry. She dressed in the flesh-coloured Shanghai gown and went to visit Walter Humphries at his house.

She trod carefully on the handmade tiles of the entrance stairs and knocked on the wooden door for the first time since he had started renovations.

'Solid teak lah,' she murmured. He had obviously been working hard on being faithful to the original.

Walter Humphries opened the door with his sarong slung below his paunch.

'Ah. The messenger of death. Come in. Tell me what you think of my renovations.'

Ghislaine appraised the situation in her usual empathic way, and told him what she knew he wanted to hear. 'More authentic than the locals' houses.' She repressed her inconvenient impulse to laugh at him as he stood there in his sarong holding his half-finished whisky stengah in his hand.

He gestured towards an ornately carved antique daybed. 'Try out the new seating. I only had it installed last week.'

'Why lah? The locals sold their daybeds to the antique dealers years ago because they took up too much space and time. Those things are for reclining on, not for sitting lah.' She wished immediately she hadn't been so dismissive.

'Wouldn't have thought that would worry you. You're good at taking things lying down.'

She pretended to ignore his comment. 'Aiya. Silk cushions. Opulence lah. You forgot to buy an opium pipe to go with it.' *Stop it. Remember I am here to declare love,* she reminded herself.

He pushed a cushion into place. 'So what brings you here? First time you've come to my place for a while.'

'I just wanted to ask you something lah.'

'Fire away.'

'You have all these rooms, all this house. You work on it inside and out. But what about deep inside *you*?'

'Oh God. Don't get spiritual with *me*, Ghislaine.'

'I mean, Walter, don't you think it would be nice to really share life with someone who loves you?' He looked out the window, but all the distance was in his eyes. 'No offence lah.' It was going to be more difficult than she had thought. *Keep it light,* she told herself, feeling suddenly heavy, tasting her overbrewed hope turn to bitterness again. He didn't reply.

'You gave me so many hide-and-seek answers last time we spoke about this. That night in the Dorchester Hotel all those years ago. Like you were camera-shy. Only got a blurry exposure of your heart lah.'

'Your English is still improper, despite the dictionary I gave you.' He fingered his collar rash. 'You're still in good shape, though. For a mother.'

'Not that lah,' she said, raising her hand gently to his lips. 'Tell me how you *feel.* About us.'

'I'm not in bad shape myself.' He undid the knot at his sarong.

'Don't. Not now.'

'Why not?'

She patted the cushion closest to her. It was at this moment she saw it, sliding from under the cushion to the edge of the wooden seat. It was only a small thing, really, but it made her so weak she felt she needed to sit down immediately. So she didn't know him as well as she thought she did. *It's not what it appears to be,* she told herself as she looked at it gleaming on the teak. But she would not sit there, so close to the evidence.

'Why not?' he said again, his hands bracketing her hips.

'Because you've never told me what your feelings for me are lah.'

'You're such a romantic, my dear.' He made it sound like an insult.

She took another surreptitious glance at the gap between the cushions and the teak. It was what she'd thought it was. *What did you expect?* she asked herself.

'It's much truer to make love with your body than with words, don't you think?' He undid the top frog fastening of her gown. She stepped back, shifted the cushion and glanced again at the gap between it and the carved backrest. She could now see there were two of them, two shiny filigree phoenixes on the end of two hairpins that had bent open and fallen at right angles to one another like a pair of wings. Two meant it was no accident. Someone else had been letting her hair down with him on the daybed. She imagined the careless deliberation of his gesture as he released the long hair to fall like a curtain across the other woman's eyes, the Nonya's icy gaze. She heard the soft, almost imperceptible sound the hairpins made as they fell on the silk cushions.

She picked up the phoenixes and handed them to him. Keeping his face closed, he put them on the table behind him.

'There's so much you've kept hidden from me, Walter.'

'Do you know what I think, Ghislaine? I think your convent education taught you hypocrisy. When all's said and done, you've been just another sleeping dictionary to more than one man.'

Did he really say that? His last words were so brittle they broke into sharp, microscopic pieces in her ears. They were no longer words, but a kind of white noise thickening her blood with a dense, invisible shame that she would carry in her veins for the rest of her life. 'Anyway, Ghislaine. Why should I tell you about things that have nothing to do with you? No doubt you were still sleeping with your husband in the highlands when you slept with me.'

'Because some time not too far gone . . .' she gestured towards the hairpins on the table behind him, '. . . the hands you've just been using on me were all over someone else. If you wish to enter me, it would be polite etiquette to let me know if you are bringing anybody else with you.'

'You are such a narrow-minded Malacca convent girl, Ghislaine. Go back to your family.'

'I had hoped we might come home to each other one day,' she said. 'I should have known. True bodies are only paper thin, after all.'

The travel writer tugged his sarong more tightly around his paunch as he looked through the window. As she walked towards his front door, he muttered: 'Did you really think you had any claim on me? I mean, look at you. You've let yourself go.'

'You're right, Walter. I've mistaken desperation for love.'

Crossing the threshold, she felt something rising from deep inside her, as if her body was releasing something long forgotten. And then she really let herself go. As she walked away, the unladylike fighter's laugh rang out from her, an inheritance from her mother, Mathilde, that cleared Ghislaine de Sequeira's path through the new Malacca day.

LONDON, APRIL 1986

With the warmer weather, couples stroll hand in hand along the paths and children run across the lawns of Kew Gardens. The honeyed scent of lime-tree blossom hangs in the air as Sunil and I use long-handled nets to scoop algae and ice-cream wrappers from the water garden in front of the Palm House. Our reflections look like those of gondoliers searching for passengers as I tell Sunil about Philip's ambivalence towards me, about his scar, his unseen other woman and their voices drifting from his bedroom.

—In this day and age, they call it an abuse of power, what your tutor's done. At the very least. You should put in a complaint to the college.

—It was just an accident, no different from what the travel writer did to my mother.

—Precisely. Accident my arse.

—We'd both been married women. People would say we were experienced enough to know better, that we knew just what we were doing. Me especially. The losses and limitations of my mother's Malaccan life aren't mine. So why did I fall for the tutor?

Sunil arches one eyebrow.

−Firstly, Isabelle, apart from your marriage, you're really *in*experienced with men. You've really only known David since you were what, eighteen? Secondly, you wanted love so much you couldn't see your tutor for what he is.

−That reminds me of a cutting about travel I found in my mother's diary. Something like the more we need to see the signs of safe arrival, the more we are likely to be deluded that we have arrived.

−Exactly. Men like Philip Border exploit that kind of weakness. He's just another connoisseur of exotica not willing to pay the full price.

From where we are standing, the Palm House's reflection on the surface of the lily pond looks like an enormous cage again.

−What a joke. I fell for a teacher who lies.

A gust of wind splinters the reflection of the Palm House.

−Strange, to think I loved him.

−You can bet he's still depending on that. You're not alone though, Isabelle. I reckon only the very lucky and the truly confident never fall for the wrong person.

We pull our nets from the pool and rest them on the barrow. Sunil wraps his arm tightly around my shoulders, as if trying to help me gather myself together.

−My mother reckons that we fall in love with the wrong people because we can't see ourselves clearly. She says it's another kind of blind spot. Her doctors told us the blind spot in the eye is essential to vision. It's where the nerve begins.

−I guess there's hope for us all in that.

※

After much urging from Sunil, I go to the grey college to lodge a complaint. The secretary behind the desk looks like someone's grandmother, her hair neatly permed and coloured, her expression impassive, as if she wishes not to offend or to be offended herself. I keep my voice low.

–A friend of mine has a problem.

–Speak up. I can't hear you.

–Who should students like my friend see when they think . . . they've been badly treated by their tutor?

–What do you mean badly treated?

I feel my throat tighten. I whisper.

–He had sex with her and . . .

The woman presses her lips together and looks away.

–Your friend wants the sexual harassment officer, she says, making the location with an X on a map of the building, pushing the paper over the counter without looking at me.

I knock on the sexual harassment officer's door, but she isn't there. I wait one minute before losing my nerve and hurrying away.

Can I really call Philip Border's behaviour towards me sexual harassment? The term sounds both too small and too big for what happened between us. What happened is so complicated I can't find the words for it. So how could I ever make a formal complaint about it?

I will simply not see him again. Nothing seems as necessary.

It takes me only minutes to withdraw from his class.

※

I tiptoe into Clara's bedroom and watch her sleeping. She makes strong, intermittent sucking sounds, as if she is dreaming of drinking from the breast. From birth she's slept with her eyes slightly open, as if she fears she might miss something whilst asleep. Her face looks even fuller and rounder in repose than when she's awake, her lips soft and open, a tiny furrow between her brows. She looks as if she's intent on divining her future. I place my cheek gently against hers. I want to speak to her dreams. *Don't worry*, I want to say, *we will find sufficient love.*

※

I'm woken while it's still dark by my heartbeat tolling my loss again, but this time so deeply my body shakes with it. *Mother,* it seems to ring like a ship's bell echoing in a harbour. *Mother.*

In those moments of waking, it seems clear that she will never be able to answer my call for help again, but it's even clearer to me as I feel my way down the dark hall to the kitchen that I do not know how to respond to the urgency of her situation.

It's four-fifteen in the morning, still hours before my mother wakes. Beyond the window, her garden gleams under a full moon. I unbolt the door and enter it by touch. The leaves of the palms stroke me as I walk deeper into them and crouch in their centre. They have survived, despite not having their trunks blanketed for winter by her for the first time ever. I stay there under the touch of their leaves, watching the moon move towards the rest of the world.

I will do none of the great things I had dreamed of with Philip Border. But, like my mother, I will try to do little things with great love.

The sky begins to lighten in the east. Clara will be awake soon.

Relative contentment is more trustworthy than rapture, I tell myself before leaving the night garden.

✳

The yellow has almost disappeared from my mother's face when I arrive at the hospital, and she's sitting up in a chair, smiling.

Unexpected surge of joy.

–You look so much better!

A teacup smashes in the corridor.

–Oh dear, tea lady will be in trouble.

–Do you want a cuppa, Mum?

–With milk and bubbles in it. Teh tarik, she smiles. –If only. Tell them not to make it too strong.

–Actually, I've brought you some Darjeeling tea. –I'll get them to give us a pot of hot water.

—What a treat. Thank you lah.

A cleaner sweeps up the smashed crockery as the tea lady, unperturbed, brings us a small metal pot of water and two thick white hospital cups with milk arrowroot biscuits poised indelicately on the edge of the saucers. The morning sun hovers between the church and the war memorial as I spoon the tea leaves into the pot.

—It's your birthday in a few days, Mum. What would you like for it?

—Oh. Don't buy anything. Like I said lah, I can't take it with me when I go.

—You're not going anywhere yet. Who will I have to talk to? What will I do without your wisdom?

I don't succeed in keeping the desperation from my voice.

—Me, wise? I don't know about that lah.

I pour the tea and hand her a cup. She lifts it to her nose.

—Lovely aroma.

Over the top of the white china, I can see my mother's eyes have dark circles under them that look almost khaki green through the pale yellow filter of her skin.

—What a lovely smooth muscatel flavour. Second-flush Darjeeling, I would say. How is the writing going, Isabelle?

—I dropped the class.

—Oh? Why?

—Oh, you know, my tutor. Guess I don't know enough about love. Guess I don't know enough about anything for him.

—You know plenty. Some men just don't want to *see* what we know.

She closes her eyes. I think: *She is remembering Walter Humphries the travel writer, or perhaps my father, Rupert Balneaves.* She opens her eyes and runs her finger and thumb along the fold of the sheet.

—As for knowing enough about love, well. Who does? One thing I know is this. Our desire for something other than what we have is what gives us our nerve. It pushed you and me out into the world, certainly. And now here we are, each one of us dying a different kind of death so many oceans away from home.

I blink my eyes fast against the prickling of tears for a few seconds.

–Yes. Did you and Walter Humphries ever really love one another, do you think?

She closes her eyes briefly again before speaking.

–Love meant such different things to each of us.

My question is out before I think better of asking her.

–Why on earth did you put up with him for so long? I still don't really understand.

She looks more stricken than I've ever seen her. She averts her face from me.

–Sorry, Mum. Grief is private. You said that. You don't have to tell me.

She turns her face slowly towards me again.

–No. I've been thinking about it again, after all. I should have shared that particular grief with you years ago. If anyone should know, you should.

All of a sudden I'm not so sure I want to know. It seems everything around me is elongating and changing shape: the pool of light cast by the yolk of the sun across the wall behind her, the moments between each word as she speaks.

–I've told no-one else this. You are very entitled to be angry with me. To say the very least.

She clears her throat.

–It seems hardly fair to be telling you now, Isabelle. I put up with him for so long because Walter Humphries was your father lah.

The burning white heat rises in my skin again. I can barely speak.

–My father? Why didn't you tell me? All these years . . .

The image of my mother wavers under a film of tears.

She places her hand on mine.

–Aiya, anak. Forgive me my cowardice. All those pages I tore from the New World diary.

—They were about Walter Humphries, right? All those mistaken stories I've been inventing about you and him because you didn't tell me before.

She nods slowly.

—I couldn't decide which would be the better of two evils, lah. To let you go on believing the lie that your father was Rupert Balneaves the tea-taster, who at least cared enough for you to leave us the Portobello Road house. Or to let you begin living with the knowledge that Walter Humphries was your real father when you've known ever since you were a little girl that he didn't care for you.

She must have hoped her lie, like the babies' blindness in the Malaccan tale she'd told me months before, would save me from seeing the father who didn't love me: the true but terrible face of my misfortune.

—Did you tell any of your friends or relations who my real father was?

—No lah. Too much shame, having a child born out of wedlock in Malacca in those days. I was pregnant before I left Our Lady Convent, can you imagine? If Grandfather Wish had known, he would have beaten us or hounded the travel writer to marry me until he left the country.

—Did Grandfather Wish ever work it out, do you think?

—Who knows?

—Would he really have beaten you, do you think?

—Well, probably not. Grandfather Wish was a gentleman. But he would've been ashamed. All that colonialism and Catholicism to prove himself against. What do they say lah? You can take a Christao man out of church, but you can't take the church out of the Christao man.

—Did you tell Rupert and . . . Walter?

—Not Rupert. Your survival and mine in the Cameron Highlands depended on that lah. I told him you were two months premature. I didn't tell Walter until he came up to the highlands to do that travel article.

−Why not before?

She rubs the lines on her forehead as if they could be erased.

−I didn't even know I was pregnant when I left Malacca for the highlands with Aunty Zeraphina and Uncle Theobald. No human-biology lessons at Our Lady. I wrote to Walter Humphries some weeks after we left. He didn't reply. I read he'd gone overseas. Rupert Balneaves came along. I knew I was pregnant by then. I was desperate. In those days most of the very few Christao girls who got pregnant out of wedlock were sent away from Malacca for their pregnancy and their babies were put up for adoption.

−What did Walter Humphries say when you finally told him?

−He told me in London that he didn't believe you were his child.

−At the Dorchester Hotel?

−The Dorchester Hotel. That's when the real coldness started. She pulls the pale blue hospital sheet up higher under her arms.

−He said I was just another sleeping dictionary cashing in on Englishmen.

Her hand is very small in mine.

−Reminds me of my writing tutor. Good at stretching the truth to cover himself.

−Yes. They use words like another skin. To protect and make themselves look good. Walter told everyone he was a travel writer, but he wrote more petty court proceedings and small-business advertisements than travel articles.

−You mean he wasn't even a travel writer, really?

−No more than most other expat journalists working in Malaysia and Singapore at the time.

−So my father was just a liar you lied about. I'll never have a true picture of him.

−Aiya, anak. I should have told you the truth when you were a child. It would have mattered to you less then. I heard a few years after we left Malacca that he died. I'm so sorry.

−But you told me he asked you to marry him.

−With impossible conditions.

—What were they?

—Aiya, anak.

—Tell me.

I can just discern the tremor in her top lip.

—Only if I put it in writing that Rupert Balneaves was your father, and sent you to live with someone else.

—I wrote your life all wrong. But not only because of the lie you told me about . . . my father. I distorted it with my own hopes and disappointments in love.

My mother puts her cup on the bedside table.

—Which history is ever true? We all bring too much of our own experience to making sense of others' lives. Any account of a life is a bit like our bodies, I guess. Informed by blindness and misperception as much as by knowledge.

An ambulance siren recedes in the street below.

—Forgive me. There's no journey between men and women without accident. And no-one loves achelessly. I'm so sorry, Isabelle. I told the lie so we could live.

All those spurned unmarried Malaccan mothers and fishermen, rowing boats strewn with limes, blossoms and holy water; rowing in faith through seasons of bad catches, trying to put distance between themselves and tragedy. The travel writer's refusal had launched us on that journey, too.

My mother runs her hands gently over my face. I can almost feel the blood pulsing under our skins. The Malacca River, rushing to meet the seas of the world.

—And because nothing is as difficult as bringing love to the story of our lives, she says.

THE TRUE BODY

✤ *Opening the eyes of the dead* ✤

Malacca darkness, viscous and candid.

'Release me,' Ghislaine de Sequeira begged the night as she walked the streets behind the ruins of A Famosa fort during her nights of sleeplessness.

On the way back from one of these walks, she met her neighbour Jamilah, the woman who'd lost her son to the English curator. She was clutching an open pale blue envelope. It was stamped with the head of the Queen of England. The woman drew a photograph from it and thrust it at Ghislaine.

'Yusef,' she said. 'Open his eyes. Can?' she asked in her broken English.

The photograph had been taken by an amateur. It was underexposed and slightly blurred. It took Ghislaine almost a minute to confirm who the photograph was, for the eyes of the adolescent boy were closed, and it had been years since the curator had taken her neighbour's son to England. Ghislaine was certain the boy was dead, for she could see the edge of a coffin in the photograph. She felt around in the envelope for a letter, a note, anything so that she would not have to find the words to explain to her neighbour what had happened to her son, but there was nothing. Perhaps the curator had forgotten the Malay word for death and the photograph was the only way he could bring himself to tell Jamilah of their child's death. Ghislaine looked more closely at the photograph. What struck her most was the crease between the boy's brows, as if he was trying to apprehend something incomprehensible.

She steered her neighbour to the seat near the front door. There were no fancy words for death in Malay.

'Yusef meninggal,' she said, as gently as possible. Nothing could be more dead than meninggal.

'I know that! I know that, you stupid woman!' Jamilah screamed as she stood suddenly and slammed her front door behind her.

Ghislaine went back inside her house and packed rice congee with extra saltfish into a container. She knocked on her neighbour's door but there was no answer. She left the container on the step.

*

Ghislaine barely heard the noise as her mind grazed between sleeping and waking early the next morning. It was an unremarkable sound, like a melon being dropped onto the road. She turned over and slept until the alarm clock went off.

When she stepped outside to buy roti for Isabelle's breakfast, she noticed a small crowd had gathered. She had to push past the onlookers to see the disarrayed limbs and the pulped face of Jamilah, who had managed, despite the impact of her fall, to keep hold of the photograph of her son in both hands. Only Ghislaine noticed the two deliberately positioned holes in the photograph where the child's eyes had been. Only Ghislaine wondered if Jamilah had meant to open her son's eyes to life one last time, or was putting them out forever.

Ghislaine saw that the tiffin container she'd left on her neighbour's doorstep the night before was gone. She hoped that meant that Jamilah had eaten a good meal before she fell to her death. But all she knew for certain was that it was time for her to say goodbye to the dead and move on.

'How would you like to go and live in your father's house in England?' she asked Isabelle when she came home from school.

'Why?'

'Well, you could see where your father came from. And there's all that tea to drink.'

※

Ghislaine de Sequeira saw Walter Humphries the day before she and Isabelle left Malacca for London to live in the tea-taster's house off Portobello Road. They met in the Melaka Kedai Kopi, the coffee shop he'd taken her to when she was still a student at Our Lady of Sorrows Convent. Laminex tables and chairs had replaced the marble and wooden ones, the old Malay proprietor's son now ran the shop in tight white trousers with his hair slicked back like Elvis Presley's, and a newspaper cutting of the Singaporean prime minister Lee Kuan Yew shaking hands with the Malaysian prime minister Tunku Abdul Rahman barely covered the greasy frame mark on the wall above the charcoal burner where the coronation portrait of Queen Elizabeth had previously basted in the oil of a decade of tiffin cooking.

'Another doomed partnership,' Ghislaine commented as she looked at the photograph of the two leaders in their sweaty, Englishman's suits, taken on the day they proclaimed the merging of their nations into one. 'I knew the merger would be over before it started.' She turned from the photograph to face the travel writer. 'Life's given me a feeling for these things.' The travel writer turned the teaspoon over in the sugar bowl. He had his camera closed up in its leather case, slung over his shoulder.

'Aiya, Walter. You never let me take a photograph of you, and you never took a photograph of me. I suppose you never thought of me as a significant enough destination lah.' She retrieved an envelope from her dress pocket and pushed it across the table to him. 'Speaking of photographs. I thought you might like this one of Isabelle. Before we go.' He pushed the envelope back towards her without opening it.

'Ai-yaah. Still don't want to believe me. Walter? What are you afraid of losing if you admit to being her father?' His eyes darted sideways before fixing on the window. She pushed down the same unladylike laughter that had resurfaced on her last visit to his house. She remembered the shame and grief of seeing him in Isabelle's tiny face during her years of marriage to the tea-taster. So much to leave behind.

'At least you're committed to your house,' she said wryly. He didn't try to grasp any possible meanings beyond the obvious in what she said. Her speech had taken on these strange nuances since he'd given her the Unabridged Oxford, but often it seemed to him that what sounded like complexities of thought and speech were due to inaccuracies in her comprehension of the dictionary's definitions.

'And what about you, Ghislaine? Will you try blending your elusive In-Between flavour again from all those teas Mr Balneaves has left you in England?'

'You remember the flavour I was trying for when I met you in Cameron Highlands again? Something with a scented liquor, smoky notes and enduring body and strength. I am certain that it is no longer worth hoping for.'

'Why's that? Technical problems?'

Ghislaine de Sequeira might have told him some things she'd learned: that there was no recipe for love. Or that even the flavours that cost most don't endure for long; that it's always the corruptible we taste with our tongues. Instead, she shrugged and said, 'Experience tells me.' She kept her tongue in her tea then, and watched him.

He was looking at the open door of a car on the street. He was already on his way somewhere else. She understood, for the first time, that his sky-filled gaze into the distance was as close as he ever came to looking into himself while she was around. She finished her tea and put the envelope containing the photograph back in her pocket. He would never see what she had seen in Isabelle's face: his own, waiting to be recognised.

For a few moments, grief almost overwhelmed her. Then she rose, pushed in the chair and smiled all the way towards the door, despite everything she knew.

❊

Ghislaine and Isabelle carried their Phoenix-brand cardboard suitcases towards the taxi. Across the road some neighbours had hung strings of red firecrackers for Chinese New Year. A sudden breeze from the south carried a few faint chords of guitar and bells.

'Listen to that, Isabelle. Someone in the Land of the Priest is playing fado. Our Portuguese ancestors' songs of fate.' The melody receded and advanced intermittently on the breeze as an old Chinese woman went past, pushing her trolley full of large cakes like rounds of beeswax.

'Lovely kueh bakul, aunty.'

'For good luck,' the woman smiled toothlessly.

'Sniff hard, Isabelle. So . . .' Ghislaine's voice faltered, '. . . you'll remember it forever.' They inhaled the good-luck cake's odour of spice, molasses and burning candles as it mixed with the sea breeze. The smell of curry devil drifted from a neighbour's kitchen. 'In two days we'll be in London, and London won't smell like this.'

They watched the old woman push her cakes down the street and out of sight as the last note of the song of fate died in the air.

LONDON, APRIL 1986

 —What happens to a true body when the mourning's over?
I ask my mother.

—It burns. And the burning of the body illuminates the way
home for the mourner.

✻

—The ache's even worse in this back molar, I tell Mr Gopalkrishnan.

He clicks his tongue when the X-ray comes back.

—It's deteriorated since your previous visit. You have an inflammation caused by one of those stress cracks. You need root-canal
work. I've had a couple of cancellations this afternoon. Want me to
do it now?

—Uh-huh.

—The gardener has a problem with her roots, nurse. Give her a
painkiller and get me the anaesthetic and the 0.5-diameter metal
files.

I float like a cloud on the painkiller, but the files keep threaten-
ing to break off in my root canals. The anaesthetic wears off before

the dentist has finished dredging. Still, I do not come down to earth as his files grate. I do not wince when his instruments meet the gum and the live nerve, or as he uses the gutta percha to fill the hole where my roots and my nerve meet.

I've rehearsed on worse pain recently.

Mr Gopalkrishnan winks.

–The gutta percha's from the rubber plantations of Malaysia. Top quality. You have very unusual roots. Instead of going straight up, they curve almost sideways in three separate directions. Swallow some more painkillers to get you home. It'll take a while to settle down. I'll take more X-rays to check on it next time you come.

When he shows me the pre-treatment X-ray as I'm leaving, I think I understand the nature of my inflammation perfectly. It's shadowed, as if trying to hide itself, or as if susceptible to silencing, but its curved roots bloom like a Holy Ghost orchid in the darkness near the base of my tongue.

❋

The painkillers wash through my blood as I enter the Palm House, its glass dome aglow with the fire of the setting sun. I take the iron stairs to the landing. Behind the tall central stand of palm trees, the refracted sun lights up the glass roof-panes into mirrors. There's a tiny, distant person glowing in the centre of each fiery mirror. They're probably analgesic-induced hallucinations, but for some moments I see Grandfather Wish, Mak Non and Rupert Balneaves reflected in the glass. Ghislaine and Mathilde are there too, the wreckage of their first marriages trailing behind them like the tails of comets: the mildewed mansions of His Majesty's Straits Settlements with their collapsing foundations and peeling walls; the abandoned menageries and spurned meals. Each person's arms are outstretched, as if to embrace, bless or beseech. As if, one way or another, they're keeping the night at bay.

Those who light the way first touch darkness.

❋

The next morning, Sunil and I share a thermos of tea in the gardens' Chinese pagoda. A scattering of crude love hearts and initials are scratched into its red-painted columns.

–I heard some woman say on the BBC this morning that history is desire enlarged, I tell him as he slurps his PG Tips.

–Interesting. I suppose people like the tutor and us are still playing out the history of the Empire.

It's difficult to swallow my tea just then. A magnolia tree frames our sweeping view of the gardens, its pale green buds curled tightly shut.

–Some of these Asian species bloom late in London, I murmur.

Sunil puts his cup down and runs his forefinger across the fate line on the palm of my hand.

–Helps them survive adverse conditions, I guess. Frosts, cold winds. Invasion by foreign bodies. Time to change the course of history, don't you think?

I have to agree. That afternoon I go straight home to my mother's little garden, because small is the way of most beginnings, and the seeds are already there.

❋

As I plant palm seeds for future clients into the trays in my mother's greenhouse, fleeting memories and images gleam at me through the leaf-filtered light:

My mother, struggling to hold on to Walter Humphries and his dictionary, apprehending both their value and their burden. All gifts have weight, especially words.

The imprint of a bird's body and wings in the film of dust on the greenhouse roof. Mistaking reflections on the glass for the sky. Did my mother and I mistake those men for freedom?

And Clara. Her eyes and her grin widening as David pushes the swing and she enters the light. Soaring so high she could almost be flying.

※

How do you choose a birthday present for someone who is dying? Something for her final journey, the morphine in her veins taking her to a destination she has never been. And how long after her birthday does my mother have left to live? I don't know whether to count the days on one hand or two.

Straight into Harrod's. A depression has been worn into the first stone step by the feet of customers. The depressions aren't so evident on the rest of the stairs, as if the first step to spending is always the most emphatic.

Between the beige tills and pillars, the mirrors reveal the lines of my face, downswept by the proximity of death. It's as if the face I had the previous year belonged to another life altogether. For a few seconds I long for Malacca. My mother's right. We look to where we come from when love seems impossible in the present.

I meander past the sheer fabrics of sleepwear, but can't bring myself to buy her any of these items. She doesn't need to be reminded of how limited her life has become.

On the chrome racks of middle-aged women's wear hang the dresses with their polka dots and stripes and lozenges, the stiff floral blouses and pastel scarves. Would it make her feel better to wear some of those? Does someone dying want to be reminded of a normal life, to dress as if she is, in fact, up and about?

I remember hearing on the radio that the sense of smell is the last to go when we die. I pause at the perfume counter.

–I'd like something a bit gentle and meditative. For someone who's dying.

The impeccably made-up shop assistant looks embarrassed.

—A warm Oriental, perhaps, she suggests.

She selects a tall smoky glass bottle and turns my wrist over. My veins show green and mauve through my paler underside skin and taut tendons. The burst of perfume is all wrong, full of that cloying ingredient they call musk. A really warm Oriental would smell of ylang ylang and gutters full of monsoon rains and spice. My sinuses block.

—Thank you. Maybe I'll come in some day when this cold has gone.

I wander down to the tiled food hall. The tutor told me they had fifty kinds of bread and sixty kinds of pickle from all over the world. Perhaps I will find a flavour from my mother's childhood. At the imported condiments counter, I ask a silver-permed shop assistant for belachan.

—What on earth is belachan?

—It's a shrimp paste, from Malaysia.

—That's a new one to me. Sorry.

Her hair hardly moves as she shakes her head.

What else might entice my mother? Her stomach's so sensitive now. All those years of loving her, and I no longer know what's good for her.

In desperation, I buy a blue canister of finest-grade Boh Gardens Cameron Highlands tea from the tea counter and a flowering gardenia plant before hurrying towards the tube station. I have so many questions about the travel writer still to ask her.

It's late afternoon when I arrive at the hospital carrying the tea and the gardenia wrapped in saffron-yellow tissue paper, but my mother's room is empty, the bed freshly made. They've moved her to another room.

I go to the nurse's station to inquire.

The nurse looks pensively at the gift and the envelope.

–Miss de Sequeira? Come this way.

We walk down a long corridor until the nurse pauses outside a room and ushers me in. I look around the doorway, expecting to see my mother's face. There are just two wicker armchairs and an arrangement of artificial white roses and lilies on a low table. The nurse motions me to a seat.

But I don't want to sit down. Something's coming to me. It approaches me as if from a great distance. I wait for it. I want to take this standing up.

–You weren't home when we rang.

I put down the presents. No-one needs to tell me now.

–Your mother died this morning. I'm sorry. Would you like to see her? She was quite a character, wasn't she? She must have known last night she was going. She left instructions with the night-shift nurse on just how she wanted to be dressed when she died. And rice powder to hide the yellow; every day after the first day her skin turned yellow, she dusted it with rice powder. She said she got it . . . I can't remember now. Wherever it was she came from.

※

My mother has a slight frown, as if she's trying to bring some broken memory together. She wears her hair out. It's lustrous and dark as molasses against the pillow. She's dressed in her silk Shanghai gown from Malacca. It is almost the colour of her skin dusted with rice powder. I sit there for five minutes staring at her before it occurs to me she is dressed as if she will meet her great love. As if he might come round the corner, at last, carrying that bouquet of long-stemmed flowers she'd never been given; after so many years, walking towards her with that devotion no suitor had ever approached her with; finally, his gaze upon her in full acknowledgment of who she is.

I press a gardenia between her long, fine fingers, stroke her brow and kiss the eyelids that have closed forever over her fading vision. Her skin is creased like paper, all her life written on it. I rest my head on her shoulder as a plane flies overhead, while the rush-hour traffic accelerates and gradually diminishes below, as the world keeps turning.

The room is in shadow when I kiss my mother one last time before carrying her gifts out into the London spring evening.

In the church across the square, the homeless woman in her black dress sings her song of yearning in front of the sandstone war memorial, her voice skittering out of pitch as two, three, four youths with their mohawked hair roll past on skates. The deep lilac sky is strewn with pieces of cirrus blown in by breezes from all directions. There is a long jagged rent in the largest veil of cloud to the east. In this twilight the gardenia petals look cold and unreal as wax, but they smell fragrant as coconut rice.

There's a sudden drop in the hum of the traffic. I leave the gardenia and the tea in front of the singer, for these presents and the world around me seem suddenly desolate and meaningless.

Who do I turn to now?

Suddenly, I think I can hear my mother's voice. *It's time to turn to yourself.* And one last word, spoken like a blessing: *Begin.*

I do not know where I am going, but I put one foot in front of the other as cars shunt along Portobello Road and the homeless woman, bowing to the gift, sings *Ave M-aariiii-i-a.* She strikes her little triangle just once at the end of her song. The last note is clear and high, fading in the air as imperceptibly as a breath.

Mother, what gift could ever have been adequate for your final journey? Who could ever have guessed your deepest desires? Goodbye, Ghislaine Evangela de Sequeira. Fly to your true body now.

I would like to say all this to her, but she is no longer listening to me with her considered silence.

DISEMBARKATION
Largah – to release, to let go

Back in my mother's London garden, the holes where I dug up my gifts for Philip Border are covered with new growth. In her greenhouse trays, the palm seeds send invisible roots into the soil.

I no longer fall open at the pages the tutor marked in me. Only during moments of great fatigue, when I am lost even to myself, do I see the apparition of a man and a woman intrigued by the differences in one another's skins and tongues.

This man and this woman could be in England or any of its colonies, yesterday or more than fifty years ago. They mark one another's bodies and words over days, months, years, as if making dictionaries or maps. It seems they are beginning to know one another, even to love each other. She learns to translate what is not spoken by him: that particular disinclination of his head, his wide range of smiles, that aversion of his gaze. But his silence spreads.

She consoles herself with a song in her old language, one she learned from her mother. It helps fill the silence. But one day, finally, she listens to its words carefully. She heeds its warning about the dangers of clinging to the wrong kind of love.

She's letting him go now. No more clinging to his words, however well-articulated; to his captivatingly foreign body, tangible as it is; to his promise of a passport to somewhere better.

In all her spare waking moments, even in her sleep, she peels off the man's marks on her like old skin, bit by burning bit. It seems it will never end, this labour of letting go. But one day she wakes to find herself revealed by this labour, re-defined. The burning has subsided. Her own body feels truer to her.

❋

I walk the narrow road that follows the contours of the Malaccan hills, Clara humming to herself in the pram, her hands gripping my mother's ashes in the London crematorium's grey plastic box. The air smells sharp as green limes in some patches, sweet with nectar in others. And from one of the last remaining tracts of jungle, a birdcall like a baby crying. There are no straight roads in the hills beyond Malacca. For miles I believe we've almost arrived.

The sun is ascending the pale sky when we finally reach the top of the hill where the road ends. Clara scrambles from the pram, clasping the box of ashes firmly against her chest. I take her by the hand towards a little shelf of rock that faces across the spires and old ruins of Malacca towards the sea.

Below us, the valley falls without pause, its deep green jungle lightly veiled by the morning mist. The quicksilver ribbon of the Malacca River runs towards the coast. Perhaps it will carry some of my mother's ash towards the world's wide oceans.

I help Clara slide open the lid of the grey box.

My mother's ashes sigh and rise on the breeze before spiralling almost whimsically down into the valley towards the stream. At first we can see them quite clearly, drifting, crosshatching the air like snow. Clara reaches out with one hand, a bright star against the dark valley.

The ashes sink below the mist.

–Gone, Clara says.

A sudden updraught blows open a gap in the vapour.

As we watch the ashes continue spiralling until they are embraced by the darkness of the valley, I feel something alight on my forehead. When I brush my fingertips across it, they come away streaked with ash that's blown back in the wind.

My mother's ashes are neither black nor white, and, in the rush of that moment, they smell of burning and sugar and salt, of bitter aching and sweet release all at once.

ACKNOWLEDGMENTS

While some of the incidents in this book are based on historical events, and while many of the places described in this book exist, it must be stressed that this story is a fiction and that the characters who appear in it are fictional.

I am especially indebted to my mother, Judith Lazaroo, my father, Ken Lazaroo, and his extended family for information about Malacca and Singapore. Joan Marbeck was boundlessly hospitable in Malacca, and shared her knowledge of Malaccan history, Christao language and culture. Joan and her daughter Elaine Cheong helped me locate and visit some of the bomohs still practising in Malacca today, accompanied me to the Cameron Highlands in Malaysia, and acted as interpreters whenever the need arose.

The scenes I wrote about Aloysius de Sequeira's 'out of body' travelling were based on experiences and beliefs recounted to me by my father's now-deceased cousin Patrick Nonis. My late aunt Theresa Trollope described taxi dancing at the Great World. My aunt Dorothy Van Heuven, of East Sussex, England, informed me of aspects of post-World War II expatriate society in Singapore. Mr Wilfred Hamilton-Shimmen of Singapore shared information about the women known as 'sleeping dictionaries' in Malaya.

Amanda and Guy Hodgkinson of Lasseran, France, were hospitable and informative about 1980s London and the Kew Gardens.

I am grateful to David T.K. Wong, Andrew Motion and the University of East Anglia, England, for granting me financial assistance through the David T.K. Wong Fellowship, which enabled me to research and develop an early draft of the novel in England. Jon Cook and the staff of the Department of English and American Studies at the University of East Anglia were supportive and hospitable during my time there.

Edith Cowan University provided me with a generous scholarship and Curtin University with an adjunct teaching fellowship during the writing of *The Travel Writer*.

I am especially indebted to Susan Ash for her astute and repeated readings of countless drafts of the manuscript, and for telling me about the wrapping of palm trunks in blankets. Sarah Lutyens, Susan Strehle, Tseen Khoo, Sari Smith, Marian McCarthy, Julienne Van Loon, Richard Rossiter, my agent Jenny Darling, publisher Nikki Christer, and editors Jo Butler, Judith Lukin-Amundsen and Jo Jarrah made invaluable comments on the manuscript. Jennifer Jacobs of Selangor, Malaysia, made precise suggestions on my use of Malay language. Fay Zwicky identified the author of the epigraph for me. Thanks to Dennis Haskell, Delys Bird and my Murdoch University colleagues Trish Harris, Vijay Mishra, Helena Grehan, Anne Surma and Cheryl Miller for their kind support, and to Ken, Sophia and Tom Rasmussen who were encouraging and patient throughout the writing of this novel.

Another version of the chapter titled 'The Dying House' was published in the anthology *Gas and Air* by Bloomsbury, London, 2002, and a briefer version of 'The Censors' White Flare' was published in *Westerly*, at the University of Western Australia, in November 2005.

My deep gratitude to all.

❋

Various texts informed the writing of *The Travel Writer.*

The epigraph is from Viktor Frankl's *Man's Search for Meaning*, Washington Square Press, New York, 1984.

The list of Relaxation House regulations in the novel is based on a list in George Hicks's book *The Comfort Women*, Heinemann Asia, Singapore, 1995.

The newspaper article about Mak Non's prosecution in court was based on an account of court proceedings found in J.N. McHugh's *Hantu Hantu – An Account of Ghost Belief in Modern Malaya*, Donald Moore, Singapore, 1955. I drew other information about bomohs and hantu from the same source.

The cooking scenes in this novel draw on Celine Marbeck Ting's book *Cuizinhia Cristang – A Malacca Portuguese Cookbook*, Tropical Press, Kuala Lumpur, 1998.

Joan Marbeck's *Ungua Andanza: An Inheritance*, Loh Printing Press, Melaka, 1995; her *Kristang Phrasebook*, Calouste Gulbenkian Foundation, Lisbon, 2004; and Father Antonio da Silvo Rego's *Dialecto Portugues de Malacca*, Agencia Geral das Colonias, Lisbon, 1942; were invaluable sources of information about Christao culture and language. Most Christao words and translations used in *The Travel Writer* are drawn from Joan Marbeck's *Kristang Phrasebook*. (However, while linguists now usually write 'Christao' as 'Kristang', I have used the former spelling in this novel to reflect a spelling used in 1940s and 1950s Malacca.)

R.C.H. McKie's *This Was Singapore*, Angus and Robertson, Sydney and London, 1942; and Donald Moore's *We Live in Singapore*, Hodder and Stoughton, London, 1955, provided expatriate experiences and views of Singapore and Malaya from the 1930s to the 1950s. The 'travel safety' quotes in Ghislaine de Sequeira's diary were informed by James Reason's *Man in Motion – The Psychology of Travel*, Weidenfeld and Nicolson, London, 1974.

Much of the tea-tasting terminology in this novel was drawn from *The Tea Companion* by Jane Pettigrew, Viking, Ringwood, 1999. C.R. Harler's *The Culture and Marketing of Tea*, Oxford University Press, London, 1958, provided information about post-World War II tea cultivation and processing procedures.